The
Temptation

MAUREEN CHILD
TESSA RADLEY
KATHIE DeNOSKY

MILLS &
BOON

Published in Great Britain 2015
by Mills & Boon, an imprint of Harlequin (UK) Limited,
Eton House, 18-24 Paradise Road, Richmond, Surrey, TW9 1SR

THE JARRODS: TEMPTATION © 2015 Harlequin Books S.A.

Claiming Her Billion-Dollar Birthright, Falling For His Proper Mistress and *Expecting the Rancher's Heir* were first published in Great Britain by Harlequin (UK) Limited.

Claiming Her Billion-Dollar Birthright © 2010 Harlequin Books S.A.
Falling For His Proper Mistress © 2010 Harlequin Books S.A.
Expecting the Rancher's Heir © 2010 Harlequin Books S.A.

Special thanks and acknowledgement to Maureen Child, Tessa Radley and Kathie DeNosky for their contribution to the Dynasties: The Jarrods series.

ISBN: 978-0-263-25202-6
eBook ISBN: 978-1-474-00381-0

05-0215

Harlequin (UK) Limited's policy is to use papers that are natural, renewable and recyclable products and made from wood grown in sustainable forests. The logging and manufacturing processes conform to the legal environmental regulations of the country of origin.

Printed and bound in Spain
by CPI, Barcelona

CLAIMING HER BILLION-DOLLAR BIRTHRIGHT

BY
MAUREEN CHILD

Maureen Child is a California native who loves to travel. Every chance they get, she and her husband are taking off on another research trip. The author of more than sixty books, Maureen loves a happy ending and still swears that she has the best job in the world. She lives in Southern California with her husband, two children and a golden retriever with delusions of grandeur. Visit Maureen's website at www.maureenchild.com.

To family.
Mine. Yours.
And to all the wonderful, irritating moments
we share with them.

Prologue

Christian Hanford refused to sit in a dead man's chair.

So instead, he walked to the front of Don Jarrod's desk and perched uneasily on the edge. The old man's study was in the family living quarters on the top floor of Jarrod Manor. Here at Jarrod Ridge resort, everything was luxurious. Even a study that the public never saw. Paneled walls, thick carpets, original oils on the walls and a massive fireplace built of river stones. Of course, there was no cheerful blaze in the hearth, since summer had settled over Colorado.

He imagined none of the people in the room felt cheerful anyway. How could he blame them? They'd lost their father only a week before and now, they'd just had the proverbial rug pulled out from under them.

Years ago, each of the Jarrod children had left Jarrod Ridge, the plush resort that had been in their family for generations, to make their own way. Their father had pushed them all so hard to succeed that he'd managed to drive them away, one by one. To come back now, when it was too late to mend fences, was a hard thing to accept.

Not to mention the fact that in death, Don had figured out a way to not only bring them all home—but to keep them there. Something he hadn't been able to do in life.

The huge Jarrod estate was to be divided equally among his children—on the condition that they all move home and take over running their legacy. Each of the Jarrod siblings had been slapped hard and none of them were happy about it. The old man had found a way to control them from the grave.

Which wasn't sitting well.

Christian watched them all, understanding how they must feel, but sworn to abide by his late client's wishes. God knows he'd tried to talk Don out of this, but the old man had been nothing if not stubborn.

Blake Jarrod and his brother Guy were the oldest. Though not identical, the twins each carried the stamp of their father. Blake was more the buttoned-down type, while Guy was a bit more easygoing. Gavin was two years younger than the twins, but he and Blake had worked together for quite a while out in Vegas.

Trevor Jarrod was the most laid-back of the bunch—or at least that was the demeanor he showed the world. Then there was Melissa. The youngest and the only girl.

Or so she thought.

Christian sent a mental kick out to his now deceased mentor for leaving him in this position. But even in death, Don had wanted to rule the Jarrod clan and no doubt, wherever he was now, he didn't really care that it was Christian getting stuck with the dirty work.

Blake stood up as if he couldn't bear sitting still another minute. Just a week since Don Jarrod's death, none of his children had had a chance to come to terms with his passing. And now they'd all been sucker punched.

They'd left the cemetery just an hour before and after reading through most of the will's bequests, emotions were running high. Well, Christian thought, they were about to go even higher.

"Why are we still here, Christian?" Guy asked from his seat, bracing his elbows on his knees. "You've read the will, what's left to say?"

"There's one more thing to cover."

"What haven't you covered?" Trevor asked, shifting a glance around the room at his brothers and sister. "Seems pretty clear to me. Dad's arranged things to get us back to Jarrod Ridge. Just like he always wanted."

"I still can't believe he's gone," Melissa whispered.

Gavin dropped one arm around her shoulders and gave her a supportive hug. "It'll be okay, Mel."

"Will it?" Blake asked. "We've all got lives separate from the Ridge. Now we're supposed to walk away from whatever we've built to come back home and take over?"

"I understand how you feel," Christian said softly and waited until all eyes were on him. "I do. I told Don this wasn't the way to handle things."

"Let me guess," Guy interrupted, "Dad wouldn't listen."

"He had his own ideas."

"Always did," Trevor mused.

"The point is," Blake said, voice loud enough that everyone settled down to hear him, "Dad split the estate up equally between the five of us. So what's left to talk about?"

There was his opening, Christian thought, bracing himself for what would come in response to his next statement. "The fact that the estate's been split, not into five equal shares, but *six*."

"Six?" Gavin repeated, glancing around at his siblings as if doing an unnecessary head count. "But there are only five of us."

"Don's last surprise," Christian said quietly. "You have a sister you've never met."

One

"Please send him in, Monica." Erica Prentice checked her hair and smoothed the front of her sleeveless black dress. She turned to glance out the narrow window behind her desk and took a quick moment to enjoy the pitifully small glimpse of the ocean afforded her.

Situated firmly at the bottom of the totem pole at Brighton and Bailey, a PR firm in San Francisco, Erica didn't exactly rate the best view. But that was okay, she told herself. She'd prove herself—both to her employers *and* her father, no matter how long it took.

But right now, she was meeting with an attorney who had refused to tell her what he wanted to see her about. Which accounted for the jangle of nerves in the pit of her stomach. She was enough her father's daughter to realize that the sudden appearance of a lawyer rarely heralded good news. The Prentice Group, one of the largest clothing manufacturers in the country, were constantly dealing with attorney-led problems. Briefly, she thought about calling her father to ask him if he knew anything about a lawyer from Colorado, but then realized she didn't have time for that.

Behind her, the office door opened and she turned to greet her visitor. But whatever she might have said died unuttered at her first look at the man standing in the doorway.

The elegantly cut dark blue business suit he wore only emphasized the muscular body beneath. His shoulders were broad, his legs were long and his dark brown eyes were narrowed on her. He had a strong, square jaw, neatly trimmed brown hair and a mouth that looked as though it didn't smile often.

It only took seconds for Erica to get an impression of cool confidence. It took even less than that for her to feel an attraction to him that sent what felt like champagne bubbles shooting through her veins.

When she was sure she could speak without making embarrassing gulping noises, she held out her hand and said, "Mr. Hanford, I'm Erica Prentice."

He crossed the room, shook her hand and then held on to it for just a bit too long before releasing her. "Thanks for seeing me."

As if she'd had a choice, she mused. He'd arrived at her office ten minutes ago, unannounced, to claim to have something important to discuss with her. The fact that he hadn't even hinted at what that might be made her wary even as her hormones continued to do a dance of appreciation.

Erica waved him to one of the two chairs opposite her desk. "I have to admit, I'm intrigued. Why would a lawyer from Colorado come all this way to see me?"

"It's a long story," he said, glancing around her office.

She knew what he was seeing and that he was probably singularly unimpressed. The beige walls of the tiny room were mostly bare but for two paintings she'd brought from home to lessen the grim atmosphere. Erica's office was nearly claustrophobic, as befitting someone just getting started on their career. Of course, she thought, not for the first time, if she'd been offered a job in the family company, things would have been different.

Though her older brothers all ran different arms of the Prentice Group, Erica's father had made it clear that she wouldn't be a part of the family business. They'd never been close, she thought, but she'd hoped that she'd be given at least a chance to prove herself, as her brothers had. But her father wasn't a man you could argue with and once his mind was made up, the decision might as well have been set in concrete.

Still, she thought, dragging her brain away from the problems of family, now wasn't the time to be thinking about any of that. As tempting as it might be to indulge in a long meeting with a gorgeous lawyer watching her through amazingly dark chocolate eyes, she simply didn't have time for it today. As it was, she'd only managed to squeeze out a few minutes from her already packed schedule to accommodate Christian Hanford. She couldn't give him more.

Leaning forward, she folded her hands on her desktop and smiled. "I'm sorry, but your long story will have to wait for another time. I have another appointment in fifteen minutes, Mr. Hanford, so if you wouldn't mind, could you just tell me what you're doing here?"

His gaze met hers and held. Erica couldn't have looked away if she had wanted to.

"I represent the estate of Donald Jarrod," he said quietly.

"Jarrod." Erica thought about the name, trying to place it, when suddenly, she made the connection. "Colorado. Jarrod. You mean the Jarrod resort in Aspen, Jarrod?"

He gave her a brief smile and inclined his head. Reaching down for the briefcase at his feet, he pulled it onto his lap, opened it and took out a legal-size, manila envelope. Sliding it across the desk to her, he said, "Yes, *that* Donald Jarrod."

Confused but curious, Erica picked up the envelope and opened it. She pulled out a document and glanced at the title. "His *will?* Why do I have a copy of the man's will?"

"Because, Ms. Prentice, you're one of the beneficiaries."

She glanced from the document to him and back again. Her stomach did a wild spin and flutter that left her feeling off balance.

"That makes no sense," she murmured, slipping the will back into the envelope and deliberately flattening the brass clasp. "I've never met the man. Why would he leave me anything in his will?"

His features tightened and Erica thought she caught a glimpse of sympathy shining in his eyes before he took the envelope back from her and slid it into his briefcase. "I told you it was going to be a long story."

"Right." She watched him close up his black leather case and wished she had the document in her hands again. She'd like the chance to read it herself before they went any further. But apparently, Christian Hanford wanted his say first. Which didn't do a thing to ease the tension flooding her system.

What was happening here? How had her average, run-of-the-mill day taken such a bizarre turn? And what did a dead empire builder from Colorado have to do with her?

"Then perhaps we can meet later, when you have more time."

She didn't want to wait, but didn't see how she could avoid it.

"Time. Yes. That's probably a good idea. I'm…" Erica shook her head, met his gaze and said, "I'm sorry. This is just all so confusing. Maybe if you gave me some idea what this was about. Why I was mentioned in his will…"

"I think it's best to get this done all at once," he said. "No point in getting into it now when we can't finish it."

He stood up and Erica was forced to tip her head back to look up at him. That frisson of attraction was still there, but now there was more. There was a sense that once she met with Christian Hanford and heard the whole story, nothing in her life was ever going to be the same.

She could see the truth in his eyes. He was watching her as if he could read her mind and knew exactly what a tumult her thoughts were in. She read understanding in his eyes and once again thought she caught a flicker of sympathy.

Nerves rattled through her and Erica knew she'd never make it through her whole day now without knowing what was going on. How could she possibly meet with clients and do the myriad other little jobs that required her attention with this mystery hanging over her head?

Nope, an impossible task. On impulse, she stood up and said, "On second thought, I think we should have that talk now. If you could give me a half an hour to clear up a few things, we could meet…"

Where? Not her apartment. She wasn't inviting a strange man into her home, even if he was a lawyer. Not here in the office. If she was about to get hit with bad news, she'd rather it wasn't done in front of people she had to work with every day.

As if he were still reading scatter-shot thoughts, Christian offered, "Why don't we meet for lunch? I'll come back in an hour and then we'll talk."

She nodded. "One hour."

Once he'd left, Erica took a deep breath in a futile attempt to steady herself. Her stomach was jumping with nerves and her mind was whirling. What in the world was going on? Once again, she was tempted to call her father and ask his advice. But at the same time, she knew he would simply tell her to think it through and make her own decisions. Walter Prentice had never been the kind of man to "mollycoddle" his children. Not even his youngest child and only daughter.

No, she would meet with Christian Hanford, get to the bottom of this and then decide what to do about it.

But before she could do that, she had to clear her appointments for the day. She had no idea how long this meeting with Christian Hanford was going to take—or if she'd be in any kind of mood to deal with business once their meeting was over. She hit a button on her phone. Her assistant, Monica, opened the office door an instant later. Her blue eyes sparkling, she asked, "What's up with Mr. Gorgeous?"

Erica sighed. Monica was more friend than assistant. They'd bonded shortly after Erica had come to work for B&B nearly a year ago. The two of them were the youngest employees in the company and they'd forged a friendly working relationship that had resulted in lots of after-business drinks and dinners. But today, Erica was feeling too jumbled to enjoy her friend's teasing.

"I have no idea."

Monica's smile faded. "Hey, are you okay?"

"I'll let you know later," she said, sitting down at her desk again. "For now, I need you to cancel today's meetings. I've got something important to take care of."

"That won't be difficult. When do you want everything rescheduled?"

"Work everyone in as quickly as possible," Erica told her. "We'll just double up a little and stay late if we have to."

"Okay," Monica said. "This does sound important. Is everything all right?"

"Honestly, I don't know." The unsettled feeling in the pit of her stomach kept warning her that things were about to get very weird.

And there wasn't a thing she could do to avoid it.

Christian was waiting for her when Erica came down the elevator and crossed the lobby of the office building. Something inside him stirred at the sight of her. He'd felt it earlier, too. The moment he'd looked into her whiskey-brown eyes, Christian had known that this woman was going to be trouble.

He didn't do trouble. Not for years, now. He had exactly what he'd spent most of his life working toward. A position of respect and more money than he could spend in two lifetimes. He hadn't worked his ass off for years to get where he was just to let it all go because his body had reacted to the wrong woman.

And Erica Prentice was definitely off-limits to him.

Not only was she the illegitimate daughter of his long-time employer…there was also the fact that any "fraternization" with members of the Jarrod family could see him lose the job he valued so much.

Hadn't ever been an issue for him before this. Melissa Jarrod was a sweetheart, but she'd never interested him.

But he had the distinct feeling that Erica Prentice was going to be a different matter altogether.

As she crossed the glossy floor, his gaze took in everything about her. Shoulder-length light brown hair, soft and touchable. Smooth, pale skin, amber eyes and a mouth that had a tendency to quirk to one side as if she were trying to decide whether to smile or not. She was short, but curvy, the kind of woman that made a man want to sweep her up and pull her in close. Not that he had any intention of doing anything like that.

Her eyes met his and Christian told himself to take care of business and get back to the jet waiting for him at the airport. Safer all around if he concluded this trip as quickly as possible.

"Sorry I'm late," she said as she joined him.

"No problem." Of course the fact that he wanted to take her hand again just for an excuse to touch her might be looked on as a problem. Shaking his head to dislodge that thought, he said, "Look, I saw a café just down the street. Why don't we go have some lunch and get this situation taken care of?"

"Fine." She headed for the glass doors and walked outside when they swished open automatically. She stopped on the sidewalk and pushed her hair out of her eyes when a cold San Francisco wind tossed it into the air. Looking up at him, she asked, "Tell me this much first. Are you about to make me happy? Or is this going to screw up my world?"

Christian looked down into eyes shining with trepidation. "To tell the truth, maybe a little of both."

Two

"You must be crazy," Erica said fifteen minutes later.

The outdoor Italian café sat at the corner of a busy intersection in downtown San Francisco. Only a few of the dozen small round tables covered in bloodred tablecloths were occupied by people stopping for an early lunch. Inside the restaurant there were less hardy souls, diners not wanting to deal with the capricious wind. Fabrizio's was one of Erica's favorite places, but now she was sure this visit was going to forever take the shine off the restaurant for her.

Staring across the table at the man who watched her through steady eyes, she repeated what she'd said only moments before. "You're wrong. This is crazy. I am *not* Donald Jarrod's illegitimate heir."

Their waiter came up to the table just as she finished speaking and Erica felt heat rush up her neck and fill her cheeks. She only hoped the man hadn't heard her. That would be perfect. She was known here. People would talk. Speculate.

They would anyway, she realized. The Jarrod family, much like the Prentice family, was big news. Even if this wasn't true—which, she assured herself silently, it wasn't—word would get out and soon Erica would be the subject of tabloid gossip and whispered innuendos from those she knew.

She could just imagine the reactions from her father and stepmother, Angela. Walter Prentice loathed scandal. He'd raised his children to believe that family business was private and that getting one's name in the paper was not something to be desired. Now, Erica thought, ancient dirty laundry would be spread out for the world to read about and enjoy and she and her family would be the punch line to mean-spirited jokes told at cocktail parties.

Oh, God, this just couldn't be happening.

"Iced tea for the lady," the waiter was saying as he divested his tray of drinks, "and coffee for the gentleman. Have you decided on lunch?"

"No," Christian said. "We need a few minutes."

"Take your time," the young man told him, then gave them each a smile and left them alone with their menus.

Erica didn't even glance at hers. She wasn't sure she'd ever be hungry again. She grabbed her tea, took a long drink to ease the dryness in her throat and then set the glass down. Keeping her voice low enough that Christian was forced to lean across the table to hear her over the discordant hum of traffic, she said, "I don't know what this is about, or what you're up to, but…"

"If you'll hear me out, I'll try to explain."

He looked as if he wished he were anywhere but there and Erica knew exactly how he felt. She wanted nothing more than to jump up, vault over the iron railing separating the café tables from the sidewalk and disappear into the crowds. But since that wasn't going to happen, she told herself to remain calm and listen to him. Once he was finished saying his piece, she'd simply walk away and put this hideous conversation out of her mind forever.

He threw a quick glance at the table closest to them as if to assure himself he wouldn't be overheard, then he looked back to Erica. His dark chocolate eyes shone with determination as he said quietly, "I realize this is a shock—"

"It would be if it were true," she allowed.

"It is true, Ms. Prentice." His voice dropped another notch. "Would I be here if this were all some elaborate joke?"

"Maybe," she said. "For all I know this is some sort of extortion attempt or something."

Now those dark eyes of his fired with indignation. "I'm an attorney. I'm here at the behest of my late employer. It was his final wish that I come to you personally to deliver this news."

Erica nodded, seeing the insult her jibe had delivered and said, "Fine. It's not a joke. But it *is* a mistake.

Believe me when I tell you, I'm the daughter of Walter Prentice."

"No," he said tightly. "You're not. I have documentation to back me up."

She took a breath of the cold, clear air, hoping it would brace her for what was coming. If this was a mistake, she'd find out soon enough. If it was all true, she needed to see proof. "Show me."

He delved into his briefcase and handed her a smaller manila envelope than the one he'd shown her earlier at her office. Warily, she took it, her fingers barely touching it, as if she half expected the thing to blow up in her hands. But it didn't and she opened the clasp and slid free the three sheets of paper inside.

The first document was a letter. Written to Don Jarrod and signed by…Erica's mother. Her heart lodged in her throat as she stared at the elegant handwriting. Her mother had died in childbirth, so Erica had always felt cheated out of a relationship with the woman her brothers remembered so clearly. Danielle Prentice had kept a journal though, one that had been passed on to Erica when she was sixteen. She'd spent hours reading those pages, getting to know the mother she'd never known. So she recognized that beautiful, familiar handwriting and it was almost as if her mother were there with them at the table.

The note was brief, but Erica felt the grief in the words written there.

My dear Don,
I wanted you to know that I don't regret our time

together. Though what we shared was never meant to last, I will always remember you with affection. That said, you must see that you can never acknowledge our child. Walter has forgiven me and has promised to love this child as he has our sons. And so I ask that you stay away and let us rebuild our lives. It's best for all of us.

Love,

Danielle

Shock faded into stunned, reluctant acceptance as Erica's eyes misted over with tears. Not once in her journals had Danielle ever even hinted at the affair she had had with Don Jarrod. Yet these few, simple words were impossible to deny even as the page before her blurred and she blinked frantically to clear her vision. Slowly she traced the tip of one finger across the faded ink, as if she could actually touch her mother. Though a ball of ice had settled in the pit of her stomach, she realized that this letter explained so much.

Walter had never been an overly affectionate father, even with Erica's older brothers. But with her, Walter had been even more…distant. Now at least, she knew why. She wasn't his child. She was, instead, a constant reminder of his wife's infidelity. Oh, God.

Christian was sitting there across from her and not speaking, and for that she was grateful. If he tried to say something kind or sweet or sympathetic, she'd lose what little control she was desperately clinging to.

She lifted her gaze to look at him and said in a last-ditch attempt to avoid the inevitable, "How do I know my mother actually wrote this letter? For all I know you've had it forged for your own reasons."

"And what could those be?" Christian asked. "What possible reason could the Jarrod family have for lying about this?"

"I don't know," she admitted as she frantically tried to come up with something, anything that might explain all of this away. Her family wasn't a close one, but they were all she had. If she accepted this as truth, wouldn't that mean she would lose them all?

"Look at the other two papers," he urged, taking a sip of his coffee.

She didn't want to, but didn't know how to avoid it. Pretending this day had never happened, that Christian Hanford had never appeared at her office, wouldn't work. Hiding her head in the sand wouldn't change anything. If this were actually true, then she had to know. And if it were all some elaborate lie, then she had to know that, too.

Nodding to herself, she looked at the next paper and froze in place. It was a letter from her father to Donald Jarrod and it managed, in a few short lines, to completely disintegrate the last of her doubts.

Jarrod,
My wife is dead, delivering your daughter. This letter is as close as you'll ever get to the child, make no mistake. If you try to get around me, I'll see to it that you regret it.
Walter Prentice

"Oh, my God." Erica slumped against her chair and looked at Christian.

"I'm sorry this is so hard." His voice was without inflection, but she thought she caught the sheen of sincerity in his dark brown eyes. Still, his being sorry didn't change anything.

"I don't even know what to say," she whispered, staring at her father's handwriting. She'd have known that scrawl anywhere. She knew it was genuine because as her older brothers had long said, what forger could ever reproduce such hideous writing?

God. Her brothers.

Half brothers.

Did they all know? Had they been lying to her, too, all these years? Was nothing in her life what she'd thought it was? If she wasn't Erica Prentice, then just who was she?

"Ms. Prentice...Erica," Christian said, "I know you're having a hard time with this."

"I don't think you could have the slightest idea," she told him.

"Fair enough," he said. "But I do know that your biological father regretted never being able to know you."

"Did he?" She shook her head, unsure just what she felt about Donald Jarrod. What kind of man was it who slept with another man's wife? Who created a child and then never made an attempt to acknowledge it? Had Walter's letter really kept Don Jarrod away? Was he that easily put off? Had his affair with Danielle and Erica's birth meant nothing to him?

As if he knew exactly where her thoughts had taken her, Christian said, "Donald's wife, Margaret, died of cancer, leaving him with five children to raise alone when the youngest, your sister Melissa, was only two."

"My sister," she repeated.

"Yes," he said, "and Melissa is eager to meet you, by the way. She's delighted she's not the only girl in the family anymore."

"I'm the only girl in my family, too—" Erica laughed shortly as she looked at him. "But then, apparently I'm not."

An icy wind blasted down the street and the sun slipped behind a bank of gray clouds. Erica shivered, but didn't know if it was the emotional reaction or the sudden drop in temperature that caused it.

Christian said, "Don met your mother at a vulnerable point in his life—"

"And that excuses him?"

"No, it doesn't," he said, his features tightening even as his voice grew clipped. "I'm simply trying to explain it to you the same way Don did for me. He knew how you'd feel hearing this news."

"I'm surprised he gave it a thought," she said. "Not one word from him my whole life and now I'm supposed to be grateful that my biological father is popping up after his death?"

"He didn't contact you because he thought it would make your life more difficult."

"Putting it lightly."

"Exactly. Don't think you weren't on his mind,

though." Christian folded his hands around his coffee cup. "I knew him for a lot of years and I can tell you that to him, family was most important. It must have driven him insane knowing you were here and completely out of his reach."

"So my father's—Walter's—threat worked. Donald stayed away from me to avoid scandal."

"No." Christian smiled a little at that. "Don wasn't worried about what other people thought of him. My guess is he stayed away out of respect for you and your father. He wasn't the kind of man to go out looking to destroy marriages."

"And yet…"

Christian shook his head. "Just before he died, Don talked to me about all of this because he knew I'd be the one coming to see you."

"So even when he knew he was dying, he didn't get in touch with me." Erica wasn't sure how she felt about that. If Donald Jarrod had contacted her, would she have believed him? Would she have welcomed him? She couldn't say. Her relationship with her father had never been a good one, but she did love Walter. He *was* her father. The only one she'd ever known.

Didn't she at least owe him loyalty?

Frowning, the man across from her admitted, "I argued with him about that. I thought he should talk to you. Tell you this himself. But he refused to go back on his word. He'd sworn to Walter he would stay away and he did, though I believe it cost him a great deal to keep that promise."

"I'll have to take your word for that, won't I?"

"I guess so." Their waiter appeared with a coffeepot to refill Christian's cup, but when he would have stayed to take their order, he was waved away again. "Look," Christian continued when they were alone again. "Just do me a favor and read the last letter in that envelope before I say any more."

She really didn't want to. What more was there to tell? What in her life was left to shake up and rearrange? Yet, morbid curiosity had a grip on her now and Erica knew she'd have to satisfy it.

Somehow, she wasn't surprised when she glanced at the bottom of the page and saw the name *Donald Jarrod* in a bold signature. Lifting her gaze to the top of the paper, she read,

My Dear Erica,
I know how you must be feeling right now and I can't blame you. But please know that if I had been given the opportunity, I would have loved you as I cared for your mother.

People—even parents—aren't perfect. We make mistakes. But if we get the chance we try to correct them. This is my chance. Come to Colorado. Meet your other family. And one day, I hope you'll be able to think of me kindly.
Your father,
Donald Jarrod

Again her eyes misted over. She had never known her mother. She'd grown up with a stepmother, Angela, who had been as distant in her own way as Walter had. Now, it turned out, she'd never known her father, either.

"Did you read these letters?"

"No. Don gave them to me in the closed envelope and they've stayed sealed up until just now."

She looked at him. "And I'm supposed to take your word for that, too?"

He met her gaze. "I'll never lie to you, Erica. That is one thing you can depend on."

Since she'd only just discovered that her entire life had been based on a lie, that should have been a comforting statement. On the other hand, she didn't know if the statement itself was a lie.

A headache burst into life behind her eyes and Erica knew it was only going to get worse. So it was best if she just finished this meeting as quickly as possible. Then she could get away. Think. Plan. Try to make some sense out of this insensible situation.

Pushing her hair out of her eyes as the wind whipped it into a frenzy, she said, "All right. Say I believe you. I'm Donald Jarrod's daughter. What now?"

He reached down for his briefcase, opened it and extracted the manila envelope he'd shown her earlier. "As a beneficiary of Don's will, you receive an equal share of his estate."

"What?"

He gave her a small smile. "The estate's been split between all six of his children."

Erica sighed and took a gulp of her iced tea. "I can imagine how news of me went over at the reading of the will."

"As you might guess. Surprise. Shock."

"Sounds like we'll have a lot in common," she said wryly, still reeling from the information overload she'd experienced.

"More than you might think," he told her as he slid the envelope across the table toward her. "There's a catch to your inheritance, though."

"Of course there is," she mused, laying her fingertips atop the will as if she needed the physical contact to assure herself that this was all for real.

"Each of you has to move to Aspen to help run the family business. If you don't…"

"If we don't, then no inheritance."

"Basically."

"Move to Aspen?" She glanced around her at the city she'd grown up in and loved. The city sidewalks were at the bottom of canyons built of steel and brick. Sly sunlight poking through gray clouds appeared and disappeared as if performing magic tricks. Crowds of pedestrians hustled along, everyone hurrying, fighting the wind and the snarls of traffic. Car horns blared, music from a street corner musician peeled out and somewhere close by, a tiny dog yapped impatiently.

The city was hers.

What did she know about Colorado?

But was that even the point? How could she *not* go? Yet, if she did, how would her father and brothers react?

Christian watched her features and knew just by looking at her that her thoughts were tumultuous. Why wouldn't they be, though? He'd known that what he'd had to say to her would shake the foundations of her life. Make her question everything she had ever known.

And he still resented the hell out of the fact that Donald had left this mess in *his* hands.

"You don't have to make any decisions right now," he said after a few long minutes had passed.

She gave him a reluctant, halfhearted smile. "That's good, because I don't think I could."

Nodding, Christian offered, "Why don't you take a few days? Make your decision, then call me." He scribbled his cell number on the back of his business card, then handed it to her. "According to the will, you've got a couple of weeks to take up your place at the resort. Use the time. Think about what you want to do."

She held his card and ran her thumb over the embossed lettering in a slow stroke that mesmerized Christian. His body stirred and he shifted uncomfortably on his chair. He didn't need this attraction to her and wished he could shut it all down.

Unfortunately, the longer he was with her, the stronger that attraction became. What he'd like to do was blow off the business talk, take her for an elegant meal and then off to his hotel where he could lay her down across his bed and they could spend a couple of hours enjoying themselves. If she was any other woman, that's exactly what he would do.

That thought made him even more uncomfortable than he had been before.

Erica Prentice was off-limits and if she ended up going

to Aspen—which he thought she would—then his body had better get used to living with disappointment.

"A decision," she said softly, locking her gaze with his. "We both know what that decision will be."

"I think I do," he told her. "You're going to accept the conditions of the will."

"How can I not?"

He smiled in approval. "You have more of your father in you than you know."

"Which one?" she asked.

"Does it matter?" he countered.

Christian studied the woman across from him and tried once again to take a mental step back from the raging lust pounding through him. He'd never had such an immediate reaction to any woman before, and it was disconcerting as hell when he was trying to concentrate on business.

Her face was an open book. Every emotion she felt was written there for the world to see and he had to admit that he liked that about her. There were no artifices. What you saw with Erica Prentice was what you got.

She was strong, as well. The kind of news he'd just delivered might have flattened most women, but she was already finding a way to deal with it. Might not be easy, but he didn't think she was the kind of woman to run from a challenge. Her whiskey-colored eyes shone with tears she refused to shed and that, too, struck a spark of admiration in him. She could control her emotions, which would be good once she hit Aspen.

Dealing with a whole new family wouldn't be easy,

but he was willing to bet she'd make it work. But he had to wonder how the Jarrod siblings were going to handle it. They'd all been shocked of course, but he'd expected that. He hadn't counted on the outright hostility he'd sensed from Blake and Guy. If they tried taking their outrage at their father out on Erica, Christian would just have to stop them.

Surprised at the thought, he realized that he was feeling…protective of her. Which didn't make a bit of sense since he'd only just met her. But there it was. She'd had her whole life turned upside down and inside out and damned if he'd let the Jarrod twins make her feel even worse about it.

"Is there something else you're not telling me?"

He looked at Erica. "What? No. Why do you ask?"

"Because you suddenly looked fierce enough to bite through steel."

"Oh." Apparently his legendary poker face, his ability to mask his emotions, was slipping today. "No, it's nothing. I was just thinking about some business I have to take care of back in Aspen."

"Right. You live there, too."

"I do." He smiled to himself, thinking about the home he had built on the Jarrod property. "I've got a house on the resort grounds. Don wanted his lawyer close by."

"Handy."

"It has been." He shrugged and expanded on that a little. "I grew up in Aspen. Worked at the Jarrod Resort as a teenager."

"So you knew my—" she stopped and rephrased what she'd been about to say "—Don Jarrod a long time."

"Since I was a kid."

"So you know his children, too."

"Sure. We didn't hang out together as kids, but I knew them. Got to know them better later on."

"What're they like?"

"You know," he said, glancing around for the waiter that had apparently given up on them ordering lunch, "we should get a meal while we talk."

"I'm not hungry, thanks."

"Oh." He should have figured she'd still be too shaken to eat. "Are you sure?"

"I am. Just tell me how they took this news. Are they furious? Am I going to be facing a firing squad in Colorado?"

He gave her a smile he hoped was reassuring. "Nothing so dramatic. I admit they were as stunned as you. But they're nice people. They'll deal with it."

She took a deep breath and blew it out again. "I suppose we'll all have to."

There it was, he thought, that thread of steel running through her slender, feminine body. "I have to say, I'm surprised at how well you're taking this. I actually expected you to need more convincing."

She shook her head and thought about that for a moment before answering. When she did, her voice was soft and low. "I've just discovered that my entire life has been built on lies." Her eyes met his and Christian felt the power of her stare slam into him. "I have to know the truth. I don't expect you to understand this, but I feel as though I *have* to go. Not for the inheritance. I don't need Don Jarrod's money. I have to go for *me*. I have to find out who I really am."

He had the oddest urge to reach across the table and cover her hand with his. His palm actually burned to touch her, but he resisted, somehow knowing that one touch would be both too much and not enough. Instead, he kept his voice deliberately businesslike as he said, "I do understand. You need to see *both* of your lives to be able to accept either one."

She tipped her head to one side and studied him. "You do understand." After a long moment, she turned her head to look out at the street pulsing with life behind them. "Until this morning, I thought my life was pretty dull. Routine. The biggest problem facing me this morning was getting through the morning meeting at the office. Now, I don't know what to think."

"Maybe you should give yourself a break. Don't try to figure anything out yet." He saw confusion and hurt in her eyes and he didn't like the fact that it bothered him. "All I'm saying is, wait. Go to Aspen. Meet your other family. Take some time."

She nodded thoughtfully. "Before I can do that, I have to go see my father," she said. "I need to hear what he has to say about this."

"Of course." He stood up as she did and held out one hand toward her. When she slid her palm against his, heat skittered up the length of his arm to reverberate through his chest. Oh, yes, touching her was an invitation to disaster. Instantly, he released her hand again. "I'll be flying back to Aspen tomorrow, so if you have any other questions, I'm at the Hyatt at the Embarcadero."

She smiled. "I love that hotel. Good choice."

"Nice view of the bay," he admitted. As she picked up her purse and the manila envelopes he'd given her, Christian heard himself say, "Call me when you're ready to come to Colorado. I'll tell you what to expect when you arrive."

"I will." She swung her purse up onto her shoulder, held on to the manila envelopes he'd given her and said, "I guess I'll be seeing you again soon, then."

"Soon." He nodded and stood there alone to watch her leave. Sunlight slanted through a bank of clouds and dazzled her hair with light. Her hips swayed and his gaze fixed on her behind so he could enjoy the view.

The next time he saw her, they would be in Aspen. Surrounded by the Jarrod family, he would be forced to keep his distance from her, and Christian didn't like the thought of that at all. He had a feeling that cleaning up the mess Don had left behind was going to be a lot harder than he'd believed it would be.

Three

Erica was always nervous when she walked into the headquarters of the Prentice Group. Of course, that was the impression her father wanted to make on prospective clients or competitors. Walter wanted people to be intimidated by their surroundings, because then he would always have the psychological advantage.

The building itself was massive, a glass-and-steel tower. Its tinted windows kept the sun at bay and prevented prying eyes in neighboring buildings from peeking in. As if that weren't enough, the décor had all the warmth and comfort of the great man himself. Cold tile, white walls and stiff, modernistic furniture set the scene in the main lobby and that tone was echoed on every floor.

Walter Prentice was a firm believer in the saying

"Perception is everything." He showed the world what he wanted them to see and that picture became reality. Erica thought about her father—or the man she'd always considered her father—for a second and felt an old ripple of anger slide beneath the surface of the confusion and hurt rampaging through her.

She'd been raised to uphold the family name. To be a shining beacon of respectability and decorum. This building was the heartbeat of the Prentice family dynasty. Where her brothers worked with their father. Where family meetings she was never included in were held. Where the men of the family made plans that the women were expected to follow. This was the place she had never felt good enough to enter.

Her father hadn't wanted her here. He'd made that clear enough. Wouldn't even consider her working in the family business, no matter how she had tried to convince him. Erica had never understood why, but she had been on the outside looking in for most of her life. Today, she had discovered the reasons behind her sense of seclusion.

Did her older brothers know the truth? Was that why they'd never really been close? As a kid, she'd wondered why her big brothers weren't like those of her friends. Sure, they were much older than she was, but still, they'd never paid attention to her. They'd never had the kind of relationship she had once wished for. Had they known the truth all along? Was she the only one who'd been in the dark?

It was time to find out.

She walked across the gleaming, cream-colored tile

floor to the security desk. The general public could just walk up to the bank of elevators on the south wall and take them up to any number of floors. But to reach the top floor, where her father's and brothers' offices were, required a stop at security where you were given a badge that would get you onto the penthouse elevator. As a child, she'd always felt "special" going through these motions. Today, she only felt even less a part of the Prentice world.

"Good afternoon, Ms. Prentice."

"Hi, Jerry," she said. The older man had been working in her father's lobby for twenty years. When she was a child, Erica remembered, Jerry had kept candy at his station so he always had some for her when she arrived. Now that she thought about it, she realized Jerry had always been happier to see her than Walter had. "I'm going up to see my father."

"That's good. Nice for a father and daughter to stay close," he said as he made a notation in his log, then handed her a badge. "Now that my Karen's moved out to college I don't see her nearly enough."

Erica smiled and hoped it looked more convincing than it felt. Fathers and daughters. She wondered wistfully if Don Jarrod had been a good father. Had her sister, Melissa, had the kind of connection with her father that Erica had always hungered for? Or had her biological father been cut from the same cloth as Walter? After all, they were both wealthy, important men. Maybe it was in their natures to be closed off and more concerned with business than with their children.

Some relationships were so much closer than others. And some, she mused, with a thought for the father she would never know, were never realized at all.

"You have a nice day now," Jerry said as she took the badge and headed for the private elevator.

Nice day. Two words rattling around inside her mind as she pushed the call button. Confusing day. Terrifying day. Nice? Not so much. In seconds, the doors swished open, she stepped inside and listened to the muted music that drifted down around her.

Now that she was here, Erica's stomach was churning. What was she going to say? What *could* she say? "Hello, Father, or should I call you Walter?"

Tears stung at her eyes, but she blinked them back. She hadn't cried in front of Christian Hanford and she wouldn't cry now. For one brief moment, the Colorado attorney's gorgeous face rose up in her mind and Erica thought if only he hadn't been there to tear down the foundations of her life, she would have been seriously attracted to him. But it was hard to notice a hum in your body when your heart was breaking.

Even now, her heart hurt and her knees were trembling. Music played on as the elevator silently streamed skyward. She should have thought this through more before coming to the office, Erica told herself. Figured out what she was going to say before coming here. But her feelings had pushed her here. That wild rush of anger and confusion and hurt was simmering inside her and waiting wouldn't have made a difference. She wouldn't have calmed down. If anything, the tension riding her would have only increased with a wait.

Besides, she thought as the elevator stopped and the doors slid open to reveal the rarefied air of the penthouse suite of offices, it was too late to back out now. She was here and it was past time for answers.

Thick, cream-colored carpet stretched on forever. Her father didn't want to be bothered by the clipping sound of shoes on tile. And what Walter Prentice wanted, he got. So the carpet was thick and the music soft. It was like stepping into a cloud, she thought. The view out the glass walls was impressive, the city stretched out all around them and the bay just beyond.

Taking a deep breath, Erica walked down the long hall to the desk of her father's assistant. Jewel Franks was fiftyish, no-nonsense and had her fingers on the pulse of the entire company. She had iron-gray hair neatly coiffed, cool blue eyes and the patience of a saint. She had to, to be able to work with Walter on a daily basis as she had for the last thirty years.

"Erica!" Jewel smiled at her. "What a lovely surprise. Your father isn't expecting you, is he? I don't have you on my list for the day...."

Erica felt a reluctant smile curve her mouth. Jewel's lists were legendary. If it wasn't written on her legal pad, it didn't exist.

"No, I'm sorry," she said. "This is a spur-of-the-moment thing, Jewel. Does he have a few minutes?"

The older woman gave her a wink. "You just managed to catch him between calls, honey. Why don't you go on in?"

"Thanks." Erica's stomach spun and dipped, as if her insides were dizzy and looking for a way to sit down.

Another deep breath to fortify already flagging nerves and she was walking to the double-door entrance to her father's office. A soft knock, then she turned the brass knob and entered.

"What is it, Jewel?" Walter didn't even look up from the sheaf of papers on his desk.

Erica took a second to study him as he sat there. All of her life, she'd looked up to this man, tried to please him and wondered why she continually failed. His hair was thick and cut short, white mingling with the black now, and his navy blue suit fit him like a uniform. Which it was, she supposed, since she had rarely seen her father in anything but a suit and tie. That tie was power-red today and as he lifted his gaze to look at her, she saw his eyes narrow in question.

"Erica? What are you doing here?"

Not exactly a warm greeting, but Walter never had cared for being interrupted at the office. "Hello, Father."

Openly frowning now, he asked, "Is there something wrong? Shouldn't you be at work?"

She watched his face, searching for some sign of warmth or pleasure, but there was nothing. So she walked across the floor, never taking her eyes from his. When she was standing opposite his desk, she said, "I had a visitor today. A lawyer from Colorado."

Walter jerked as if he'd been shot. Then he stiffened in his chair and set his sterling silver pen onto the desk top. His features went deliberately blank.

"Colorado?" He repeated the word without the slightest inflection in his voice.

"Don't," Erica said, staring into those distant green eyes of his as she had her whole life, hoping to see love shining back at her. But again, she was disappointed. "Don't pretend to not know what I'm talking about."

His eyes narrowed as he sat back in his chair and gave an impatient tug to his suit vest. "Young lady, don't take that tone with me."

Erica almost laughed and would have if her heart wasn't aching in her chest. She hadn't heard that particular phrase from him since she was seventeen, and telling her father she was going to a concert with her friends. Of course, she hadn't gone to the concert, since he'd refused permission and sent her to her room. She wasn't a rebellious girl anymore though, fighting her own nerves and her father for the right to spread her wings. And she no longer needed his permission to do what she felt she had to do. She was all grown-up and she deserved some answers.

"Father," she said quietly, "the attorney told me some things. Things I need to talk to you about."

"I can imagine he did. But I'm not going to discuss this with you." His jaw jutted out, his eyes narrowed and he silently dared her to continue.

"I need to know, Father," she said, doing just that. "I have the right to hear it from you. I have to know if everything he said was true."

"You want to talk about rights? What about my rights to not have this distasteful matter resurrected?" he muttered, tapping his fingers against the desk in a nervous tattoo. "You're Erica Prentice. My daughter, and by heaven, that should be enough for you."

God, she wished it were. She wanted it to be enough. But just looking at Walter's face told her that there was so much more she needed to know. All her life, she'd loved this man. Wanted him to be proud of her. Had strived to be the best—at everything—just to win his approval.

Now, she wanted him to tell her this was all a mistake. Some cruel trick. Yet even before she'd come here, she'd known it wasn't. "Father, please. Talk to me. I don't even know what to think about all of this."

He ground his teeth together, his jaw working furiously before he said, "That bastard Jarrod. This is all his fault. Even from the grave he tries to steal from me."

"What?" That was not the opening she'd been expecting.

Walter pushed back from his desk and stood up. "He left orders in his will to contact you, didn't he?" He shoved one hand through his hair, startling Erica. It was the first time she'd ever seen him actually rattled.

"I knew he would," Walter was muttering. "It was the one sure way he could get around me. Should have known he wouldn't keep his word."

This was getting more confusing by the moment. "Don Jarrod left me an equal share in his estate."

Walter snorted derisively. "Of course he did. He knew I couldn't stop him and this was the only way he had left to stick it to me."

"To you?" Erica shook her head and felt the sting of tears she wouldn't allow burning in her eyes again. "This isn't about you, Father, this is about me."

"Don't you fool yourself." Walter stabbed his index finger at her. "This was always about Don Jarrod and what he could take from me. No better than a damn thief, that man."

Heart sinking in her chest, Erica watched as Walter's features went florid with the rush of temper. Even knowing it was foolish, she'd been harboring one small flicker of doubt inside her. The hope that this was all wrong. That Don Jarrod had made a mistake. That Walter was her father and really did love her. So much for hope.

"So he really was my father?"

"Yes." Walter bit the word off as if it had tasted foul. "The bastard." He glanced at her, then looked away again and stalked across the room to stare out at the gloomy view of gray sky and sea. "Your mother and I were having…problems. No point in getting into them now, it's over and done years ago. But we separated for a time. I went to England for several months, setting up the European branch of the company. Thought it best if Danielle and I each had some space. Some time to consider what we wanted."

She stared at his broad back as he kept his gaze fixed on the window and the world beyond the glass. He couldn't even look at her as he spoke and that ripped another tiny shred out of her heart.

He had thought it best to leave her mother for a while, Erica told herself and wondered what her mother's wishes had been. Then Walter was talking again and she paid attention.

"Don Jarrod was here, in town, supposedly buying

up a hotel or two. They met at the theater. Introduced by mutual friends," he said that last word with a sneer, as if the sting of betrayal were still too sharp. Then he inhaled deeply and exhaled on a rush of words. "The bastard took advantage of her. I was out of the country, and Jarrod saw she was vulnerable, sad. He romanced her, seduced her and got her pregnant."

Erica swayed unsteadily, but kept standing. It all sounded so awful. So…tacky. How was she supposed to feel about this? She was the unplanned result of a hurried affair. Not the sort of thing a woman wants to hear.

Walter was still talking. "Of course," he told her, with a glance over his shoulder, "I didn't realize your mother was expecting you until after we'd reconciled…."

That's when it hit her. "So you were separated when—" It didn't really make it better, but at least her mother hadn't been cheating.

"Hardly matters," Walter argued. "We were still married. Not that Don Jarrod would care about that. I loved my wife. I wanted our marriage back. Danielle assured me the affair was long over. Jarrod had returned to Colorado and we put it behind us. When she discovered she was pregnant, she went against my wishes and told him because she felt he had the right to know about his child."

"He knew all these years."

Walter snorted. "Yes. Naturally he got in contact. He wanted to be a part of your life—as if I would ever have allowed that. The scandal of it would have rocked this city. Ruined business, cost me clients. I couldn't have that."

"Of course not," she whispered, feeling another sharp slice of pain. Scandal was the one thing Walter wouldn't tolerate. The idea of his friends and business associates knowing about his wife's affair would have been unbearable for him. He hadn't hidden the truth because of his desire to protect and love her, but to save himself embarrassment.

This explained a lot, she told herself, her mind racing, darting from one thought to the next so quickly she could hardly keep up. As a girl, she had dreamed of a daddy who doted on her. After all, she was the youngest in the family by quite a bit. The youngest of her older brothers was still fifteen years older than she. Erica had grown up practically an only child. Her brothers were out and building lives of their own by the time she was a teenager.

But Walter had never been the kind of father she'd yearned for. At last, she knew why. And Erica wondered sadly if Don Jarrod would have been any different. He was—or had been—much like Walter, a businessman first last and always.

And yet…

"He wanted me," she said softly, more to herself than to Walter.

"He wanted to ruin *me*," Walter told her flatly. Some of the hot color drained from his features. "He tried to convince your mother to leave me. Go with him to that backwater out in the country. But she knew what was best. What was right." He nodded with satisfaction. "Besides, I told her I wouldn't hold her mistake against her."

"No," Erica said softly. "You held it against me."

He stared at her. "I beg your pardon?"

Erica's pain was enveloped by a rising tide of regret and sadness. "Father, my whole life you've looked at me with barely concealed revulsion."

"Not true," he said, but his gaze slipped to one side, avoiding her eyes.

Even now, he couldn't look at her. Couldn't meet her gaze and admit to the truth. But she wouldn't play the game anymore. She finally understood why she'd always been a little less worthy than her brothers and that in itself was liberating.

"Yes," she said, "it is. I used to wonder what I'd done that was so wrong. So awful to make you dislike me so much."

"I don't dislike you, Erica," he said, surprise coloring his voice. "I love you."

She wished she could believe that, but with her heart aching it was simply impossible. "You've never acted as if you do."

He squared his shoulders and lifted his chin. "I'm not an emotional man, Erica, but you should be well aware of my feelings."

"Until this moment, I wasn't sure you had any," Erica snapped, then lifted one hand to cover her mouth, almost as stunned as he was that she'd said such a thing.

He looked at her as if she was someone he didn't even recognize, and to be fair, Erica thought, she could understand his reaction. In her whole life, she'd never once spoken back to him this way. Stood up for herself. Always, she had tried to be the perfect daughter. To win a smile or a nod of approval from him. At this moment though, none of that meant anything to her. Right now, all she felt was her own hurt. Her own disappointment. Her own wish that things were different.

"Erica," he said, that deep voice rumbling out around her as it had since her childhood. "I *am* your father in every way that matters. Haven't I always been here for you? Didn't I raise you? Have you *ever* wanted for anything?"

"Only your love," she said, voice catching as she finally admitted to him that she'd felt that lack her whole life.

"How can you say that?" His shocked expression told her exactly how surprised he was by her words.

The tears that she'd managed to hold at bay all day finally began to show themselves. Irritated by their arrival, Erica quickly swiped them away with the backs of her hands.

"I'm sorry, Father," she said at last. "Maybe my coming here wasn't a good idea. I didn't want to upset you. Didn't want us to tear at each other."

He took a single step toward her, then stopped, clearly unsure of his next move. Which was, she thought, another first.

"Erica…" He paused as if gathering his scattered thoughts, then said, "Your mother wouldn't want you to go. She'd want you to stay here. With your family."

Would she? Erica wondered. Or would her mother understand the need to discover her roots? God, what a clichéd way to think of this. But wasn't it true? Wouldn't she be exploring her past so that she could figure out her future?

"I do love you, Father," she told him. "But I'm going to Colorado. I have to. To meet my brothers and sister. To find out if I belong there any more than I do here."

"What's *that* supposed to mean?" His bellow was completely unexpected. Walter Prentice never lost his temper. Or at least, he'd never allowed anyone to witness it. "Of course you belong here, this is your home. We're your family."

"So are they."

"You will not do this thing." He folded his arms across his chest. "I forbid it."

Erica had to smile through her tears. Typical of this man, she thought. If he couldn't sway, he would command, fully expecting that his opposition would fold and do exactly as he wanted.

Still, she loved him and wished he would sweep her up into his big arms and tell her this was all nonsense. That of course he loved her. Always had. Always would. She wanted to be cuddled against her father's broad chest and reassured about her place in the world.

But that wasn't going to happen.

Sadly, she faced him. "You can't stop me, Father, so please don't try." Erica walked to the door and opened it but before she could slip through, his voice halted her.

"If you don't find what you're looking for there?" he asked. "What then?"

She glanced back at him and suddenly thought that he looked so…lonely, in his plush office surrounded by the symbols of his success. "Honestly? I just don't know."

"So what is she like?"

Christian looked up from the desk in his office at the Manor and smiled at Melissa Jarrod. She wore a pale yellow silk blouse tucked into a short, dark green skirt. Her heeled sandals gave her already five-foot-eight height three extra inches and her blue eyes were sparkling with excitement. She shook her long fall of blond hair back from her face, planted both hands on the desktop and leaned toward him.

Looked as though he wouldn't be getting much work done, he told himself. Melissa was bound and determined to get information on her new sister and until he surrendered to the inevitable, Christian knew the woman wouldn't be going anywhere.

"Come on, Christian, give a little," she prodded.

"I already told you she seems very nice," he said.

"Nice doesn't tell me a lot." She straightened up and paced around the room. "Is she funny? Boring?"

He didn't remember her being boring, Christian thought. Would have been easier on him if she had been. But no, Erica Prentice had to be strong and intelligent and—not helping, he told himself. "She's…nice."

Melissa laughed. "Honestly, you're hopeless. You make a terrible spy."

"Good thing I'm a lawyer then," he said and shifted his gaze back to the papers on the desk. His brief hope that he'd satisfied her curiosity and would be allowed to get back to work was shattered a second later.

"Fine. As a lawyer, give me a description. Tell me how she reacted. What she's thinking. Something," she begged.

Sitting back in his chair, Christian looked across the room at the youngest Jarrod sibling—well, now thanks to Erica, she was the second youngest. Melissa hadn't taken long at all to decide to come home to Aspen. She'd quit her job managing a trendy, luxurious day spa in Los Angeles and had taken over at the spa here at the resort. Since she was also a yoga instructor, she had plans to include yoga retreats at the spa, as well. She'd slipped back into mountain life as if she'd never left it.

"What do you want to hear?"

"I don't know," she said, laughing again. "I have a sister I've never met. Is she fun? Does she smile a lot? Is she stuffy? You know, more into business than anything else? Because really, with my brothers, I'm hoping she's not."

"She didn't seem to be," he said, thinking back on that one day he'd had with Erica. Not like he hadn't been doing a lot of thinking about her ever since they first met. On the long flight home, he'd almost convinced himself that the instant attraction he'd felt for her wasn't as overwhelming as he'd believed. But then Erica had called him that night to tell him she would be arriving in just a few days.

All it had taken was hearing her voice and his body was tight and hard and… Christian cut those thoughts off fast. Melissa was pretty damned intuitive and he didn't need her picking up on what he was feeling for her sister.

"She was," he said, before Melissa could prod him again, "surprised. As shocked as all of you were to hear about her connection to the family."

"Poor thing," Melissa murmured, her soft heart showing. "I can't even imagine having that curve ball thrown at you."

"You did have it thrown at you," he reminded her.

"Yeah, but I already knew I was a Jarrod. She's coming into this cold and it had to be hard to find out you're not who you think you are."

Christian smiled at her again. She was going to be an ally for Erica. A safe harbor in a strange new world. And that was a good thing. He had a feeling she was going to need friends. In their communications with him, Blake and Guy weren't exactly warming up to the idea of a new sister. And as for Gavin and Trevor…he'd know when they arrived what their attitude was going to be.

"I think it's safe to say it hit her hard. She's strong though," Christian told her. "Every bit as tough as you are. But she's got a soft side, too," he mused, remembering the sheen of tears she'd managed to keep at bay when they'd been talking.

"Do I detect some interest there?" Melissa asked.

"What?" He straightened up and glared at her. Damn it, he couldn't afford to relax his guard for a minute around her. She was way too perceptive. "No. You don't. Besides, that would be inappropriate."

"Oh, for heaven's sake, Christian," Melissa said with a sad shake of her head, "you sound like a Puritan or something."

"I'm not and I'm also not discussing this with you. Don't you have a spa to run?"

Frustrated, she huffed out a breath. "Honestly, men are the most bizarre creatures."

"Thanks so much. Goodbye."

"Oh, I'm going," she said, smiling now as she headed for his office door. "But don't think this ends the conversation, Christian."

Once she was gone, he leaned back in his chair again and told himself to shape up. He couldn't afford to show any of the Jarrod siblings that he was attracted to Erica. With the board of directors due to meet in a few months, he couldn't afford to start rumors.

Dating a member of the Jarrod family was one sure way for an employee to find himself quickly unemployed. It was there in the contracts they all signed, since Don had been adamant about protecting his family. Don's will ensured that the fraternization clause would stay. The board of directors would follow Don's directions until new ones were put in their place. Christian couldn't count on the Jarrod siblings doing anything to change the status quo. And he wasn't going to give up the job he'd worked so hard for and loved so much for any woman.

No matter how much he wanted her.

Four

Three days after her lunch with Christian, Erica was on a private plane headed to Aspen. Strange how quickly she'd managed to pull this together. Erica had taken a leave of absence from her firm, closed up her condo and put her car into storage. When she called Christian Hanford to tell him her plans, he'd insisted on sending the family jet for her. She'd argued with him of course, but Erica thought as she looked around her, she was glad she'd lost that argument.

The plane was furnished with both elegance and comfort in mind. Thick, sky-blue carpeting covered the floor and the dozen seats were in pale blue leather and more comfy than any first-class accommodation she'd ever tried. There was a flat-screen TV on the bulkhead, a selection of movies for the DVD player and a stereo outfitted with dozens of CDs. There was also a uniformed hostess who had served Erica a delicious breakfast before disappearing into the front of the plane with the pilot and copilot.

She had the cabin to herself and Erica was grateful for the respite. She'd been doing so much thinking and considering over the last few days, had had so many people talking to her and at her, it was nearly a vacation to have some quiet time to herself.

Although, with all of this quality thinking time, she was starting to make herself crazy wondering what exactly she was getting herself into. Christian had said that her new family was eager to meet her.

She had to wonder about that. He was probably just being nice. Why would they be taking this situation any better than her older brothers had? She hardly saw her siblings unless it was at some family function, but only the day before, the three of them had descended on her en masse to try to talk her out of this move.

Erica leaned her head back against the seat and closed her eyes. She could still hear her brothers' voices, alternately pleading, arguing and demanding that she stop hurting the man who'd loved her and raised her. Strange how they were all so interested in protecting Walter from a truth he'd known all along. None of them had given much thought to what *she* was having to deal with.

Even with her brothers coming at her from all sides, that confrontation hadn't been as bad as the one with her stepmother. Angela, to give the woman her due, loved Walter to distraction. She'd made him happy,

Erica knew, and she'd even tried, in the beginning, to foster a relationship with Erica. But the woman really wasn't very maternal and Erica had been old enough to resent a woman who wasn't her mother trying to take over her life. So they'd never really connected. And that wasn't likely to change now, she thought as she remembered that last scene with her stepmother.

"You're hurting him with this, Erica," Angela had *said softly, her tone and expression clearly showing her disapproval. "He doesn't deserve this sort of treatment from you."*

"Angela, all I want to do is find out who I am," she *argued patiently.*

"And you believe your father resents your choice."

"Are you saying he doesn't?"

Angela took a long breath and let it sigh from her lungs. Picking up her clutch, she tucked it beneath her left arm and slowly shook her head. "You've never looked past his brusque exterior to the man beneath, have you?" Not waiting for an answer, she said, "One day you will, my dear. And you'll see that Walter's heart aches for you. He loves you, Erica. It doesn't matter that Don Jarrod donated his sperm to your creation. It's Walter Prentice who is your father."

Was Angela right? Or was she only defending her husband as she always had? Erica didn't know, but she couldn't allow anything to stop her from this quest.

"So basically," Erica whispered to no one, "I'm on my own. Probably about time, too," she added under her breath.

Heaven knew this was the greatest adventure she'd ever undertaken. Unlike her friends, she hadn't back-packed through Europe after graduating from college. She hadn't taken a year off to "find" herself. Instead, she'd done exactly what was expected of her. She had gotten a job at a well-regarded firm and began the process of building a respectable life. In fact, Erica had never done a single thing on impulse. She had been the good little girl, doing the right thing. The proper thing. All because she had been trying to prove herself to a father who had never noticed her. Now though, it seemed she was making up for all of that.

Pulling up stakes and moving halfway across the country to live with people she didn't know and help run a resort she'd never seen.

It was crazy. Made zero sense. She should be terri-fied.

But she wasn't.

Erica looked out the window at the earth far below and watched the view change from city to mountains and plains and felt a stir of excitement rise up inside her. This was new. Fresh. She had a chance here that few people ever had. An opportunity to completely reinvent herself. She was going to do the best she could with it. She was going to find her way and figure out who she was and when that was done, she'd be able to face her father again and hold her head high.

She picked up her cup of coffee and sipped at it. But for the muffled roar of the engines, the inside of the jet was quiet. She wasn't interested in watching a movie or listening to the selection of music they had on board. In fact, she was actually too restless to sit still. The only thing keeping her in her buttery-soft leather chair was her instinctive fear of flying. And as the time ticked away, Erica's excitement turned into nervousness and she worried about the reception she'd be receiving once she landed.

Friends? Or enemies? And how would she be able to tell?

The pilot's voice crackled over the speaker, interrupting her thoughts. "Ms. Prentice, please make sure your seat belt is fastened. We're beginning our initial descent and will be landing in Aspen in about twenty minutes."

She nodded as if the man could see her, then smiled at herself.

Only twenty minutes until her new life started.

He was waiting on the tarmac.

Christian Hanford looked different than he had in San Francisco, Erica thought as her heartbeat sped into a gallop. For one thing, he wasn't wearing a suit. And if she'd thought him gorgeous in that elegantly cut business suit, it was nothing to how she felt now.

He was wearing dark blue jeans, black boots and a red pullover collared shirt. His short dark hair ruffled in the wind and his lazy stance as he leaned against a black BMW only added to the "dangerous" air about him.

He walked to meet her as she came down the retractable stairway. A half smile on his face, he stopped at the bottom of the staircase and looked up at her. "How was your trip?"

"Fabulous," she said quickly. "Thank you for sending the jet for me."

"Least we could do," he said and held out one hand to help her down the last few steps. His thumb traced lightly over the back of her hand and his touch felt like licks of flame. His dark eyes locked with hers and Erica felt a nearly magnetic pull toward the man. For one split second it was as if they were the only two people in the world. His square jaw was shadowed with a faint trace of whiskers and his mouth was still curved in that half smile as he added, "It's the Jarrod family jet. You're family."

She laid her free hand against her abdomen in an attempt to still the butterflies that had suddenly decided to swarm inside her. It was a wasted effort. With excitement came nerves and she didn't expect either to let up anytime soon.

"How about a quick tour of Aspen before we go to the resort?"

"I'd like that," she said, tearing her gaze from his really gorgeous dark chocolate eyes long enough to look around her. Once she did, she gasped.

She glanced around the small—compared to San Francisco—airport and the mountains surrounding them. The sky was so blue it nearly hurt to look at it and the white clouds scudding across that sky could have been painted on, they were so perfect. The air was sharp and clean and the relative quiet was nearly deafening to a woman used to the sounds of a city.

"It's beautiful," she whispered, staring out at the mountains that towered over them like guardian angels.

"You know," he said, and she turned to catch him looking at her, "it really is." Then he shook off whatever he was thinking, and gave her hand a tug. "Come on, city girl. Let me show you around."

She was too damn beautiful; that was the problem, Christian told himself. He'd hoped that his memory of her was exaggerated. That she hadn't really had eyes the color of finely aged whiskey. That she didn't smell like peaches. That her softly layered hair didn't really lift in the wind until it looked like a halo around her head. He'd hoped that his desire for her would be something he could tuck away and ignore.

But just touching her hand had set off explosions of want inside him and now Christian knew exactly what he was up against.

Temptation.

He kept her hand tucked into his as he led her toward his car. The top was down and it was a perfect day for her to see her new home. When he opened the car door for her he took an extra second to enjoy the view. She wore white linen slacks, a dark blue shirt and black leather flats, and managed to look more beautiful than any woman had a right to. Oh, yeah. He was in deep trouble.

He closed the car door and said, "We'll drive through town, let you get your bearings."

"What about my luggage?"

"They'll deliver it to the resort."

"Right." She nodded. "Okay then."

He hopped in on the driver's side, fired the engine and drove out of the airport.

"I can't believe the mountains are so close," she said, pushing her windblown hair out of her face.

"I've lived here my whole life so I guess I don't really take the time to look up at them much."

"I don't know how you could do anything else," she admitted.

He followed her gaze briefly, allowing himself to admire the sweep of green that climbed up the mountains ringing Aspen. Like most citizens of Aspen, he more or less took the natural beauty of the place for granted. When you grew up in the middle of a painting, you tended to think everyone else lived with those kinds of views, too.

Christian gave her a quick grin. "I give you two weeks before you stop noticing them, just like the rest of us."

She glanced at him and shook her head. "I'll take that bet."

As he drove into the city, he rattled off the names of the businesses crowded along the streets. On Galena he pointed out the old brick buildings, several of the shops and Erica noticed the flower boxes lining the walkways between stores. Down Main Street, he showed her the *Aspen Times,* one of the town newspapers, and she smiled at the small blue building adorned with old-fashioned gold lettering across the front.

He knew what she was seeing, but he had to admit

that like the mountains, he tended to take for granted the charm of the city he'd grown up in.

It was modern of course, with plenty of high-end boutiques and shops for the megawealthy and celebrities who flocked here every year. But it was also an old mining town. Brick buildings, narrow streets, brightly colored flowers in boxes and old-fashioned light posts that were more atmospheric than useful. It was a mingling of three centuries, he supposed.

"In Aspen, we've sort of held on to the old while we welcomed the new."

"I love it," she said, her head whipping from side to side so she could take it all in.

He threw a quick look at her, saw pure pleasure dancing in her eyes and wondered how he was going to maintain a strictly business relationship with the youngest of Don's daughters. As his mind wrestled with his body's wants, he tried to focus on the road and not the way she lazily crossed her legs.

"It's so big," she said after another minute or two.

"Aspen?" He gave her another quick look. Coming from a city the size of San Francisco, he was surprised to hear she thought Aspen was big. "It's not, really. Population's around five thousand with a hell of a lot more than that every winter for the skiing and in the summer for the food and wine gala."

"No, not Aspen itself," she corrected. "Colorado. It's all so…open. God, the sky just goes on forever." She laughed a little and shrugged. "I'm more used to fragments of sky outlined by office buildings."

"Which do you like better?"

"Well," she said as he stopped at a red light, "that's the question, isn't it? San Francisco is beautiful, but in a completely different way. I feel so out of my element here."

The light changed, he put the car in gear and stepped on the gas. Keeping his eyes on the road, he said, "You're Don Jarrod's daughter, so Colorado's in your blood. Your family goes back a long way here."

"Tell me," she said, focusing on him now more than the city around them.

"I'll do my best," he said, thinking back to everything he'd heard Don talking about over the years. "Don's great-great-grandfather started the resort. He was here for the silver mining boom that started the city back in 1879. Bought himself some land and built what he called the biggest, damnedest house in Colorado."

Erica smiled. "No shortage of self-esteem in the Jarrod family then?"

"Not at all," Christian agreed with a chuckle. "Anyway, by 1893, Aspen had banks, theaters, a hospital and electric lights."

"Impressive," she said, half turning in her seat to watch him as he spoke.

"It was. Then the bottom dropped out of the silver market, mines closed and people moved out by the hundreds. Eli Jarrod refused to go, though. He kept adding on to his house, and opened it up as a hotel. There were still plenty of people back east who wanted to come out here on fishing and hunting trips and Eli was set up to take care of them."

"Smart."

"Not a shortage of brains in the Jarrod family, either," he told her. "Anyway, Eli managed to hang on. The Depression wasn't easy for anybody, but then the resort really took off in 1946. Then people were discovering the mountains for skiing and the Jarrods were prepared to handle the tourism trade."

"Right place, right time?"

"I guess," he said, "though they hung on through the lean years when everyone said that a hotel in the middle of 'nowhere' was a bad idea. So maybe you could just put their success down to pure stubbornness."

He steered the car past a delivery truck and along street after street. Businesses gave way to bungalow homes set far back on wide lots dotted with pines. Soon they left the city behind and turned onto a road guarded on either side by tall trees and open space.

"Tell me about the resort."

Christian nodded. "Like I said, it started out as just the family home, though your ancestor made sure it was the biggest house for miles around. As he turned it into a hotel, the place got even grander. Wings were added off the main building and the Jarrod resort was born." He took a sharp left and steered the car across the bridge spanning the Roaring Fork River. "And the resort just kept growing. The main hotel is out front and the top floor is the family residence. That's where you'll be staying."

She took a breath and nodded. "Okay, what else?"

"There are lodges built on the grounds, some of them actually going up the slope of the mountain. There are standard log cabins, some stone ones. Most of the lodges are small and cozy, one-family deals, but there are much bigger ones too, fully staffed with butlers, maids and cooks."

Her eyebrows rose. "Wow."

"Oh, yeah." He steered the car down a narrow road lined with stands of trees so thick she could barely see through them. "I think you're about to be amazed, Erica Prentice."

She laughed. "What makes you think I haven't been already?"

"It's about to get better," he assured her.

The long drive up to the resort unfolded in front of them. An acre of neatly tended lawn bordered by banks of flowers spilling color and scent lay in front of the truly impressive Manor.

Erica felt her mouth drop open. "It's a castle," she whispered, her gaze sweeping up and over the main stone building, then encompassing the wings jutting out from either side. Flowering green shrubs crouched at the base of the Manor and gleaming window panes shone in the sun like diamonds. There were peaked roofs, balconies with iron railings and the aged brick of the structure itself was the color of roses.

It would have seemed like a postcard, but for the bustle of employees around the circular drive making the whole place come alive. A doorman in a sharp, navy-blue-and-gold jacket spouted orders like a general and bellmen raced to follow them. Luxury cars idled beneath an arched stone covering over the gravel drive as guests stepped from them to be escorted into the hotel.

"This is…" she whispered, still stunned.

"I told you," Christian said. "Amazed."

"That's really not a big enough word," she told him as he pulled under the archway and stepped out of the car. In a moment, Christian was at the passenger side, helping her out. She stood up and did a slow turn, trying to take in everything at once.

It was impossible. She thought she'd need weeks to get the whole picture of the Jarrod resort. But what she had seen, she loved. Erica had never seen anyplace like it. It was as if she had stepped into a fairy tale. All that was missing was the handsome prince riding up on a black charger.

Then her gaze shifted to Christian. Handsome man in a black BMW. The modern version of the fairy tale then, she thought with an inner smile. But he wasn't a prince and she wasn't in need of rescuing. Or was she?

Shifting her gaze to scan the yard, then turning to peek through the open double doors into the lobby, Erica couldn't avoid a quick jolt of nerves that shot from her stomach up to her heart and back again. She was here. About to meet a family she'd never known and there was no going back.

"Second thoughts?"

She turned to look at Christian and found him watching her with a bemused expression on his face. Funny, she hadn't even met him a week ago and now, he was the one spot of familiarity in a rapidly changing world.

"No," she said firmly, taking a deep breath as she

did so. "No second thoughts. I made the decision to come here and I'm going to stick with it."

A flash of admiration lit up his dark eyes briefly and Erica felt warmed by it.

"Good for you," he said, then waved one arm out toward the interior of the hotel. "Ready to see your new home?"

"As I'll ever be," she told him and started walking.

The honey-colored wood walls and floors shone like a jewel box in the overhead lights. Framed photos of the mountain taken during every season dotted the walls and there were tables and chairs scattered around the wide lobby. A hum of conversation rose and fell as people wandered around the room and through it all, there was an almost electrical air about the place.

Erica swiveled her head from side to side, looking at everything as Christian guided her across the lobby to an elevator off by itself. "This is the private elevator to the family quarters," he told her and took a card from his pocket to slide into the key slot.

The door slid open and they stepped inside. Again, honey-colored wood set the tone, making Erica think not only of a mountain cabin, but warmth and luxury.

"Your key will be in your suite, waiting for you," Christian was saying. "Your luggage probably beat us here, since we took the scenic route. You'll find everything you need in your suite. There's even a small efficiency kitchen there and it's been stocked with the basics."

"Okay."

"There's also a main kitchen on the family level,

if you really feel the urge to cook something. But the hotel restaurants will deliver, so you don't have to worry about that if you don't want to."

"Oh, I like cooking," she told him as the elevator stopped and the door opened.

"Well, then, you and your brother Guy should get along just fine. He's a chef." Christian stepped out and held the door back for her. "He was, anyway. He owned his own restaurant in New York before coming back to Aspen and now he's pretty much taking over running the resort restaurants."

"A chef," she mused with a smile. "I'm not in his league, then. I said I like cooking. Didn't promise I was good at it."

"Make me dinner some night," he said, then stopped and frowned to himself as if he already regretted the words.

Judging by his expression, Erica ignored what he said, stepped into the hall and sighed as she looked around. "It just keeps getting prettier."

The hallway they stepped into was wide, leading off in two directions. Wood floors, walls the color of fog and a narrow table boasting a cobalt vase stuffed with roses and hydrangeas greeted her. Every few feet, an arched window let in sunlight and provided a view that was breathtaking. But she didn't have enough time to look around and enjoy it.

Christian pointed to the left. "Down there are four suites, and just past them, along the hallway, is the family room."

"Okay…" She noted that the private quarters

followed the line of the hotel, only the windows here looked out over a palatial pool area. The aquamarine water held a few guests lounging on rafts and on the flagstone area surrounding the pool, cabanas, tables and chairs with brightly colored umbrellas offered places to sit and chat. There was a bar tucked into one corner of the space and uniformed waiters and waitresses hurried back and forth seeing to the guests' comforts.

No doubt about it, she had walked into a very different world in Colorado than the one she was accustomed to. Then she realized that Christian was still talking and she turned around to watch him and listen.

"Past the family room is the original family quarters. The master bedroom and bedrooms for your brothers and sister when they were kids."

She tried to imagine growing up in this place, but it was hard to envision. So much space. So much open land for children to run and play. Smiling, she recalled that as a girl, she'd thought the park her nanny had taken her to was a veritable wilderness.

"As his kids got older," Christian said, "Don had the place rehabbed, building each of them their own suite and a few extras for guests."

It sounded as though Don Jarrod had done everything he could to keep his children at home. Yet each of them had fled Colorado. She had to wonder why.

Erica took a breath and nodded. "Are they all living here now?"

As if he could read the trepidation on her face, he smiled and said, "No. Right now, there's only Guy in one of the suites and Guy's twin, Blake, and his assistant living in two of the others. The rest of your family are here—staying in different lodges."

Only a couple of siblings to worry about facing every day then. That was good. Erica would prefer to settle in a little before she was forced to deal with Don Jarrod's other children. But if Guy or Blake and his assistant were there at the moment, now was as good a time as any to get the first of the introductions over with.

"Are any of them here now?" Erica tried to steel herself for meeting the first of her new family. Though now that she thought about it, she wished she had a minute to drag a brush through her wind-tossed hair and to put on some makeup and—

"No," Christian said, interrupting her frenzied thoughts. "Blake's gone for a few days at the moment. He and Samantha have been flying back and forth a lot to Vegas, wrapping up loose ends in the business and getting ready to take over here. Blake and your brother Gavin have been building hotels, mostly in Las Vegas and they've done exceptionally well out there."

"And they're giving it up to come back here?"

"Yeah," Christian said. "Like you, your brothers and sister have closed down their old lives and are here to start over again."

But they were returning to something familiar at least. She, on the other hand, felt as though she'd fallen into the rabbit hole. Nerves rattled through her again, but resolutely, she fought them down.

"What about Guy?"

"This time of day, he's probably downstairs in the main restaurant."

She drew a breath and let it go. "What about Gavin? Is he in Vegas with Blake?"

"No, he's here. But he's living in one of the private lodges on the grounds." Christian shrugged. "He wasn't interested in moving into the Manor."

Erica was beginning to understand that none of her brothers and sister were exactly thrilled to be back in Aspen. Yet, they'd all come, putting aside their plans and lives outside Jarrod Ridge to return and take up the family resort again. That told her that despite what were probably mixed feelings about their father and this place, their loyalty to family meant more than their reluctance to return. And that knowledge made her feel better, somehow. If family was everything to these people, then eventually, she might be able to have a relationship with all of them.

"What about the others?" she asked. "Where are they living?"

He led her down the hallway in the opposite direction from Blake's suite as he continued.

"Well, like I said, Trevor has his own place in Aspen, but he's here most days. Guy stays here mainly because he's working here at the Manor. And Melissa…" He paused. "She lives in Willow Lodge. It's the farthest lodge from the Manor, but anyone here can tell you where that is. She also runs the hotel spa, and you'll find her there most days."

"How big are the family quarters?" she suddenly

asked, astonished at the length of the hallway in both directions.

"As big as the top floor of the hotel. Including wings," Christian added with a smile.

"Amazing," she murmured as she followed after him.

"Yeah, it is. Down here is your suite, plus two more. Farther along this hall, you'll find the kitchen, the great room and what was Don's office. My office is down on the main floor, but I do most of my work at home."

"Right. You don't live at the Manor. Where's your place from here?"

He steered her toward one of the high, arched windows lining the hallway and pointed. "See the red roof just past that tall pine?"

She did. The building couldn't be more than a five-minute walk from where she was standing. "Close."

"It is. So if you ever need anything…"

He was standing so near, she felt heat radiating from his body toward hers. He smelled so good, she wanted to breathe deeper and when she looked up into those chocolate-brown eyes, she had the strangest desire to lean in and… *What* was she thinking? Didn't she have enough going on in her life at the moment?

"Thanks," she said abruptly, taking a safe step back from him. "I'll keep that in mind."

He watched her for a second or two and Erica wondered if he could tell what she'd been thinking. If he could see that she had been wondering what he would taste like. If his lips were as soft and warm as they appeared to be.

But if he did know, then he was as determined as she to not draw attention to it. He scrubbed one hand across his face, then waved one arm out in front of him in silent invitation to continue on down the hall. He walked beside her and the heels of their shoes sounded out like gunshots in the stillness.

When he finally stopped in front of a door and opened it, Erica stepped past him and stopped dead on the threshold.

It was gorgeous, which shouldn't have surprised her. Everything about Jarrod Ridge was breathtaking. But somehow, she hadn't expected her room to be so... wonderful. After all, she was the stranger here and from what she could tell so far, her new brothers and sister had been no more thrilled to hear of her existence than she had been to hear about them. She'd half expected an ordinary hotel room, lovely, but generic. This, she told herself as she walked farther into the room, was anything but generic.

The living room was done in various shades of blue. Pale blue walls, dark blue, overstuffed furniture, cobalt vases stuffed with flowers dripping heavy scent into the air and navy blue drapes at the arched windows. The wood floor was dotted with braided rugs in shades of blue and cream and even the fireplace was fronted by tiles that looked like delft.

"Wow," she said and even that word was just so insignificant to the task.

"Glad you like it," he said, moving into the room behind her.

"What's not to like?" She did a slow turn, trying

to see everything at once. Then her gaze landed on Christian again. "To tell the truth, I wasn't expecting anything like this."

He grinned briefly and something inside her twisted up tight in response. Really, the man had an almost magical smile. Good thing he didn't use it often.

"What were you expecting? A cell in a dungeon?"

She smiled and shrugged. "No, not that bad, but nothing so..."

"Melissa suggested you stay in this suite. She thought you'd like it and your brothers had no objection."

"No objection." Well, that was something, she supposed. "It was thoughtful of Melissa."

"You'll like her. She's looking forward to meeting you."

"And my brothers?"

He paused for a long moment before he said, "They'll come around."

"Just one big happy family, huh?" Funny, her excitement-driven nerves had become anxiety-driven in the blink of an eye. It seemed there were plenty of hard feelings for everyone to get through before they could even begin to relate to each other.

"You have as much right to be here as they do," he told her.

"Do I?" Erica shook her head and frowned as she threw out both hands as if to encompass the entire resort. "They grew up here. I'm the interloper. This is their *home*."

"The home that every one of them escaped from the minute they got the chance."

Her hands fell to her sides. "Why did they? Was Don Jarrod such a bad father?"

"Not bad," he said, crossing the room to stand by her side. "Just busy. Opinionated." Christian smiled ruefully. "He wasn't even my father and he was full of orders about what I should do with my life and the best way to do it."

"Sounds familiar," Erica mused, strolling to the window and staring out at the pool area and the mountains beyond. "I grew up with a father much like him. Ironic, isn't it?"

"Maybe that insight will make it easier for you to understand your siblings."

"I guess we'll see. Seems strange that this lovely place is practically empty. It's sad, somehow. That none of the Jarrods want to live in their family home."

"Well," Christian allowed, "like I told you, Don wasn't the easiest father in the world. Most of them have issues with the place and aren't very happy about the way their father arranged getting them back to Aspen."

She sighed a little. "So, we've got father troubles in common, anyway."

"You could say that." He shoved his hands into the back pockets of his jeans and watched her as she walked to the sofa in her new home. "Speaking of your father, how'd it go when you spoke with him about all of this?"

Erica shot him a look. "As I expected. He didn't want me to come."

"Why did you?"

She stopped, leaned over and picked up a throw pillow. She ran her fingertips across the heavily embroidered fabric, then set it down again. "I had to. I had to come and see and…"

"Find yourself?" he offered.

She laughed a little. "Sounds pompous, doesn't it?"

"Not really. I've been lost before. It's not always easy getting found again."

Erica tipped her head to one side and studied him. He looked so in control. So at home. So sure of himself, it was hard to imagine that he might have suffered self-doubt or anxiety. But she supposed everyone did from time to time. The trick was to not let those times get the best of you.

She turned around and let her gaze slide across the room that would be her home for who knew how long. There was a hallway off the living room that she assumed led to the bedroom and— "You said there was a stocked kitchen?"

"Yep." He pointed. "Right through there."

She went to investigate and off a short hall, she found a two-burner stove, a small refrigerator and several cupboards. The fridge was stocked with water, wine and soda along with fresh vegetables. There was a bowl of fruit on the abbreviated counter and she noticed that the window in the kitchen overlooked an English-style garden.

"You hungry?" Christian's voice came from directly behind her.

MAUREEN CHILD 79

She turned around to look at him and admitted, "Actually, I am."

"Why don't we go get some lunch downstairs? I can answer your questions and you can meet one of your brothers at the same time."

That brother being Guy, she reminded herself. The chef. Well, that meeting just might kill her appetite, but gamely she said, "Give me one minute to freshen up and I'm ready."

Ready for all of it, she added silently.

Five

Guy Jarrod had once been a sought-after chef, with a reputation of excellence, but when he opened his own restaurant, he'd stepped out from behind the stove so to speak. He'd learned to love the business of running the restaurant even more than he had the actual art of cooking.

Now, he hired and fired chefs, made sure everything ran the way he wanted it to. But being back at Jarrod Ridge doing what he did best hadn't been on his agenda. Trust his father to make sure he eventually got his way where his children were concerned…even if it meant he had to die to do it.

Still irritated at being managed from beyond the grave, Guy had to admit that running the five-star restaurant at the Ridge was turning out to be a better gig than he'd expected it to be. He had big plans for the place.

Over the years, the restaurant and the general manager of the hotel had become, not lax, exactly, but complacent. They stayed with what worked rather than trying out new things. That was about to change.

All he had to do was get accustomed to being back here again.

"Excuse me, Mr. Jarrod?"

"What is it?" He looked up as one of the servers rushed into the wine cellar off the kitchen. A young kid who looked familiar, Guy hadn't had time to learn all their names yet.

"Mr. Hanford's in the dining room with a guest. He asked if you could come out to speak with them."

Christian. Well, part of being back in Aspen was going to entail dealing with his brothers, his sister—sisters, he reminded himself sternly—and Christian. They'd been friends once, Guy reminded himself. Now, they were business colleagues all because of one old man's stubborn refusal to let go of his children.

"Fine. Tell him I'll be right there." He left the wine cellar where he'd been taking a personal inventory—he wanted to know exactly what the restaurant had on hand and didn't trust anyone else to do it right.

That thought brought him up short. Maybe he was more like his old man than he'd ever thought.

He stalked through the kitchen, out into the main dining room, his gaze constantly shifting. He checked on the servers, on the table settings, on the flowers. He noticed the tablecloths and the flatware and the shine on the silver and brass espresso machine. He had a sharp eye, no tolerance for sloppy work and he intended to make good use of those traits now that he was back running this place the way it always should have been run.

Guy spotted Christian sitting at a booth in the back. As he got closer, he saw that across from him was a trim, pretty brunette with amber eyes. She looked vaguely familiar to him, but he couldn't place her. Which meant, Guy thought suddenly, *this* was the long-lost sister they'd all been waiting to meet. Her familiarity was simply that she had something of the Jarrod family stamped on her features.

They hadn't noticed his approach yet, so he took that spare moment to observe her. Pretty, he thought again. But she looked on edge. And hell, who could blame her? All of them had been dragged back to Jarrod Ridge whether they liked it or not.

Yet she had the worst of it, he thought. At least he and his siblings had each other. She was the stranger in a strange land. Despite a flicker of sympathy for her, though, Guy agreed with his twin. A newly acknowledged sister didn't deserve an equal share of the estate.

Christian caught Guy's gaze as the man approached. He also noticed the appraising gleam in the man's eyes as he gave Erica a quick once-over. He knew Erica was nervous about this meeting, but Christian was glad she would be starting out by meeting Guy. This Jarrod sibling had always had a cooler head than most of the others.

Well, except for Trevor. There wasn't much in life that shook Trevor.

"Christian, good to see you," Guy said, but he wasn't looking at him. Instead the man's eyes were locked on Erica. "And you must be my new little sister."

She flushed nervously, but she lifted her chin, stuck out her hand and said, "That's me. But I usually go by Erica."

"Good one," he said and shook her hand briefly. "So, you getting settled in?"

"I am, but I think it's going to take me a while to be able to find my way around."

"I'm pretty sure the front desk has maps," he said, giving her a smile. "What do you think of the Manor?"

"It's gorgeous," she blurted, looking around the half-full dining room at the guests gathered there. "It must have been a wonderful place to grow up."

"You'd think so, wouldn't you?" Guy tugged at the edge of the tablecloth, smoothing out a tiny wrinkle in the fine linen. "Christian told us you were in PR back in San Francisco."

"Yes, I was."

"That'll come in handy, then." A server slipped up behind him, whispered something and then drifted away again. "I'm sorry. There's something in the kitchen I need to handle. Christian, good to see you again. Erica…" He shifted his gaze to hers and held it for a long moment before smiling. "I'll be seeing you around."

When he was gone, Erica blew out a breath.

"Wasn't so bad, was it?" Christian watched her as she reached for her water glass and took a sip. Guy could have been a little more welcoming, but on a scale of one to ten, ten being a warm hug and one a shotgun reception—he'd scored about a five.

"A little nerve-racking, but all in all, not bad," she admitted. Then she asked, "What did Guy mean, my PR skill will come in handy?"

Christian had wanted to give her a day or two to get used to being here, but there was no point in putting things off. There was a lot coming up and since she was now expected to take her place in the Jarrod family, she might as well get her feet wet right away.

"The food and wine gala is coming up in a few weeks," he said. "It's a big deal in Aspen. Held every year, lasts several weeks and has foodie and wine lovers in the country and in Europe coming into town to enjoy themselves."

"I've read about it," she said. "And seen some coverage on the news every year, too. It's practically a Mardi Gras type thing, isn't it?"

"Close enough," he told her. "The city depends on the tourism dollars and the gala the Jarrods sponsor is a big part of that. As one of the Jarrods, you're right in the middle of this one."

Her eyes went wide, but she nodded and said, "Tell me."

Again, he had to admire how she was able to go with

the flow. She was strong, but she had the tendency to
bend, not break. Most of the women he'd known in
his life would still be sitting in San Francisco trying
to come to terms with everything she'd dealt with in
the last few days. Not Erica Prentice though. Once her
decision was made, she gave it her all.

For a tiny thing, she was formidable.

Her gaze was locked on him and he found himself
getting distracted by those amber depths. By the way
she chewed at her bottom lip when she was thinking.
Hell, he was distracted by her, period.

Grumbling to himself, his voice was brusque and
businesslike as he said, "Your brother Trevor is the
marketing expert. He's been running his own company
right here in Aspen for years. Now, he's taking over the
marketing for Jarrod Ridge."

"Big job."

"It is," he said, "and so is yours. You'll be the new
head of the Ridge's PR department."

When she looked startled, he added, "You'll be
working with Trevor directly on most of it. You'll have
your own office at the Manor, so you'll be on site more
often than Trevor. The two of you will probably see a
lot of each other over the next few weeks."

"Won't that be fun."

Worry had crept into her voice again and he reminded
her, "Trevor's pretty laid-back. He's not going to be a
hard-ass, so nothing to worry about there."

She took a deep breath. "Hope you're right about
that."

"I am. Just as I'm right about thinking you'll handle yourself well here."

"Right into the deep end then?"

"Any reason to think you can't swim?" Christian asked and watched as she seemed to consider his question.

Finally, she shook her head, gave him a fierce, bright smile and said, "I'll swim."

"I bet you will," he said, staring at her as she picked up her leather-backed menu and perused the offerings. He wished to hell he didn't find her more and more intriguing with every passing minute. What was it about this one small, curvy woman that had his body tied up in knots and his brain overheating?

Was it the lure of the unattainable?

He didn't think so. There had been plenty of women when he was younger who had been out of his league. A townie kid with a single mom didn't really have the means to play in the ball games of the rich and famous. But he wasn't that kid anymore and he could have the pick of any woman he wanted.

What he couldn't figure out was why that didn't seem to matter.

The one woman he wanted was also the one woman he couldn't have.

Two hours later, Erica was alone in her suite. Sunset was deepening into twilight but here in her rooms, the lamplight was bright and she was too wrapped up in what she was doing to even notice the end of her first day in Colorado. Christian had gone back to work after their early meal—excusing himself as quickly as possible with a claim of having to get some work done before morning. Once she was on her own, Erica had done a little exploring.

Now, she sat on the couch in her new living room and looked at all of the magazines, books, postcards and brochures she had spread out around her. She'd practically bought out the gift shop downstairs, buying up every item she could find pertaining directly to Jarrod Ridge.

And there had been plenty to choose from. The brochures listed every activity to be found at the resort and the book described the history of the place. She'd stared at the black-and-white photos of her grandparents and biological father with a fascination that had kept her captive for nearly twenty minutes. The grainy images of men in worn jeans and cowboy hats were so far removed from the tidy heritage she'd grown up hearing about, it was fascinating. She'd looked for resemblances between the people in those old pictures and herself and she'd found them. The shape of her eyes, the curve of her mouth. It was odd to see something of herself in people she had never met.

Yet in a weird way, it was almost comforting.

Her family was bigger than she'd ever imagined. They had been adventurers, dreamers. Men and women who had come to the middle of nowhere and built a life, a legacy that had lasted. Their dreams had grown and blossomed and had become something very special.

And she was a part of it.

A very small link in a lengthy chain.

When a knock sounded on her door, she was at first surprised, then a second later, a little worried about who might be dropping by. But then, she thought, it might be Christian. He might have decided to come back and take her on a little tour of the hotel. That thought spurred her off the couch and toward the front door. She fluffed her hair, smoothed her shirt and smiled to herself at the prospect of being with him again.

But when she opened the door, there was a woman standing there, holding two bottles of wine.

"Red or white?" she asked, walking past Erica into the living room.

"I'm sorry?" Confused, Erica just watched her.

"Red or white? Which do you prefer?"

"Uh, that depends, I guess..."

The woman grinned at her. "Good answer. I'm your sister, Melissa. And I've just stolen some wine from our brother Guy's private reserve so that you and I can get to know each other."

Hard to feel out of sorts or uncomfortable with Melissa Jarrod beaming goodwill toward her. Although the woman did manage to make Erica feel a little frumpy in her wrinkled clothes. Melissa was wearing sleek black jeans, an off the shoulder, silk turquoise top and black sandals that were really nothing more than three slinky straps and a three-inch heel. Her long blond hair hung loose down her back and her wide blue eyes were sparkling with challenge and welcome.

"You stole the wine from Guy?" Erica repeated, closing the door, then turning to face her sister.

"Sure did. There may be hell to pay tomorrow, but tonight, we party."

"That actually sounds like a great plan," Erica said, smiling.

Melissa grinned right back. "Just so you know," she said, "if we both drink it, we both face Guy's wrath. A united sister front."

"Sisters," Erica repeated.

Melissa wrinkled her nose then shrugged. "I know. Sounds weird still, doesn't it? Does to me, too. But I think you and I are going to make a terrific team."

Erica felt a bit of her earlier tension slide off her shoulders. Looking into her sister's eyes, knowing that this welcome was genuine, made her feel that maybe making a home at Jarrod Ridge wasn't going to be as difficult as she had thought it would be.

"You know," Erica said, "I think you're right. So, do you know if they stocked wineglasses in my new kitchen?"

Melissa led the way and threw back over her shoulder, "Since I'm the one who ordered the stocking done, I happen to know that wineglasses were first on the list."

"Excellent," Erica said following her into the tiny kitchen. "I'll make some popcorn, so let's start with the white. What do you think?"

Melissa set both bottles down onto the counter, then turned and held out her hand to Erica. "It's a good choice. Guy stocks the best sauvignon blanc anywhere in Colorado."

"And how will he feel about us helping ourselves?"

Erica asked as she took Melissa's outstretched hand in hers for a shake.

Shrugging, Melissa said, "Guess we'll find out. Together?"

"Together," Erica agreed and for the first time since she'd arrived in Colorado, felt that there was a real chance she would be able to make her own place there.

Then the two women moved companionably in the small kitchen, getting to know each other as they worked. Halfway through the second bottle of wine—they'd decided to open another bottle of white that had been stocked in Erica's fridge—the two women were well on their way to being fast friends.

"You make excellent popcorn," Melissa announced.

"Thank you. I told Christian I could cook."

"And was he impressed?" Melissa shook her head. "No, never mind. Probably not. The only things that impresses Christian are ledgers, files and injunctions."

"You've known him a long time?" Erica asked, settling back into the couch and curling her feet up beneath her.

Melissa was tucked into the opposite corner of the couch. "Forever," she said. "Since we were kids. Of course, back then, Christian was working for the resort and dear old dad didn't approve of family and employees hanging out together. But I saw him all the time and the boys and he were sort of friends even back then. When Christian was a teenager, my father took an interest in him." She frowned, took a sip of wine and said, "Dad loved to point out that Christian didn't have any of the advantages that *we* had and yet his drive to succeed eclipsed ours." Shaking her head at the memory, she said, "Let me tell you, there was a lot of irritation toward the great Christian when we were kids. Dad dangled his accomplishments in front of us like a perpetual taunt." Melissa shook her head in memory. "Good thing Christian was such a nice guy or things might've gotten ugly. Anyway, my point is, once Dad noticed him, Christian was around the Manor a lot more."

Erica's mind drew up a picture of a young Christian, battling for success, trying to find a place for himself amidst the Jarrod family. It seemed she and he had a lot in common. Here she was, after all, trying to do the same thing that he had so many years ago. But it wasn't only his adapting into the Jarrod world she was curious about. She wondered what his life had been like before Don Jarrod. In fact, she just wondered about Christian in general. Thoughts of him were never far from her mind, even though she told herself that now was definitely not the time to indulge in an attraction. She had to find her own footing here. Did she really have time to explore a relationship? And did she dare risk trusting someone so new in her life? Besides, it wasn't as if Christian had made a move. Maybe she was alone in feeling the draw toward him. And if she was, then she'd keep it to herself.

"So," she said, "your father took an interest in Christian and then what?"

"*Our* father," Melissa corrected with a brief smile. "He helped him get into college, then hired him when he got out of law school. He's worked for the Ridge most of his life, I guess. Dad made up his mind that Christian was going to be the official Jarrod Ridge attorney and that was that. Our father wasn't someone easy to walk away from." Then she cocked her head to one side. "Hearing me call him *our* father must be very strange for you."

"It is." Erica thought that was the biggest understatement of all time. She had hardly had time to wrap her own mind around it. Now finding herself sitting here with her *sister* was just one more oddity in a world suddenly turned upside down. But despite the craziness, she liked the camaraderie that Melissa had instigated. "Though you're making it easier."

"Happy to help. Trust me, I'm glad to have another female in the Jarrod ranks."

"Thanks," Erica said and meant it. In all the strangeness of her new world, it was good to have at least one person here who seemed to be on her side. Why Melissa had decided to be an ally seemed clear enough. Heaven knew that Erica would have loved to have a sister to help her stand against her older brothers occasionally.

"Now," Melissa asked, pointing at the piles of brochures and pamphlets scattered across the coffee table, "what are you doing with all of this stuff?"

Laughing, Erica scooped up one or two of the forgotten pamphlets. "I was trying to learn all I could about Jarrod Ridge."

Melissa took a sip of wine. "There's an easier way. Just ask me."

"Okay, I will as soon as I figure out what to ask."

"Deal. So, Christian told me you're in PR?"

Glad for a respite of talking about her now tangled family ties, Erica said, "Yes, and apparently that's what I'll be doing here, too."

"That means working with Trevor. You'll like him. Easygoing, hard to ruffle," Melissa said, "unlike the rest of the bunch."

"I met Guy this afternoon."

"How'd that go?"

"Cool, but polite."

"That sounds about right," Melissa told her. "Of the twins, Guy's more reasonable. Blake not so much. But he'll come around. Just don't let him scare you off."

That didn't sound promising, Erica thought, now even more reluctant than ever to meet Blake Jarrod. But there would be no way to avoid it and now, knowing for sure that he was going to be less than welcoming, it gave her a chance to prepare. To be ready to stand up for herself as she'd had to do most of her life.

"I'm here and I'm not leaving," Erica told her. "If Blake's unhappy with that, he'll just have to get over it."

"Good for you!" Melissa grinned at her, obviously pleased at her new sister's inner strength.

If only she knew, Erica thought, that right now, her strength was little more than a carefully constructed front. Inside, she was quavering. But she, too, would get over it.

"Now then," Melissa was saying, "there's Gavin to deal with, too. He's sort of shut-off emotionally, so probably won't be much trouble. But good luck getting a smile out of him."

"He sounds a lot like my older brothers."

"That's right. Christian told me that you're the only girl in your family, too. What do your brothers think of you being here?"

"They tried to talk me out of it—as did my fa—" she caught herself and amended what she had been going to say. "Walter."

Melissa reached out and patted her hand, sending her a commiserating smile at the same time. "It's going to get confusing with all of the fathers around here, isn't it?"

"I suppose."

"Look, my dad may have been your biological father, but Walter's still the man who raised you," Melissa said softly.

"I know, it's just…" How to explain her need to stand alone, to find answers? To live with the feelings of guilt and betrayal she had for turning her back on Walter, despite the fact that she'd never really felt any real warmth from him?

"So, are you and Walter close?"

"No," she answered quietly, wishing she could say otherwise. "How about you and your dad?"

Melissa sighed and shook her head. "No. I was two when my mother died and my father didn't really know what to do with me, I guess. So he did nothing." She smiled ruefully. "I know how it sounds, poor little rich girl. The truth is though, Erica, you got the better end of this bargain. You weren't raised here."

"At least you had this place," Erica told her. "It's so beautiful here."

"A golden jail is still a cell." A long moment of silence passed during which Erica didn't have a clue what to say or do. She'd have liked to offer her sister comfort, but wasn't at all sure it would be welcome. Besides, she knew all too well that sympathy didn't always salve ancient hurts. Sometimes it only made it worse. So she kept quiet and waited until Melissa came out of her musings herself.

"Anyway, ancient history for both of us, right? Moving on. So, PR girl…what do you think about helping me design a new menu of services for the spa?" She grabbed the old one off the coffee table and glared at it. "This one is so generic it's tired. I'd like something splashy. Something bright. Oh, and something about the yoga classes I'm going to be teaching. Do you do yoga?"

Erica laughed at the rapid-fire statements, grateful that they'd left the subject of their fathers and sad, lonely childhoods behind. Shaking her head, she said, "Yoga? No thanks. I'm just not that bendy. But I'd love to work up a new brochure with you. If I have time with the food and wine gala preparations…"

"Oh, yeah." Melissa sighed in disgust. "True. Okay, once you get that going, then we'll tend to my little slice of Jarrod Ridge."

"Sounds good."

"So," Melissa said, and lifted her wineglass in a toast. "Here's to us. Sisters by birth, friends by choice."

"Here's to us," Erica said and clinked her glass against the rim of Melissa's. She could only hope that the remaining meetings with her siblings would go even half so well.

Six

The next morning, Gavin walked into the Manor to meet Erica Prentice in Christian's office.

Sister?

Not as far as he was concerned. She was a stranger who shared a little Jarrod DNA. Logically, he knew that she, too, was being manipulated from the grave by Don Jarrod. But it didn't make her being here all right.

He wasn't sure how he felt about this new sister taking up a place at Jarrod Ridge. Hell, he wasn't even happy about having to be there himself. But for him it was different. The Manor was filled with memories, good and bad. He felt his father's presence everywhere in the old building and knew that wherever Don was now, the old man was enjoying watching his children wrestle with the terms of his will.

"Just like him," Gavin muttered as he walked through the crowded lobby, discounting the low roar of dozens of voices locked in conversations. He continued on along the hall toward Christian's office, resenting the fact that he was here at all. He'd made a life apart from the Ridge and his father had known it. But then, he thought, that would have been half the fun for Don. Upsetting his children's plans to ensure that his own worked out as he wanted.

"Nothing Don liked better than stirring things up and seems like he's done a great job of it this time," he told himself.

He'd already talked to Guy and Melissa about their new sister and while Guy was withholding judgment, Melissa had, of course, come down on Erica's side. Though he appreciated the input, Gavin would make up his own mind and he believed firmly in not putting off what could get done today.

Unlike Blake. He knew damn well that Blake had left for Vegas deliberately this time, not wanting to be at the Manor when Erica arrived. As for Trevor, well, he was supposed to be here this morning but he'd do whatever felt right for him at the moment.

As if his thoughts had conjured him out of thin air, Gavin's youngest brother pushed away from a wall and lifted one hand in greeting.

"Wasn't sure you'd come in," Trevor said.

"I told you I'd be here."

Trevor smiled. "And you're always exactly where you're expected to be."

"There something wrong with that?"

"No," Trevor answered with a shake of his head, "But don't you ever get tired of leading such a regimented life?"

"It's not—" He broke off, clearly not interested in rehashing the same old discussion.

Trevor admired his oldest brother. Hell, as a kid, he'd practically worshipped him. But now that they were all grown, Trevor thought Gavin's life could use some shaking up. Coming back to the Ridge was a start, but he needed more. The man was wound too tight, Trevor told himself sadly. While he, on the other hand, took life as it came, did as he wanted and planned to have no regrets when it came time for him to check out.

Just another reason he'd gone along with his late father's machinations to get them all back to the Ridge. Not that Trevor had gone far from the Jarrod family home. And why would he have? He loved skiing and he'd never find better than what Aspen could offer. Besides, he had his house in town, his own company and too many friends to just pack up and disappear.

So he'd stayed in Colorado while everyone else had gone. He'd missed his brothers and sister, though, so despite how it had happened, he was glad they'd come back.

As for his new sister, Trevor was willing to give her a shot. After all, it wasn't her fault Don Jarrod was her father.

"So, you ready to meet her?" Gavin asked.

Trevor snorted a laugh. "You don't have to make it sound like we're going to a hanging."

His brother sighed. "And you don't have to turn it into a social event."

"It *is* a social event, man. We're going to meet our long-lost sister and unless you're trying to scare her off, you might want to paste a smile on your face."

"You smile enough for both of us."

"You're hopeless, you know that, right?" Trevor asked and then, more seriously, said, "She's probably more upset by all this than we are, Gavin. Maybe you could cut her a little slack?"

"Fine. Slack for the newcomer. No slack for you."

Trevor laughed.

Grumbling, Gavin fell into step alongside his brother and swung past the hotel's business center. They walked on to Christian's office. The man didn't have a secretary guarding his gate. Instead, he used the employees of the business center to take care of whatever tasks he needed done. Which made dropping in on him even easier.

After a brisk knock, Gavin opened the door and stepped inside, with Trevor just a pace behind him.

Looking up from his paperwork, Christian smiled. "She's not here yet."

"Late, huh?" Gavin pointed out.

"No," Trevor corrected with a sigh and shake of his head. "We're early." Then he walked into the room and dropped into one of the available chairs. Looking at Christian he asked, "So what's the newest Jarrod like?"

Christian leaned back in his chair and studied the two men. Gavin was standing off to one side, his arms folded across his chest. Trevor, on the other hand, looked the picture of relaxation. The two of them had offered to come in to meet Erica together and Christian had agreed, hoping Trevor's presence would be enough to mitigate Gavin's penchant for aloofness.

"What's she like?" he mused, and instantly his mind filled with images of Erica. Her eyes, her mouth, her delicate, but curvy figure and just how much he wanted her. But an instant later, he shut those thoughts down as quickly as he could. Not exactly the description he could give Erica's brothers.

"She's smart. Funny. Strong." His gaze shifted from Gavin to Trevor and back again. "She's nervous, as anyone would be, but she's determined to make this a success."

"Why is this so important to her?" Gavin asked.

"Hate to admit it, but good question," Trevor agreed.

Frowning, Christian said, "You know what your relationship with Don was like. Well, that's what she had with the man who raised her. From what I can gather, she was cut out of their family business and now that she's been brought into this one, she's focused on making it work."

"Focused."

Christian looked at Gavin. "She knows that you guys aren't exactly ready to throw her a welcome-to-the-family party. And from what I can gather, she's used to that kind of behavior from her older brothers."

"Well, that's telling us," Trevor muttered. "So we

can play nice or we can be the bastard brothers she's accustomed to."

"Exactly," Christian said with a nod. It was important to him that they understand. That they give Erica the chance she deserved. He wasn't willing to explore *why* it was important to him, though. Point was, "She's innocent in this, you know. If you're pissed that your father had an affair with her mother, be pissed at *him*."

Gavin shifted position uneasily as if he were feeling the stirrings of guilt and didn't like it a damn bit. "I didn't say I blamed her for any of this. It's just a difficult situation. For everyone."

"It is," Erica said softly.

Christian's gaze snapped to the doorway and the woman who stood poised, alone, watching them. He stood up and said, "Erica."

She spared him a quick smile, but it was gone too soon in Christian's opinion. What was it about this woman that grabbed at him? Why was he having so much trouble reminding himself that as an employee of Jarrod Ridge, the Jarrod family was off-limits to him?

Trevor came lazily to his feet and Gavin turned to face their younger sister.

"I didn't mean to interrupt," she was saying as she walked into the room, with her chin tilted defiantly. "But I couldn't help overhearing. Since I was the topic of conversation anyway, I thought it was as good a time as any to introduce myself."

Christian spared brief glances at both of the Jarrod

men and he saw Gavin trying to think back and figure out if he'd said anything he should apologize for. While, at the same time, Trevor's mouth was quirked in an approving smile.

"Erica," Christian said, coming around his desk to align himself at her side—both physically and figuratively. "These are your brothers, Gavin and Trevor."

She returned Trevor's smile, then looked at Gavin. They stared at each other for a long minute and Christian could actually feel the tension building in the room. And then suddenly, it was gone as Gavin stepped forward, held out his hand to her and said, "Welcome, Erica."

She only hesitated an instant before shaking his hand. "Thank you. I heard you say this was difficult and you're not wrong. This whole situation has been just as hard on me as it has been on all of you."

"You're right," Trevor said as he came up to join them. "And whatever you heard before you came in, pay no attention. Everybody's a little on edge, being back at the Ridge, and that's bleeding over into everything else."

"I appreciate that," she told him.

Christian felt that stir of admiration for her again for how well she stood up to brothers who clearly weren't eager to have her in the family. Whether she was wanted to be here or not, she had a place at the Ridge. Through birth. Through blood. Because Don Jarrod had wanted to bring *all* of his children home.

"Once you're settled in, come and see me," Trevor

was saying. "We've got the food and wine gala right around the corner now. Most of the marketing and publicity is already lined up and in play. But there are a few things we can still do to give it that final push."

Erica nodded. "I've heard about the gala for years, though I've never attended. I'm looking forward to being a part of it this year. Last night, Melissa showed me some of what you'd been doing and it's really fabulous."

He grinned, apparently satisfied.

"But," she added, "I've got a few ideas we might want to try."

His eyes narrowed on her thoughtfully, then after a moment, he gave her a grin. "I like confidence, so yeah, I'd like to hear your ideas. Tomorrow work for you?"

"Tomorrow's great."

Gavin interrupted them. "I know this isn't easy on you, being here. Being thrown into the middle of something you didn't even know existed a week ago."

"No," she said, "it's not."

He nodded. "I came in here prepared to not like you," he admitted and smiled when she stiffened. "But I've got a lot of respect for anybody who's not afraid to stand up for him—or herself."

"And I respect anyone who's trying to protect his family," Erica told him. "As for standing up for myself, I've been doing that my whole life."

"I'm getting that," Gavin said with an approving nod. "I think you just might make a place for yourself here…little sister."

Erica gave him a careful smile, pleased but clearly

not willing to relax her guard just yet. Then the moment was over and the Jarrod brothers were excusing themselves.

Christian couldn't take his eyes off of her. He hardly noticed when his friends left. All he saw were two amber-colored eyes watching him with a mixture of nervousness and satisfaction shining in their depths. She was pleased with the way she'd handled herself and damned if he wasn't, as well.

He'd set this meeting up specifically so that he would be there when she met her brothers. So that she wouldn't be alone. Not that he didn't believe the Jarrod siblings, even if they were angry about the situation, would be anything but polite. It was only that Christian had wanted her to have his support and *know* that she had it. He didn't ask himself why that was important to him, he only accepted that it was.

She was still nervous, but the others wouldn't have been able to tell. Funny, but he'd once thought her features easy to read. Now he knew the truth. Though she might be quaking in her shoes, she'd never let anyone know it.

Their first meeting had been different. She'd been taken off guard and her shock and stunned surprise had been impossible to hide. But he'd learned since that the only real hint to what Erica Prentice was feeling lay in her eyes. There, her emotions shone out loud and clear.

Despite her lifted chin and firm voice, those eyes of hers showed him that she was silently battling her own fears. Yet despite everything, every time she went into battle, she came out victorious. He admired the hell out of that. Almost as much as he wanted her.

Desire was now a constant companion. Haunting him through his sleep, torturing him during the day. Thoughts of her were never far away and his body was in a constant state of arousal. He'd never before felt such a powerful pull toward any woman. And every moment he spent with her only intensified those feelings.

"Gee, that went well," she said after a moment or two of silence that practically throbbed with unresolved tension.

"Believe it or not, it did," Christian answered. "I think you impressed both of them."

Her gaze fixed on his. "I wasn't trying to impress."

"Maybe that's why you did. Just by being yourself. They respect strength."

She smiled ruefully. "Good thing they couldn't hear my knees knocking then, isn't it?" She walked across his office and looked out the window behind his desk at the sweep of lawn that seemed to stretch all the way to the mountains. "You arranged that meeting specifically so I wouldn't stumble across my…brothers on my own, didn't you?"

"Yeah," he admitted. "I thought it would be easier if I were around."

She turned her head to look directly at him. Her gaze slammed into his. "It was. Thank you."

He stared into her eyes and it was all he could do to keep from going to her, sweeping her into his arms and kissing her until neither of them could breathe. But somehow he managed. "You're welcome. You've still got Blake to meet and deal with, but he should be back in a couple of days."

"From what everyone says, I'm not looking forward to meeting him."

"Blake's all right," Christian told her, not wanting her to be anxious over the last Jarrod hurdle she had to face. "He's not really happy with the situation, but he knows none of this is your fault."

She blew out a breath. "What do you think, Christian? You're the objective observer in all this. Do you think this is going to work out?"

"You being here, you mean?" When she nodded, he walked closer to her. "Yes, I do. You're already making a place for yourself here. Your sister likes you. Your brothers will come around."

Erica shook her head and her light brown hair lifted from her shoulders, then fell back again in soft waves. Christian curled his hands into fists to keep from reaching for it. To keep from threading his fingers through that mass and turning her head toward his—

"Why are you on my side in this?" Erica asked. "Melissa says you've known the family since you were a kid. And you were Don's personal attorney. I'd think that would make you more prejudiced in their favor rather than mine."

He backed up a step, leaned against the corner of his desk and said, "Don Jarrod was a hard man to know. He helped me when I was a teenager. Offered me a job here when I got out of law school. But," he added, "that said, I don't owe him or his memory my soul. Just the best job I can do. My allegiances are my own."

She tipped her head to one side and looked up at him. "And you've decided to be my ally."

"Yeah."

"Why?"

"Do you really have to ask?"

"Shouldn't I?"

He shrugged, though it cost him. He wanted her to trust him, but couldn't say that he trusted himself around her. He wanted more than friendship or an alliance with her. But if he took more, he'd risk everything he'd already built.

"Let's just say that whatever I owe the Jarrods, I owe myself more. So I'm on your side because I've had a hand in throwing your life off kilter."

"So you feel responsible? You don't have to," she told him. "Like I said earlier, I can take care of myself."

"I've noticed," he said, then forced a smile. "Let's get out of here. How about a tour of the grounds?"

"I'd like that," she said and took the arm he offered before walking with him out of the office and the hotel.

They walked for what felt like miles.

Erica was overwhelmed with everything. She was on sensory overload. Jarrod Ridge had to be the most beautiful place she'd ever been and it was staggering to realize that she was a part of the legacy that had built it.

The resort was like a small town in and of itself.

Narrow walkways, cement pathways bordered by vibrant flower beds, wound past tiny bungalows and lavish cabins. Christian had stopped by his own home to give her a quick tour and Erica had loved everything about it. From the honey-colored log walls to the braided rugs on the polished wood floors to the overstuffed, brown leather furniture.

He had a river stone fireplace big enough to stand up in and the huge windows in his kitchen overlooked the forest and the mountain beyond. She could imagine stepping out onto the back porch, sitting in one of the rocking chairs there and sipping a morning cup of coffee as she watched the world wake up.

Seeing his home had given her more insights into Christian the man and she relished them. He was neat, but not to the point of craziness. He had actual pots and pans in his kitchen, which meant he at least tried to cook occasionally rather than subsisting on room service or takeout. He had framed family photos hanging on his wall and seeing him as a younger man with one arm thrown across his mother's shoulders told her that he was someone to whom family meant a lot. All good things. And all of those things combined made him even more intriguing to Erica.

When they left his house, Erica was more captivated by him than she had been before. She took his arm as he led her on through the resort. He pointed out the cabins where Gavin and Melissa lived. He'd shown her the gift shops, the jewelers, the on-site bakery and the ice cream parlor. He'd taken her past the pools—both the indoor and outdoor, not to mention the pool built just for kids.

Guests in swimsuits, tennis gear and even riding outfits streamed over the property in a never-ending flood of humanity. Children raced each other across manicured lawns and a couple of elderly guests sat on a padded iron bench beneath a gorgeous cluster of aspen trees.

The sun was out, the sky was blue and she honestly felt as though she'd stepped into an alternate world. Everything was almost too perfect.

Including the man at her side. He wasn't wearing a suit and tie, just black jeans, a white, long-sleeved shirt open at the throat and a pair of black boots that looked as though they had seen a lot of wear. He looked handsome in a well-cut suit, but Erica thought he looked even more so in casual clothes. It was then a person realized that his personal power wasn't shaped by any outward appearance—not his clothing, his car or his job—but by his own innate strength.

And that, Erica thought, was about the sexiest thing in the world.

She loved how people knew him. Smiled, waved, stopped to speak to him as they walked. He introduced her to managers and housemaids, all with respect and deference. He treated everyone the same and she found that sexy as hell, too. She'd been raised by a man who believed in the perception of status. Walter would never have introduced a friend of his to a maid—but Christian was a different sort of man. The kind she'd been looking for before her life turned upside down.

Now, she had to wonder if part of her attraction for him wasn't because he was the only familiar face around her. But no, even as she considered that, she put it aside. There was much more to what she was feeling for Christian Hanford.

"So what do you think?"

She looked up at him and loved how the wind had ruffled his short dark hair onto his forehead. She just managed to catch herself from reaching up and pushing it back. "Um," she said, gathering up her scattered thoughts, "I hate to keep using the word *amazing....*"

He grinned, and her breath locked in her lungs. Seriously, when the man flashed an unguarded smile, he was a danger to any woman with eyes.

He pointed off in the distance. "The stables are down there, alongside a paddock, and there are riding trails through the woods. Tennis courts are over there and the golf course is back at the opposite end of the resort."

She laughed to herself. "It's like a little city all in itself."

"Exactly how Don saw it, too," Christian said. "We've even got a small clinic on site. Joel Remy runs it. He's got a nurse who helps out and they can take care of any minor situations the guests might have. Of course, anything more serious is treated at the hospital in Aspen."

"Our own medical staff. Wow." She turned from him and stared out at the surrounding cabins and lodges.

"That's the first time you've said 'our' about this place," he commented. "Starting to feel more connected?"

She looked back at him. "I guess I am. It's a little nerve-racking, but I'm excited about it, too, you know?"

"I do," he said, then looked around as she had, as if he were seeing it for the first time through her eyes. Finally, he turned his gaze back on her. "You'll make your place here, Erica."

"Yeah," she said, giving him a smile that lit up her eyes. "I will."

He nodded as if he sensed her commitment, and said, "A long time ago, I decided to make this my place. To carve out my own slice of Jarrod Ridge."

"Why? I mean, what drove you to want this?" She asked the question quietly, not wanting to disturb the intimacy of the moment. Despite the fact that they were surrounded on all sides by happy, chattering guests, it felt as though they were alone, just the two of them.

He smiled to himself and tucked his hands into his jeans pockets. "I told you I grew up here. Well, in Aspen."

She nodded but didn't say anything, encouraging him silently to continue.

"My first job was as a busboy in the main restaurant in the Manor." He glanced back over his shoulder at the palatial mansion, its rose brick walls nearly radiant in the bold, summer sunshine. "I loved it. Well, not working in the restaurant, but being here. Being a part of it all." He paused, as though he were gathering up stray thoughts and straightening them out. "My dad died when I was three. My mom worked constantly, but it was hard, you know?"

Erica nodded, caught up in the soft cadence of his words, the faraway look in his eyes.

"Anyway…" He took a long breath and released it again. "I knew what I wanted. I wanted to belong at a place like this. So I worked my ass off in school, got a scholarship and eventually, with Don's help, went to law school."

"Why did he help?" she asked, curious now about the father she would never know.

"To tell you the truth, I don't really know," he admitted with a half smile. "There was never any telling what Don would do or why. I like to think he saw something in me he thought would work well here. That he knew I'd do the job for him."

"Sounds like that's exactly what he thought," she told him.

Christian sent her a glance. "Maybe. I'll never know for sure. I do know that he helped shape me into the kind of lawyer I am. And I helped him reshape this place into the growth it's enjoying now."

"Then you did what you set out to do," Erica said. "Made a place for yourself. Ensured that you belong here."

"Yeah, I did. And I owed Don a lot—which," he added wryly, "he never let me forget."

"What's that mean?" It didn't sound good and by the look on his face, Christian wasn't happy about whatever he was going to tell her.

"It means, that in my contract with the resort, Don laid it out just the way he wanted it. Hell, he even made sure the codicil was in his will, just in case I needed reminding."

"What?" A curl of apprehension settled in the pit of her stomach. Erica had the distinct feeling she wasn't going to like what he was about to say.

Christian locked his gaze with hers. "For me to keep my invested shares in Jarrod Ridge, I'm to remain loyal to the business."

"That doesn't sound so bad."

"Then there's the added warning to stay away from his daughters."

"What?" Erica shook her head as if she hadn't heard him right. "Say that again."

Christian huffed out a breath. "He didn't put it in those words, exactly, but the meaning's clear enough. I might be a big-time, rich lawyer now, but Don still saw me as the poor kid looking for a chance. And he didn't want that kid anywhere near his daughters. Either of them. Bottom line, Erica? You're off-limits."

Seven

"But that's ridiculous," Erica argued, astounded at this turn of events.

He shrugged. "That's Don."

"It's medieval." She took a step away from him, turned around and came right back. Looking up into his chocolate eyes, Erica felt that bone-deep hum she always did when she was around him. She knew he felt it, too. She could see desire in his eyes, feel heat rippling off him in thick waves. Erica looked up at him. "Why are you telling me this?"

"You know why," he said and his eyes darkened even as his mouth tightened into a hard line. "Because there's something between us."

"So you want to stop it."

"Didn't say I wanted to," he corrected with a shake

of his head. "But this is my life. One I worked damn hard for."

"That's right," she countered. "*Your* life. And *mine*. Don Jarrod has nothing to do with this."

He snorted a laugh. "The fact that you can say that and mean it just goes to prove you didn't know him."

"No, I didn't. But even if I had, I wouldn't let him make my decisions for me," she snapped. Anger shot through her and she let her words ride the wave of it. "I didn't let Walter decide whether I'd move here or not. I won't let Don decide who I become involved with or not."

"You think I like this?" he asked, reaching out to grab hold of her shoulders. "Do you think I like dancing to Don's tune? I don't. It goes against everything that's in me."

"Then why?"

"My mom worked hard her whole life," he said tightly. "Thanks to my work here, my shares of Jarrod Ridge, she'll never have to work again. I bought her a condo in Orlando. She has friends. She plays golf. She gets her hair done in a fancy salon and she buys her clothes at the best boutiques in town. She takes cruises with her friends and she has *fun* for the first time in her life."

Her heart twisted in her chest as everything nebulous that she'd felt for him over the last several days solidified into something bigger. More important. Staring up into his eyes, she saw the kind of man she used to hope she'd meet. The kind who saw loyalty as a virtue. The kind who took care of his family no matter the cost to himself. The kind who put his own needs last behind everyone else in his life who mattered.

"No matter what I feel for you, or might feel for you," Christian said, "I won't take that away from her."

"I wouldn't ask you to."

"So you understand that this can't go anywhere."

"No," she said, "I don't. But I understand why you believe that."

He hissed in a breath, grabbed her hand and said, "Come with me."

She refused to move when he would have tugged her along. "Where?"

"We need to talk this out and…I want to show you something." His gaze searched hers for a long moment until he said, "Please."

Erica nodded and went with him, her fingers curled tightly around his. He led her off the concrete path and down a short slope that ran behind a short row of shops. In the distance, the forest loomed, green and filled with shadows, and he was walking right for it.

"Where are we going?" She held on to his hand and quietly enjoyed the rush of heat that linked them together.

"Thought I'd show you something here that Don Jarrod had nothing to do with building."

"You're kidding, right?" she asked as she ran to keep up with him. "I thought this was completely his."

"Most of it," he said, glancing back over his shoulder. "But this part was here first."

He led her through the trees, his steps sure as he continued on, deeper into the cool gloom. The farther they got from the resort, the quieter it became. Erica heard birds high overhead and from a distance, there was a muted roar of sound that got louder and louder as they approached.

Erica looked back over her shoulder and couldn't see the resort at all. The trees were so thick it was as if a dark green wall had been erected between them and the grounds of Jarrod Ridge.

When Christian at last came to a stop and released her hand, she was simply staggered by the beauty around her. A river rushed past them, growling and roaring over stones in its path. Lined on either side by thick stands of trees, and a narrow ribbon of rock and sand, the water was frothy and beautiful and completely untouched. It was an oasis of privacy in a sea of people and Erica loved it.

She walked closer to the water's edge, her sandals sinking and sliding on the sand. She felt the spray on her face as a soft wind kicked up, rattling the leaves of the trees until they sounded like whispered conversations.

"This was my spot when I was a kid," Christian said softly as he came up behind her. "When I needed to think, when things got bad, I came here and everything felt…all right again."

"I can see why," she said and wondered how anyone could be sad or depressed if they had somewhere so beautiful to go. She looked at him and asked, "And how many women have you brought here, I wonder?"

"Counting you?" he asked, gaze fixed on hers with

an intensity that shot a lick of flame through her center. "Just one."

"Why did you bring me?" she asked, her voice as breathless as she felt. "After everything you told me about Don and the will and everything…why did you bring me here?"

"Because," he admitted, his gaze moving over her face like a caress, "I had to."

Then he pulled her in close and kissed her.

He took her mouth with a hunger he'd never known before. Instantly, her lips parted, allowing him access, welcoming him into her warmth. He'd known, somewhere deep inside him that it would be like this with her. Known that the pulse of electricity between them would erupt into a shower of light and heat the moment he got close enough to her.

With a groan, he surrendered himself to the sensations pouring through him, refusing to think about anything beyond this moment. This kiss.

This taste of her that was filling cold, dark corners within him.

Their tongues tangled together, breath mingled and her soft sighs gave him all the encouragement he could have wanted. Sweeping one hand down her back, he traced her curves and wished he could peel her out of the dark red shirt she wore. Instead, he settled for tugging the hem of her blouse free of her crisp, white linen shorts and then slid the palm of his hand across her bare skin. She shivered as his fingers caressed the line of her spine, up and down and then up again. He needed the feel of her as badly as he needed her taste in his mouth.

Her arms came up and wrapped around his neck as she leaned into him. Her breasts flattened against his chest and he felt the hard points of her nipples pushing into him. He groaned again, felt his body go hard and ready and ground his hips against hers, looking for ease, but only managing to torture them both.

Christian kept his mouth on hers as he lifted her off her feet and deepened the kiss further. Slower, longer, hotter, he wanted all, wanted everything. For days now, his mind, his body had been clamoring for just this and now that he had his hands on her, his mouth on her, he didn't want it to end.

The roar of the river was right behind them, the insistent rush of it playing counterpoint to the thudding of his own heartbeat. When he finally tore his mouth from hers and dragged in a ragged breath, she smiled up at him.

"So much for medievalism."

His breath strangling in his lungs, he nodded. "I've never had to work so hard to stay within the rules. But I've wanted to taste you since the moment we met."

"Good to know," Erica said, moving one hand to cup his cheek in her palm. "I felt the same way. I still do. I want you, Christian."

His body tightened even further and he wouldn't have thought that possible.

"You're not making this any easier," he said, setting her back on her feet, keeping his arms around her, one hand on her bare back.

"I'm glad. It shouldn't be easy. It should be damned hard to walk away from whatever it is that's between us."

"It is. That's why I brought you here. I need to have you to myself. If only for today."

"And that would be enough for you?"

"No," he admitted, sliding both hands under her shirt now, moving over her skin to cup her breasts over the lacy cups of her bra.

She gulped an unsteady breath.

Through the lace, his thumbs and forefingers toyed with her nipples, eliciting another soft moan from her. "I've thought about tasting you, touching you. I've dreamed of having you alone and under me, over me."

"Oh, my…"

Slowly, he moved his hands until he reached the waistband of her shorts. She took a shallow breath as he deftly undid the snap and zipper.

Her gaze locked with his and Christian couldn't have looked away if it had meant his life. Suddenly the entire world, or at least all he wanted to know of it was there, in her amber-colored eyes.

"I need to touch you," he whispered, his voice almost lost in the thunder of the swift-moving river.

"Yes," she said, leaning toward him again, giving him all the welcome he needed.

He snaked one arm around her waist while his other hand dipped down, over her belly, beneath the thin elastic band of her panties. Then lower still, inch by glorious inch, past the tight curls at the juncture of her thighs. She gasped and stiffened, holding herself perfectly still as his fingers smoothed over her heat.

A low-throated groan slid from him as he felt her wet warmth and knew it was all for him. That she wanted him as desperately as he did her.

Then she jolted in his arms and a tiny, want-filled sigh slid from her lips. Her eyes closed as he dipped his hand lower still.

He touched, he caressed, he explored her delicate folds, learning her, learning what pleased her, what sent her soaring. He watched her face as he took her and her every sigh fed the flames of his own desire. He claimed her with a slick stroke across that single bud at the heart of her. That one spot that was the most sensitized and she trembled in his arms.

As sunlight played down around them and the world went about its business, Christian took Erica on a fast ride to pleasure. His fingers deft, he drove her relentlessly until she whimpered and pleaded his name on sighs torn from her throat. Her hips rocked into his hand as she sought release only he could give her. She parted her thighs wider, hoping he would take more, silently offering the invitation.

And he did. Dipping his head to the line of her throat, his lips and teeth left a trail of flames along her skin as he dipped first one finger and then another deep into her heat.

"Oh, Christian!" She swayed against him, but then held still as if afraid he'd stop.

He wouldn't. The feel of her beneath his hands was magic. Everything he'd dreamed and more. He wanted to lay her down and take her body with his completely, right here, on the soft, warm grass under the shelter of the trees. But he wouldn't. Couldn't risk someone stumbling across them. So he would settle for this stolen moment. This one instant when the two of them were alone and nothing was more important than the next sigh.

He took her higher, his fingers moving over her most tender flesh. She gasped, she sighed, she shivered against him and still he pushed her on, dragging out the sensations, taking her to the edge and then drawing her back. Lifting his head, he looked down at her and she opened her eyes as if needing to see him as tension coiled tighter and tighter within.

"Let go," he whispered, bending to brush her mouth with his. "Let go and come for me now."

Her fingers curled into the fabric of his shirt and clung to his shoulders as if she were half-afraid she would slide off the edge of the world.

"Christian…" His name came on a breath as she trembled against him.

His thumb caressed her again and then she shattered in his arms. Her body quaked and shivered, her eyes slid closed. She held on to him as pleasure rippled through her again and again until finally, the last waves died away and she was left nearly boneless.

He held her closer, wrapped both arms around her middle and held her pressed tightly to him. His own heartbeat was crashing in his chest and matched hers beat for beat. This was so much more than he had thought it would be. He felt so much more than he'd expected.

Somehow, he had thought that touching her would bring him satisfaction. That having her in his arms, sighing his name, would ease the need that had been gnawing at him for days. But it hadn't. If anything, that need was sharper now, clawing at his insides, demanding more. Demanding all.

Christian's head fell back and he stared at the sky as he realized that something incredible had just happened. Something life-changing.

But the question was, did he want his life changed— and was it too late to stop it?

For the next couple of days, Erica hardly saw Christian, but she almost didn't have time to notice. Her new life was racing straight ahead and she was forced to run just to keep up. There was a lot of work still to be done to prepare for the opening of the gala and she was working at a disadvantage, since she was coming in at the tail end. She had to catch up with Trevor's plans, and with the marketing scheme he'd devised and already had in motion.

Working with Trevor was more fun than she'd expected it to be. She knew about PR. How to market a product so that a customer would be not only slavering to have it, but instantly convinced to buy it. Working the ins and outs of a gala as big and splashy as the Jarrod Ridge affair was, at its heart, no different. There were posters to see to, artistic signs, menus for some of the out-of-town vendors and professionally shot photos, showing impossibly perfect people at play.

Jarrod Ridge was about to become the center of the food and wine industry for several weeks and Erica was right in the thick of it.

She couldn't remember being happier.

Her office on the ground floor of the Manor was bigger than her old one in San Francisco and bright with sunlight pouring in through a bank of windows. There were fresh flowers in the room, and a top-of-the-line computer and printer. She had all the assistance she needed from the employees at the business center and she had Trevor to bounce ideas off of and to argue with occasionally, as well.

What she didn't have, she thought now, was Christian.

He'd made himself scarce the last couple of days. She'd barely caught a glimpse of him. Erica stood up from behind her desk and looked out her window at the English-style garden beyond the glass. Scrubbing her hands up and down her arms, she forced herself to accept the fact that he was deliberately avoiding her. But why?

Those stolen moments beside the river rose up in her mind as they'd been doing regularly in every spare second. And in a heartbeat, she was back there again, his mouth on hers. His hand touching her intimately, pushing her into a pleasure so deep it was like nothing she'd ever known before.

It had been the most incredible encounter of her life.

So why wasn't he coming to her again?

Did he really mean to stick to Don Jarrod's ridiculous rules? Would he turn his back on her and what they might find to keep his job? Okay, yes, she could understand wanting—needing—to keep his mother safe and happy. But wasn't *he* allowed to be happy, too?

Or, she thought miserably, maybe he was happier without her. Maybe what they'd shared on the banks of the river hadn't touched him as it had her. Maybe he hadn't felt a damn thing. Maybe it hadn't meant anything from the start and he was just—

Her office door opened behind her and she whirled to face… "Christian," she said. "I was just thinking about you."

"Erica." His voice was cool, polite.

She nearly caught a chill from across the room. But two could play at this game, she told herself. If he wanted to pretend there was nothing simmering between them, then that's what they would do. Be damned if she would show him that she was hurt. That he was stomping on her heart even now with his professional air and distant tone. No, she wouldn't give him the satisfaction.

"Can I help you?" Her words were as polite as his. Her tone every bit as cold.

"I've come to introduce you to—"

"Me," another man said as he walked into the office and looked at her. "I'm Blake Jarrod."

"It's nice to meet you," she said, maintaining the professional manner she'd begun with. Erica saw no warm welcome in his eyes, so she wasn't going to act as though they were any two siblings greeting each other.

Blake studied her and could see what his twin had already mentioned to him. Their newest sister did have the look of the Jarrods about her, so there was clearly no mistake made. He could see it in the defiant tilt of her chin. In the flash of her eyes. Hell, she probably had more of Don in her than Blake did.

But that didn't mean that he'd welcome her into the family like the prodigal daughter. Or that she deserved a share of the estate. Being blood didn't mean jack if you didn't earn your place, he told himself. Everyone else might be willing to give her a chance, but he wasn't so easily taken in. She'd have to prove herself to him.

Not that he had anything against her personally. And judging from what Melissa had had to say on the subject, he would probably like her. Eventually. But for right now, she was the intruder. Pushing her way into a family already hip-deep in problems and not really needing any extras.

"Getting along all right, I see," he said, giving her office a quick scan.

"Everyone's been very helpful," Erica told him, then came around her desk and took a few steps closer. "Look, I know how hard this is for all of us. And I'm not expecting us to be one big happy family anytime soon."

He folded his arms across his chest and nodded.

"I do, however, expect you to give me a fair chance," she said.

"You do."

Erica looked directly at him and refused to be cowed by his steely stare. She'd already been warned that Blake would be the hardest nut to crack, so to speak. That this one of her new brothers would be the least welcoming. So she would stand her ground and if she needed to show him that she meant to make this place her home, then that's what she'd do.

Besides, Christian was standing right there, watching her, and she wasn't about to look weak or pitiful in front of him.

"That's right. Just as you would any new employee," Erica said. "I think that's fair."

Blake thought about it for a long moment before he nodded and walked forward, offering his hand. "It is fair. Okay, a chance it is."

"Thanks." Erica shook his hand and stepped back.

"Now, I've got to go find Gavin and talk to him about some business. If you two will excuse me…"

Blake left, shutting the door behind him and suddenly Erica and Christian were alone. Silence dragged out for what seemed like forever. Finally though, Christian said, "You handled him well."

"Thanks," she said, her words clipped, "is that all?"

"Erica…"

"I really don't have time to talk right now, Christian.

Trevor's expecting to see the new poster I've designed for the gala and—"

"I've missed you."

She whipped her head around to glare at him. "Couldn't have been easy to miss seeing me. I've been right here."

He blew out a breath and took the few steps separating them. Now that he was closer, Erica could see the shadows under his eyes and realized he hadn't been sleeping well. That made two of them. She wanted to reach out and touch him, but wasn't sure he would accept it, so she kept her wants buried under a layer of anger.

"It's complicated," he said.

"Not as far as I can see. You haven't spoken to me since…"

"You think I don't want to?" His voice was low and hard. "You really believe I'm not thinking about you every damn minute?"

Her heartbeat felt faint and fast. The look on his face was haunted, his eyes were blazing with fury and desire. "How would I know that when you've been avoiding me?"

"Because if I don't avoid you, this is what's going to happen." He closed the distance between them, grabbed her and pulled her close, wrapping his arms around her so tightly she could hardly draw breath.

And she didn't care.

Didn't care because his mouth was on hers, his breath driving into her mouth, his hands scooping up her back into her hair. His body pressed into hers. She felt the hard, thick ridge of him that proved exactly what he was feeling for her.

She moved in even closer, giving herself up to the feelings only he could engender. Her body was hot, her blood felt as if it were boiling in her veins. So when he released her abruptly, Erica staggered back a step before she recovered her balance.

Lifting one hand to her lips, she stared at him, trying to understand just what kind of game he was playing. And why she was allowing it.

"Yes," he said, his eyes fierce, his voice a deep groan of need, "I want you. So damn much just being around you is painful." He shoved one hand across the top of his head. "But you've got enough going on in your life right now. You don't need this as an added distraction."

Erica blinked at him. She couldn't believe what he was saying and wasn't sure he believed it, either. "So you're backing off for my sake, is that it? Making a grand sacrifice so poor Erica doesn't get confused by too many things at once?"

He winced, either at her words or the sharp slap of how they were delivered. "All I'm saying—"

She interrupted him because she'd heard enough. "I'm sick and tired of people deciding what's best for me. My father and brothers did it for years. And if you think I'm going to allow *you* to jump in and do the same, then you couldn't be more wrong."

She was trembling, her body shaking and quivering, not only from the rush of anger. Once again, he'd turned her body into an inferno of desire only to shut it down before it could fully erupt.

"That's not what I'm trying to do," he ground out.

Frustration and fury mingled inside her.

"Oh, no. All you're saying is thanks but no thanks. You've made that clear." She turned her back on him and walked back to her desk. Once she was safely behind the rosewood barrier, she looked at him again. "Well, I'm just so grateful for your help, Christian. With so many things going on in my life, I don't know what I would have done without you there to help me keep things straight."

He looked just as angry as she felt, and she was glad to see it. At least she knew that his ridiculous decision to pull away from her was making him as crazy as it was her.

"Erica, damn it—"

"Just stop it, okay? I've got a lot of work to do and I'm guessing you do, too."

He stared at her for a long second then nodded as if accepting that the conversation was over. "Fine. We'll leave it. For now. But neither one of us is going anywhere, so you can be damn sure this isn't finished."

"Isn't it?" Erica asked. "How is it that *you* suddenly get to decide how this relationship will go? When did you get the controlling vote?"

"Excuse me?"

He sounded angry—his voice was low and taut. *Well, good,* she thought. Why should she be the only one furious here?

"Do you seriously think so little of me to believe that I'm incapable of making my own decisions?"

"Of course not. That isn't what I meant at all."

"It's what you said. Poor Erica. Too many new things in her life."

"Damn it, you're deliberately misunderstanding."

"Oh, I understand more than you think I do."

"What's that supposed to mean?"

"Just that this isn't about *me* at all, Christian. You can tell yourself that if it makes you feel better. But this is really about you playing by a dead man's rules."

A muscle ticked in his jaw and she saw the flare of anger in his eyes. She recognized it because she knew that same emotion was shining in her own. She'd spent the past several days torn between anger and misery, but now the fury was spilling over.

He reached for her, but she scuttled back, not trusting herself to allow him to touch her right now. She might shatter. Need swam inside her and battled her own pride. It was a toss-up at the moment which would win.

"I told you," he said, letting his hands fall to his sides, "I can't risk what I spent my life building. But it's also true that you've got too much going on in your own life right now. You don't need me making things even more complicated."

"Oh, stop it," she whispered, shaking her head. She'd already trusted him too much, risked too much. She couldn't chance feeling even more. Trusting more. He'd already pushed her aside. How much clearer could he make himself?

"Wish I could," he admitted, coming around her desk, walking closer and closer still. "Wish to hell I could put you and what's between us out of my mind, but it won't go."

She laughed sadly, thinking of the past few days when he'd avoided her at all costs. "It seems you've been doing a fine job of that."

"No. You're in my mind all the damn time. You haunt me, Erica, and I'm not sure how to deal with that." He reached out, and this time she didn't move away. Couldn't make herself do it.

He cupped her face between his palms. Staring into her eyes, he said, "What's between us won't be denied and neither one of us can wish it away."

"Can't we?" she asked, her voice soft as she met his gaze searchingly. "Isn't that what's been happening lately?"

"No," he countered. "This is what's been happening."

Then he kissed her. Hard and deep, pouring into that kiss everything she'd been needing for so long. Her head swam, her heartbeat quickened into a racing gallop and by the time he broke away, she was laboring for breath.

Yet at the same time a tiny corner of her heart was erecting barriers, ready to defend her.

"Don't," he said softly. "I can feel you pulling away even when I'm holding you."

"Haven't you been doing the same thing these last few days?"

"No," he answered, releasing her and taking a step back. "I'm doing what I have to do."

"Because you won't risk caring for me."

"Because this is my life," he reminded her, and his features were hard.

"It's my life, too," she told him, stiffening her spine. "And I won't be used then discarded on a whim. You can't run hot and then cold on me, Christian. I refuse to play that game."

"You're wrong about me," he said tightly. "I'm not playing games, Erica. I wouldn't do that to either one of us."

She scraped her hands up and down her arms, trying to chase away the chill that was swamping her. But it was bone-deep and she was suddenly sure that she'd never be really warm again. What she felt for Christian was going nowhere. Because he would continue to refuse what lay between them. Once again, Erica thought sadly, she just wasn't wanted badly enough.

When he was gone, Erica slumped into her desk chair, turned it around and stared out at a sunlit day that had gone, for her at least, suddenly dark.

Eight

Despite their argument, over the next week, Christian spent time with Erica every day. He continued to be her guide as she grew more and more accustomed to her new life. But somehow he managed to keep their conversations centered on business, or the resort itself. He refused to bring up anything personal and she must have come to the same conclusion. She was polite. Cool. She treated him as she would have a distant acquaintance.

And every minute he was with her was a session in torture.

He'd never wanted anyone with the fierce desperation he did her. Thoughts of her plagued him constantly. He couldn't lose himself in his work anymore. Couldn't stroll through the Manor without seeing her, hearing her—or hearing someone else talk about her.

She'd charmed the staff and had settled into her new position as if she'd been born to it. And in a way, he supposed, she had. She was a Jarrod, after all. Which was the major problem for him.

If she weren't a member of the Jarrod family, he wouldn't be doing his best to ignore her.

Stopping by her office, he knocked, then walked inside to find her hunched over her keyboard, gaze fixed on the screen. Even here, he thought, when she was unaware that anyone was watching her, she looked… alluring. Her hair was tucked behind her ears and long, twisted shards of gold hung from her lobes. She was chewing at her bottom lip as her fingers flew over the keys and didn't look away even when she reached out blindly for a cup of coffee on her desk.

She'd given herself up to this job. This place. She'd jumped in with both feet and, true to her word, was definitely making a place for herself.

He wished that place was with him. But damned if he could see a way to make that happen.

As if she sensed his presence, Erica looked up then. Backlit from the window behind her, her amber eyes were shadowed, but he could still see the trepidation on her features as she looked at him. "Hi. Was there something you needed?"

"Loaded question," he muttered, then said more loudly, "Actually, yeah. There is. I wanted to know if you approved the design for the gala's setup on the main lawn."

"Yes, I did. I sent the papers over to Trevor this morning."

"Fine. I'll check with him again. He couldn't find them earlier, but that's not saying anything. He probably misfiled them."

She smiled slightly. "That does sound like Trevor."

"You like him," Christian said.

"It's impossible not to," Erica told him as her smile slowly slipped away. "He's got this flair for living that I really admire. He is who he is and makes no excuses for it. He simply lives and enjoys every minute of it."

Christian stiffened a little at the inherent comparison between himself and the easygoing Trevor Jarrod. "Trying to tell me something?"

She glanced up at him and shook her head, her soft hair swinging in a gentle arc that made Christian want to reach out and bury his fingers in the softness. "No, Christian, I'm not. I think we've already said everything there was to say."

"Impossible," he told her, walking toward her desk. "We couldn't have, because there's still too much unsaid between us."

"And it should probably stay that way," she said.

"Maybe," he agreed, reminding himself that it was *he* who'd put up the wall between them. He had been the one to take the first step back from what they might have found. And though it infuriated him to acknowledge even privately that she might have had a point when she accused him of being unwilling to face up to a dead man's wishes…she hadn't been far wrong.

If Don Jarrod were still alive, it would be different. He could go to the man, tell him how he felt about Erica. Make the old bastard see that she was right in saying that the fraternization clause was medieval. But with Don gone, the board of directors was in charge, and with the codicil in Don's will insisting that the clause remain in effect, they wouldn't be making changes anytime soon.

And how the hell could he go to the Jarrod siblings and insist that *they* change it? He couldn't be sure that they wouldn't side with their father.

Christian felt as if his hands were tied and his heart was being ripped in two. What he wanted was vying desperately with what he'd spent his life working for.

"Let's not do this again, Christian," she said quietly as she stood and came around her desk. "At the very least, we can stop torturing each other."

He tucked his hands into his slacks pockets to keep from grabbing her. God, he missed the feel of her pressed against him. The taste of her. The scent of her. He was making himself crazy with wanting her.

Then she reached up and smoothed his hair back from his forehead and the soft slide of her fingertips against his skin sent flames rushing through him. He inhaled sharply, deeply, and she instantly let her hand drop to her side again.

"Sorry," she said with a shrug she no doubt meant to look nonchalant. "As angry as I am at you, it seems I still have to remind myself not to touch you."

"I know the feeling all too well," he admitted, calling on every ounce of his will to keep from holding her and damn the rest of the world. Screw his job. Screw the Jarrod family. Screw Don Jarrod in particular for creating this hell for the two of them.

"I guess we'll just have to work on it, won't we?"

"Right." He nodded, but it cost him. "I'll just go check with Trevor about those papers."

"I'll go with you," she said. Tugging her white, long-sleeved shirt down at the hem, she smoothed her denim skirt.

Her legs looked long and tanned and her feet were tucked into dark blue heels that made her legs look even longer. Hell, she didn't even have to try to make him crazy.

Erica walked past him into the hall and he fell into step beside her. Blake and Gavin were standing near the elevator, locked in a conversation that was suddenly halted when they drew near.

"Hey, guys," Christian said. "What's going on?"

Blake shot Erica a wary look and said, "Nothing. Just talking. What're you two up to?"

Erica said, "Just checking on some paperwork with Trevor."

"Right. Well." The elevator door opened and Blake stepped in. "We'll see you later."

As the doors whisked closed again, they both heard Gavin say, "For God's sake, Blake, lighten up with Erica, will you? She's not the enemy."

"That went well," Erica said wryly as they continued on to Trevor's office.

"Blake will come around." Christian took her

arm and pulled her to a stop. "It's a big change for everyone."

She looked down at his hand on her arm until he released her. Then she shifted her gaze to his. "I don't mind Blake's feelings. At least he's honest."

Heading into Trevor's office alone, Erica didn't look back at him. So she didn't see Christian's dark scowl as he was left standing alone.

The main spa room at the Ridge was so opulent it was nearly decadent. Which made it perfect. A curve of aquamarine water followed the circumference of the room. Jets built into the walls of the pool produced frothy bubbles of pure relaxation and the only sounds were from the jets and the rhythmic splash of the overhead waterfalls spraying heated water down into the waiting pool.

Erica felt loose and limber and almost guilty for taking an entire day to do nothing but be pampered. Still, since it had been Melissa's idea to have a quiet day of sisterly bonding, Erica thought she could let the guilt go just this once. Besides, after the long week she'd had, it felt good to just relax, away from the Manor, away from Christian.

"You're seriously making us all look bad," Melissa told her with a sigh. "I mean, really, you don't have to be Jarrod Family Member of the Year right off the bat."

Erica smiled and hid the hurt that seemed to be a constant companion. Yes, she was making great strides at her new job. Her brothers and sister were coming around—she'd even managed to talk to Blake without him glaring at her. And she'd had dozens of compliments on her plans for the splashy welcome she'd designed for the opening of the gala.

For the first time in her life, Erica felt as though she was being accepted for who and what she was. For what she could contribute. And it felt great.

Or would have, if there wasn't a shadow clinging to her thoughts. Christian hardly spoke to her anymore. Not since that last kiss they'd shared in her office a week ago. She saw him at the Manor, of course. The offices were all too close together for them to completely avoid each other.

Though that might have been easier all the way around. How much harder was it to see him and not be able to touch him? Talk to him? But she refused to be the kind of woman who threw herself at a man when he had already made it clear that there couldn't be anything between them.

"Okay, what's wrong?"

"Hmm? What?" Erica jolted as she realized her thoughts had wandered off while Melissa was talking to her. "Nothing. I'm just thinking about work."

"Uh-huh." Melissa shook her head and reached out to pat Erica's shoulder.

The two of them had indulged in a luxury spa treatment. They'd already been through the facials, the massages and now, they were stretched out side by side in the narrow curve of the pool, relaxing. Or they were supposed to be.

"I know that look," Melissa said. "And it's not a 'work' look. It's a 'man' look. So spill."

She automatically shook her head. She'd never been one to share secrets with her girlfriends and there was simply no way she wanted her new sister to know that she was lusting after a man who wasn't interested. "I really don't think—"

Melissa gave her a dramatic pout. "What's the point of having a sister if you can't bare your soul and get free advice—or sarcasm, as the situation demands."

In spite of everything, Erica smiled. It did feel good to have a sister. Even two weeks ago, she never would have believed that she'd be able to use the words "my sister" in a sentence. Yet here they were, and astonishingly enough, the two of them had actually formed a bond that Erica hoped would only get stronger with time.

Sister wasn't just a word anymore. It was real. And it was good.

"Okay," she said, and glanced around to make sure they were still alone.

"Relax. The place is ours for the afternoon. I run the spa, remember?"

"Right." Erica lifted one arm and slid it through the water, letting the jetted bubbles pulse against her skin. "Okay, say there was a man I'm having a problem with."

"Yes, let's say that." Melissa leaned back and floated, allowing more of the jets to beat against her body. "Now let's say some more."

"Okay, this man, he's interested, but he's not willing to get involved."

"What's his problem?"

"It's a long story," Erica said, not wanting to give Christian's name or his reasons for pulling back from her. She wasn't sure if they knew about the fraternization clause.

"One you don't want to share."

"Not exactly."

"Is he married?"

"No! of course not!" Erica frowned at the other woman. "If he was, I wouldn't be making myself nuts over him."

"Okay, so do you want this man?"

"Yes, damn it."

Melissa laughed. "So go get him. Or at least try."

"What about dignity?" Erica countered. "Pride? Am I supposed to chase him down like a dog with him protesting the whole time?"

Straightening up, Melissa shook her wet hair back from her face and gave Erica a pitying look. "Little sister, men are simple creatures. He wants you. That's the point here. He's trying to stay away for whatever reason, but he doesn't want to. So make it a little more difficult for him to ignore you. For heaven's sake, why would you make it easier on him?"

"I don't know…" Erica sighed and shifted in the water, letting the heated water push into her back, easing tension she hadn't even really been aware of.

"Up to you of course," Melissa told her. "But for me, if there was a guy I wanted, I'd go get him."

Her words were said so forcefully Erica had to wonder if there was a particular man her sister was talking about. But an instant later, the timer for the jets shut off and silence dropped over them.

"I'll think about it," Erica said, climbing out of the water and reaching for a fluffy white towel.

"Less thinking, more kissing is probably the way you want to go," Melissa advised, "but maybe that's just me."

Maybe Melissa was right, Erica thought as she and her sister toweled off and moved toward the locker room to get dressed. Because really, why was she making it easier for Christian to ignore her? Could be that what she *should* be doing was spending more time with him, not less. Talk to him. Lean into him. Keep him so close that he wouldn't be able to pull away from her.

After all, ignoring him hadn't hurt him and had been driving her insane. So, she'd turn the tables on him. Take Melissa's advice and make him so miserable that he wouldn't be able to avoid her. And, since she'd just spent the last three hours being buffed and polished and styled, today was the perfect day to set this new and much more interesting plan in motion.

Christian threw a rock into the river and watched it hit the water and sink. Just how he felt, he thought. He'd been carrying around a sinking feeling inside him for the last two weeks and it was only getting worse.

Being here at Jarrod Ridge had always given him a sense of satisfaction that he'd found nowhere else. He'd studied back east and had been eager to get back to Colorado. He'd traveled the world and never found another spot as beautiful as this one. But now…

There was an unsettled feeling inside him.

And its name was Erica Prentice.

Hell, he couldn't even enjoy standing alongside the river anymore. Because he saw her here, now. She was everydamnwhere in Aspen, and no matter how hard he tried, he couldn't get away from her.

"Well," a too familiar voice said from behind him, "you look furious."

He turned around to watch Erica approach him. The sunlight was fading as twilight edged closer. She wore a short, lemon-yellow skirt that stopped midthigh and a pale green short-sleeved T-shirt that displayed her tanned, toned arms and clung to her narrow waist. Her hair was soft and shining in the last of the light and her eyes were locked on his.

"So," she asked as she came nearer, "did you want to be alone with your fury or can you stand some company?"

"Alone," he ground out, because he knew if she came any closer, he wouldn't be able to stop himself from reaching for her.

"That's a shame, because I prefer company," she said. She whipped her hair back from her face and continued down the slope, passing within inches of him as she walked to the water's edge.

"What're you doing here, Erica?"

She glanced back at him and shrugged. "I came to look at the river."

"And you could only see the river from here. This one spot. On the whole resort."

She smiled slowly. "I like this spot."

His hands fisted at his sides and he deliberately relaxed them, taking a long, deep breath into his lungs at the same time. Unfortunately, that only brought him a whiff of her scent, which made his insides tighten into knots. She smelled like peaches and flowers and all things soft and beautiful.

"Fine," he said. "Enjoy the view. I'll go."

"Okay, so will I." She turned and headed back toward him.

"What are you playing at?" he demanded when she stood right in front of him.

She shook her head and looked up into his eyes. "I'm done playing, Christian. No more games. No more teasing. I'm here because I want you and you want me."

His teeth ground together and he hissed in a breath, hoping to find some equilibrium. He didn't.

She lifted both hands to his shirt front and smoothed her palms over his chest.

His body went from hard to aching in under a second. He caught her hands in his and stilled them. Then he stared into her eyes and whispered, "Why are you doing this?"

"Because you won't," she said and went up on her toes to slant her mouth over his. Once, twice, a soft brush of her lips to his and Christian felt the heat of her rush through him.

He knew he was a dead man. He had to have her.

Couldn't have turned away now if someone had a gun to his head. She was everything he wanted, needed. She was all he could think about. All he cared about. It didn't matter if he would regret this later or not. Or, if being with her would only make the situation between them harder.

For now, he was lost.

He grabbed her then, as if half-afraid she might disappear on him if he didn't hold on to her tightly. Pulling her up close to him, he took her mouth with a desperation he'd felt clawing at him for days. Again and again, his tongue delved deep, claiming her in a mimicry of what his body wanted to be doing to hers. In and out, he dazzled, he took, he gave, his heartbeat racing, his blood pumping, he gave himself over to the demands of his body, clamoring to meet her demands.

As a soft summer wind caressed them both, Christian took the hem of her shirt and pulled it up and over her head. She threw her head back and laughed in delight as the air touched her heated skin. In that moment, Erica looked more beautiful to him than she ever had before. He unhooked her bra and spilled her breasts out into the palms of his hands.

She sucked in a breath as he cupped her, rolling her nipples between his thumbs and forefingers. She sighed, arching into him, offering herself to him as the sun's last golden rays played across her skin.

Her eager response fed the fires within him and Christian groaned, bent his head and took first one nipple and then the other into his mouth. Her skin was soft and smooth and smelled of peaches. His lips and tongue and teeth nibbled and suckled at her, drawing sighs and moans from deep in her throat. Her fingers slid through his hair, holding his head to her, as if worried that he would stop, that he would suddenly pull away and tell her no, they weren't going to do this.

But that wasn't even a glimmer in his brain.

They'd passed that line and there was no going back.

If he didn't have her *now,* he knew he'd die of the want.

With one last, lingering draw on her nipple, Christian straightened, caught her hand in his and said, "Come over here."

"What? What?" Dazed and unsteady, Erica followed him, her hand tucked into his. "Where?"

"Right here," he said, picking a blanket up off the ground and spreading it out beneath the trees.

She laughed a little, surprised. "You came prepared?"

He grinned, feeling lighter than he had in weeks. "Sometimes I sleep out here on warm nights. Good to have a blanket handy."

"It is," she agreed and went to him eagerly. She wrapped her arms around his neck and held on, kissing him deeply, slowly. Until finally, Christian growled, pulled his head back and lay her down on the blanket.

"Let's get you out of those clothes."

"You, too," she urged and immediately wiggled out

of her skirt and pushed her panties down and off. She kicked out of her sandals and lay across the pale blue quilt like an offering from the gods.

Christian took seconds to strip and join her on the blanket, going up on one elbow to kiss her while his left hand stroked up and down the line of her body. He defined her curves, explored every valley and took the time to tease her rigid nipples until she moaned into his mouth.

Her hand moved over his back, sliding across his shoulders and down the length of his spine. Every touch inflamed him until his body was so hard and tight, he could hardly think beyond the need hammering at his mind, his heart.

He slid his hand down over her belly and past the nest of curls to find her center. She gasped and lifted her hips for his touch. He obliged, sliding his fingertips across those heated folds, finding her damp warmth and realizing that she was as ready for him as he was for her. He dipped one finger inside her and stroked those inner muscles until she whispered his name with a hunger that matched his own.

"Christian, don't wait. Take me now, be inside me now. I need this. I need *you*."

"No more waiting," he promised and shifted to cover her body with his. He knelt between her thighs and parted them wider, opening her up to his gaze.

She twisted beneath him. "Christian," she said, licking her lips, "please. Now."

"Now." He pushed his body into hers with one long

stroke and instantly experienced the wild rush of being a part of the only woman who mattered to him.

She was tight and hot and caressed his length every time he withdrew only to surge forward again. Her legs came up, wrapped around his middle and took him deeper on every stroke. She curled her fists into the blanket beneath her and lifted her hips, rocking into him, following the rhythm he set and matching him move for move.

"Open your eyes," he ordered, staring down into her face as he took her. Her eyes flew open and met his. He read his own desire reflected back at him and saw in those amber depths the passion he'd waited too long to see.

She released the blanket so she could touch him, scraped her palms up and down his chest, up and over his back and dug her fingernails into his shoulders as he increased their pace. Hips pistoning, he took her higher, faster than either of them had ever been before.

Together, they raced toward a completion that had been waiting for them for weeks and together, they crashed over the edge and fell.

Nine

Erica was spent.

Every cell in her body was whimpering with release and pure pleasure. Her legs were trembling and her arms felt as if they weighed a ton. Christian was sprawled on top of her and though he was heavy, she didn't want him to move. Didn't want to lose this connection they had. She wanted to keep his body joined to hers for as long as possible.

Staring up through the thick branches overhead, she spotted small slices of a deep purple sky. The sun was down and the first stars were coming out. Beside them, the river rushed on, and here, on this blanket, the world was standing still.

"I want to roll off of you," he muttered, his voice

muffled against her skin. "But I don't think I can move."

She smiled, delighted that she'd brought such a man to his knees, so to speak. Christian was more than she'd thought when she first met him. Then he'd seemed so locked away, so suit and tie and cool distance. Now she knew what he kept hidden beneath that very businesslike exterior. And she didn't ever want to lose him.

"I don't want you to move anyway. I love the feel of you against me. In me."

Love.

Erica's breath caught in her chest and she smiled to herself as she realized it was true. She did love him. Why hadn't she realized it before? It all seemed so simple now. So clear. It didn't matter how fast it had all happened. It was as if she'd been heading here. To Colorado, to *him,* her whole life. Days, weeks, time had nothing to do with it. When it was right, it was right, she told herself firmly and gently stroked her hands up and down his broad, muscular back.

He groaned and lifted himself up onto his elbows. Looking down into her eyes, he rolled his hips against hers and she sucked in a gulp of air. His body stirred inside her, thickening, hardening. She sighed at the sensation and suddenly she was more than ready for him.

"You touch me and I can't think," he admitted, moving again, slowly, pushing deeply into her.

But in a heartbeat he went perfectly still and stared

down into her eyes. "Can't think. *Didn't* think. Erica, we didn't use any protection."

She gasped, stunned that the thought had never even occurred to her. She'd never done anything so irresponsible in her life.

"I'm sorry. I should have— Damn it."

"Stop," she said quickly, reaching up to cup his face with her palm. "It was my mistake as well as yours. But as long as we're both healthy, it should be all right."

"I am, I swear," he said, concern etched on his face. "But are you sure you won't get—"

"Pregnant?" she finished for him. "I can't be absolutely positive, of course, but it's the wrong time of the month, so…"

"Good. That's good."

But he didn't sound relieved, she thought. He sounded almost…sorry.

"But we shouldn't risk it again."

"Probably not," she admitted, "but if you pull out of me now, I'll have to kill you."

He grinned, lowered his head and kissed her. "I'll risk it if you will."

"Oh, yes," she said, sliding her hands up and down his back, over his shoulders and down the front of his chest. "Thinking's overrated anyway."

"Right," he murmured, dipping his head for a kiss. "Just feel. Just experience."

"Experience is good," she agreed, already feeling the fires burning, building within.

"New experience is even better," he said and leaned back, wrapping his arms around her, drawing her up with him, keeping their bodies joined. He sat back on his heels, with Erica on his lap.

She gasped and threw her head back, loving the feel of him impaling her so deeply. Instinctively, she twisted her hips, grinding her body against his, increasing the friction between them until he groaned her name and clamped both hands at her hips, holding her still.

In the soft light of the early evening, Erica looked down at him. Cupping his face in her palms, she took a kiss and then one more before sliding her hands down his neck to his shoulders. Then she moved on him, easing herself up and down in a slow, lazy rhythm, driving them both relentlessly onward. His hands at her hips, he kept his gaze locked with hers as she moved, taking him deep, releasing him, only to reclaim him again.

Over and over, as tension built, as need spiraled inside her, she moved, rocking, swaying, twisting her hips at their joining. Her hands at his shoulders, she felt it when he neared completion and surrendered to her own climax. As the first, electric ripples of pleasure dazzled through her, she heard him shout her name just before he let go and gave himself completely to her.

It was perfect.

What could have been hours passed before Christian said, "Are you cold?"

A chill swept along her spine, but it had nothing to do with the cold. It was his deep whisper resonating in her ear that affected her so. "No. Not cold."

"Still…" Christian reached across her, grabbed the edge of the blanket and drew it up over her.

Erica snuggled into his side and laid her head on his chest. Running one hand across his warm skin, she tangled her fingers through the soft dark hair until he laughed and the rumble sounded loud in his chest. "Touch me like that and we're not going to ever go back to the Manor. I'll have to keep you here all night."

"Not a very good threat," she admitted with a smile. "It actually sounds fabulous." She tipped her face up to look into his eyes. "I don't think I could ever have enough of you."

He lifted his head, gave her a quick, hard kiss, then lay back down again, one arm tightening around her, holding her close. "I don't know what to say to you."

"Say you don't regret it."

"I'd be a damn fool if I did," he muttered.

She smiled to herself and sighed a little, enjoying the moment. The soft wind rustling through the trees, the grumbling river just a few feet away and the soft summer night close around them. It was all perfect. Her life finally felt…right.

"Not that I'm complaining," he said, "but how did you know to find me here?"

"Hmm? Oh, Melissa suggested it. She said you came out here a lot on clear nights."

His hand on her arm stilled and Erica sensed that something had changed, though he hadn't said a word. Silent tension spilled out between them and though he was still beside her, Erica knew that he was already pulling away. "Christian?"

He scrubbed one hand across his face, released her and sat up to stare out at the river. "Melissa? Melissa knows you were going to come to me?"

"She knows I was looking for you, sure." Now she was cold. Despite the warmth of the evening air she felt as though ice crystals were settling on her skin. She tugged the edge of the blanket around her and stretched out one hand to touch his back.

He flinched at the contact.

"Great. That's just great." He stood up, grabbed his jeans and tugged them on. Then he snatched up her clothes from where they'd fallen and tossed them to her. "Get dressed."

Hurt and feeling at a complete loss, she only stared at him. "What is wrong with you? Why are you acting like this?"

"Unbelievable." He muttered something else under his breath, but she couldn't catch it.

Erica grabbed the clothing he'd tossed her. She slipped her bra on, then tugged her T-shirt on over her head. When she stood up to pull on her panties and skirt, she turned her head to look at him. He was searching for his shirt and finally found it hanging from a tree limb where he must have thrown it earlier.

Disgusted, he snatched it down and Erica was more confused than ever, so she blurted, "What is going on?"

He pulled his shirt on then ran his fingers through his hair. Glaring at her he said, "I told you, I couldn't be with you. I work for the Jarrod resort. *You're* a Jarrod.

Word of this gets out, I'll lose everything. And what do you do? You tell your sister."

Erica inhaled sharply, feeling as though he'd slapped her. This was what had him so tense? Knowing that she'd spoken to Melissa? Was he really that worried that someone might know they were together? Was his job really that important?

Stung to her soul, she snapped, "Your reputation's safe, Christian. Melissa didn't know why I wanted to see you. It's not like I advertised or printed a pamphlet alerting the residents of Jarrod Ridge that I was going to try to seduce a man who's been trying to keep me at arm's length!"

"Damn it, Erica…"

"Relax," she told him hotly. "You don't want people to know you were with me? Rest easy then, because I'm in no hurry for anyone to find out about this moment."

He faced her and though his teeth were gritted, he still managed to say, "It's not that I don't want them to know. I can't *let* them know."

"Oh." She nodded and gave him a wry smile. "Big difference. Thanks for clearing that up."

"You don't get it, do you?" He stood, legs far apart, arms folded across his chest as if he were trying to hold himself in place. "I've worked my whole damn life for what I've got here. I won't risk it. Won't lose it. You can't understand because you've always had this…" He threw his arms wide as if taking in all of Jarrod Ridge. "With either the Prentice family or the

Jarrods, you're one of them. I don't have that. I *made* my way on my own."

"And I haven't?" She snorted in disgust. "You saw my office in San Francisco. Bottom of the food chain. You know why? Because my father never wanted me involved in the Prentice family business. So what I had I made. On my own. And coming here didn't change that."

"Erica—"

"No, you had your say. Now it's my turn. I told you what it was like where I grew up. Never accepted. Never let into the inner circle. It's only here that I've begun to find my way and even then, I wasn't exactly met by a ticker tape parade."

He shook his head and sighed. "That's different. Whether the Jarrods were happy about it or not, you were one of them. You belonged. Like I said, you don't get it."

"I'm not one of them. I might be. One day. I hope so. But if that happens it'll be because I *made* it happen," she countered. "I wasn't handed anything. You think it was easy to come here? It wasn't. I walked out on the only family I knew. I gave up my job, my home, my *life* to try for something new. Something better."

"I'm not going to argue with you," he told her quietly.

"Of course not," Erica muttered. "You might lose."

"I'm doing what I have to do and you'll never understand it."

"Oh, I get it," she said softly. "Finally I get it. You're a coward."

He took the two steps separating them and grabbed hold of her upper arms. His hands were strong, each of his fingers digging into her skin as he dragged her up on her toes, so they could be eye to eye. "I'm no coward and you don't know what you're talking about."

"Yes, I do," she said. Erica wasn't afraid of him. Even with his eyes nearly glowing with fury, he wouldn't hurt her. It wasn't in him. He was a closed-up man hiding a passionate nature, but that passion didn't include brute force. "I can see it in your eyes. You're already pulling away from me, from what we found, planning on how you can avoid me in the future."

He let her go instantly and backed up, muttering under his breath. Then he said, "When we're around others, nothing has to change. We just won't be doing… this again."

"Oh, is that all?"

God, how was she breathing? Everything inside her was still and cold. Her lungs, her heart. Even the blood running through her veins felt icy.

Erica grabbed her sandals and hopped on one foot then the other to tug them on. Once she was dressed completely, she threw her hair back from her face and stared daggers at him. "After what we just experienced you can actually stand there and say to me that you don't want us to be together? That you'll walk away from this? From what we might have?"

* * *

No, Christian thought wildly, he didn't want to say that. Didn't want to think it. With Erica, he'd found more peace, more excitement than he'd thought possible. When he held her, she was the world. He couldn't imagine never having her with him again. Couldn't even see his life without her in it.

These last few hours had been more precious than anything he'd ever known before. From the moment she'd approached him, it was as if they'd stepped into some dream world where they were the only two beings in existence. He'd forgotten his hard and fast rules. He'd turned his back on what he'd made of himself over the years and lost the essence of who and what he was in her. The magic of her.

But magic wasn't real.

And eventually, dreamers woke up.

He wanted her desperately. But if he acted on what he wanted, then he stood to lose everything he'd ever worked for. Everything that had made him what he was. How could he turn his back on his life? On the man he'd become? If he did, what would he have left?

Who would he be?

"You're going to do it, aren't you?" she whispered. "Even after everything that happened tonight, you're going to be the good corporate drone and go back to your cubicle."

He sighed. What the hell could he say to her? He couldn't even explain it to himself. "Erica…"

"No, don't bother." Her voice was low, almost lost in the roar of the river. But somehow he heard every word and felt the power of them hit home as if each one was a blade.

"You're going to regret tossing me aside," she said.

He stared into her eyes and couldn't quite bring himself to tell her that he already *did* regret it. Standing here, so close and yet so far away from her, he felt as if all the life was draining out of his body. But he couldn't say what she wanted—needed—to hear.

"You'll regret it, but it'll be too late. I feel sorry for you, Christian. Because I would have loved you forever." With a sad shake of her head, she turned and walked away from him.

Christian watched her go and felt his heart go with her.

She was gone the next morning. Back to San Francisco on the family jet. According to Melissa, Erica was only going back for a visit, but Christian couldn't help but wonder if he'd managed to drive her away from her legacy.

Two days later, he felt on edge. He was miserable. He hadn't slept. Couldn't close his eyes without seeing her. Work wasn't the salve it had always been. He couldn't concentrate on any single task because his mind kept drifting to Erica and the way she'd looked at him just before she walked away.

He never should have let her go.

"What the hell is wrong with you?"

Christian shook his head and glared at Trevor. They were in Trevor's office and had been working on the layout for the gala and somewhere in there, Christian's mind had taken a sharp left turn. "Nothing. Can we just finish this? I've got other things to take care of."

"You know what? Never mind. I'll finish it myself."

"Good." For the first time in years, Christian wasn't interested in Jarrod Ridge or its gala. He didn't care about the tourists flocking to Aspen or the businesses depending on the Ridge to increase their profits. He was damn sick and tired of living his life by the wants and needs of the Jarrod family.

Hell, he was still following Don Jarrod's edicts even after the man was in his grave. So Christian's life had now come to the point where a dead man was controlling his actions.

Was he really going to allow this to continue? Could he really risk losing the only woman who'd ever gotten under his guard?

Would he give up his future to assuage his past?

Furious with himself and the whole damn situation, Christian turned to go, but stopped when Trevor spoke up again.

"What's eating at you, man? You've been terrorizing the staff and *me* for the last couple of days."

Yeah, he had. Wrestling with your demons didn't make for a good time and there were bound to be innocent bystanders caught up in the fight. But Trevor wasn't his enemy and it'd be best to remember that.

Christian looked back at his friend and said, "I've got some things on my mind, that's all."

"Want to talk about it?"

"Not really," he said. He had to get things sorted out

for himself before he could speak to any of the Jarrods about this.

Trevor stared at him, then nodded. "All right. I figure a man's entitled to his secrets. But if you change your mind, I'm here."

"Appreciate it." And he did. He had friends here, Christian knew that. What he didn't have was Erica. "I'll see you later."

Blake walked in the door almost at the same instant and jumped out of the way before Christian could crash right into him. "What's his deal?"

"I don't know. He won't say. Clearly something's bugging him though." Trevor sat down at his desk, ready to dive into the paperwork again.

"I know how he feels," Blake said.

The tone of his voice more than anything else had Trevor looking up. "Why? What's wrong?"

"Not sure. But I just saw Melissa with Shane McDermott. They looked…cozy. Have you heard anything?"

Trevor leaned back in his desk chair. "No. But if our friendly neighborhood rancher is interested in our little sister, I suggest we keep an eye on things."

"Just what I was thinking," Blake agreed.

Three days holed up in her old condo in San Francisco and Erica was no closer to knowing what to do than she had been when she arrived. She'd cried herself silly for the first several hours until her sorrow had faded into fury. Anger was so much easier to deal with.

Erica stood up and moved to the balcony off her

living room. She had a view of the bay and the Golden Gate Bridge and she'd spent most of her days with the sliding glass door open to let in the frigid wind blowing in off the ocean.

After so much time in Colorado, with the sky so wide and open and so much space around her, she felt… caged in the very home she'd once loved so much.

Strange. She'd only been gone three weeks but this place no longer felt like home. She looked at the soft, pastel paintings on the walls and couldn't figure out what she'd seen in them. She wasn't the same woman who had lived here. She'd changed. Grown. She'd reshaped her life to suit the woman she'd become.

Now Erica knew what it was to finally find her place. She had discovered what it was like to love someone and lose. She knew what it was to go on with your heart breaking and not have a clue what to do next.

She'd found more than a home in Colorado.

She'd found herself. And the woman she was today needed answers to questions she was no longer afraid to ask. She hadn't run from Christian; she'd run *toward* her past. After leaving him at the river, Erica had realized that she couldn't enjoy a future without first dealing with her past. And so she'd come back to San Francisco. To tie up the loose ends of her life so that she could return to the place she belonged.

Okay, yes, she hadn't immediately gone to face her father. But she was going to. She'd simply needed a few days to sort out her own feelings. That didn't mean she was turning tail and running. And she certainly wasn't going to hide here in a condo that wasn't really *hers* anymore.

She was going back.

Just as soon as she found what she needed to know.

Ten

The very next morning Erica marched into her father's office and faced him, for the first time not as his daughter, but as an adult who demanded respect.

"Erica," Walter said, standing up and moving out from behind his desk. "You didn't tell me you were coming."

"No." She studied his familiar features and saw with surprise that he looked older than she remembered. And not as intimidating, either. Was it her imagination? she wondered. Or was it that she was no longer looking at him as a child would?

"Are you all right?" He came to her, gave her a brief, awkward hug, then stepped back.

The embrace was over so quickly it was almost as if

it hadn't happened at all. Erica felt the sting of tears in her eyes and inwardly groaned. She fought to hold those tears at bay as she asked, "I need to know something, Father, and I need the truth."

"Of course."

"Did you ever love me?"

"What kind of question is that?" His eyes narrowed and his scowl deepened. "Is this what they've been telling you in Colorado? Those Jarrods have been filling your head with nonsense and you've been listening?"

Shaking her head, Erica felt her heart sink. "They haven't said a word about you, Father. This is something I need to know. Did you love me? Ever?"

His mouth tightened into a straight, grim line as if he were deliberately holding back the words she needed to hear.

Walking past him, she dropped her cream-colored leather bag onto the nearest chair, then turned to face him again. "I'm tired, Father. And hurt. And a little miserable, too. I'm finally figuring out who I am, but to finish doing that, I have to know who I was. Was I *ever* a daughter to you?"

As if all the air had left his body suddenly, Walter Prentice seemed to shrink in size right before her eyes. His shoulders slumped, his head dipped until his chin met his chest. Tiredly he lifted both hands to rub his face, then dropped them again and looked up at her.

She walked toward him, drawn by the naked pain on his face. Erica had never seen this side of her father.

Never known him to be emotional at all. She took a shallow breath and held it.

"You're more like your mother than you know, Erica. You have her beauty, but more important, you have her heart." Leaning forward, he took her hands in his and held them gently. "I do love you, child. Always have. I couldn't love you more if you were my own blood."

A great weight eased off her heart and Erica took her first easy breath since walking into his office. "Then why? Why have you always kept me at a distance? Why would you never let me get close? You wouldn't even let me work here, Father. I thought you believed I wasn't good enough to join the family business."

"Ah, God, I've made so many mistakes," he muttered, his grip on her hands tightening. "But I swear they were made with the best of intentions. For years I was afraid that Don would try to take you from me, so I tried to keep an emotional distance from you. Fearing that if I did lose you, the pain would be too great to bear." He sighed heavily. "Then the years passed and I kept you tucked away, out of the family business, to protect you from Don Jarrod."

"What? That makes no sense."

"It did to me. I was terrified that he'd come back, you see. Try to take you from me as he stole your mother. I couldn't bear the thought of that."

"Oh, Dad…"

He squeezed her hands. "Do you realize that's the first time you've ever called me that? To you, I was always 'Father,' not 'Dad.'"

Erica sighed and let go of the pain and misery she'd been carrying around for most of her life. Sad as it was, it was also sort of comforting to know that neither one of them had deliberately shunned the other. Mistakes had been made, true, but by both of them and for far too long.

Leaning into his warm embrace, she wrapped her arms around her father's neck and let the tears flow. He patted her gently and whispered words of comfort that were too soft for her ears to catch—but her heart heard and slowly began to heal.

"Are you happy out there?"

Erica sat across from her father and smiled. It was the first time she could ever remember her father being concerned with her happiness. But then, there had been a lot of firsts today. She felt lighter, freer than she had in years. She'd accomplished so much in just leaving, taking her own life in her hands. She'd found who she was meant to be. She'd reconnected with the father who had loved and raised her. And she had found—and lost—Christian.

Her smile faded, but she forced it back into place. "I really am. I know it's strange. I can hardly believe it myself, to tell you the truth. But it's so gorgeous there, Dad." Funny how easily that name spilled from her now that she knew her affection was welcome. "I don't just mean the resort, but Colorado itself. It's huge and open and so beautiful it's almost hard to look at it. I hope one day you'll come to visit me there."

Clearly uncomfortable at the thought, he was quiet for a moment, his brow furrowed and his eyes narrowed. "I'll come. Don Jarrod's ghost won't keep me away from my daughter, Erica. I'm not going to risk losing you again."

Her heart opened even further as love swept in, chasing away years of regrets and misery. "You won't lose me, Dad. You can't. I love you."

He reached across the table and took her hand in his for a quick squeeze. "Does my heart good to hear that, I don't mind telling you. But the most important thing is you're happy, right?"

"I was.…" How to explain to him what a mess she'd made of everything? She couldn't actually confess to her father that she'd seduced a man who didn't want her, after all.

"What changed?"

She folded her linen napkin and set it on the table. Then sitting back in her chair, she said, "I fell in love."

"And this makes you miserable?"

"No," she said on a short laugh, "it made me happier than I've ever been before."

"But…" Walter encouraged her to talk just by patiently waiting.

Smiling, she acknowledged, "You've still got the intimidation knack."

"It's a gift," he said with a wink. "Now, tell me what's wrong with this man that he doesn't see what a wonderful girl you are."

"There's nothing wrong with him," she said, Christian's face rising up in her mind to taunt her. "He just doesn't want me enough."

"Well, why the hell not?"

"It's complicated, Dad. I think he does care for me. But he won't let himself." Irritation spiked inside her and she had to take a deep breath just to calm herself. "So the question is, how am I supposed to live there and see him every day feeling the way I do?"

"What's the alternative?" he asked briskly. "Run away? Hide? Pretend you don't feel what you do?"

"I don't know," she whispered.

"Well, I do," Walter said, standing to come around the table. He pulled her from her chair and stood her up in front of him. With the tips of his fingers, he tilted her chin up until she was looking directly into his eyes. "You're a Prentice, Erica. And we don't run. We don't put our heads in the sand when things don't go our way, either. If you love that dolt, then find a way to make him admit he loves you, too."

Throwing her arms around his neck, she hugged him tightly and sighed when Walter's arms came around her with a fierce embrace.

"I love you, Dad," she whispered and his embrace tightened in response.

"I love you, too, little girl," he whispered. "Guess you'll be leaving right away?"

She pulled back and smiled up at him. "I really should. The gala opens next week and there are a million details to see to—not to mention the fact that there's a certain man I have to see and talk to."

"Do I get to know his name?"

"As soon as I straighten him out, I'll introduce you," she promised, then gave him an extra hug for good measure. Grabbing up her purse, she raced for the door, but stopped dead when her father called out her name.

"Yes?"

He wagged a finger at her. "Just don't you forget who you are, little girl. You're Erica Prentice. *My* daughter. And you can do anything you put your mind to."

She grinned at him. "You're damn right I can."

Christian refused to live like this any longer. He hadn't seen or spoken to Erica in days. For all he knew, she could have decided to forego her inheritance and move back to San Francisco. That thought drove spikes through his mind and heart. What if she didn't return? What if she decided that staying at Jarrod Ridge would be too painful because *he* was an idiot?

His stomach felt like a ball of lead had settled in it, while at the same time, his chest felt hollowed out. He scrubbed both hands across his face and stood up. Turning, he faced the window and didn't even see the spectacular view. Instead, he saw Erica as she'd been their last night together by the river.

Naked, open, holding her arms out to him, taking him into her body, her heart. He could see the warmth in her eyes and the soft smile wreathing her face. His insides twisted and his mouth dried up. He loved her.

He loved Erica Prentice.

And he'd not only let her walk away, he'd been ass enough to ruin what had been the best damn night of his life. The question now was, was he going to let that mistake stand? Or was he going to do everything in his power to correct it?

"Screw this," he said out loud to no one. He turned and looked around the interior of his office. The one he'd worked so hard for—and all he saw was emptiness. In his mind, his future stretched out in front of him and that, too, was empty.

Pointless.

What the hell good was the job of his dreams if the woman he needed wasn't a part of his life?

Furious with himself for taking this long to realize what was the most important thing to him, Christian jumped up from the desk chair and marched out of the room. He needed to talk to the oldest Jarrod sibling and he knew exactly where to find him.

Twenty minutes later, he was searching for Blake Jarrod amid the throng of people wandering around the site for the gala. The man was out here somewhere directing the crews setting up. When he spotted him, Christian headed right at him.

"Christian," the other man said with a nod of greeting. "What are you doing out here? Giving up law to come swing a hammer with us?"

"No," he said, barely glancing at the crew. "Blake, I need to talk to you."

"Sure," he said, heading to a less crowded part of the lawn. He stopped and crossed his arms over his chest. "What's this about, Christian?"

The only way to handle this was to jump right in.

"I'm resigning as family attorney as of today," Christian said and felt a weight slide off his shoulders. Damn, it felt good to be a free man. He'd been living an indentured life and he hadn't even realized it until just this instant.

All along, he had thought he was steering his own course. Plotting his own life and destiny. But in reality, Don Jarrod had still been in charge. Even from the grave. But not anymore. And never again.

"What?" Astonished, Blake reached out, grabbed Christian's upper arm and dragged him a little farther away to make sure no one would overhear them. "You can't resign. Are you nuts?"

"Not anymore," he said, grinning. "And yeah, I can resign. Watch me."

"We can't run this place without you, Christian!"

"Not my problem as of today, Blake. Sorry, but this is how it has to be."

"Sorry?" Blake threw his hands high and let them slap down against his thighs. "You're *sorry* that you're walking out just as we all get back and have to deal with mountains of crap?"

"You've got each other. You'll do fine. This is your home, Blake."

"It's your home as much as it is ours."

Christian looked around, letting his gaze scan the familiar grounds, the guests and the well-trained staff. True, this was his home. But it didn't mean a damn to him without Erica. Decision made, he turned back to Blake.

"I'll type up a formal letter and leave it with your assistant," he said. "If you want, I can make some recommendations about who I think would work well here."

"I don't want your recommendations," Blake muttered with a dark frown. "I want you here, doing your job. Like always."

"Can't do it, Blake," Christian said. He wasn't thinking about Blake. He was thinking about Erica. He had to tell Erica he loved her and that he was willing to risk everything in his life *except* her.

"You have to do it. We can't afford to lose you." Blake took a deep breath, bit back his frustration and demanded, "You've always been happy here, Christian. Where's this coming from?"

"Things are different now."

"Since when?" Blake's eyes narrowed on him.

He hadn't intended to say anything. But how could he not? Blake was a friend and the brother of the woman he loved. Why the hell should he hide his feelings now? He took a breath and plunged in.

"Since your sister."

"Melissa?"

"No." Christian laughed out loud at the stunned

surprise on Blake's face. Clearly he'd done a very good job of keeping his feelings to himself. "Erica."

"Really?" Blake shook his head. "Huh. I didn't have a clue."

"Nobody does," Christian told him. "That's the point. I've been hiding how I feel about her because of my responsibilities here."

"What?" Now Blake just looked confused. "Why would you do that?"

Christian sighed. "You know as well as I do how your father felt about what he called 'fraternizing.'"

"Oh, for God's sake—"

Christian kept going. "I get involved with your sister, I lose my position here and any shares I have in the company. The board of directors will take care of that at their next meeting."

"So you're just gonna walk away from everything you've ever known instead."

"Rather than lose her? Yeah. In a heartbeat."

Blake nodded and grinned at him. "I can see that. What you didn't think about is, the Jarrod family won't let you resign."

"You can't stop me."

"No, but I can hire you again the minute you quit," Blake told him. "And when I do, there'll be no restrictions, Christian."

"What are you saying?"

"I'm saying what everybody knows. Don Jarrod was a hard man. I'm not him. And neither are my brothers." Blake laughed aloud. "God, Christian, Melissa would kill us all if we let you leave over something like this."

Christian shook his head as if he couldn't believe how this conversation was going. He'd been prepared to lose everything to keep Erica. Now it seemed he was going to have it all. If he could convince the woman he loved that he deserved her.

Slapping him on the shoulder, Blake said, "We'll write up a new contract between you and the Jarrod Resort whenever you're ready."

"I don't know what to say."

"I think that's a first," Blake told him with a laugh. "So you and Erica, huh?" His eyes went cool and serious for a moment. "I've had my issues with the new sister, but bottom line here is, she *is* my sister. So just to put you on alert—if you're not actually planning to marry her—you won't have a job to worry about. None of us will stand by and let anybody hurt her."

"I don't want to hurt her. I want to marry her. All I have to do is convince her to say yes."

"Good luck, man." Blake held out a hand toward him. "And welcome to the family."

Christian shook his friend's hand and hoped to hell his talk with Erica would go as well.

By the time the Jarrod jet landed at the small strip in Aspen, Erica was a woman on a mission. She was focused. Determined. She had her plan on facing down Christian all worked out and was eager to get on with it.

But her lovely, well-thought-out plan dissolved as she disembarked from the plane and saw a car waiting for her. The driver, an older man with grizzled black-and-white hair, smiled as he held out an envelope.

Curious, Erica opened it while the driver stacked her luggage in the trunk of the car. The note inside was short and in Melissa's handwriting. *Get in the car and don't ask any questions.*

A spurt of irritation briefly shot through Erica, because now she'd have to wait to take care of the most important confrontation in her life. But just as quickly, she let go of her disappointment and told herself that her conversation with a hardheaded man could wait a while longer. If Melissa had gone to this much trouble, she must need Erica for something.

"Okay, then," she said, smiling at her driver, "guess we should get going."

"Yes, ma'am." He opened the car door, saw her settled, then climbed behind the wheel. In a few minutes they were on the road to the resort and Erica was wondering what Melissa was up to. She had called her sister to let her know that she was coming home, so if there had been something wrong, wouldn't Melissa have told her about it already?

Home.

That word settled in her heart and she had to smile. Oddly enough, after only three short weeks at Jarrod Ridge, the place *had* become home to Erica. She wasn't the same person she'd been when she arrived. Now, she was officially an *ex* big-city girl. She'd officially quit her job. Oh, she'd have to go back to San Francisco soon, to arrange for the sale of her condo and to have her furniture shipped west. But she'd take care of that and get back to Jarrod Ridge as quickly as possible.

This was where she belonged now.

Her gaze scanned the scenery as it passed in a green-brown blur, her mind racing, dragging up image after image of Christian. She worried over how their talk would go and told herself that no matter what else happened, she would at least have the satisfaction of knowing she'd told him how she felt. If he still chose to walk away from her—well, she'd just make his life a living hell until he changed his mind.

In no time at all, the car was pulling through the resort's front gate. But instead of heading toward the hotel entry, the driver drove off on what had to be a service road. She looked behind her as the Manor receded into the distance and was then swallowed up by the cloud of dust flying up from behind the wheels of the car.

"Just where are we going?" she asked, despite Melissa's note.

"Only a minute or two more, miss," the man said.

The trees were thicker here, lining either side of the road like soldiers at parade rest. She didn't recognize this area and realized that there was still a lot of the resort for her to explore and come to know. But she hadn't planned on doing it right now.

Finally the car came to a stop on the rutted road. The

driver helped her out, pointed to the tree line on her left and said, "Just head right through there, miss."

Before she could ask any questions, the driver had hopped back into the car and disappeared down the road. "Perfect. What is going on?"

She headed off to her left and cocked her head to listen when she heard a familiar roar of sound. It was the river. Her heart started pounding and a tiny curl of nerves unspooled in the pit of her stomach. Still, she walked on, until she rounded a bend and saw a blanket spread out under the trees. Her breath caught in her chest as she realized that the driver had brought her to Christian's spot alongside the river. Since they'd taken the back way in, she hadn't recognized the place until now.

On that blanket was a silver ice bucket holding what looked like a bottle of champagne, and a picnic basket, its lid partially opened to allow a baguette to spear up.

Erica took a deep breath and when Christian stepped out from behind a tree, she felt hope and confusion tangle inside her. When she could speak without her voice breaking, she asked, "What's this about, Christian?"

"I needed to talk to you and I thought the best place to do that was here. In our spot."

Our spot. Not his. *Ours*. That brief flash of hope she'd experienced began to shine more brightly. But even as it did, she wondered if maybe he'd brought her here to tell her he'd never love her. Maybe he had chosen this particular spot to soften the blow of goodbye. So before he could speak, she did. "I have a few things I want to say to you, too."

He came toward her, stepping out of the dappled shade into the wash of golden sunlight. "First hear me out, Erica."

"No." She skipped back out of reach of him, because she knew if he touched her, the words would dry up in her mind and she'd forget everything but the feeling of having his hands on her again. "Let me say this. I've been rehearsing it all the way here and I need to get it out."

"Okay, then. Tell me."

Nodding, she pointed at the picnic he'd set up in the shade and said, "First, let me say if you've brought me here to tell me goodbye, you can forget it."

"Goodbye?" Christian reached for her, but she moved back and away again, frustrating him beyond belief. "I'm not—"

"Because I'm not going anywhere," she said, lifting her chin and glaring at him. "I'm going to be right here. Every day. You'll have to see me, work with me, talk with me. Every day. And every day I'm going to remind you of how good we are together. Of what we could have had together if only you'd made the right choice. And I'm going to keep on reminding you of that until I convince you that we should be together even if it takes me another twenty years."

Tears were shining in her eyes and that alone tore at Christian's heart and soul. "Don't, Erica. Don't cry."

"I'm not crying," she argued. "I'm arguing, and arguing makes me emotional."

"I can see that," he said, smiling now because she still loved him. Still wanted him. He hadn't ruined everything after all. "Now, will you listen to me?"

She sniffed, cast a look at the champagne picnic, then turned back to him. "I suppose."

"Good, because you're not going to have to remind me for twenty years. Not even for twenty minutes."

"I'm not?"

He walked to her, closing the distance between them with three long steps. He looked down into her whiskey-colored eyes and saw everything he had ever wanted shining back at him. How could he have thought for even one minute that he would be willing to do without her? That he would be *able* to be without her?

Not a chance.

"I went to Blake while you were gone and I quit my job as family attorney."

"What?" She pushed at him. "You can't do that! I won't let you give up everything you worked for just because Don Jarrod was a medieval warlord. And Blake shouldn't allow it, I'm going to—"

Christian laughed as she turned from teary to warrior in the blink of an eye. God, life with her was going to be fascinating. "You don't have to do anything. Blake refused to let me resign. Said he'd just hire me again without all the qualifiers his father insisted on."

"So you're not leaving?"

"No."

She watched him warily. "And you're not going to pull away from me again?"

"No." He pulled her into his arms and held her tightly to him until he felt her return his embrace, her arms winding about his waist as she clung to him. Then his world righted and Christian knew everything was going to be all right. "I'm never letting you go again. I love you, Erica. Have from the moment I met you. When you left…"

He pulled back and stared down into her eyes. He lifted one hand to cup her cheek and then smoothed his fingers through her hair, loving the cool, slick slide of it against his skin. "When you left, you took my heart with you. I knew then that nothing I had, nothing I had worked for, was worth anything without you in my life."

She sighed, and a soft, amazingly beautiful smile curved her mouth as she looked up at him. "Christian, I love you so much."

"Thank God," he muttered.

She laughed a little. "I thought for sure I'd have to argue for hours to convince you that you loved me."

"No arguments necessary," he said. Then he reached into his pocket, pulled out a small, dark red velvet box and opening it, held it out to her.

Sunlight danced off the enormous diamond and shone in her eyes as he watched her. He took the ring from the box and slid it onto her finger, all while she simply stared up at him, with a bemused smiled on her lovely face.

"I finally figured it out."

"What?" she asked, glancing down at the beautiful promise glittering on her hand.

"That all I need is you. If I have you, I have everything. Without you, there's nothing."

"Oh, Christian…" Tears fell, sliding along her cheeks, but her smile was as brilliant as the diamond on her finger.

"Marry me, Erica. Make a family with me."

"Yes!" she shouted the single word, then laughed in delight. "Yes, I'll marry you and I swear, I will love you forever."

He kissed her hard and fast, then drew back and grinned at her. Erica threw her arms around his neck and hung on for all she was worth as he swung her into a dizzying circle. The world rushed by, a blur of color and sound, but in the center of it all, they were together.

As they were meant to be.

* * * * *

FALLING FOR HIS
PROPER MISTRESS

BY
TESSA RADLEY

Tessa Radley loves traveling, reading and watching the world around her. As a teen Tessa wanted to be an intrepid foreign correspondent. But after completing a bachelor of arts degree and marrying her sweetheart, she became fascinated by law and ended up studying further and practicing as an attorney in a city firm.

A six-month break traveling through Australia with her family reawoke the yen to write. And life as a writer suits her perfectly—traveling and reading count as research, and as for analyzing the world…well, she can think "what if?" all day long. When she's not reading, traveling or thinking about writing she's spending time with her husband, her two sons or her zany and wonderful friends. You can contact Tessa through her website, www.tessaradley.com.

For my cousin Merope
The only person I know who can find a restaurant
where sinfully rich chocolate cake is served
first on the menu
and entrées appear on the dessert menu described as
something to fill the space left over!

One

Everything was running smoothly.

Well, almost everything, Guy Jarrod amended as he strode into the cobbled square that lay at the heart of Aspen's famous Jarrod Ridge resort.

Erica Prentice, his newly discovered half sister, had sprung the unwelcome news on the family at breakfast this morning that Art Lloyd, one of the Food and Wine Gala speakers, had called yesterday to cancel his appearance because of a bad bout of influenza. Apart from the minor headache of finding someone to replace Art, the annual festival was on track and the tall, snowy-white marquees that lined the square on three sides hummed with activity.

If his old man had been here, even he would've admitted that the spectacle was impressive.

Heaviness pressed down on Guy's heart. Don Jarrod, his father—and an Aspen legend—was gone. Forever. Yet Jarrod Ridge remained a monument to his father's life's work.

A large shadow floated over Guy. Squinting skyward, he saw awestruck faces peering down at him from baskets that hung below brightly hued balloons drifting lazily across the morning sky. Guy's mood lifted and he raised a hand to wave before making for the nearest marquee that, even this early in the day, was already crowded.

He could see Erica huddled next to Gavin, one of his two younger brothers, her finger stabbing the air as she emphasized a point. And over to the right, beside the wine-tasting tent where an early-bird charity auction was already happening, his twin brother, Blake, was talking to—

The press of people opened for an instant, long enough for Guy to catch a tantalizing glimpse.

He blinked.

It couldn't be.

The crowd shifted again.

It was.

His gaze homed in on an achingly familiar blond head and a petite curvy feminine body that should've been nine hundred miles away in California.

His twin bent courteously to hear what the blonde was saying, and Guy's eyes narrowed dangerously when her slim hand pushed a pair of designer sunglasses to the top of her head. The action revealed the curve of a cheek he'd stroked with his fingertips under the cover of darkness, the corner of a lush, smiling mouth he'd kissed until all smiling had ceased and she'd moaned instead.

God, he remembered those moans....

Little mewing sounds that had clawed at his groin and made him go wild with hunger.

So what the hell was Avery Lancaster doing staring up at his twin in that intent fashion?

Without conscious thought, Guy began to move, long

strides that ate up the ground. All too soon he was looming over the Barbie-blonde who barely reached his shoulder.

She must have sensed his approach. It took only one startled glance from those wide china-blue eyes for Guy to feel the imperceptible tightening of his skin, the rippling of the muscles below. A slight shudder quaked through him before he remembered to breathe and sucked in a lungful of air. Being this close to Avery had always made him feel invincible, like some kind of superhero.

Not anymore.

Yet, for once, Avery looked rattled, too.

"Guy!"

In the month and a half—okay, so he'd kept count—*forty-nine days*—since he'd last seen her, Avery's sorcery hadn't diminished a whit. In her absence, Guy had half convinced himself he'd imagined it. No woman had that much power.

But standing beside her brought home that he hadn't imagined a thing. A once-over showed that her composure was back—if indeed it had ever slipped. Avery looked like she'd stepped from the pages of a glossy magazine that would have every female reader rushing to buy the floral dress she wore. Her soft honey-gold skin tempted his touch. Only the blond tendrils that had escaped the restraining sunglasses broke the model-like perfection and made her look tousled—and very, very kissable.

"Avery," he responded with just enough frost to cause Blake to raise an eyebrow.

"You two know each other?"

"Avery helped me review the wine list at Baratin."

His glare dared her to contradict him. Avery's gaze fell beneath the force of his—as he'd known it would. Traitor. It felt like a lifetime since the day she'd swept into his life with the force of a hurricane—and proved to be every bit as destructive. In reality little more than two months had passed since the day they'd met. Fourteen hours after that first meeting she'd been in his bed. The next day she'd moved out of the hotel where she'd been staying into his apartment. Two weeks later she'd been gone.

Yet instead of boasting about what a fabulous job she'd done at Baratin, Avery now turned her head away, presenting him with a smooth, flawlessly tanned cheek, and fixed her attention firmly back on Blake.

Over my dead body.

Guy's lips tightened. She could forget about seducing his brother. One Jarrod would have to be enough.

Blake grinned. "I remember you mentioning employing a freelance sommelier—you didn't tell me she was gorgeous."

Avery hadn't spared Guy another glance—he might as well have been invisible. And his normally brisk-and-businesslike twin hadn't taken his eyes off Avery. Irritation spiked through Guy as a rosy flush spread over her cheeks.

Could she have faked that?

A dimple appeared beside her mouth, and a little husky laugh followed. "Flatterer," she said to Blake, her polished fingertips fluttering like butterfly wings against his brother's arm.

Guy started to frown.

She'd better damn well stop flirting with Blake or he'd drag her away and send her packing back to Napa Valley. He wasn't having destruction follow in her wake as it had before.

He was onto Avery Lancaster.

She chose that moment to remove her hand from Blake's arm and flick the bangs off her forehead. The crossover neckline of the dress printed with pink roses—without a warning thorn in sight—pulled tight. Guy's lip curled. No magical illusion there, just plain feminine wiles, as old as Eve.

It infuriated Guy that even he wasn't immune. Giving himself a mental shake, he forced his eyes away from temptation, only to discover his charismatic twin still assessing her with amused interest.

Damn.

"You two must be brothers." The breathy voice that had once made him shiver with longing held a note of discovery.

Guy suppressed an annoyed growl as Blake instantly responded, "Guy is my twin."

"I knew there was something familiar about you—"

"Fraternal twins," Guy bit out, determined to make Avery stop examining Blake as if he was a juicy cut of filet mignon. "Not identical."

The gaze that switched to meet his with startling directness was carefully blank. "Funny, I didn't even know you had a brother, much less a twin," she murmured. "Or that you were one of the Aspen Jarrods."

Funny? They'd had an affair. Passionate. Explosive. Nothing remotely funny about it. Then she'd walked away. There'd been no obligation to bare his soul, dammit.

"Now you know—and, since you're obviously interested, I have two more brothers as well." Gavin and Trevor were every bit as eligible as Blake.

Despite the curve of her lips, her vivid blue eyes had dimmed, and held none of the sparkle he remembered. Only an unfamiliar wariness.

She should be worried.

Unless she was a fool. And, despite the sexy-Barbie exterior, Avery had never been dumb. In truth, the way it had played out *he'd* been the dumbass; *she'd* played him for the fool.

Guy snorted at how he'd fought a primal, gut-deep fear and tried to do romance. For her. How he'd planned the most romantic birthday gift he could dream up. An extravagant meal of all the foods he'd learned Avery loved. Shrimp tempura. A light salad with walnuts, blue cheese, pear and a hint of ginger. Cherries. Tiramisu. Baratin's frenetic Friday night bustle had been replaced with the intimacy of soft candlelight. Twenty-seven white candles—to match her birthday—glowed around one solitary table, with all the other chairs and tables packed away.

Surrounded by the aroma of the fluffy rolls he'd baked himself and the fragrance of cut flowers in tall vases filling the air, Guy had waited.

And waited…

And while he waited, his heart more exposed than he'd ever allowed, Avery had been seducing Jeffrey Morse.

The big romantic gesture had cost Guy more than a night's takings. It had cost him a week's sleep and most of his self-respect. And nearly two months later his pride still smarted.

Of course, if Avery had known he was one of the Jarrods from Jarrod Ridge, Aspen, Guy doubted she would have switched her attentions to Jeff, his Go Green business partner, so readily—despite Jeff's sizeable trust fund.

But the subject of his family had simply never come up. There hadn't been time. They'd either been talking about wine and work—or tumbling into bed. And Guy was suddenly, savagely glad that she hadn't known before he'd gotten a chance to discover exactly what she was.

Gold digger.

Well, there'd be no Jarrod gold for her here….

Forcing himself to ignore her considerable physical endowments, he speared her with a cold stare. "What are you doing at Jarrod Ridge?"

The instant he bit out the words Guy wished he'd kept his mouth shut. What the hell did he care why she was here? He despised her. It was obvious that she'd come to Jarrod Ridge to prospect for another wealthy fool at a festival renowned for attracting the rich and famous. Jeff had sent her packing once guilt at the way he'd betrayed a friend had set in. Guy knew he should be grateful for his own lucky escape, that he'd found out Avery was looking for nothing more than a wealthy man.

Except gratitude was not the emotion that filled him as Avery's pink tongue slid across her pouty kiss-me-senseless bottom lip. In another woman the gesture might have suggested anxiety; in Avery it was pure feminine seduction. Her tongue retreated and Guy breathed again. Then her lush lips parted. Guy couldn't have glanced away if there'd been a gun against his head. Right now all he cared about was sexy Avery and her provocative, pink mouth.

Clenching his fists at his sides, Guy swore a silent streak.

Poor Jeff hadn't stood a chance.

And this time her wiles were clearly directed at his twin. Eyes narrowing, Guy leaned closer. If Blake was to be her next target, she'd miscalculated. Yet, as he opened his mouth to growl at her to back off, he caught a whiff of the sweet, intoxicating floral scent that was all she ever wore to bed. Hot blood rushed through his veins, pooling in his lower belly.

Ah, hell!

If only his body hated her, too…

With grim realism, Guy shut his mouth with a snap and decided it was just as well the resort was full to capacity. The crowds would make it easier for him to avoid her.

"Art sent me."

"Art sent you?"

The question must have betrayed his dazed disorientation

because Blake spoke from beside him, reminding Guy that he and Avery were not alone and that he'd asked Avery what she was doing here. "Avery is Art Lloyd's niece—even though she doesn't resemble him in the least."

Avery flashed a quick smile at Blake, and Guy could've sworn the woman fluttered her eyelashes at his brother. Damn her.

"You're Art's niece?" Disbelief was certainly better than following through on the overwhelming impulse to shove her away from his brother.

"Uh-huh." Avery nodded, and the wispy bangs shimmered with the lustre of gold in the sunshine. "I'm sure you're aware he was scheduled to speak at the gala, but he's ill. Flu on top of asthma and a weak chest. The doctor says he can't possibly fly in that condition."

He could've sworn he read apprehension in her wide, Barbie-blue eyes. Not that he blamed her. Even now, seven weeks after she'd run out on him, he wanted to shake her.

Instead he shoved his fists into his pockets and said, "I'm sorry to hear he's ill. I like Art."

He didn't need to add that he detested *her*. Avery wasn't stupid—if she didn't see it in his face, she'd be able to draw that inference herself.

She inhaled sharply.

Guy couldn't help himself, he looked down. The pink roses moved, her sweet floral scent surrounded him, and he could've sworn his world tilted, too.

From a distance he heard her say in that breathy, bedroom voice that drove him crazy, "Well, I'm here to speak in Art's place."

Hell!

Inside the snowy-white bower of the grand marquee the Friday night oyster-and-champagne cocktail party that launched the Food and Wine Gala each year was in full swing. Waitresses circulated with trays piled high with hors d'oevres, while dinner-jacketed waiters refilled tulip glasses that glinted in the light of the glittering crystal chandeliers overhead.

"Erica has outdone herself," Guy said with grudging approval to Blake as he scanned the chattering crowd who'd paid top dollar for tickets to tonight's event.

"It's the food that's got the crowd talking," said Blake, "and that's your domain."

Guy inclined his head in acceptance of the compliment. "It helps that every available ticket was sold," he pointed out. "The more people here tonight, the more media coverage the festival will get, and the more word-of-mouth buzz will spread."

"She's certainly better at public relations than we ever expected," his twin conceded. "But I was always certain there wouldn't be any tickets left over to give to the local business suppliers as Erica suggested."

"The gesture would've won Jarrod Ridge plenty of local goodwill." Guy had joined his twin in vetoing the suggestion when Erica had made it. Deep down Guy suspected he'd done it more because he resented his illegitimate half sister's very existence, rather than for sound business reasons. It was a suspicion that made him decidedly uncomfortable, one that he was not yet ready to confront.

"Anyway it would've made the function too big—lost the exclusivity." Blake sounded certain.

"We could've limited the number of speakers who gained complimentary entry." Guy's brooding gaze settled on the woman whose arrival earlier had turned his hard-won peace on its head. Avery didn't look like she had a care in the world. But he would've breathed a lot easier without her here tonight.

"Dad always gave festival speakers free entry to the opening night cocktail party. Mom set the tradition."

Blake's point hammered the final nail in the coffin. And Guy resisted the urge to argue that none of them had done what Don Jarrod wanted in life. So why the reverence for his opinion now that he was dead?

But the night of the official opening of the Food and Wine Gala was certainly not the time for friction with his twin.

Particularly not with Avery nearby. A sideways jerk of her head warned him she'd seen them. Guy edged closer to his brother. He fully intended to save his twin from Avery's irresistible advances tonight. And damn irresistible she was, too, in a dress the color of summer sunshine. Every time she moved diamond drop earrings sparkled through the pale gold feathers of her hair. Even in this celebrity-studded crowd she attracted attention.

After giving them a brief smile of greeting, Avery showed none of this morning's interest in Blake. From the corner of his eye Guy watched her intercept a tall, well-built stranger. His mouth twisted as she flung her arms around the man and kissed him on the cheek, before stepping away with a beaming smile.

It certainly hadn't taken her long to find company.

"Who's the man beside Avery Lancaster?" he demanded. His twin knew everyone worth knowing. Blake's networking skills and business acumen were unsurpassed.

"Looks familiar." Blake frowned with concentration. He snapped his fingers. "Got it. A vintner. From California—I think. But I can't recall his name."

"Which winery is he with? Does he grow good grapes?" It seemed important to establish a flaw in the stranger who stood too close to Avery for Guy's comfort.

Blake shook his head. "Can't remember. It will come to me. Why the interest?"

Guy refused to admit that he was fishing. Whoever Avery's quarry was, his highly polished Italian shoes and the avant-garde designer-label tuxedo he wore were a testimony to his wealth. It would be good to know that he had some weakness that could be exposed when needed. "Always good to know who's making the best wines."

"Information always gives us an edge over the competition," agreed Blake.

At that moment Avery threw her head back and laughed at something the Californian said. Her earrings danced and her eyes sparkled.

Unexpectedly, anger ignited in Guy's belly.

He swung away and told himself he should be relieved to be rid of a gold digger like Avery. So why the hell was he so damned annoyed? He'd always been easygoing about relationships, shrugging philosophically when they ended. And usually remaining friends with his former lovers.

But this time it was different.

Blake asked him something. He grunted his assent without any idea about what he'd agreed to. Then he told himself Avery had declared war by running out on him in New York without an explanation of why she'd seduced his business partner, his friend. He'd deserved to know. *She* might think it was over between them. But *he* wasn't through with her yet.

Not by a long shot.

No one betrayed him, then ran out on him…and Avery was about to learn that.

When Erica joined him and Blake, Guy shifted to get a clear view of Avery again as she accepted a glass of champagne that a waiter offered. She didn't take a sip.

A heartbeat later, Avery's head turned his way. Guy found himself blurting out to Erica that she'd done a great job with tonight's cocktail party before Avery could catch him staring at her with puppy-dog eyes. He didn't even notice his half sister's flush of surprised pleasure or Blake glaring daggers at him, reflecting the uneasy relationship between the Jarrod brothers and their new-found half-sister.

Another furtive glance showed that Avery had set her untouched glass of champagne down on the edge of the table behind her and was talking, gesturing with both her hands to illustrate what she was saying. When her fingertips settled on her companion's jacket sleeve, anger stabbed deep in Guy's chest. Forgetting to pretend disinterest, he assessed the easy familiarity of the gesture through narrowed, bitter eyes.

Maybe not a stranger after all.

A former lover? Someone she'd been pursuing even while she passed time in his own bed?

Bile rose in the back of Guy's throat.

"What's wrong?"

Guy started. Erica was gazing at him with concerned eyes.

He glanced around.

"Don't worry, Blake's not here. He's gone to fetch me a glass of water. I'm hot and thirsty. It's been a long day."

That made him feel curiously uncomfortable. He hadn't been aware of Erica's discomfort. Or his twin's departure. Because he'd been too damned busy devouring Avery with his eyes. Was he so transparent that even the half sister he barely knew could read him like a book? He pressed his lips together and glanced away without responding, discomforted by the sudden flush that heated his face.

"Who is she?"

"Nobody," Guy bit out.

Erica blinked. "Hey, I only wanted to help. You looked… unhappy."

Unhappy? Not at all. Instantly Guy forced a smile. "I'm fine."

She didn't look convinced.

"Truly, I am."

"Okay, I'll butt out." A smile softened the words.

His own smile widened into a relieved grin. "Thanks."

The lines of strain around her eyes eased, and a wave of remorse flooded him. It was time to cut Erica some slack. She'd done a damn fine job with the festival so far. Yet before he could offer an olive branch he caught sight of Avery and her companion heading for the exit. The tension that had been winding tighter ratcheted up another notch.

She wasn't ending up in the other man's bed tonight. Not under his nose, on his turf.

A well-known food writer stepped forward to greet Avery's companion, causing him to pause. Guy made his move.

"Excuse me," he murmured to Erica, before rapidly shouldering his way through the throng, unaware that his half sister watched him go, a bemused look on her face. His sole focus was on Avery.

"I want to speak to you." He cut Avery away from her partner as neatly as a wrangler.

"Guy! What are you doing?"

Placing his arm around her, he bent his head toward her. To an onlooker it would have appeared intimate. Even cozy. But his growled warning was anything but lover-like. "Now's not the time for a scene, Avery."

"Scene? I'm not making a scene—you are," she objected, her voice rising as he swept her along with him. "*Let go of me.*"

He leaned closer still—and instantly her sweetly sexy floral scent surrounded him. Savagely fighting the sudden blast of raw desire, Guy lowered his voice and murmured into her ear, "Hush. I have no intention of kidnapping you."

Two

Avery wasn't so sure.

It only took one glance to reveal that there was a determined—even ruthless—set to Guy's jaw that she didn't recognize. His arm, heavy and unwelcome, tightened around her waist. She would've given anything not to be so spine-tinglingly aware of his proximity as he hurried her away from Matt.

She'd known this confrontation was coming from the moment he'd realized she was here to speak in Uncle Art's place. She'd tensed, waiting for the outburst that had never come.

If she'd realized that *her* Guy Jarrod was one of the Aspen Jarrods she'd have done whatever she could've to avoid coming here. Heck, even though it would've meant breaking her word to her uncle, she'd pleaded with Matt this afternoon to take his dad's spot so that she could catch the first flight out. But Matt had to be back in Napa Valley by tomorrow. And not even her desperate pleas had swayed him.

As she shot her nemesis a sideways glance, her breath snagged in her throat. From the opposite end of the grand marquee he'd been eye-catching, but up close Guy Jarrod was utterly devastating. His six-foot plus height suited the tailored tuxedo, the broad shoulders tapering to a lean waist, while the white dress shirt only emphasized the masculine perfection of his handsome profile.

I should hate him…he deserves it.

To hide the humiliating effect his body had on her, she wrinkled her brow, hoping she looked convincingly puzzled. "What did you want to talk about?"

Guy clearly wasn't fooled. His lips firmed into an impatient line as he stopped in the back corner of the marquee beside a table laden with trays of oysters. He turned to face her. "You taking Art's place."

"Is it a problem?"

Of course it was. His reaction earlier had shown that. What she couldn't work out was why he didn't want her speaking at the Food and Wine Gala. Well, she was no doubt about to learn.

Avery forced herself to smile faintly—and very politely—at him before helping herself to a glass from a passing waiter to give her hands something to do. She took a delicate sip of the pale liquid and pretended to savor the crisp dryness on her tongue.

Guy's gaze dipped to her mouth. The eyes that met hers a moment later had gone dark. In the past he'd sometimes poured a glass of champagne for them to share after—

No! She wasn't thinking of the countless abandoned glasses of untouched champagne or the passionate encounters that had followed.

Her lashes fell, and Avery fixed her attention on the square

black snaps of his dress shirt. She recognized those snaps…
one evening she'd yanked them all loose—

Oh, heavens!

She jerked her head back and focused on his jaw instead.
It was a hard jaw, a determined j—

"You're not listening."

"Of course I'm listening." Please don't let him ask her to
repeat whatever he'd just said.

"You're not even interested."

"Not in you," she muttered rebelliously.

Only a few inches separated his mouth from the area of
jaw line she'd been examining, and she watched his beautiful
lips flatten into a hard line. To her exasperation, her heartbeat
kicked up. This close he smelled so familiar. Of sandalwood
soap, a green hint of moss…and man. But this recklessly
rash awareness of the man didn't alter the fact that he was a
first-class bastard.

One she would be wise to avoid at all costs.

"How typical of a woman not to be able to separate her
emotions from her work."

What? "That's not true—" Avery broke off. Or maybe it
was. She'd made it personal by disavowing any interest in
him. "Okay, I shouldn't have made that crack." Especially
when her reaction suggested it was patently, horrifyingly
untrue.

She was pathetic.

Hadn't she learned what kind of scum Guy Jarrod was,
despite the fancy French restaurant he owned in New York
and his high-society family?

God help her.…

He rocked back on his heels and the extra inches of space
allowed her respite to breathe again without drowning in
his scent. For an awful moment she thought he was going to
pursue exactly how much of a lie her denial had been.

To her relief, he let it slide.

"No, you shouldn't have. And I'll accept that as an apology."

She wouldn't have gone so far as to call it an apology. Annoyance made her bristle like a cat stroked the wrong way. "That's big of you."

He expelled an impatient sigh. "You know, this isn't going to work. Go back to California—I'll find someone else to stand in for Art."

Avery stared at him, aghast. This was what she'd wanted… but now that he was telling her to go, she knew there was no way she could ever tell Art she'd let him down. "I promised Art—"

Guy was shaking his head. "Art and I were scheduled to do two talks together," he said, "and it's clear that you're not going to be able to cooperate."

Oh, dear God, what had Art gotten her into? He'd muttered something about a panel on wine selection and a presentation about the importance of superior service in a world-class establishment but that had been all. There'd been no mention of a joint presentation with anyone, let alone Guy Jarrod.

She should never have come….

Uncle Art's pleading voice played through her head. She hadn't had a choice. To think she'd considered speaking at such a prestigious event, the opportunity of a lifetime. But this wasn't about her…it was about what she owed Uncle Art and Aunt Tilly.

She'd never lived up to Aunt Tilly's hopes. But Uncle Art was proud of her. He'd taken her in after his sister and brother-in-law—had died in a sailing accident. He'd loved her, cherished her, supported her. For her uncle she would walk across burning embers—barefoot. Except he'd never asked that of her.

He'd run interference on her behalf with Aunt Tilly when

she'd refused to attend another beauty pageant or talent show. He'd supported her when she'd bailed out of drama school. He'd never asked anything of her.

Until now.

Her shoulders sagged. "Of course I'll cooperate with you." Within reason. *No sex with his friends and colleagues.* More to the point, no sex with Guy Jarrod. Period. "Just tell me what you need me to do."

"Have an oyster."

They'd decadently shared oysters in bed one memorable Monday when Baratin had been closed. They'd risen late. He'd fed them to her...interspersed with kisses...it had ended up in one of the most erotic encounters of her life. Surely he wasn't referring to that?

It took a moment for the shocked daze to clear and for Avery to realize he was holding out a platter where oysters on the half shell nestled between fat wedges of lemon and translucent ice cubes.

"They're perfectly shucked. I oversaw the preparation myself. No sand or broken shells. Just succulent flesh with a hint of juice."

For a brief second she caught a glimpse of the Guy she'd thought she'd known so well. Wicked mirth sparkled in his gray-black eyes and warmed her.

Irresistible, damn him.

She resisted the charm with a toss of her head. "No, thanks. I'm quite sated."

The laughter evaporated. "I'm sure you are."

The platter disappeared into the hands of a hovering waiter. Avery searched Guy's face but could find no trace of the bitterness the words suggested. She must've imagined it.

"My schedule for the next couple of weeks of the festival is ferocious." Guy continued as if they'd never shared that crazy moment. "Art offered to do most of the work to put the first presentation together."

That got her back on track. That's why he didn't want her speaking? He considered her too inept, did he? Believed she couldn't do what Art had undertaken to do? Avery suspected she was going to regret not leaping at the opportunity of escape Guy offered. Instead, her innate love for a challenge surged, and she found herself saying, "I can do that."

He didn't look convinced. In fact, he looked downright dubious. "Not only was Art doing two talks with me, he had a solo presentation planned."

"On the importance of superior service—I know."

"And he was contracted to look over the resort's wine lists and compile a report of his findings about service levels," Guy continued as though she hadn't interrupted. "It will have to wait until he's fit to come out here himself."

"No, it won't. Art and I discussed this, I'll do it in his place. That won't be any problem at all."

A waiter offered Guy a glass of champagne. Unconsciously Avery noted that the waiter's white jacket was pristine and carefully pressed, his handling of the tray deft. The resort staff were evidently well-trained.

Guy glanced at her still-full glass before helping himself from the proffered tray. "It's a pity I don't share your confidence," he said in a clipped voice, and Avery's approving smile to the waiter froze.

She turned her full attention back to the man whose reappearance in her life had caused such inner turmoil, caused so many memories and emotions, which she'd thought she'd suppressed, to waken.

"Oh?"

Avery cringed and dropped her gaze to stare at the bubbles rising merrily in the pale golden liquid in her own glass. *Oh?* Was that the best she could do? What had happened to her intelligence? Her wit? Her sass? Was she going to let this arrogant jerk walk all over her?

She was the one with a problem, not him!

She *hated* him.

Blindly she set her glass down.

She would be professional. Reasonable. And blow him away with her expertise. "Look, I've overhauled plenty of wine lists, I've trained junior sommeliers and other staff, I've done lots of public speaking." She jabbed her right index finger against the fingers of her left hand as she counted off the list. "I've taught, and I've even had my own TV show. That should boost your confidence a little."

"The TV show lasted all of four episodes."

Avery colored. The show had been axed. Because the ratings hadn't been good enough, she'd been told. She suspected there could have been more episodes—if she'd been prepared to sleep with the producer, when he'd made that suggestion. But that price had been too high. Avery had quit—despite Aunt Tilly's disappointment. And the producer had found another—more accommodating—sommelier. It hadn't surprised Avery when that show had ended in scandal and tears. Losing the program hadn't been the first time her sex-kitten looks had mucked up her life.

Even Guy was giving her the kind of once-over that left her enraged…and uncharacteristically flustered. But by the time his gaze came back to meet her own furious gaze, his was filled with contempt. And something else. Something that caused her heart to leap.

Avery resisted it.

There was no room for this…this…unwanted feeling. She was over Guy Jarrod. He was a bastard. And she had no intention of ever returning to the misery he'd caused her.

She could do this. She knew it. But first she had to convince him.

Lifting her chin a notch, she readied herself for a fight. "*Cuisine* stated that the new wine list at your New York restaurant had been put together 'with artistry and sophisticated style'. I wouldn't deliver anything less here."

"This isn't Baratin, Avery. Jarrod Ridge has four restaurants and six bars. The selection of wines, beers and alcoholic beverages served in each of those needs to be overhauled, as you put it. Don't forget I've read your résumé. You've never handled a project of this scope."

He didn't blink as he delivered his verdict in a calm, controlled voice. Avery knew he didn't believe she was up for the task. She forced herself not to look away from that alarming scrutiny. "I'm sure I can discuss whether I'm capable of completing the task with whoever is in charge of overseeing the menus and service requirements."

"That would be me." His crooked smile held no amusement, even if it did cause two nearby women to give him admiring glances. "I'm looking at introducing new dishes, and the beverages need to be matched to give a perfect selection."

"I'd be working with *you?*"

He nodded and raised his glass. "Do you want to toast to the success of our partnership?" The irony was acute.

Two could play that game. Avery reached for the glass on the table behind her and raised it with bravado.

"To success!"

Champagne splashed out, almost landing on her yellow silk dress.

"Careful!" Guy gripped her wrist with his free hand and the crisis was averted.

"Thanks," she murmured. "I would've hated to have ruined this dress."

"That didn't augur well." He quirked an eyebrow. "Still want to stay?"

In truth, she was ready to run. She'd never admit that. Especially not to him.

"Of course." She tilted up her chin. "You won't get rid of me that easily."

A fierce and stormy emotion flickered across his face. Then his thumb moved against her wrist, and his hold eased a degree. The frisson of awareness that shot through her was as unwelcome as the knowledge that they'd be working together—far too closely for Avery's comfort—for the duration of her stay.

It would be an impossible situation.

She raised her hand, his fell away, and she took a gulp of champagne. Then sneezed.

"Steady."

Her eyes were streaming.

"The bubbles always make me sneeze."

"How unfortunate for a sommelier!"

She wiped her tears away with her fingertips. "That's what my family thinks, too. It's one downside of the job."

"That's why you've barely drunk any tonight—and why you never wanted champagne in the past."

Arrested by his statement, Avery stared at him. He'd been watching her. For how long? And…why?

How could she work with a man she'd once upon a time hoped she was falling in love with? A man to whom her body unfurled like a sunflower to the sun. A man she now hated.

"Here, let me take that."

Numbly she opened her hand and relinquished the glass. Guy set it back down on the table behind them.

How could she let Uncle Art down? He'd been the rock in her life. How could she turn her back on him when *he* needed *her?*

Avery swallowed. The short answer was, she couldn't.

"So—" Guy faced her again "—you're staying then."

She swallowed her objections. "I can take the heat in the kitchen," she said rashly, "can you?"

There was a moment of throbbing silence. Then he said softly, "I can take anything you care to dish out."

"You're the chef, you're the expert at dishing out."

Avery didn't care if he heard her disillusionment. Between Guy and his friend Jeff they'd shattered the dreams she'd spun around the man in front of her, the man she'd convinced herself was her perfect life partner.

That night Guy had sent Jeff to her for her birthday had made her grow up….

Pushing past him, she said, "Now, I need to go find Matt."

Three

Day one down…just over three weeks more to endure.

Yet despite her dread about Guy's presence, Avery had managed to successfully avoid him and her first full day at the Jarrod Ridge Food and Wine Gala had passed in a buzz of excitement. She'd found herself indulging in celebrity spotting like some wide-eyed teenager. There'd been the handsome hero of a popular soap, a pop diva with rainbow-streaked hair and a hunky, tanned tennis star.

In the afternoon, she'd sidled in to listen to the presentation her cousin Matt was giving, and joined him in the trendy sky lounge on the covered rooftop of Jarrod Manor for a too-quick drink afterward.

"This is the kind of world Mom always wanted for you, pumpkin." Matt stretched his legs and lounged back in the leather armchair. "She was certain you'd be a star."

Avery wrinkled her nose. "Despite all the classes, I never had any acting talent. I would've made an awful beauty queen—too short. And you know I hate being called pumpkin. I'm twenty-seven years old." But there was no heat in the objection that had already been made a million times before.

Matt chuckled—as she'd known he would. "You really did look like a pumpkin when you arrived to live with us. Chubby and wearing orange dungarees—don't know why Mom ever thought you'd win any of those baby pageants."

"Chubby? Oh, you!" But she laughed up into his teasing face. "I was two—hardly a baby. And it's your fault Aunt Tilly craved a little girl, you were all such hooligans." As much as the four scruffy boys had overwhelmed her in the beginning, she'd grown to love them all—even her well-meaning aunt. El Dorado, the boutique vineyard her uncle had acquired shortly before her arrival, had become home.

"When do you leave for home?" Her cousins still based themselves at El Dorado—as did she when in California.

"I fly out first thing in the morning." Matt unfolded himself from the armchair and rose, yawning, to his full height. "I've still got to prepare for my meeting tomorrow."

Avery scrambled to her feet.

"I wish you could stay longer." A wistful note crept into her voice. It was cowardly wishing Matt would stay to help her cope with Guy. Yet his departure felt like a desertion.

"No chance, pumpkin." Matt threw an affectionate arm around her shoulders. "It was hard enough taking these two days out my schedule, but it was worth the exposure that today's talk gave the business."

"You did great."

She gave Matt a fierce hug and hoped he hadn't detected the desperation behind it. Those hopes were dashed as he held her at arm's length and studied her face.

"Dad will be okay." All teasing vanished, leaving his

expression unexpectedly serious. "Don't wear yourself down with worry."

He'd sensed her unease but he'd attributed it to the wrong cause. Immediately guilt constricted her chest. She'd been so busy fretting about Guy, she'd hardly spared a thought for her uncle. Selfish!

Taking a deep breath she said. "Make sure your dad looks after himself. I don't like that he's ill."

"He's a tough old codger." Matt gave her a squeeze. "He'll be fine—you'll see. Mom will coddle him to death. But I'll give him your love when I see him tomorrow."

Over Matt's arm Avery found herself looking into a pair of stormy eyes. Guy Jarrod. Then the shutters came down, and all expression leached out, leaving her wondering if she'd imagined the flash of emotion.

Ignore him, she commanded herself. He's not worth the heartache. She hoped she'd be able to follow her own advice in the weeks to come.

Avery made herself glance away from Guy's blank stare to give her cousin a wobbly smile. "I've decided to spoil myself. I've booked a massage at the resort spa and I'll have a soak in a hot tub afterwards. That should guarantee I'll sleep like a baby tonight."

"I suspect you haven't done enough of that lately."

"What do you mean?" She stared at her cousin in surprise.

"I'm not going to pry, but you came back from New York looking like a wraith. It was all we could do to stop Mom interrogating you."

Avery felt herself flush. "You're joking!"

"We love you, pumpkin. You're family. If I ever meet the man who put that bruised look in your eyes, I'll be giving him a few bruises of his own."

Matt's tone was light but his eyes were deadly serious. She

didn't dare glance past him to see where Guy was. If Matt knew that Guy had expected her to sleep with his friend, before returning to join the ménage à trois himself, her cousin would be ready to kill him.

She gave a dismissive laugh. "He was nothing!"

"Get over him," Matt said gruffly.

"Oh, I intend to." She smiled at him. "When you see me again I'll be heart-whole and fancy-free. Who knows, later in the week I might go shopping…do a little sightseeing."

"Or find yourself a hot lover."

"Matthew!"

"If you're going to live it up, pumpkin," Matt grinned down at her, "Aspen is the place to do it. Indulge yourself. No regrets. And, don't worry, I'll keep you updated about Dad."

"Thanks, you're the best." She stood on tiptoes and brushed her lips across his cheek in a gesture of gratitude and affection.

Giving up on wrestling her foolish need to search out Guy, Avery turned her head. To her relief the man who had haunted her nightmares was nowhere to be seen.

The sight of brass letters on the wall announcing Tranquility Spa was enough to ease some of the diabolical tension that had been building ever since Avery's encounter with Guy yesterday.

The first thing Avery noticed was the calming sound of water as she entered the spa. Water trickled down stone fountains set in wall panels along the reception area. Between the fountains scenic paintings formed vistas of incredible beauty.

Two women were talking behind a long counter carved from pale, polished wood, and one turned as the front door clicked shut.

"Avery?"

The gold badge the woman wore read Melissa Jarrod, Manager. With her long, wavy blond hair and blue eyes there was little resemblance to Guy's dark hair and metallic, almost black, eyes. Perhaps Melissa Jarrod was a cousin or married to one of his brothers.

Giving a hesitant smile, Avery said, "Yes, I have an appointment for a massage."

Melissa glanced at the flat computer screen on the desk, and said to the nervous-looking woman beside her, "Rita, would you let Joanie know her client is here? I'm going to leave now, I'm so tired I can barely stand." With a sweet smile to Avery she said, "Let me show you where your treatment room is."

Melissa did look pale, Avery thought as she followed the other woman down a corridor where smaller wall fountains were set between wooden doors.

"You're in the Red Room," said Melissa. "The saunas and steam rooms are further along. I'd recommend fifteen minutes in one of the steam rooms after your massage, followed by a soak in a hot tub."

"Sounds fabulous." Avery had every intention of following that advice.

Melissa pushed the next door along open, and Avery glimpsed an interior painted a shade of welcoming red ochre. A huge seascape of a dramatic sunset dominated one wall, while a dark red massage bed with a soft throw stood in the foreground. Farther back sprawled a large, wood-paneled hot tub with an ice bucket resting in a black wrought-iron stand beside it. Three fat white candles cast a soft glow, adding to the womb-like warmth of the room.

"Oh, wow!"

The other woman laughed. "You may have gathered that our mission at Tranquility Spa is to ensure that you relax."

Avery stepped into the embrace of the warm, sensuous room and gave a sigh of contentment.

"Can I pour you a glass of champagne?"

"No, but I'll definitely help myself to some of those while I soak." Avery pointed to the tray of dark chocolate truffles at the side of the tub. "What a heavenly, decadent treat."

"You can change out of your clothes." Melissa was smiling as she handed Avery a soft towel. "Joanie will be here in a few minutes to give you your massage."

The massage passed in a delightful haze of well-being. Avery felt her muscles easing as the pent-up tightness dissipated under Joanie's skilled fingers. Guy had loved stroking his hands along her back when they made love....

Yes, if she was brutally truthful, she'd missed the passion they'd shared. Missed laughing with him at the end of a day when they sat in the massive tub in his starkly modern apartment after sating themselves in his king-size bed. But she hadn't been prepared to pay the cost that Guy had demanded.

A cost she'd never expected.

His promise that he had a surprise in store for her birthday had caused a surge of hope...after all, she'd fallen for him like a ton of bricks. Even though she'd sensed his reticence about commitment, she'd hoped...

He'd promised a surprise.

It was her birthday.

Maybe...

Avery had been almost too scared to hope.

Yet when she'd opened the door of Guy's apartment that evening, the last thing she'd expected had been Jeff. She'd met Guy's business partner twice before. Briefly. He'd seemed pleasant enough. What she had managed to piece together was that Guy and Jeff had started Go Green fueled by a desire to create a place where consumers could find all-green cookware and cooking technology for a green, clean diet. Avery loved the concept…and Guy was convinced that the corporation was already making a difference to people's mindsets.

Yet the Jeff bouncing up and down on the doorstep hardly resembled the mild man she'd encountered previously.

"Yes?" she asked.

"Guy asked me to drop in, he's been held up at Baratin."

Typical. Guy had gotten into the workaholic groove at his beloved Baratin and spending time with her on her birthday had been shoved onto the back burner.

Quashing her qualms about letting Jeff in, Avery stepped back. "Come in."

Jeff followed her through the sky-lit lobby where the white walls were lined with modern abstracts into a spacious lounge with polished dark-wood floors, leather furniture and floor-to-ceiling windows.

"I'm to escort you down to Baratin for your birthday dinner in—" Jeff glanced at his ornate watch "—just under an hour."

So Guy hadn't forgotten about her birthday. The leap of joy was quickly followed by a feeling of letdown. He hadn't cared enough to collect her himself for their date.

"Thank you, that's very kind of you."

Jeff flung himself down onto the closest couch and grinned up at her. "I try."

"Can I get you a drink?"

"Bourbon. Neat. On ice. Thanks."

Avery crossed to the tallboy that housed Guy's bar. The clink of ice cubes followed by the gurgle of bourbon filling the glass broke the silence. When she turned it was to find Jeff examining her in a way he'd never done before.

A frisson of discomfort feathered along her spine.

Stop it. He's Guy's friend, his business partner, someone he trusts, she told herself. She handed the drink to Jeff. Before she could retreat his free hand snaked out and he hauled her onto his lap.

Then he was kissing her, wet, alcohol-drenched kisses that made her stomach turn, muttering fantasies that made her cringe. A furious struggle, and she was on her feet.

"Get out."

He stood. "Don't be so hasty, sweetheart."

Avery was trembling with outrage, fear…and something else.

"Go, and don't come back." She backed away. A glance showed her that her cell phone lay on the sideboard. "I'm calling Guy."

Jeff laughed. "That's not going to help you."

"What do you mean?"

"He knows, sweetheart."

Avery froze, her heart thumping in her chest. "Knows what?"

"He sent me, remember?"

"To play taxi driver." She tossed her hair back.

"Oh, you are an innocent." It didn't sound such a good thing the way Jeff said it—and the way his eyes roved over her made her feel grubby. "Despite that fantastically sexy little body."

"Guy wouldn't want to hear you saying things like that."

He laughed again. "Guy sent me. I'm your birthday present."

Horror shook her. "What do you mean?"

"Guy sent me to pleasure you. I'm to chauffeur you to Baratin when we're done. Then we were going to feed you your favourite foods." He licked his lips suggestively. "Afterwards all three of us were going to share dessert." There was no mistaking his meaning. "Guy wanted it to be a birthday you'd never forget."

Jeff reached for her.

"No!" She slapped his hand away.

His face contorted. "Come here."

As his hands clamped down on her shoulders, Avery kicked him in the shins.

"Ouch, you—"

She didn't wait to hear more. The front door seemed a mile away but she made it. Once outside she looked both ways before bolting for the stairwell. And cocked her head to listen, while her heartbeat slowed, until she was sure that Jeff hadn't followed.

Then she brushed her fingers across her eyes, surprised to find no residue of tears.

This had been Guy's surprise?

Even now, lying facedown on the massage bed, surrounded by the soft light of scented candles, she could still remember the maelstrom of emotions that had shaken her that night. By gifting his friend to her for the evening of her birthday and expecting her to sleep with Jeff, Guy had destroyed her trust.

Yet meeting him again here at Jarrod Ridge had proved she wasn't immune from his effect on her, that she still desired him.

That discovery horrified her.

What kind of woman did that make her? How could she lust after such a jerk? And how could she reconcile that with her most secret desire for a loving husband and a clutch of tow-haired kids?

"Here's a terry robe."

Joanie's voice stirred Avery from the conundrum threatening to short-circuit her brain. "Thank you."

Turning away, the masseuse said, "I'll fill the tub with hot water. The steam rooms are down the hall from the massage rooms. You can leave your belongings in here. I'll give you an access card to get back in."

The next fifteen minutes passed in a haze of heat. Avery couldn't help thinking of the conversation she'd had with Matt.

"Get over him," Matt had said.

And Avery was determined to do just that. By the time she left Jarrod Ridge it would be without a backward glance. She would exorcise this wretched awareness of the man. She would banish him from her thoughts…no matter what it took.

By the time Avery exited the steam room, filled with resolve, a sheen of moisture dewed her skin.

As she reached into the pocket of the robe for the access card to the treatment room where she'd had her massage, a masculine hand came down on the door in front of her, blocking her entry. Avery found herself face to face with the man who'd occupied so much of her recent thoughts.

"I've been looking for you. Rita said you were here." Guy's face was harder, more remote, than she'd ever seen it. The only evidence of the humor and amiability that had been so dear to her back in New York lay in the laugh creases around his eyes.

For a fragment of time her heart ached for what had been, what might have been, what was now forever lost.

No sign of laughter lingered in the steely gaze that roamed her giving no quarter. Avery became conscious that her face was cleansed of makeup and the spa's white robe ended inches above her knees.

"I see you've already managed to find yourself a rich lover."

Avery froze. Then, not deigning to answer, she knocked his hand off the door and pushed past him, seeking the sanctuary of the private room.

But Guy was quicker. Before she could slam the door in his face and lock it, he was inside, and his foot kicked the door shut behind him.

Balmy steam from the hot tub cocooned them, adding another dimension to the tension that pulsed between them. The warm reds that had appeared so welcoming suddenly seemed sensual and sultry. Avery's heart started to pound. An acute feeling of vulnerability swamped her. She drew the toweling robe more tightly around her.

"Get out, Guy."

Guy stalked closer. "Yesterday I thought it was my brother you were after. But by last night you'd found someone else. Did he share your bed?"

"What?"

"The Californian."

"Californian—" Realization dawned. He was talking about Matt.

"Did he touch you? Love you?" The darkening eyes smoldered in the glow of the candlelight. "Pleasure you?" His hand came up and stroked her skin, causing a rush of shivers to follow in its wake.

Guy thought Matt was her lover.

Avery almost laughed. Then she took in the tight-pressed mouth, the flexing muscle in his jaw.

Help…he believed it. And it had made him furious.

His fury ignited her own.

What right did he have to judge her? To leap to conclusions? She launched into attack. "Why?" she asked softly. "Are you jealous?"

The dark tumult in his eyes turned to flame.

In that instant a truly outrageous realization stunned her. Guy *was* jealous! Not because he cared for her, but because he thought she was sharing her body with someone else. Someone he hadn't sanctioned…

Bastard!

"You—" His grim voice broke off as he advanced on her.

A thrill of all-too familiar and totally unwanted electricity shot through Avery. She stood her ground, refusing to back away. He was close, so close that she could feel the force of his breath, smell the tangy male scent of him, all intensified by the steam rising from the freshly filled hot tub.

His hands gripped her shoulders. Before she could protest, his mouth slanted across hers.

Mindful of her resolve to free herself of his thrall, Avery kept her lips primly shut, yet Guy made no attempt to force entry. Instead, after the first press, his lips softened, teasing hers, pressing little kisses along the sensitive seam. Despite her determination to resist him, he was too seductive. Every bit as good as she remembered from the halcyon days before it had all turned to dust. The familiar warmth lazily uncurled in her stomach and spread through her, leaving her craving more.

Too soon he'd raised his head.

"Did *he* kiss you like that last night?"

Before she could tell him that Matt wasn't her lover but her cousin—almost a brother—that she'd grown up with, Guy's mouth was back on hers. Hot. Voracious. Devouring. Her hands crept up around his neck, caressing the smooth male skin with her fingertips. He pulled back and sucked in a shuddering breath.

"No one kisses like that," she whispered into the cavern of space that separated them.

The vibrating tension in his body eased a fraction. A hand cupped her cheek and he tilted her head back. Avery closed her eyes…waiting…waiting for his mouth to descend again.

"Look at me!"

Her lashes fluttered up. Reluctantly she met his gaze. An indefinable emotion lurked in the turbulent depths. Despite the warmth of the spa room, and the steam swirling around them, Avery shivered. This was not the easy-going restaurateur she'd thought herself in love with. She didn't know this man.

"Not even Jeff?" he asked.

"What?" Avery blinked up at him in confusion.

"Forgotten how he kisses already?" There was a caustic bite to his tone.

"N-no."

Forgotten? *Guy sent me. I'm your birthday present.* Then Jeff had breathed over her with boozy breath and touched her with hands that made her feel unclean. The words that had spewed from his mouth had made her feel dirty to her soul. *I'm to chauffeur you to Baratin when we're done.*

How could she ever forget?

Was Guy jealous of the man he'd all but pimped her to? Well, she hoped he'd suffered the tortures of the damned. He'd destroyed her illusions. If he was jealous now, it was his own damn fault for opening a forbidden box that should have stayed shut.

He deserved to suffer.

The temptation to inflame his sexual possessiveness was too much. Avery gave him what she hoped looked like a seductive, kittenish smile. "I never kiss and tell."

"You did more than kiss Jeff. You slept with him."

She stretched her eyes wide. "Why the curiosity? Wish you'd been there? We almost called you to join in."

The instant the words left her lips, Avery experienced a rush of regret. She'd thrown away the opportunity to tell Guy the real truth about how much she'd hated what had happened that fateful night.

But how could she recant now? How could she tell him her

sarcasm had been prompted by hurt and anger at his ready acceptance that she'd slept with a man he'd sent to her? Pride wouldn't let her.

He could go to hell.

Guy didn't love her. Had never loved her. It was enough to make her want to weep.

"Jeff told me that you'd been chasing him for weeks, and that night he couldn't resist what you were offering."

What?

Had he not sent Jeff to her? She gazed at Guy, searching for a chink in his shuttered face. But the only softness came from the flickering candlelight that danced over his skin, causing shadows to lurk under his cheekbones.

"That I offered?" she prompted.

Guy pushed a hand through his hair. "I was busy—"

"You were always busy."

His jaw tensed. "Jeff called just as I was about to ring you to ask you to catch a cab. He offered to make the call for me and get the cab so I could finish what I was doing. I thought it was important." His mouth twisted in a parody of a smile.

"So Jeff called me," she said flatly.

"And you asked him to pick you up—only when he got there did he find out what you had in mind."

"Of course." Avery felt numb. He'd believed Jeff.

The man must be dumb. How could he not know what they'd discovered was special? Something she'd never found with another man? Yet he believed her capable of sleeping with Jeffrey…and Matt…at the drop of a hat.

She shivered.

"You're cold."

Not cold. Goosebumps from reaction. She was hurting, exposed and vulnerable. Unlike him.

"Get into the hot tub," he ordered.

"With you here?"

He raised a dark eyebrow. "Why not? There's nothing I haven't seen many times before."

The biting sarcasm made her see red. All the objections that threatened to spill over fizzled out when he hit a button on the control dial and the jets started to froth.

Why not?

She'd told Matt that she was going to exorcise him.

No time better than the present.

With a reckless awareness of playing with fire, Avery dropped her terry robe. She was naked beneath. She heard Guy suck in air, but refused to turn her head to gauge his response. Instead she stepped over the lip of the tub into the churning water of the sunken spa.

And wondered if she'd ventured too far…

Guy could've sworn his heart ceased when Avery's robe slipped down her glorious body.

Any hope he'd nursed that Avery had not been playing cruel games with him and Jeff as her pawns had been extinguished by the brazen admission that she'd seduced poor Jeff.

It only took a glimpse of her naked form for the rage to flare into mind-blowing sexual hunger. Given that she was so little, Avery had the longest damned legs he'd ever seen. His eyes followed the sleek bare length to the delectable curve of her butt. She was perfect. Absolutely god-dammed perfect.

He wanted her. Damn, he ached with wanting. It had been too long….

The tub swallowed her as she settled down, the long legs and curvy body disappearing beneath the frothing water that gleamed in the light of the candles. She leaned her head against the edge of the tub and gave a sigh.

Only the top of her breasts were visible, yet even that was enough to make him hard.

After her betrayal he'd told her he never wanted to see her again. He'd been certain if he saw her, he'd throttle her. Famous last words. No doubt she planned to make him eat them, morsel by morsel. Well, here he was achingly aroused and dying to kiss that sassy provocative mouth again.

Damn.

She was here for the duration of the Food and Wine Gala. Why not sate this inconvenient hunger for her that gnawed at his gut like a wild, feral beast? This time he would make her as mad for him as she'd made poor, broken Jeff. The fool had risked everything for her. His friendship with Guy. Their business, Go Green.

Guy had been ready to plant a fist in Jeff's face for his perfidy until he'd realized how bad his friend had it. Jeff had told him about how Avery had teased and tempted him for weeks, until he'd been unable to resist her summons.

What would he have done if Avery had opened the door in nothing more than the bustier and G-string Jeff had told him she'd worn to welcome him?

Guy could understand Jeff's desperation. Would he have reacted any differently to her seduction? Hell, if he climbed into that spa beside her, he'd touch her and it would be over in moments.

Dragging in a breath he wrestled for control. Instead of allowing himself to be drawn into her trap, he dropped to his knees beside the sunken tub and started to knead her shoulders. This time it would be on his terms.

Avery started, she moaned.

"Good?"

"Mmm."

"Relax, let the warm water ease all the cricks."

"I already had a massage—that helped," she murmured so softly he had to bend forward to catch the words. "But how can I resist?"

Guy could see the edge of her pouting mouth. Her hair fell in soft tendrils about her face, and her features had relaxed.

He growled, a rough, throaty sound. "I better tell my sister to start a service offering neck rubs in the tub."

"Melissa is your sister? You mentioned brothers yesterday. I didn't even know you had a sister."

"You never asked," he pointed out.

"I suppose."

"We had better things to talk about."

It was true, he realized as he massaged her flesh. Their focus had been on the white-hot passion that had exploded between them, consuming them in an affair that had erupted before they could draw breath—let alone get to know each other.

But her silence made him feel a pang of guilt. Maybe they should've talked more…

"I've got another sister, too," he offered. "Erica. She's my half sister actually." He still wasn't sure how he felt about Erica. Until now he'd maintained a friendly, but definitely cool, distance. "We only discovered her existence after my father died."

"I heard about your father. I'm sorry."

His father had died less than a week after she'd slept with Jeff and walked out on him. It had been the worst week of his life. But Avery didn't need to know that.

"We weren't close." Guy dismissed her sympathy.

"It must've still been hard to discover he had another child."

"It was." Guy forced himself not to be abrupt. "The knowledge that my father had an affair so soon after mom's death was—" He broke off, reluctant to supply the words that might reveal any lingering vulnerability.

After a moment's pause, Avery said carefully, "It must have been hard for Erica, too."

Her voice held no judgment, she simply stated a fact. He wished he could see her expression. "It couldn't have been too bad for her. She inherited an equal share in Dad's estate. She's a wealthy woman now."

"Money isn't everything."

Avery of all people expected him to swallow that?

Guy found a knot and rubbed it, and Avery winced. He slowed his movements, his fingers lingering on flesh that had taken a golden glow under the candlelight.

"Erica found love, too." A note of cynicism entered his voice. "She's engaged to Christian Hanford now. The family lawyer," he tacked on, in case he wasn't making sense. Stroking her skin had that effect on him. Touching her made him forget everything else existed.

She was undoubtedly a sorceress. A magic woman who held him trapped in her secret sensuality.

"Where are you staying?" Guy changed the subject. He didn't want to talk about Erica, about the uncomfortable emotions his father's affair aroused and the sense of helpless loss that his father's death evoked.

"At Jarrod Manor," she replied, a little drowsily.

"So am I."

Avery stiffened under the stroke of his fingers. "Oh."

"Relax," he said. "It's the largest lodge. No danger of finding me—unless you want to." He didn't add that he was staying in one of the family suites on the top floor, which had their own card-access elevator. There was little chance of Avery's finding his suite by accident.

"But you only need to ask reception to find out where I'm staying—you're a Jarrod, they'd tell you whatever you wanted."

His hands stilled. "Do you want me to ask?"

"No!"

The water swirled around her as she moved in agitation. For a brief instant Guy caught a glimpse of pale pink nipple before she hastily sank beneath the bubbling water.

"On second thought, you probably don't even need to ask, do you? You'd have access to all the computer and reservation systems—and key cards."

"I'd never enter your room—or any guest's room—without an invitation." Guy was appalled by her assumption that he'd abuse his position—or the privacy of a guest. "You'd have to ask."

"Promise?"

The look she slanted up at him almost undid him. "Yes!"

She relaxed with a sigh, her head dropping back against the lip of the bath, the candlelight giving her blonde hair a rich patina. "I believe you."

I believe you. Her instant trust caused a rush of elation. Wordlessly, he rubbed his fingers in little circles along the apex of her shoulders, seeking out the tell-tale knots, massaging them. Her flesh was soft and supple beneath his fingers, and he savored the subtle, flowery scent that clung behind her ears, released by the sultry, heat of the steam, tempting him to set his lips against the silken skin.

Guy let out the breath he'd been holding. The tendrils at her nape lifted, and a rush of gooseflesh danced across her skin.

Unable to resist, he bent his head and placed his mouth against her nape.

Avery gave an audible gasp.

But no objection followed. He parted his lips and planted a row of open-mouthed kisses on her water-dewed skin, aware of the sound of her quickening breathing. His hands slipped forward around the curve of her body, and his fingers trailed over the soft, rounded mounds of her breasts.

She drew a sharp, jagged breath.

"Avery," he whispered, "invite me to join you in that damned tub."

Four

The one thing that Avery had learned about Guy in the month she'd shared his apartment in New York was that every inch of his body was pure, sinful temptation…and she was incapable of resisting any of it.

Tonight was no exception.

But tonight she knew exactly what she was doing…knew that this was not about dreams—only desire…and getting over Guy. She'd think of it as therapy.

"Join me?" she invited, her pulse skittering. "There's plenty of space."

"I thought you'd never ask."

He was already on his feet. The jeans and T-shirt he wore were discarded in a flash. He kicked off his boxers, and stepped into the tub.

Once he stood inside, the tub shrank. He was tall and big…six feet one inch of honed male muscle. Aroused male muscle, Avery noted with an awed, heart-stopping glance. Her nipples peaked. Her pulse picked up, and the air surrounding them became heavy with unspoken messages.

Perhaps this hadn't been such a good idea, after all.

But it was too late to undo the dare she'd instigated the moment she'd dropped that robe. If she told him she'd made a mistake, he'd laugh. Or accuse her of being a tease.

Her best choice was to tough it out. A few minutes of polite, uneasy silence, then she could chicken out with dignity, climb out the tub, say goodnight, and that would be that.

Avery sank lower into the water, and shut her eyes.

Except it wasn't quite that easy.

Images of his naked form warmed by soft candle flame danced across her eyelids. The smooth golden skin. The sculpted muscles. His burgeoning erection…

This was how she was getting over the man?

She bit back a gasp, and concentrated on mentally ranking the merlot wines she'd tasted today. She lost interest after rating the third wine. Ears straining, she tried to figure out what he was doing.

Was he looking at her?

The silence throbbed like a writhing beast. Unwanted memories of the nights she'd spent in Guy's bed, making love, entwined her. Now he was naked, a foot away from her, probably eating her alive with his eyes.

Avery couldn't breathe.

She knew she had to exorcise him. Forever.

"Did you get a chance to make some notes for our presentation today?" When Guy finally broke the silence, she jumped, and wavelets lapped at her throat.

He wanted to talk business?

Avery cracked one eye open and sneaked a peek through the billowing steam. She didn't know whether to laugh or scream. Guy was lying back, his eyes closed, looking utterly relaxed. She'd steeled herself to resist him—tell him to go to hell—and the damn man was practically asleep.

And here she was back to being all knotted up, fully expecting him to leap on her!

Cheated.

It wasn't—couldn't possibly be—disappointment that crawled through her, could it? She was relieved that she didn't have to fight him off. Wasn't she?

Hmm. If she were absolutely, confidentially truthful she was a teensy-weensy bit miffed.

It made *no* sense.

"So did you?"

"Uh, yes. I made some notes."

Collecting her scattered wits, she tried to remember what the thrust of them had been. And gave up. While she'd been scrambling for her sanity, Guy had opened his eyes. His gaze locked with hers. Lord only knew what he'd seen in her eyes, because his mouth curved up into a slow, knowing smile.

"Miss me?"

"Today?" She tried to laugh it off as a joke. "I didn't get a chance. Especially since I used the few spare minutes I had to work out what we were going to say."

"Pity." Under the water his hand landed on her bare thigh.

A rush of emotion filled her. Desire. Confusion. Anger. All tangled up in a mass of contrary, conflicting feelings. Avery reminded herself of all the reasons why it was a bad idea to let this happen. For sure, she would get hurt again.

But her desperate caveats didn't help. His fingers trailed up…along her belly. Her breath caught as they skirted precariously close to the underside of her breast.

Guy Jarrod was a drug and her body craved its fix.

She knew she should be telling him "No".

Yet insanely when his fingers snagged hers, and tugged,

she allowed him to draw her through the bubbling water toward him.

"I thought about you."

Her insides melted. "I doubt it," she said snippily. "You had too much to do."

"Oh, I'm not talking about today—I'm talking about the past seven weeks."

At the admission, blood roared in her ears. Guy had kept count of time? Her resistance crumbled a little more.

"I keep remembering this…."

His fingers surrounded her nipple, and the little traitor hardened.

Guy groaned. His other arm came round her and he drew her close until her body slid over him breast-against-chest, her nipples brushing the water-sleek muscle under his skin.

"So responsive," he murmured into her ear, and shivers feathered down her spine. "How could I ever forget this?"

The hope plummeted.

It was the sex he'd thought about—not her.

A cold, dampening wave of disappointment swamped her. What had she expected? An avowal of love? For him it had always been all about sex, nothing else. Guy had no idea of the fantasies she'd woven around him.

Fantasies involving love…family…and forever after.

She must've been dreaming. Or drugged. By sex? Yet right now, sex was almost enough.

Sensation shuddered through her as his mouth closed on her tight nipple. Something close to ecstasy coursed through her blood, and she gave a moan of dark delight.

Nothing wrong with sex.

Especially since this time there'd be no emotional component. It would be nothing more than an exorcism of a very bad habit.

Her legs entwined with his. Breaking the connection of

his mouth on the tingling bud of flesh, Guy linked his hands behind her neck, and she again came into full, too-tantalizing contact with him. The softness of her breasts again brushed against his chest, and arousal spiraled. He pulled her head down, and she could no longer resist.

His tongue swept across her bottom lip. Lust surged through her when the tip of her tongue met his. He sucked it into his mouth, and then plundered the warm heat of her mouth, seeking out every corner.

His fingers explored the indent of her spine, then moved under her belly and slid between her legs. At the first intimate touch she stiffened reflexively, then her legs parted. She was twenty-seven years old, too old to fool herself that Guy could make all the silly, romantic dreams of love-for-life come true. She'd left those behind the night of her birthday.

She was a woman, not a girl.

With a woman's wants.

It was time to recognize that her desperation to find love was nothing more than a ticking biological clock—an animal need to find a mate to help her raise the brood of children she'd always yearned for.

The kiss ended. His touch did not. It was expert, knowing, and gave exactly what she craved. Opening her eyes, she saw that the taut mask of desire had transformed Guy's face. Not even candle glow could soften the hunger.

He wanted her.

She wanted him.

At least there was honesty in desire.

Tonight she'd settle for lust…and deal with the fallout tomorrow.

Stretching out a hand, her fingers lightly stroked the hard, bold length of him beneath the silken water.

Guy stopped caressing her, and used both hands to yank

her up. "Stop! If you do that it will all be over way too soon."

She gave him a wicked smile. "And we can't have that."

"No," he growled.

Avery bent forward and outlined his lips with the teasing tip of her tongue. His arms tightened around her, bringing her softness in contact with the hard rock-like ridge of his arousal. He raised his hips, and the friction was exquisite.

Another shift, and her body sheathed his.

His head went back, the tendons on his neck drew tight. Leaning forward, she tongued them, tasting the moisture of the water, the slight tang of salt from his skin.

He was moving below her, his body sliding within hers, heat twisting into a blaze of unbearable pleasure. The pressure built and built until her climax rushed toward her, at the same time as Guy shuddered beneath her.

Avery was floating on a cloud of pleasure.

Her skin was flushed a rosy shade, and her body was soft and pliant. She felt like she'd died and gone to heaven.

"So what about making this a more lasting arrangement?" Guy whispered, cupping her chin with his hand.

The dreamy, heavenly feeling evaporated. Her eyes popped open and, shocked, she gazed down into Guy's smiling eyes.

"A more lasting arrangement?"

Avery almost forgot to breathe. This was what she'd wanted…hoped for…those two toe-curling weeks in New York, before the rug had been ripped out from under her on the night of her birthday.

What was wrong with her? Did she want to marry a man who thought her easy, a conniving gold digger? A man who'd wanted to share her in a tryst with his friend?

The Guy she'd imagined herself in love with didn't exist.

"Marriage is a big decision," she said finally, slithering off him to sit beside him.

His hand fell away.

"I never meant marriage?" Guy's smile slipped. The intimacy between them widened into a chasm. "Don't make more out of it than it needs to be, Avery. There's no reason why we can't enjoy each other for as long as it lasts."

Avery's jaw dropped. This only demonstrated one more difference between them. A more lasting arrangement had different meanings to her and Guy. For him it hardly lasted past tomorrow…nothing more than hot sex with the gold-digging ex. For her it had meant a surge of hope.

Stupid.

Emotionally, Guy wasn't available. To be fair, he'd always made it clear that he wasn't in the market for a long-term relationship. She'd simply believed she could change his mind.

Her mistake.

Say no. Now!

Yet if she did say no, she'd always wonder…

What if…

No regrets.

Drowning herself in dead-end yearnings wasn't going to get her over the man. What had Matt said last night? *If you're going to live it up, pumpkin, Aspen is the place to do it. Indulge yourself.*

Avery bit her lip.

She didn't want to indulge herself with just any one…she wanted Guy. Her body wanted Guy. So why not give in? And get over him?

"So what do you think?" His hand brushed her leg under

the water. Clearly he'd decided she would go along with it. Her indignation flared up all over again.

Her good sense returned. "And what happens when the festival ends? When it's time for me to leave?"

He shrugged. "Does it matter? Let's take it one day—" his eyes grew slumberous "—and one night at a time."

Yes, an affair would suit him just perfectly.

"I'd want to think about that."

His look of surprise would've been comical if Avery had felt like laughing.

"I'm sure there's enough work in all the exclusive Aspen resorts and restaurants to keep you busy for a while. I'm sure I can help you secure some contracts."

"I'm sure you can," she muttered, her irritation with him escalating. Didn't he have any idea how that would look? People would take one look at her, at her obvious closeness to Guy and she'd be written off as a millionaire's paid-for mistress. The professional reputation she'd worked so hard to establish would be gone in a puff of smoke.

Of course, it was partially her own fault. She should never have fallen into his bed so quickly. But she'd been unable to resist him. She'd thought he was her soul mate.

Damn. Damn. Damn.

Discovering Guy still set her on fire would make it so easy to agree. She wasn't caving in so easily this time. She stood up and the water streamed off her. Conscious of Guy's smoldering gaze, she squared her shoulders. "I'm not sure I want to stay in Aspen."

"Why not? You know you want to." The corners of Guy's mouth curled up. He reached up and ran a finger down her leg until it came to rest in the hollow behind her knee. "I'm here."

His arrogant certainty took her breath away. She stepped away, over the lip of the hot tub. Picking up her terry robe she slid her arms into the sleeves and yanked the sash into a knot, then said brightly, "And so will I be—until the end of the month but I can't guarantee anything past that."

"Maybe by then the flame would have burned itself out."

She could only hope…

"Maybe," she agreed. "And maybe I'll be homesick for California."

"There's that, too." Reserve entered his tone and the slumberous warmth seeped out of his eyes. "Not even this kind of chemistry will survive the distance. In terms of my father's will, I have to stay in Aspen. So we'll only have the time you're here."

Lifting her shoulder, Avery let it fall carelessly. "Working with me every day, you'll have had enough of my company."

"I'm sure you're right." But Guy's expression was brooding.

So he wasn't happy about that? Good. Because she wouldn't concede more than she already had. Even though she was unbearably tempted to settle for the affair he offered.

Sashaying away from him took every bit of nerve she possessed. She tossed her reply over her shoulder. "I'll consider your offer. But don't hold your breath." He deserved to sweat.

Avery didn't know what she was going to decide. One part of her, the part full of defiant bravado, was dying to say yes…have glorious get-over-him sex and walk away, sated and smiling. Cured. The other more cautious part of her was terrified she'd be addicted for life.

And where would that leave her?

At the door, his voice arrested her. "Uh, I meant to ask. Any consequences?"

"Consequences?" She swung around and stared at him

blankly. He'd almost broken her heart. Did that count? Or did that only rank as mere collateral damage and therefore… inconsequential?

"Pregnancy," he said a trifle impatiently from the steaming tub as she continued to gaze at him.

Oh. "I'm not pregnant."

Thank heavens for that!

"Good." He gave her a thin smile. "That's one complication neither of us need at this stage of our lives."

Speak for yourself. But Avery knew better than to voice her soul-deep yearning for a child…a family. Guy would never understand.

The water swirled as he rose. Avery's eyes widened, but she forced herself not to look away from the sight of the water droplets running down his chest…over his flat, muscled stomach. Despite everything he'd done, she really did still want him. God. She was not going to survive this.

"I almost forgot. Art was going to come along to the first of the balloon landings tomorrow—we do a champagne breakfast on landing and I have some ideas for a new menu." Her breaking dismay must've shown on her face because Guy added with a mocking smile, "You don't need to come if you don't want."

How early could it be?

"I'll be there," she said, pursing her mouth. "What time?"

"The ascent is at dawn." His grin deepened at her horrified groan. "I haven't forgotten you're not a morning person. Dress for comfort—jeans, boots and a jacket work best."

In one bound he was over the edge of the hot tub. Avery didn't wait another second, she fled.

Five

To Guy's surprise Avery was already waiting in the lobby early on Sunday morning, studying the framed photos of the celebrity guests that had been taken every season since the resort opened.

She must've sensed him because she swung around at his approach. To his surprise, the Avery who peered at him resembled a sleepy, fluffy owl rather than the svelte, petite doll he was more accustomed to. She was even wearing spectacles—something he'd never seen her don in daylight.

At his curious look, she said, "I didn't get enough sleep for my contact lenses to be comfortable. I'll put them in later."

"You don't need them."

He suspected she'd suffered lack of sleep for the same reason as he had. That quick coupling in the spa hadn't been nearly enough; he'd wanted her in his bed, all night long. Lust bolted through him. Just in time he stopped himself from babbling that she looked just as beautiful with glasses as without.

Not flattery, but true, he realized with a slight sense of shock as he inspected her.

Wearing figure-hugging white jeans and a cropped denim jacket, she glowed with vitality. The glasses simply added a scholarly twist to the sexy package. The hint of studious, good girl added by the glasses only served to accentuate the simmering sexuality that her pouty mouth and curvaceous body radiated.

To his relief, the group booked to go ballooning trooped into the lobby, providing a much-needed distraction from just how much of his thoughts Avery consumed. But not before Guy took in the appreciative smile one of the men bestowed on her. A sharp pang of annoyance caused him to turn away, before he snarled at a guest of the resort.

Hot damn but he had it bad.

Shoving his hands into his jeans' pockets, Guy hunched his shoulders and headed through the open, double glass doors, past the sleepy doorman in blue-and-gold livery, and out into the crisp, cool dawn air. Autumn was not yet here, but soon it would be.

To one side of the Manor Lodge, on a wide concrete apron that doubled as a helipad, he made out the figures of three pilots and a few members of the chase crew tending to the colorful nylon envelopes spread out on the concrete, while wicker baskets waited for passengers. The rest of the chase crew, including the resort staff who would be attending to the state-of-the-art catering, stood around joking and chatting and drinking coffee from paper cups.

An engine-driven fan droned to life and the red envelope of the closest balloon began to inflate. Minutes later the burners started to hiss, heating the cold air, and the envelopes rose above the baskets amidst whoops of delight from the guests. Twenty-odd guests quickly sorted themselves into three groups and entered the baskets to pose for last-minute photos and wave to well-wishers.

Once the first balloon started to ascend, the others swiftly followed.

"Isn't that simply stunning?"

Avery spoke from behind Guy as fingers of sunlight poked over the mountain ridge behind them and caressed the vivid balloons with morning light, brightening the dawn sky to a blaze of red, magenta and yellow.

Guy turned. The blue of her eyes was blinding, and her smile caused a fresh rush of heat. He swallowed. "You can go up one morning if you want," he said, his voice sounding hoarse even to his own ears.

She shook her head. "Never in a million years. I'm afraid of heights."

"You?" Guy gave a choke of laughter. "I can't imagine you afraid of anything."

Although Avery might be delicate and fine-boned, she could be as fierce and fiery as a tigress with cubs. That thought caused him to grin—because Avery was the least maternal woman he'd ever met. It had been a major reason for his attraction to her back in New York. She was so focused on her career—which suited him just fine. He'd made a habit of steering clear of starry-eyed women with marriage written all over them in diamond-bright letters.

"I get dizzy," she said with clear regret. "So you'll never catch me up there."

"In a balloon you don't get that vertigo feeling."

"Oh, sure."

"Really! The ride is smoother than I can ever describe. You move with the wind. No swaying or jostling. So never say never."

"Forget it, Guy!"

"Sometimes one needs to take risks, walk a little on the wild side."

She took a step away from him and wrapped her arms around her stomach. "I've done some dumb things in my life, but this sounds too wild for me."

Her face had closed up.

Was she talking about sleeping with Jeff…or what had happened last night between them? He had no intention of discussing Jeff—the anger hadn't yet settled. "I never pegged you for a 'fraidy cat,'" he taunted gently in an effort to bridge the chasm that suddenly yawned between them.

"Too bad. You're not talking me into this." She hunched her shoulders. "I'm too risk-averse."

Risk-averse? Avery? Puzzled, he frowned at her. "Not sure I swallow that."

She glowered at him. "Because I leapt into bed with you the first day we met? Not my smartest move, I'll admit. It's contaminated everything you think about me."

Did she count their affair as one of the dumb mistakes she'd made? That offended him.

"Contaminated? Hardly!" He moved closer to her, and lowered his voice to a husky growl. "Hey, let me tell you, there was nothing wrong with what we did together in New York. It was one of the most memorable times of my life. And last night was pretty damned amazing, too."

He wasn't lying.

He'd missed her, dammit.

Laying a hand along her cheek, he cupped it in his palm. "You're so honest in bed, there's none of the pretence women often play at."

For a moment he thought she was going to fling herself into his arms. There was a luminous expression in her eyes that made his chest tighten in a way that was new…and more than a little disconcerting.

She started to say something, then she pulled away. "Not here, Guy, we're in public."

Annoyance jabbed him at her stubborn insistence to keep him at a distance. "Are you too scared to let anyone know that we're—" he searched for a word to describe the scorching electricity they shared "—lovers?"

She snorted. "Lovers? That implies an intimacy we don't share."

Her dismissal was like a burr beneath a quarterhorse's tail. "Nothing wrong with the pleasure we've shared. And which we could continue to share." If she stopped being so darned pigheaded. But he didn't add that.

Nor did he point out that for someone as risk-averse as Avery claimed to be they'd taken a hell of a risk last night. It had been out of character for him—not because he feared risks, but because he took responsibility for his actions. All his actions. Last night was the first time in his life that he'd had sex without a condom—he'd never done that even in his most reckless teen years.

While he knew from their past that Avery protected herself against pregnancy, he'd risked his own health.

It wouldn't happen again. Ever. He didn't need the kind of consequences that might flow from such spur-of-the-moment stupidity.

But damn, it had been good....

Instead of looking at him, she tipped her head back. The early morning sun turned the ends of her eyelashes to gold. "I don't need to experience life from up there," she said, changing the subject. "I can do it perfectly well with both feet on the ground."

"Then you'll never see the fields rolling out under you, never touch the leaves on the treetops, nor see the elk grazing on the mountaintops—and that's losing out as far as I'm concerned." From the set of her chin, he could see he didn't appear to be getting anywhere. "If you tried it, you might find it worth it. The view is fantastic from up there—a whole different perspective. You can see for miles in every direction."

"Sounds like you enjoy it."

"I go every year during the festival." Except that wasn't true. Not anymore. "At least, I used to take a ride every year," he amended. "I haven't been home for a while."

At last she looked at him, her scrutiny intense, making him shift uncomfortably.

"I was busy." The unspoken question in her eyes caused him to prevaricate. "Come on, the chase crews are on the move."

Striding across the concrete, he reached in his jeans' pocket for the keys to a black SUV with the name Jarrod Ridge emblazoned on the side. Once they were both inside he started the vehicle and pulled in behind the second minivan that contained the catering crew.

Avery was perched on the edge of her seat. The tight lines had left her mouth and he could sense her rising excitement. "Is the landing spot pre-arranged?"

Guy laughed. "If only! The crew in the first vehicle are in radio contact with the pilots and have a rough idea where the balloons will come down. But it's never exact because the pilots are at the mercy of the winds."

She snorted. "And that's supposed to reassure me about going up there?"

"The pilots are very experienced—they're also in touch with air traffic control at the local airport."

Avery fell silent for a few minutes. When she spoke again it was to sigh and say, "It is beautiful out here."

Guy had to agree. The sun was rising quickly, illuminating the meadows in the valley and the jutting mountain peaks.

"Just wait a few weeks until fall arrives and the aspens turn gold—it's spectacular."

"I'll be gone by then."

Not if he had anything to do with it. Avery owed him—and he wasn't going to let her go until he was good and ready.

"We'll see," he growled. "I'm still holding my breath."

There was an uneasy pause.

Finally Avery broke it. "You clearly love it here. What kept you from returning all those years?"

So she intended to avoid the tension that bristled between them? Guy was itching for a confrontation...one that might explode into passion. Make her say yes. Maybe her course was wisest. For now.

Keeping his focus on the road, he said in the most even voice he could muster, "Work. After leaving school I studied haute cuisine in France, then worked for several years in London, before returning to the States to open Baratin. There wasn't time to come to Aspen."

"'The finest French restaurant on the east coast'. Or at least that's what *Cuisine* magazine called it."

The accolades didn't ease Guy's guilt. "This past month was the longest I've spent home in almost two decades."

Home, funny that he still thought of Jarrod Ridge as home. Yet he'd only returned because of the terms of his father's will. If he and his brothers and sisters didn't stay, they would lose out on their inheritance.

None of them were ready to forfeit that.

Her hand brushed his leg, hovered, then settled on his thigh. Oh, hell. His muscles clenched involuntarily under the tantalizing pressure of her fingertips.

"Guy, your father knew you loved him."

Her words wiped out the pleasure her touch had bestowed. Unerringly, she'd honed in on the crux of his guilt and pain. "Did he? I'm not so sure."

"You saw him before he died?"

"I was too late."

And not for the first time.

He couldn't stand to see the pity in Avery's eyes. God help him if she saw all the way to his soul and the festering regret.

If only...

"But you spoke to him while we were—" she hesitated "—together. I even took a message for you to call your dad." She sounded rueful. "You know what? I never even realized I was talking to the legendary Donald Jarrod."

Just as well.

Otherwise he might never have discovered that all Avery wanted was a man made of gold. She would've taken care to hide her avaricious streak from him, would never have gone after Jeff. He didn't voice the cynical thought. Instead he swung the SUV left into a lane lined with poplars.

"I saw my father not long before I met you. He came to New York." Because Guy had refused to go to Aspen. "He wanted me to take over running all the bars and restaurants at Jarrod Ridge." He gave a crooked smile. "I refused. Then he died. Now I'm doing what he asked, anyway."

"And you wish you'd told him yes while he was alive."

Bull's eye.

Guy swung the wheel, pulling the SUV onto the shoulder of the road, then turned in his seat to face her.

The understanding and empathy that glimmered in her eyes nearly undid him. He forced out a shuddering breath, and a heartbeat later he hauled her into his arms.

"Your father knows you loved him," she murmured against his parka.

That uncertainty lay at the root of Guy's guilt. He'd resisted all his father's calls to return. Deep down he'd blamed his father for driving them apart after his mother's death. "I doubt it—even though I tell myself that one day we'll meet again, I'm not even sure that I believe that either. But thanks."

With a sigh, he set her away from him.

Then, narrowing his gaze until he located the minivans in the distance, he put the SUV back into gear and trod on the gas to close the gap.

"Guy, my parents died in a boating accident when I was a two-year-old."

"I didn't know that." She'd never told him that—he wondered what other vital, formative information she'd withheld.

"Uncle Art used to tell me I carried them with me, in my heart. They were with me all the time. But that worried me—I didn't want them in my heart, I wanted to know they were up there." Avery pointed through the windshield to the blue sky overhead. "It's so perfect, so blue, so clear. How could there not be heaven and angels? I used to tell Uncle Art that one day I'd go there to visit them."

So she still believed in angels and ever-after. How'd he missed this softer, more idealistic side to her? Guy wondered what other illusions she still clung to. "You wanted to visit them up there even though you're scared of heights?"

A quick sideways glance revealed her smile and the dimple in her cheek. "You know, I never gave that a thought—I told my Aunt I could catch a plane from LAX."

Guy couldn't help himself, he gave a shout of laughter.

High above where the balloons floated sunrays glinted off a plane. "Matt is somewhere up there," Avery said suddenly.

He sobered. "Matt?"

"My cousin." There was an odd note in her voice. "You've seen him."

He couldn't remember meeting her cousin. One thing his father's death had brought home was it was often better to say nothing than to mouth an inane bunch of platitudes at someone's loss. First her parents, then her cousin, Matt. He decided to keep it factual.

"I don't remember meeting him. Was it in New York?"

"No, last night. In the sky lounge."

Confused, he slowed and turned his head to stare at her.

"Dark hair. Tall." She held her hand above her head, almost touching the roof of the SUV. "We shared a drink. You came in. And left before I could introduce you. He was at the champagne-and-oyster party the previous night, too. He flew home today."

Her cousin. He switched his attention back to the road. The man who'd hugged her...was her cousin Matt.

Not dead.

And not her lover.

Guy felt himself flush. After a moment of feeling like a complete idiot, he laughed. "You should have told me."

"And ruined your fun?"

The agony of emotion that had stabbed him when she'd embraced Matt last night had been anything but funny.

"Not nice," he said reprovingly.

Avery sounded unrepentant. "Serves you right for jumping to conclusions."

"When you said he was up there, I thought you meant he was dead. Like my father."

He nosed the SUV through an open gate into a field and came to a stop beside the chase vehicles. By the time he got to the passenger door, Avery was already on the ground.

"Guy—" she touched his arm "—I'm so sorry."

Guy wished he'd kept his mouth shut. He didn't want her feeling pity for him. He wanted her teasing humor back. Everyone had been pussyfooting around the family since his father's death almost six weeks ago.

"There's a lot to do," he said gruffly. "And almost two dozen hungry people who have just come off the high of a lifetime to feed."

Guy was right. It was hectic.

After the balloonists landed the pilots shepherded them together for a celebration ceremony. Avery was conscious of the wonder on the faces of the new initiates, but there was no time to watch the ceremony as Guy and members of the Jarrod Ridge catering crew whipped up a scrumptious gourmet breakfast.

Mimosas—the orange juice and champagne fizzing in tall glasses, slices of melon, eggs Benedict, and bagels with smoked salmon and cream cheese were among the delicacies spread out on the tables that had been set up and laid with white linen and gleaming silver cutlery.

"How artistic it looks." Avery stood back to admire the effect. "I don't know why you think the menu needs overhauling. It's perfect."

"Delicious, too, I hope."

She laughed at Guy's droll comment. "That's a given. Food always tastes better outdoors."

"That so?"

She nodded emphatically. "Definitely so."

"We'll have to test that theory out sometime."

The first of the balloonists arrived at the tables, their faces glowing with excitement and their hair windblown.

"But not now," Guy added, as he moved to stand behind where the serving tables were set up.

A tall Canadian loaded up his plate and paused beside Avery. "Where are you sitting?"

Avery smiled at him. He'd greeted her back in the lobby. He had a friendly grin and appeared popular with the group. "I'm only—"

Before she could complete the sentence and tell him she was part of the resort's crew, Guy spoke from behind her, "Avery is with me."

The heavy-handed male warning was enough to make Avery see red.

<u>Six</u>

Avery stalked away from Guy, and found herself saying,
"Is there space at your table?"

The Canadian, whose name turned out to be Todd,
introduced her to his group of friends and they all started
to rave about how awesome the flight had been. But Avery
found it hard to concentrate.

All she was aware of was Guy's smoldering presence at
the next table.

Why did she care? He had no right to behave like
a complete idiot over Todd. She and Guy weren't even a
couple, darn it. He'd been the one who'd always made sure
she tendered no hopes in that direction.

She had a job to do and she would do it. She wasn't about
to let Uncle Art down. Nor was she going to put up with Guy's
arrogance.

Avery speared a piece of melon and chewed.

At the back of her mind she was conscious that she wasn't

being totally fair on Guy. She'd allowed him to provoke her into saying and doing utterly stupid things—because he infuriated her.

You're so honest in bed, he'd said on their way here, *there's none of the pretence women often play at.*

If only he knew...

Instead of grasping the opportunity to admit how she'd misled him about Jeff, she'd chickened out.

Maybe she was the 'fraidy cat Guy had called her. It was impossible to explain what had driven her to imply that she'd slept with Jeff. It had been such a stupid thing to do—heck, she didn't even understand the foolish impulse herself.

Draining the hot, aromatic coffee, she set the empty cup down on the table.

All she knew was that she'd wanted to hurt him as he'd hurt her with his belief that she was an easy little gold digger. But that was no excuse. When she'd discovered he'd never pimped her to Jeff she should have cleared up the misunderstanding then and there. Instead, she'd discovered a deep yearning for him to trust her unreservedly. When Guy had eyed her with disgust, she'd lost all sense.

And the damage had been done.

Oh, what a tangled web.

Now he had her back up with his dog-in-the-manger attitude about Todd. Again she'd instantly reacted, rebelling against his dark, thunderous glare. And proceeded to dig herself deeper into the mess she'd created.

What did Guy think she was going to do, in heaven's name? Sleep with Todd?

The frustration and anger cut deep.

Guy didn't trust her.

At the heart of it all, that was what hurt most. That was what made her act so perversely. Her disappointment at his lack of trust about Jeff...then Matt...and now Todd. God, she'd just told him he'd been wrong about Matt, but did he learn? No, he simply leapt to the next wild conclusion about her.

If he knew her at all, Guy would never have believed her capable of that kind of betrayal. If he'd known anything about her he would've found it impossible to believe. She was really quite proper in her way. Not a wild wanton at all. But he hadn't cared to find out who she was. All he was interested in was a sexy body in his bed. Coupled with his distrust, that made her loath to tell him about her stupidity.

Yet despite her annoyance with Guy she found herself tasting the food and observing the guests and keeping mental notes about what they ate and what they pushed away.

Still annoyed an hour later, Avery escaped the ride back with Guy by hopping in one of the other resort minivans with the balloonists on the way back. But when they pulled up in the courtyard, Guy was waiting for her, his eyes still stormy.

"I'll introduce you to Louis Leclere, the chef at Chagall's."

"I met him yesterday, at one of the talks I listened to," Avery said. "He told me that you and he are old friends."

The Frenchman had confessed that Guy had lured him to Jarrod Ridge just over a month ago.

Guy's mouth tightened. "Let me introduce you to the resort's head barman then."

"Oh, I met him, too. Louis thoughtfully introduced us. In fact the three of us are meeting—" she glanced at her watch "—in thirty minutes. They're going to show me around the cellars. I better go change into something more suitable." She gestured to the dust on the hem of her white jeans. "Otherwise I'll be late."

"Avery," Guy put a restraining hand on her arm, and

glanced meaningfully at Todd who was hovering nearby, "Louis tends to have a devastating effect on women. We have a policy that staff don't date guests—I've told him that already. But I wouldn't want you to tempt him to break the rules."

Angrily, she shook off his hand. "Well, since I'm neither a guest nor staff but an independent contractor, that shouldn't affect me. Of course, that won't affect me asking Louis out on a date—he's staff, and I've always had a thing for French accents."

Guy glowered.

Jerk.

Avery spent the rest of the day avoiding Guy. Until he finally cornered her late that afternoon in the Sky Lounge where she was studying the proposed drink list for the winter ski season and jotting down notes into a moleskin notebook.

"I shouldn't have said what I did this morning about staff and guest liaisons," he said abruptly halting beside the bar counter.

"No, you shouldn't," she agreed, gazing unseeingly at the list in front of her. "You should've trusted me to behave with professionalism."

Her rebuke was met with silence.

"Truce?" he said at last.

He had a long way to go. Setting the list down with a snap, Avery glanced up to find that Guy's confusion was written over every hard line on his face. "If you're not prepared to trust me, then so long as you treat me with the respect you accord other employees and contractors we have a truce."

Heat flared in his eyes, turning them a smoldering, smoky gray. "Impossible. I can't treat you like I treat everyone else. We're lovers."

"Shh!"

Avery glanced around to see if he'd been overheard. But the nearest group, three young women and two men, were clustered around the bar counter sipping margaritas and flirting furiously, showing no interest in her and Guy.

"Not any more."

"But we were. We will be again. Soon."

He brushed his fingers across her cheek and she flinched away. He couldn't help remembering how demonstrative Avery had been in New York, always ready to touch him, stroke him. With the exception of last night, all she'd seemed to have done since she came to Jarrod Ridge was back away from him.

"I don't want people knowing we had a relationship."

That made it sound like she had no intention of considering his suggestion that they enter a more lasting arrangement during her stay.

He drew a deep breath. He wasn't going to accept that. They were not through yet. No woman walked out on him. "Avery, it's nothing to be ashamed of."

"Not for you. Everyone will just think 'what a stud', while I get the sniggers."

"It won't be like that." Guy raked his hand through his hair, but the dark, shaggy strands sprang stubbornly back.

After a pause during which her blue eyes dueled with his night-gray ones, he said, "Tell you what, let's have dinner at Chagall's tonight."

Avery shook her head. "Can't you understand? I don't want to be seen out with you, Guy."

"We need to talk more about what you'll be doing at Jarrod Ridge over the next few weeks."

Avery had been dying to sample the dishes at the resort's premier restaurant. But she got the feeling that dinner was less about setting up a professional work relationship than trying to get her back into his bed.

Why was he bothering to pursue her? It wasn't about her agreement to step into Uncle Art's shoes. Guy had been averse to that from the start, and he could easily contract another sommelier. Nor did she flatter herself that he wanted only her in his bed. He'd made his opinion of her clear. Finding another lover would be equally easy for a man like Guy. It had surprised her that he hadn't already acquired a new lover, until she'd realized that his father's death and the terms of his will had left Guy with no time to find a new girlfriend. How fortuitous for him that she'd turned up, saving him the bother.

No, the only attraction she held was the fact that she wasn't falling over herself to get back into his bed. How galling that must be when he'd already labeled her easy and a gold digger....

With a jolt she took in Guy looking at her expectantly, no doubt waiting for her to agree to dinner—and to serve herself up as dessert.

"No thanks, not tonight. It's been a long day, and I need a good night's sleep. Alone," she added pointedly.

By the tight line of his lips she knew he'd gotten the message.

"Then I won't be seeing you for a few days," he said. "One of the national supermarket chains is interested in stocking Go Green products, and Jeff and I are meeting with them in New York to hammer out an agreement."

Avery forced herself not to react to the mention of Jeff-the-Jerk's name. What would it help? It wouldn't repair the damage she and Jeff between them had done or encourage Guy to trust her. He'd made it more than clear that his loyalty lay with Jeff, and the friendship and business relationship they shared.

All she said was, "Well, I hope your meeting is productive."

"No reason why it shouldn't be. Oh, and speaking of meetings," he added, "on the afternoon I get back we'll be having a progress briefing about the Food and Wine Gala before Blake flies out back to New York. You should be there." Guy pointed to her notebook. "Some of the information you've collected will be very useful."

By Thursday morning, Avery had convinced herself that she didn't care if Guy's loyalty lay with Jeff. All she wanted was a professional relationship with a man she'd been dumb enough to almost fall in love with. Her notebook clutched in her hand, she scanned the family room on the top floor of Jarrod Manor with interest. Forcing herself to ignore the impact that seeing Guy again had on her, she inspected the high beams, the woven rugs scattered over the landing, the wood finish that all combined to give a cozy, homey feel.

The Jarrods were seated around a sunken conversation pit in front of a fireplace, which in winter would give the room a warm ambience.

Blake patted the table to get everyone's attention. The group slowly fell silent. "Gavin…Trevor…you're both here. Anyone missing?"

Gavin and Trevor were remarkably similar-looking in coloring and build and even mood, Avery noticed. Much more so than Blake and Guy. She compared the twins. Their dark hair and determined jawlines were the only resemblance they shared.

"Except Melissa," said Erica from an armchair set to one side. "She was feeling off color and went home."

"She's been tired a lot lately," said Christian, Erica's fiancé, who was perched on the arm of her chair. "Perhaps she should go see a doctor."

Guy shuffled a pile of papers. "Okay, let's get down to business."

Nothing could've more effectively made Avery realize how wrong he was for her. All he cared about was business…and sex.

Even his sister's health was of little concern to him.

Nothing about him made him a good prospect for the husband she wanted, for the father of the family she yearned for. So why had she wasted three whole days pining after the darn man?

He didn't want a family. Look how relieved he'd been when she'd told him there had been no consequences to their affair. If she'd had any sense she might've told him about the very light period she'd had and made him fret a little.

In fact, it was probably worth purchasing a pregnancy test just to make sure there'd been no slip. Not that she expected there to be a baby, but the two weeks she'd spent in Guy's bed in New York had been over her most fertile time of the month. She'd been on the Pill then, even though she was off it now.

She doodled on the pad on front of her. A row of daisies with smiling faces. She told herself that it was for the best that she couldn't have conceived. That she should be as happy as the daisies she'd captured on the legal pad.

After the meeting was over she'd go into town. Just to make sure.

Guy couldn't find Avery anywhere.

He'd unexpectedly missed her in the days he'd been gone, and now she'd vanished into thin air.

Rita confirmed Avery wasn't booked for a treatment in the spa. Nor had Louis seen her all morning—much as it galled him to ask his friend if he'd seen her. So she hadn't been to

Chagall's. Reception said she hadn't used her card to access her room.

He was dying to tell her about the success he'd had with Go Green. Jeff hadn't made the meeting in the end, and Guy had been left to do all the wheeling and dealing alone. It was the first time that Jeff had let him down, and Guy knew it could only be because his partner still felt awkward about having slept with Avery. The relationship between them had become strained.

Despite Jeff's absence, the supermarket chain had placed a large order, but there were tough deadlines and production would have to get moving. Now Guy found himself wanting to watch Avery tip her head to one side as she evaluated the progress he'd made, to hear her arguments against it. And watch her eyes widen and her head bob if she considered the opportunity as good as he did.

So where the hell was she?

Grumpily, Guy took his cell phone out from the chest pocket of his white business shirt and located her number. Three rings later her breathy voice greeted him. Instantly desire curled in his groin.

"Where are you?" he asked more brusquely than he'd intended.

"In town."

She'd gone to town? Why? "You didn't tell me you were going."

"You didn't ask."

"Why the big secret?"

"It's not a secret."

A chill feathered along his spine at the defensive note in her voice. Avery was not being completely truthful with him. *Why?*

What was she hiding?

Was she meeting someone—hell, be honest—he wanted

to know if she was meeting Todd. He swallowed the bile in the back of his throat. Had they become an item in his absence?

Guy suspected he was being unreasonable...he'd never reacted with this kind of unwarranted jealousy with his other girlfriends. But then he'd never experienced this degree of turmoil over any of them.

"I wanted to talk to you," he said finally.

"What about?"

Suddenly it all felt flat. This call wasn't going the way he'd planned. "It doesn't matter."

"We can talk when I get back—sorry, I have to go now."

Guy stared at his BlackBerry in disbelief. She'd killed the call. No woman ended a call until *he* was good and ready...it was always he who cut the woman short. In New York Avery had been openly admiring, now she barely had time for him. He didn't like the role reversal one little bit.

But why the hell did it matter?

He didn't want her to love him. The last thing he wanted was a needy woman—he'd made it his life's mission to avoid them. All he wanted was sex. Good sex. No, he wanted more, he wanted great sex. The kind of sex he'd always had with Avery.

But that didn't explain this sudden pressing need to talk to her about how the Go Green meetings had gone.

Guy shook his head, confused.

The sooner he got Avery back into his bed the better. In his experience sex fixed everything.

Seven

Back in her hotel room, Avery stood in the bathroom and stared at the applicator stick.

The emotion that surged through her at the sight of the single pink line was not the relief she'd expected. Instead she felt unaccountably sad.

Her throat was tight and achy. She wanted to cry.

There'd been two tests in the box she'd driven to Aspen to buy earlier. Both had given the same result.

One pink line.

Not pregnant.

It's for the best, she tried to convince herself. It was what Guy had wanted. What she should've wanted, too. If she'd had any sense.

She ought to be dancing around with delighted relief. Not staring at the second stick praying for the second pink line to appear.

Because she wanted a baby. She longed for a family.

And, damn it, she wanted Guy, too. All in the same breath. Even though she knew such pie-in-the-sky dreams were utterly impossible.

Pink. She felt downright blue.

A knock sounded on the door of her room.

Avery stuck the traitorous stick back into the box and hurried out of the bathroom.

Wrenching the door open she found Guy on the other side.

Horrors. For a moment she couldn't marshal her thoughts. All she could think of was the telltale pregnancy test sitting on the bathroom slab, incriminating evidence of all her dashed hopes.

"Aren't you going to invite me in?"

"Wh-what are you doing here?" she stuttered. For a wild moment she considered slamming the door in his face.

"I came to help you move your stuff."

"Move my stuff?" She retreated into the room, and barely noticed that he'd followed.

"Didn't Reception call? I've changed your room." He frowned as he scanned it. "I didn't know you were given a room in this wing. The view isn't great."

"It doesn't matter—I spend so little time here. Frankly, I'd be grateful for a broom cupboard, I know how scarce accommodation in Aspen is."

"Now's not too bad, but during the ski season it's diabolical."

She didn't bother to remind him she wouldn't be here for the ski season.

He strode across the room.

"Where are you going?" she squawked, intent on distracting him before he entered the bathroom and discovered the telltale stick. She'd already told him she wasn't pregnant, she didn't want him doubting her.

Instead he stopped just to the left of the door to the bathroom, and threw open the wardrobe doors.

Avery's breath whooshed out in a gust of relief.

He spoke into the wardrobe. "It shouldn't take you long to pack up."

"I'm not packing up."

"If you don't want to move into another room, you can move in with me. Because you never did give me an answer. And I've been very patient, I've given you more time than you need."

She stared at his back, achingly conscious of the shaggy length of his hair where it brushed the collar of his T-shirt.

"I'm not moving into your quarters."

"The view is far better from my suite upstairs."

She wished she could see his face. "I'm sure it is. But as I just said, I'm not in my room enough for it to matter."

He spun away from the wardrobe.

Avery caught a glimpse of tumult in the dark gray eyes, before his jaw firmed, and he moved toward her with long, swinging strides.

Hooking his arms around her shoulders, he bent his head until his forehead touched her hair.

"I want you with me," he said into the cave of space between them.

Oh, dear heaven. How was she supposed to resist this?

If only he'd been a different kind of man...

A family man.

But he wasn't. And she had to be strong. She had to resist.

"I'm not going to have an affair with you."

"And I'm not going to accept no for an answer."

Her breath whooshed out in frustration. "You have to accept it. You can't force me to move in with you."

"I can certainly use every advantage I have to persuade you." His lips brushed hers in a light teasing kiss.

"I need some space," she said desperately.

"Why? Just admit you want me." He kissed her again, his mouth lingering on hers.

Unfair!

"We're working together. Trying to keep a professional distance." Her breath mingled with his. "We're both going to need space, time away from each other. Otherwise we'll drive each other crazy." And she refused to let herself fall in love with him all over again.

"I don't want any space between us…." He pulled her up against his body. "Almost a week has already slipped away, I want to spend every remaining minute we have together."

He sunk his tongue into her mouth in a primitive act of possession that sent a thrill of desire along Avery's bloodstream.

The sentiment was all well and good, but Avery knew he didn't mean it. Not in the way that she needed him to mean it. All he was talking about was sex.

He wanted her within reach all night long.

And first thing in the morning, if it came to it.

Guy was a demanding lover. He'd take whatever she gave, without giving much of himself in return. Having her in his bed, at his convenience, didn't mean he wanted to be close to her.

Not in any of the ways that really mattered.

Avery drew away. "No. I'm keeping my stuff in my room. This room. I'm not your lover anymore. I don't want special treatment. I don't want the staff, your family, thinking that I am your lover."

His hand brushed her hair off her face, his touch so gentle her throat thickened. "I'm not going to give up until you agree."

She was going to have to spell it out this time. So that he'd understand and never ask again. She couldn't bear this.

"Because I've worked damn hard to get where I am. And I'm not having anyone denigrating my efforts by saying that I got there because I slept with one of the Almighty Jarrods."

"That didn't matter to you in New York."

"Because I didn't know you were a Jarrod then—not one of these Jarrods." She drew a steadying breath, refusing to be provoked. "And in New York I didn't know anyone—I was on temporary assignment. Here, at the Food and Wine Gala, there are a lot of people I know. People who respect me. People who may offer me work."

She tilted her head back and gazed up at him.

"How long do you think their respect will last once they know I'm living in your penthouse suite?"

"It won't be like that."

"It's always like that. Everyone will think me a lucky little gold digger who landed a rich lover—exactly what you accused me of only a few days ago."

His gaze fell before hers.

"I apologize, I shouldn't have said that."

"No, you shouldn't. Your apology is accepted. But it doesn't change the fact that I'm not moving in with you."

There was a long pause. Avery tensed, waiting for an argument, for him to sweep her up in his arms, for something.

But he only said, "We need to work on the presentation we're giving tomorrow."

Back to work. The professional relationship that was all she could ever afford to share with him.

So why did she want to sag with disappointment that he'd accepted her decision? At least she knew she could deal with Guy on the work front.

Hurriedly she said, "Well, we might as well talk about both presentations." The second presentation was next Wednesday, less than a week away. "Give me an hour, I'll come up to your suite." She made herself give him a cheeky smile. "Have dinner ready, but don't think that you can change my mind about staying the night."

Avery was true to her word.

The intercom buzzed exactly an hour later—and Guy activated the private elevator for her to come up, then opened the door to his suite.

She stepped into his living room, a tote slung over her shoulder and a bright smile on her face. She was wearing high-heel slides, a pair of her trademark white jeans and a strawberry-ice silk blouse that clung to her curves. She looked good enough to lick.

"Come in," said Guy huskily.

"Oh, that looks good."

Her attention had homed in on an array of mouthwatering tapas spread on the low square coffee table where two sofas sat beside the empty fireplace. "Funny how the sight of food always seems to remind me of how long it's been since I last ate."

"Room service," he said laconically.

She slid him an amused look as she sat down on the nearest sofa. "And there I thought you'd been slaving in the kitchen preparing our meal. You still owe me a meal—you promised to make me one in New York, and you never did."

Never again. He'd done that on the night of her birthday… and had been left cooling his heels while she entertained herself with Jeff.

"We've got a lot of work to get through," he said tersely. "Let's get started."

She didn't take the hint. "You know, while I stayed with you most of our food was take out from Baratin's—"

"What's wrong with that? Most women would kill to never have to cook."

"I cooked."

"Very occasionally—and then only breakfast." He tipped his head to the side. "Now that I think back, it was toast and cereal most mornings."

"Do you have any idea how intimidating it is to cook for a chef? Obviously not! Except you never cooked—I'm seriously beginning to wonder if you actually know how to cook, or whether you're just a fraud." She slanted him a teasing glance from under those fluttery eyelashes.

Despite the gloom that the memory of her birthday had cast over him, Guy found himself laughing. She'd always been able to charm a smile from him.

"Avery, that's something I sometimes wonder myself. I employ chefs these days. I seem to spend more time doing paperwork and juggling numbers than cooking. The business courses Dad insisted I take are being used more than my chef credentials."

"I'm always impressed when I watch food shows." She leaned back on the couch, folding her hands behind her head. With her glinting eyes half closed, she was all temptress. "Those so efficient chefs, chopping onions without weeping, producing masterpieces in minutes. You'll have to show me how it's done."

Guy suppressed the urge to rush to the kitchen, don an apron, anything to impress her. Been there, never again. "Maybe one day."

But he had no intention of exposing himself that way again.

Avery kicked off her slides. Guy caught a glimpse of pink-tipped toes before she tucked her feet underneath her. From her tote, she drew out a black notebook and a pen.

"Okay, so where shall we start?"

Guy was still admiring the picture she made, the way her white jeans clung to her thighs, and fantasizing about feeding her strawberries that he'd flambéed to impress her then licking the flavour from her lips.

Caught off guard by her businesslike demeanor he found himself stuttering, "Uh...I have a PowerPoint presentation that will provide some material."

She tipped her face toward the flat-screen television that dominated the wall across from where she sat, then looked expectantly back at him. "Let's watch it."

Hell, he hadn't linked his laptop.

Guy rubbed the back of his neck. "When we've finished talking."

She shifted, a little wriggle that had Guy clenching his teeth in frustration, before she settled again.

He barely knew what they talked about for the next twenty minutes, except that Avery seemed to take copious notes... and make numerous suggestions—none of which he was likely to retain.

Not when she was such a tempting distraction.

Finally, Avery closed her notebook with a snap and said, "Good, that should wrap it up."

Guy was simply relieved that the torture was at an end. Until she reached for a toothpick and speared a piece of spicy chorizo with it. Popping it in her mouth, she chewed, head tilted to one side, then said, "That was very tasty. There's a smoky flavor that would go well with an oaked and well-aged red made from tempranillo grapes."

"That would be a great match."

A frown furrowed her brow. "I detect a spice I can't place."

Guy tried to tell himself that this was still work. Matching food and wine. But his body refused to believe him. All he could do was stare at her mouth like a hungry hound after a meal.

"Have you eaten?"

He shook his head, not trusting his voice.

"You should."

With delicate grace she took a second toothpick out of the white porcelain holder and spiked a piece of chorizo then added a sun-dried tomato, and offered it to him.

His heart thumped.

He bent his head, took it from her fingers, aware of the unconscious eroticism of the gesture.

The sweetness of the tomato and the spicy sausage complemented one another.

"What do you think?" Her brow had crinkled. "Can you identify that elusive spice?"

"Pimentón," he said huskily, watching her help herself to a shrimp cake. "Spanish paprika."

She snapped her fingers. "You're right." Then she speared a fat, shiny black olive. "So," she said, "what thoughts do you have about the menus for the restaurants?"

This was work, what Jarrod Ridge was paying her for. No doubt she'd be keeping track of every second to bill the resort. He forced himself to concentrate. "A total re-vamp."

Another olive went the same way as the last. Guy almost growled. But he managed to feed himself and stanch some of the physical hunger. Too soon the platters on the table were empty.

"When are you going to put the PowerPoint on?"

She had to be joking, right?

One glance revealed she wasn't. The notebook was propped against her thigh, and a pencil twisted between her fingers. She expected them to work. Guy suppressed a sigh and hooked his laptop up to the flat screen. Then he settled down on the couch beside her.

He put his hand on her leg.

"Hey."

He took it off. This time he sighed loudly.

With no choice he focused on the screen, conscious of every move of her hand as she scribbled the occasional note.

The room grew darker. There were a couple of clips of interviews and Avery put her pad and pencil down on the coffee table.

"Seen enough?"

She shook her head. "I want to watch it all."

Guy's thoughts wandered. He'd seen parts of the presentation countless times. He was tempted to flick it forward, speed it up.

Dammit, he'd had enough of work.

He ached to kiss Avery. It had been too long. When her head brushed his shoulder, his pulse surged and he slung an arm around her. She rewarded him by snuggling up against him. Guy couldn't wait for the program to finish.

Her breathing grew more regular. Guy peered down at her through the dim light, and suppressed a groan.

Avery had fallen asleep!

She looked so young, so innocent, with her dark lashes falling against smooth cheeks. Guy stroked the feathery bangs off her face with gentle fingers. She stirred, and he stilled, but instead of waking she only burrowed closer.

Emotion bolted through him, fierce and primitive and defying him to put a name to it.

With one hand he pressed the remote and the screen went black. Scooping Avery up into his arms, he rose and headed for his bedroom. Muted light spilled from the bedside lamp. There, surrounded by the burgundy and muted gold décor, he laid her down and gently arranged the covers over her, before shedding his shirt, dropping his jeans and lowering himself beside her.

Instantly she curled into him.

The spontaneity of the gesture pierced his heart. Guy gathered her close, and closed his eyes. Nuzzling at the soft fluff of her hair he was conscious of a welcome sense of contentment seeping through him.

This time he wasn't going to let her go.

She woke in an unfamiliar room.

Avery blinked against the shaded glow of the bedside lamp. Shifting, she became aware of the warmth of a body in the bed beside her. Guy! They'd been in the sitting room of his suite, she'd felt replete and pleasantly tired. Then nothing…

They hadn't made love. She would've remembered that.

Her body was curved into Guy's spoon-fashion, her legs tangled with his. She suspected his were bare—unlike hers that were still clad in jeans.

At least he hadn't undressed her.

He'd retained that much decency.

Nor had he made love to her.

Okay, so what did that prove? Only that Guy wasn't a necrophiliac. She stifled a giggle and eased herself away from him. He groaned and rolled onto his back.

Avery slipped quickly out the king-size bed, her bare feet sinking into thick carpet. Guy's arm was flung out above his head, his dark hair mussed. In sleep he looked younger, carefree, more like the Guy she'd met…what?…could it be only ten weeks ago now? She couldn't remember what her life had been like before Guy.

A sigh escaped. Once the Food and Wine Gala ended, so would her time with Guy.

For a moment she contemplated diving back into the soft, welcoming bed and cozying up to him. They could make love. Add another treasured memory to the trove in her heart to take away with her when she left. Then she squared her shoulders.

She wasn't going to spend the night with Guy...and have the world know about it. She wasn't going to become his lover—at least not until he began to trust her. Really trust her.

Far better to sneak out like a thief in the night now than to face that humiliation in the morning when the staff came on duty.

Swinging about, Avery headed into the darkened sitting room to find her shoes, her notebook and her tote, before she risked her self-respect.

Guy stirred, and reached out an arm...only to discover an expanse of smooth sheet. An empty expanse. His eyes shot open, and he rolled over.

The bed was cool, no residue of body warmth lingered. The only signs that Avery had been there were the slight indent on the pillow beside him and the lingering scent of her perfume.

Despite Avery saying that she would not move into his suite, Guy had comfortably expected to be able to change her mind last night—once he got her there. He hadn't banked on her falling asleep, but he'd certainly expected her to still be in his bed when he wakened. Hell, he'd been arrogantly sure that he could persuade her to stay.

Her absence was a significant shock.

He'd planned to convince her that her scruples were insignificant, to pull her into his arms and make love again... and again in the shower...as they had for those two passionate weeks in New York.

Not to awaken to this void of emptiness.

Nothing was going the way he'd planned. In the past two months his life had been turned upside down. What with Avery's betrayal, Jeff's weakness in the face of temptation, his father's death, the discovery that he had a half sister he'd never known…his world had gone crazy.

For the first time in his life, he didn't have the answers. He'd expected to hate Erica, to be able to forgive Jeff, to cope easily with his father's loss—after all it had been years since they'd spent time together. Most of all he'd been certain of his ability to persuade Avery to resuscitate their smoldering affair, until he grew bored.

But Avery had changed….

And so had everything else around him.

Eight

Avery stood behind the presenter's podium in the grand marquee waiting with some trepidation for Guy to join her. She took a sip of water and pretended to scan the notes she'd typed up on her laptop in the hours before dawn, when she should've been fast asleep.

It was not the prospect of facing a crowd that was responsible for her trepidation, only the thought of seeing one man. *Guy*. She'd sneaked out like a thief in the night. And paid the price by her inability to doze.

No doubt he'd slept like a baby.

When she caught sight of him coming her way, her heart did a somersault.

He was wearing dark trousers ironed to a knife-edge, and a white shirt that hung out giving him a rakish look. There was a faint line of stubble on his jaw that should have made him look untidy, but only made him more irresistible.

His gaze caught hers, and for a moment they both stilled,

then he gave her a faint smile. It widened, full of charm and promises. Empty promises…

Avery glanced away as he wound toward her side, checking around to see if anyone else had noticed that moment of jolting awareness between them.

No one sitting in the rows of seats appeared remotely interested.

She relaxed a little.

"You ran out on me."

The whisper as he placed a laptop on the podium beside her notes caused Avery to shudder.

"Hush!" She slanted him a frown. Then ruined it by adding, "You looked like a baby, all innocence and eyelashes."

A flush stained his cheekbones. "I can assure you, I didn't feel nearly as innocent as a baby when I woke up this morning…."

The loaded words caused a rush of heat. For a moment she half wished she'd given in to the reckless temptation to stay in his bed all night long. For sure she would've slept better in his arms than she had alone. She'd missed him from the moment she'd left.

Avery had a sinking feeling that she was about to cave to his demands. She reminded herself she simply wasn't the kind of woman who could sleep with a man without an emotional connection. And tried to convince herself that her hurt and anger at Guy had broken the emotional connection that had bound her to him.

She could never do pleasure for pleasure's sake.

Yet she knew she lied to herself. Because Guy still drew her like a moth to flame. God. How could she feel something so self-destructive about a man who felt nothing for her?

"…only to find that you'd gone."

His murmur was so low she barely heard it, but it was enough to make her stiffen her spine. He might not love her, and she might feel a lot more for him than she wanted, but she couldn't afford to forget that he only wanted her for sex—however much he wrapped it up in pretty words.

"Guy, stop it! This is my career, it's important to me."

She couldn't afford to compromise her career, her own professionalism for a relationship that was headed nowhere. She had to make him understand that.

"Yes," he said impatiently. "I accept that."

"Good."

But was this what she really wanted?

There would be no more nights of illicit passion. It would all be over. She would be well on her way to getting him out of her system—out of her life. She would never be the butt of a host of insinuations about a little gold digger sleeping with the boss.

It was all for the best.

She had to stick to her guns...and not cave in to his demands or her desires. Those would only cause her harm—even though the hold Guy had on her heart would make it all too easy to assent.

By contrast their second presentation five days later was all business.

Yet it belied the fact that Avery and Guy had fallen into a routine since the night she'd fallen asleep in his suite. Each day they would spend several hours going through recipes Guy wanted to add to the menus and seeking the perfect wine and beverage match. Avery also spent a couple of hours each day reviewing and training the restaurant and bar staff. In the evening, she and Guy would order in room service to Guy's suite and analyze the day's progress. There was a delicious domesticity about their relationship, and Avery stored up every memory.

After their speech, a trio of foodies came up to talk to Guy, and Louis, the French chef from Chagall's, told Avery that they'd done a great job. Then Trevor and Gavin were both there adding to the crowd.

Trevor took her hand and shook it. "Good job. You had me wanting to visit some of those California vineyards you mentioned."

"Thanks," she smiled at him when he dropped her hand. "Start with El Dorado, it's a winery I know very well—I grew up there."

Erica arrived with Christian, and the talk quickly turned to the December wedding they were planning.

"I thought we could serve champagne cocktails to the guests as they arrive. What do you think, Avery?" Erica asked.

"You could add a hint of cassis."

"Christian suggested I talk to you, Trevor, about where to hold the service since you live here."

"Hey, I'm a freewheeling bachelor. What do I know about weddings?"

Everyone laughed at the expression of mock horror on Trevor's face.

"But as president of marketing you're the perfect person to ask," Erica retorted. "Besides, apart from Christian, you're the only one who actually lives in Aspen."

Trevor spread his hands. "Of course I'll help. Hmm, your wedding will be in December, why don't you have Blake and Guy dress up as twin Santas?" Trevor suggested with a twinkle in his eye.

"I heard that," said Guy from the other side of the trio he was talking to.

Erica laughed. "They'd both need big white fluffy beards. I've gotten to know a few of the local vendors, I'm sure Dorothy from the yarn shop could organize something."

"Forget it," ordered Guy. And everyone laughed again.

"On a serious note, Christian and I will be using as many locals as we possibly can to help us prepare."

Guy had been watching Erica, but at this he broke in. "They'd like that. It's a good idea to include them—and it will have the bonus of garnering a lot of goodwill for Jarrod Ridge. Although I know that's not your primary motive for including the locals in the celebration."

Erica beamed at him, and Avery's heart turned to marshmallow. Any resentment that Guy might once have harbored toward his half sister had clearly been set to rest.

Discussion continued about the wedding for a few minutes more before Avery excused herself. As she walked away, she was aware of more than one pair of eyes on her retreating back.

"That woman is good-looking," Louis commented as Avery sauntered away.

Guy groaned, attracting Christian's sharp gaze. "You don't think so, Guy? Or is it just that you've been too busy to notice?"

Hell. "How could I not notice?" he retorted in response to his future brother-in-law's sly observation.

"Ah, so you have noticed." Christian's eyes crinkled with laughter. "What do you intend to do about it?"

Mentally Guy crossed his fingers. "Nothing."

"Then you're a fool," Trevor entered the discussion. "A sommelier and a restaurateur has to be a match made in the industry heaven."

"Now you're starting to sound like Dad. Who said I want to always be talking work to my lover?" Guy protested.

"At least you'd be doing something you love—think of me stuck here, torn away from everything I've achieved over the past decade." Gavin sounded utterly frustrated. "What was

Dad thinking setting his will up in such a fashion? I feel like I'm being buried alive."

"And think about how much you and Avery would have in common." Erica added her weight to the argument after a short pause.

Guy felt under siege. He could hardly disclose the one thing that would stop his family from matchmaking him with Avery. Once they knew that she'd cheated on him, they'd close ranks against her. But he'd never admit what a fool he'd been. "Just as well Blake has gone back to New York, otherwise you'd be canvassing him for an opinion, too."

"We can still ask Melissa," Erica grinned at him, an infectious smile that had Guy wanting to smile back.

"I haven't seen her all morning," Guy said as he thought about his sister. In fact he'd barely seen much of her all week, and when he had she'd been much more quiet than usual.

"She's probably run off her feet at the spa," Erica said, ever practical.

"She wasn't there when I went to the gym earlier," said Christian.

"She'll turn up." Guy raised an eyebrow. "Then you can start matchmaking her with some man—so start looking for someone suitable."

They all laughed, and to Guy's great relief talk turned away from Avery and back to Erica and Christian's Christmas wedding.

It was late afternoon before he caught up with Avery again.

"I wanted to talk to you more about the brief for the restaurants," Guy said to her as they walked up the pathway lined with a profusion of colorful flowers on the way back to Jarrod Manor.

"We can talk later."

He got the feeling she was about to disappear again. "Tonight. Come up when you're done."

"Let's meet in the sky lounge," she said quickly, "I'm still working on adding some more variety to the beer list for the Christmas season."

Didn't she know that anyone seeing him with her would be unable to miss the attraction she held for him? Even his family had noticed. "Maybe it would be a better idea to go check out some of the competition—we'll go to town, hit the bars and restaurants."

Avery's eyes lit up. "That sounds like fun."

Guy thought so too, and that way he wouldn't have to be so on his guard against his family's well-meant teasing. Nor would he have to disillusion them about what kind of person Avery really was. Although it was getting harder and harder for him to remember that himself…

She truly had bewitched him.

Avery decided she could easily fall in love with Aspen. Main Street was buzzing with activity. Pickups, Porsches and even a lovingly restored old Cadillac filled the lanes. And the stores—there was everything from Gucci to Macy's and burgers to up-market restaurants that the rich and famous were known to frequent.

Guy parked the SUV and Avery emerged from the passenger door to stare around like a wide-eyed child in a candy store. Couples strolled along the sidewalk, people spilled out of restaurants, families bundled together. Guy came round to her side. Avery scarcely noticed when he threaded his fingers through hers.

He pointed to a sign ahead. "There's the first bar where I thought we might conduct some covert espionage."

She wrinkled her nose at him. "Maybe I can get some business from them, too." It was a thought. That way, if things were going well between Guy and her perhaps she could stay longer than the month they'd agreed....

God! What was she contemplating?

"Not until you've completed your contract with Jarrod Ridge." He gave her a mock frown. "I'll have to get that signed and sealed as soon as we get back."

She gave a gurgle of laughter.

The next second she was spinning into his arms. His lips slanted across hers. Avery's laughter dried up. For a moment she responded, then she pulled away, and shook her hand free of his.

Oh, my, she was even holding hands with Guy.

To cover her confusion, she said, "Oh, an art gallery. Let's have a look." At that point even an abattoir would've elicited a squeal of delight. Anything to escape the confusion of being thoroughly and publicly kissed in the midst of Aspen's main street by Guy Jarrod.

"We're almost at the bar."

"I want to have a look." She needed a moment to regain her composure. "You can wait outside if you want. I won't be long." She dived through the door into the gallery, grateful for the respite. There was a row of touristy watercolor paintings of the town, and the gallery keeper was securing a round, red Sold sticker to one of them. Avery walked quickly past.

To the right was an alcove—it would've been a misnomer to call it a room. On the far white wall, plumb in the center, hung one canvas.

Avery stopped dead.

The power of that single painting sucked the breath out of her lungs with its sheer poignant beauty.

It was a while before she became aware of Guy standing silently beside her.

"Isn't this piece amazing?"

"Amazing."

There was a peculiar note in his voice. Avery glanced at him, a little resentful that he didn't share her enthusiastic admiration. His face was taut…pale.

"Guy?" Concern gripped her. "What's the matter?"

"I'll wait for you outside, okay?"

He shoved his hands into his pockets and turned away, his shoulders hunched as he headed for the door as though he couldn't get out fast enough.

What had evoked such a response? Was he annoyed because she'd pulled out of his too-public embrace? Or did his reaction have something to do with the gallery? She glanced back at the painting she'd been admiring when he'd come up beside her.

The painting was riveting. But disturbing enough to arouse such a strong reaction in Guy? Avery studied what should've been a peaceful subject. Perhaps. It was an abstract of a river. A swollen, moving river. There was turbulence in the dark, raging colors and the brush strokes. It was full of raw power… and anger. She couldn't take her eyes off it.

"It's compelling, isn't it?"

"Yes." Avery didn't glance up as the gallery keeper came up beside her. She was still trying to fathom what it was about the painting that aroused such strong emotions.

"Margaret Jarrod loved to paint the Roaring Fork—but this is one of her last works of the river."

Now Avery looked at him. "Margaret Jarrod?"

"Don Jarrod's wife." He pushed the round wire-rimmed glasses up his nose and glanced through the sheet window to where Guy was pacing the sidewalk. "I thought you knew it was her work."

Avery shook her head numbly.

"The whole town was very sad to hear about Don's passing."

"Yes, it was a tragedy for the family."

Questions swirled around her head. Guy had never mentioned his mother. She wanted to know everything. But it seemed…invasive…to ask the gallery owner while Guy cooled his heels outside.

"For everyone. The resort helped draw people to Aspen. The Food and Wine Gala that's on now is only one of the events that Don set up to benefit everyone in the town. There are fears that his children might abandon the resort—or, God help us all, sell it to outsiders."

Avery didn't know how to reply. "I'm here for the festival— and it's been wonderful" was what she settled for. With a smile she excused herself, "I must go, Guy is waiting."

Outside, Guy's face still wore that closed expression that had perturbed Avery.

With a burst of sudden longing she wanted the man who'd planted that joyful kiss on her lips back. But he'd vanished under the mask of stony indifference. Avery was determined to find him again.

She had a feeling it wasn't going to be easy.

But she'd always relished a challenge.

Best would be to put him off guard. To that end, she threaded her hand through the crook of his arm, "Lead the way. I'm ready to examine the competition."

The bar Guy took her to had attracted a well-heeled, casually-dressed crowd, where jeans were the order of the day. Mostly designer brands—Diesel, Calvin Klein. Although Avery also spotted the odd pair of working Levis—and footwear ranged from Jimmy Choos to dusty cowboy boots. But certainly these Colorado cowboys were ranch owners rather than hired hands, and the glitter at women's throats were diamonds rather than rhinestones.

The bartender took their order, and Avery turned her

attention to the cocktails chalked up on the blackboard behind the bar, then inspected the wine and beer list.

"Not bad," she said at last. She smiled her thanks when her drink arrived, while Guy paid for the round. Expenses, she told herself, suppressing the urge to object. This wasn't a date. He stuffed his wallet into the back pocket of his jeans and settled himself onto a wooden barstool.

"But you'd do better." He made it a statement.

"Of course." She set the wine list down on the counter and met Guy's gaze with confidence.

"Tell me how."

"I'd add some of the newer wines that are taking the country by storm." She warmed to her topic. "Then I'd look to add some international flair. What they've done here is to stick to the well-known Napa Valley wineries. They've done the same with the cocktails—the names might be risqué but there's nothing here that's new and refreshing. No imagination."

"What you're telling me is they've played it safe."

"Exactly!"

"You'd take more risks?"

The smile that tugged at his lips warned her of the trap she was headed for. "Forget it. I'm not going to go ballooning, Guy. I've got too much imagination."

The smile widened into a grin that had her innards melting.

"Did I even ask you to?"

"You didn't need to…I know where this is going." He was the most persistent devil she'd ever met. But she could be even more stubborn…and she would prove it.

Their next rendezvous was one of the most popular bar-and-grills in town, located in a brightly lit mall. They strolled along Mill Street, which gave Avery a chance to admire the store frontages. As they passed a busy eatery, Avery was startled by the loud sound of metal clanging.

"What's that?"

"Probably a bear."

"A bear?" She stopped and stared at Guy. "You're joking, right?"

He shook his head. "Nope. About a year back they started moving into town."

Just then two boys ran around the corner, one of them brandishing a Stop sign. Guy gave them a quelling look.

"Where did you get that?"

"Sorry, mister, we'll put it back."

With a scuffle they disappeared back around the corner, the sound of giggles following in their wake.

"Well, there goes your bear. Hope the little devils put it back."

"I'd say they were first-time offenders," Guy replied. "They didn't look sulky enough to be hardened miscreants."

"You recognize the difference?"

"I was a boy once upon a time."

"Well, at least it wasn't a bear this time," Avery said as Guy held a door open for her. "Boys I can handle—even in a place like Aspen which seems too glamorous for kids. But bears?" Halting at the bar, Avery wasn't ready to let the subject go.

The bartender had come over to greet Guy and take their order, and overheard her amazement. "You're hearing about our black bear problem?"

"So Guy wasn't having me on."

"Oh, no!" The bartender crossed his arms. "There was even a bear in the tree in front of the courthouse."

Avery blinked.

"In front of the courthouse?" Laughter bubbled up in her

throat. "Does that mean the sheriff had to arrest him for trespassing?"

Guy shook his head. "Nor the momma bear that stood watch while her cubs raided someone's kitchen after momma had broken the door down."

"Wow." Avery knew her eyes must be as wide as saucers.

"Don't feed any bears you might see."

"Don't worry, I won't." Avery loved Guy's honesty, his determination to protect the bears, and his insistence that people should take responsibility for their actions. "Trust me, I've got no intention of getting within a hundred yards of any bear."

"Ever the risk taker," said Guy.

And Avery gave him a sweet smile.

Sensing he'd missed out on a private joke, the bartender said, "Now what can I get you two to drink?"

"Make mine a strawberry margarita," said Avery. "I think I need it after all that bear talk."

"I'll have a beer." Guy made his selection and set the wine and beer list down.

Avery studied Guy, committing every feature, every nuance of his expression to memory. She watched as he brushed back the lock of hair that fell forward onto his face. "Have you ever seen a bear in the wild? That must be amazing—so long as it's a decent distance away."

"Plenty of times. And guess what?" Guy grinned across at her. "If you go up in a balloon you've got a good chance of seeing one too—and from a safe distance."

"Forget it!" She stuck her tongue out at him. "I'd rather be on the ground wishing I were in the air than in the air wishing I were on the ground."

He chuckled, his eyes warm and filled with humor.

"Let's study these menus, and see if the opposition is doing anything better than us."

Nine

Guy said no more about whatever it was that bothered him at the gallery during their outing. But an opportunity to learn more about him presented itself unexpectedly several days later.

"There's something I want to show you," said Guy interrupting the train of thought that Avery had been tapping into her computer while sitting at a table beside the sparkling resort pool.

She stretched lazily. She was feeling particularly content. A call from Matt had updated her on her uncle—he was almost back to normal. And earlier that morning her solo presentation had gone off without a hitch. "What is it?"

"You'll have to shut down your computer, because it will take a while."

Guy's gaze raked over her and Avery became conscious of how her blouse had pulled tight over her breasts. She lowered her arms.

"How much is a while?"

"My, but you're full of questions today."

The only way she was going to find out was to go with Guy. And her curiosity had been whetted. Busying herself with shutting the computer down, Avery packed it into its case, then rose to her feet. Guy led her through the spacious lobby scattered with tables and chairs and into an elevator.

"But this is the way to my room," she said as the doors opened to her floor. "What are you going to show me here?"

Avery followed him up a short flight of stairs, until he halted outside her room. "Open up."

She dug in her toes. "What's going on?"

"Get your swimsuit and a towel, we're going on a picnic."

"A picnic?"

He grinned, looking like he had no cares in the world. "Why not?"

"Haven't you got work to do?"

"It's Monday, the slowest day at the resort. The sun is shining, it's eighty degrees. The perfect day to show you the best swimming hole in Colorado. And test your theory that food tastes better outdoors."

"I suppose you've prepared the perfect picnic feast?"

"Uh…Louis did."

"In that case perhaps I should go on a picnic with Louis." Then she tensed at her stupidity and tried to think of an inane comment that would take the edge out her words.

But Guy didn't react with the suspicion she'd half expected. "No go. I organized the food, no one is hijacking my picnic."

Avery laughed and relaxed a little. If he was starting to trust her then they were making progress.

Better she accept that Guy was not going to cook for her.

Not because he hadn't had sufficient opportunity, but because for some reason he didn't want to.

She wished she could read him better, understand what drove him.

Today he was back to the easy charm that had attracted her that first day she met him. But she'd learned that the easygoing attitude also hid a reluctance to commit his heart. Avery didn't want the shallow charmer any longer; she wanted the complex, passionate man she'd glimpsed beneath.

Maybe a picnic would help unearth him.

Swiping her access card, she opened the room door. "Give me two minutes to drop off my laptop and change into a swimsuit."

Guy parked the black SUV under the trees and led Avery down an overgrown path to where the river flowed lazily into a calm pool in the lea of a large rock.

"Best kept secret in Colorado," he said.

"Gosh, the water is like a mirror." The willows along the river bank and the wide cobalt sky overhead were reflected in the flat surface.

"Not on the southern side of the rock, there's a waterfall there." With the picnic basket in one hand, Guy reached for her fingers with his free hand. "Come."

A bolt of pure happiness shot through Avery as his fingers threaded through hers. This was what she yearned for. This sense of companionship and contentment…with no hint of suspicion and distrust.

Near the edge of the river bank, in the green space under the largest willow, Guy set down the basket and let go of her hand. Then he tugged off his T-shirt and Avery caught her breath at the sight of his broad chest, his stomach tight with muscles that rippled in the sunlight.

Before he could see the effect his body had on her, she

turned away and stripped off her jeans and tank top to reveal the lime-green bikini she wore. By the time she reached the river bank, Guy was already moving across the ledge below the large, flat rock. He took three running steps and leapt into the water.

Avery edged down the bank until she stood knee deep in the swimming hole.

"Brr." She crossed her arms over her breasts to hide her puckering nipples. "It's cold."

"Of course it's cold. What did you expect? A hot tub?"

That brought back memories she didn't need revived right now, and a wash of heat replaced the water's chill. But when the water crept up her midriff, Avery forgot about hot tubs and nipples and squealed out loud.

"You should've jumped in while you had the chance."

Avery took one look at the wicked gleam in Guy's eyes as he swam toward her and sank hurriedly under the water.

"You beast." She came up stuttering at the shock of the river's chill. "You'll pay."

She splashed a wide arc of water at him.

He retaliated and within minutes they were engaged in a water fight, the cold forgotten, until they ended up under the stream of bubbles from the waterfall.

"That was wonderful." Finally worn out, Avery hauled herself out of the pool. Spreading her towel out on the grassy bank, she lay back in the sun, closing her eyes. Her stomach rumbled as hunger started to set in.

Peering through her eyelashes, she could see Guy sitting on his towel. Drops of water ran down his chest, causing her to follow their pathway over his chest, and belly…lower… to the waistband of his trunks. Those drops looked totally lickable.

She flushed, and jerked her gaze back to his face. "You always promised you'd cook for me one day."

"Did I?" His expression was impenetrable.

"Don't you remember?"

He shrugged. "I'm too busy to prepare food these days."

"You told me that back in New York." She braved his sarcasm. "You also said you missed it. That conjuring up dishes for your patrons didn't bring the same satisfaction as feeding friends and family."

Did he really not remember? Or was this another way of closing himself up to her?

"Sounds like I said entirely too much."

"Don't you recall the conversation?" Perhaps he had forgotten. Or never taken much notice to the promise he'd made. It only went to show how little their relationship had meant to him. It irked her that she was so forgettable he couldn't even remember their conversations.

Every word he'd spoken to her was engraved on her soul.

Don't call me again. Ever.

And she hadn't. If it hadn't been for Uncle Art falling sick, she'd very likely never have met Guy again. She'd sworn never to take an assignment in New York. Even among the millions of people the risk of encountering Guy was too great.

So maybe she was a 'fraidy cat.

Yet here she was trying to remind him he'd once promised to make her a meal. A fierce and stubborn determination crept in. "You said it the day that—"

"I vaguely remember."

Vaguely? That was even more insulting. Before she could object to his choice of words Guy had moved away to unpack the hamper.

"There's a selection of cheeses, a baguette, some pickles made at the resort, grapes and a nut terrine that is irresistible." Guy spread them out on a checked blue-and-white rug. Then he dug back into the hamper. "As well as a bottle of Pinot

Noir from the Sonoma Coast. No champagne today—I don't want to make you sneeze."

At least he'd remembered that! While it might not be exactly the same as having Guy prepare food for her, the spread looked heavenly. Avery's mouth started to water.

"I suppose I could settle for that."

Reaching forward, he tore off a piece of bread and scooped a little terrine on to it. "Try this." He offered it to her.

She took it daintily, closed her eyes, and chewed.

"Good."

Her eyes opened, and caught him watching her. "What are you staring at?"

"You're a pleasure to feed," he said simply.

"So feed me."

Guy's pulse leaped. But he took her at her word. Within minutes they'd demolished the contents of the basket.

"Just as well there wasn't more." Avery grinned at him and desire clawed at his gut in a way that was only too familiar. "A full stomach and warm sunshine would guarantee that I wouldn't move for a week."

He forgot about work. He forgot about the menu that Louis was waiting for him to finalize for the black-tie fundraiser for the coming Saturday night. His whole world consisted of Avery's sparkling blue eyes, and her wicked smiling mouth.

"There's still dessert," he murmured.

"Oh, I couldn't eat another thing."

"I think you'll find space for ripe black cherries." Guy shifted closer to her. The blue of her eyes deepened as she realized his intent.

"I love cherries."

They'd talked about cherries one evening at Baratin. She'd said she'd match the sweetness with a sauce of bitter chocolate. He'd argued that honey drizzled over would match better—he'd been teasing, his gleaming laughter-filled eyes had told her that much.

"There's a bottle of honey to complement it."

Her heart sank a little. No, he didn't remember. Or if he did, he didn't care enough to take her suggestions to heart. Avery felt unaccountably crushed.

"That will be nice," she said, subdued.

He took a glass bottle out the basket.

"But that's—" Her startled gaze shot to his.

"Chocolate. Bitter and dark." There was humor in his eyes. "I must have selected the wrong bottle." His brow wrinkled. "Silly me."

He hadn't forgotten!

That he'd remembered, taken the trouble to arrange something she'd said she liked was suddenly, overwhelmingly significant.

Avery helped herself to a cherry. "Definitely tastes better out here under blue skies. Sweet and juicy, all it needs is the chocolate."

His eyes darkened. "Very tasty."

"You haven't even tasted it yet."

"I don't even need the chocolate." He leaned forward and placed his lips against hers. His tongue swept across her lip. Slowly. Sensuously. Tasting the sweet juice of the cherry she'd eaten.

Her heart jolted, and began to race.

"Now I have," he whispered against her lips.

Avery pulled back. She had a feeling she was going to regret this later. For heaven's sake, he didn't even trust her. "Guy, where is this going?"

"All the way." His eyes were intense.

That wasn't what she'd meant. But she let it pass as he drew picked up the rug and drew her into the shadowy hollow under the willow. The rasp of his breath as she arched her back was enough for now, Avery told herself. When he was ready he would tell her why he shied away from intimacy.

It was up to her to convince him there was nothing to fear.

She put her arms around him and pulled him close. "Make love to me, Guy." *Love not sex.* Out here, feeling so close to Guy, she needed to make herself believe it was more than only sex. Even if she was deluding herself.

He didn't protest.

Instead he dropped his head and swirled his tongue through the valley between her breasts. Avery moaned. Her head tipped back, and the next moment she felt the stroke of his tongue against the arch of her throat.

She shuddered.

"Let's get this wet suit off." His voice was hoarse.

That gave her pause. "What if someone comes?"

"Oh, someone will come, all right," he growled.

Avery gave a shuddering laugh. "Don't joke."

"No joke." The eyes that burned into hers were scorching hot. "I promise."

For a moment her natural caution reared its head. Then passion took over. Under the canopy of the willow they were out of sight. Avery pushed all worries about interruptions, about tomorrow…next week, out of her head. Guy filled her vision, her world.

Lifting her hands she rested them on his shoulders. His skin was sleek and smooth under her touch, his muscles firm. She gloried in the warm hardness of him. He felt so vital, so alive.

"I'll hold you to that promise," she murmured as her hands traveled down and stopped at the barrier formed by the waistband of his board shorts. Languorously she tugged the laces undone. Slipping her hands inside the waistband she pushed them over his hips and down his legs.

By the time the wet bathing suit landed on the ground, he was hard and quivering. Avery sank down onto her knees, and heard him gasp as her mouth closed on him.

Seconds later he was tumbling her onto the rug, spreading her thighs. Touching her...stroking her with hands that shook. Until her body started to sing. Just when she feared she could take no more he slipped between her thighs and sank into her, filling her until she could think of nothing.

Except Guy.

Avery arched her back and gave a breathy moan of pleasure.

He lifted his head. "Okay?"

She nodded. "Oh, yes."

His lips curved. "I'm glad—for me, too."

She wanted to say that it could be even better. If he could only relax his guard, let her into his heart, and learn to trust her.

But she knew that if she voiced the intense thoughts his smile would vanish, he'd withdraw. Because the reality was that Guy didn't want a lasting relationship. Now was all that mattered to him. She was a fool to want more with a man who didn't even trust her.

So she bit her lip instead, closed her eyes, and focused on the connection they had.

Then he started to move and she forgot everything. Except the pure blinding silver pleasure of the moment.

Afterward they sat out on the sunny river bank and ate dessert.

The cherries and rich chocolate dipping sauce might as well have been stale bread and cold broth for all Guy cared. It tasted bland. Prosaic. It was Avery that he hungered for, her skin, her lips that he craved. Not food.

He couldn't take his eyes of her. She'd pulled a tank top on with the lime bikini bottoms. She looked so breathtakingly colorful, so alive. And she'd been so passionate, so giving… everything a man could ever desire.

Yet one part of him still hung back, knowing that she would never be what she promised.

There'd be other men. And in the end she would leave again. He had to steel himself. He couldn't afford not to keep a part of himself carefully in reserve.

"Guy—" she hesitated "—we need to talk."

"Let's enjoy the sunshine."

She fell silent. Then, "There's something I need to tell you."

No.

Whatever it was he didn't want to hear. "I don't need confessions." It came out more harshly than he'd intended.

He felt her grow stiff in his arms and he suppressed a sigh. Why couldn't she just be satisfied with what they had? With the joy of the moment? Why did women always have to complicate everything?

But he sensed this was important to her. That she needed to get whatever it was she wanted to talk about off her chest. Guy told himself he could take whatever it was. Hell, he'd already gotten over her fling with Jeff, hadn't he? He could get over whatever else she was about to reveal, too.

It wasn't as if he were emotionally invested in her.

They were lovers, not soul mates—he'd always scorned the very idea of those.

"Tell me," he said with a touch of weariness.

"Maybe now isn't a good time."

Typical. Guy stifled a burst of impatience. "Don't go all feminine on me. You can't start something then pull back."

"You're not making this easy."

He suppressed the urge to groan. They made fantastic love. All he wanted was to spend the afternoon lazing in the sunshine with Avery beside him. She had to go wreck the mood with her urge to make a confession he had no desire to hear. And she said he wasn't making it easy?

She drew a deep breath. "It's about that night with Jeff."

Heaven help him…this he most definitely did not want to hear about.

She must've read the reluctance on his face, because she said hurriedly, "That night, you need to know—"

"No. I don't need to know anything about that night," he interrupted. "It's over. Forgotten."

If he told himself that often enough he might start to believe it.

"It's not over," she said stubbornly. "It hangs between us all the time."

"Nothing hangs between us, as you put it."

Guy wanted to end this discussion. He hated the thought of her with Jeff, responding to his friend with the same glorious abandon she'd just responded to him with. He didn't even want to think about it, much less do a postmortem on the distasteful topic. Nothing would take away the pain of Jeff telling him what a wildcat she'd been in bed.

"Of course it does. I implied I'd slept with Jeff, when I hadn't."

He went still. She wanted him to believe she'd lied? "Why would you do such a thing?"

How the hell was he supposed to believe this when she'd just admitted to lying to him once already?

She glanced away. "Surely that's obvious?"

"Nothing is obvious." He rolled away from her and, propping his arms behind his head, gazed up through the bent branches of the willow to the fragmented pieces of bright blue sky beyond. He refused to feel relief…or hope. Jeff had told him she'd seduced him, and Avery had confirmed that. Now she was changing her story. The chances that Jeff had lied, too, were too remote to even consider. "Why don't you spell it out?"

"I was angry with you."

"With me?" Guy turned his head and stared at her incredulously. "What did I do?"

"You put your business ahead of me—just like you always do."

"Hold on a minute. Do you know how I worried about you? Waiting for you at Baratin—and you never arrived."

For a moment Avery caught a glimpse into the depths of hell. Her fury evaporated. That night in the spa he'd told her that he'd asked Jeff to arrange a cab for her and to let her know. Instead Jeff had decided to collect her himself. And she'd run. So why had Guy worried? "But Jeff told you I seduced him. Why should you worry about me?"

"He told me over two hours later. I came back to my apartment to see if by any chance you were there—even though you weren't answering your cell phone or the apartment phone—only to find a devastated Jeff."

"I left my cell phone behind on the sideboard in my hurry to escape."

"It wasn't in the apartment."

Avery searched for a logical explanation. "Then Jeff must've taken it."

"Every explanation you offer comes back to blaming Jeff."

Avery let the accusation go. "When did he tell you about the supposed seduction?"

"When I found him drunk as a skunk in my apartment. He was torn up with guilt for sleeping with my girlfriend."

"Who seduced him," she said with a snap of her teeth. Jeff had been very clever.

Guy's gaze bored into her. "He begged my forgiveness."

Another brilliant touch. "After he'd convinced you it wasn't the first time I'd tempted him." Oh, she could see how Jeff had played it. "He manipulated you."

He'd manipulated her, too. She'd never even paused to call Guy and check his story out. She'd been too outraged and hurt. So she'd simply cut her losses and run. Exactly as Jeff had probably intended.

Guy had deserved more.

Guy was shaking his head. "I don't think so. He was crying—it really cut him up. He blamed himself. He was even making statements that sounded dangerously suicidal."

More manipulation.

Yet how could she place all the blame on Guy for being taken in? She'd believed Jeff, too. Had it given her a convenient excuse to run? Deep in her heart she'd known that she and Guy would never last…he wasn't looking for a wife, a family. He'd told her, too often, how happy he was with his life just the way it was.

Taking in the shadows under his eyes, Avery decided he didn't look terribly happy now.

He looked strained…and tired.

She'd been so angry on the night of her birthday because he'd put work before her. She needed to try to get that frustration across to him.

"You told Jeff to get me a cab so I could meet you at Baratin." Even now it annoyed her that he hadn't bothered to leave his precious business and pick her up for their date. "At the time I thought you'd forgotten all about my birthday. Until Jeff arrived and told me you'd sent him to pick me up because you were too busy—"

"Wait a minute—"

Avery discovered she was shaking. "He made it clear he was supposed to be the appetizer for our dinner date—that he was the special surprise you'd promised me for a birthday I would never forget."

Guy straightened.

"What?"

The stormy expression on Guy's face only made her shake harder. He wanted her to bare her soul to him, while he watched her from behind slitted, shuttered eyes?

Sure thing.

Clearly he didn't believe her. She'd taken a risk telling him, and lost everything. In his eyes she was a gold digger, a slut, a liar. So what was she still doing here?

Avery stumbled unsteadily to her feet. "Take me back to the resort." His disbelief had withered the last bloom of hope. "I'll leave tomorrow."

It was all over.

She couldn't work with Guy anymore, couldn't bear to see him. There was too much love lost, too much hurt and heartbreak.

She'd find a way to explain to her uncle. At least the two presentations were over. She'd done Uncle Art proud….

"You can't—"

"I have to. I can't stay here." It was going to damage the professional reputation that she valued so highly to walk out in the middle of a contract. But she couldn't endure Guy's distrust any more.

Guy's hand closed around her elbow. "Avery, listen to me!"

She froze within his grasp.

The warmth of his fingers was at odds with the harshness of his tone. She glanced up.

"I'm listening."

"I never sent Jeff to have sex with you."

She started to laugh uncontrollably. She already knew that Jeff had lied to her. But there was a certain irony in saying, "I suppose you expect me to believe that? After all, Jeff told me, and you trust Jeff implicitly. Why shouldn't I?"

Guy's fingers tightened on her wrist and his skin stretched taut over his face.

"He lied."

"So you say. Did Jeff show you the bruises where I kicked him in the shin? He should've been limping, I can't believe you didn't notice."

"I didn't see him for a few days after he told me—" Guy paused "—that you'd begged him to make love to him. That it wasn't the first time."

"Now that is a lie." Avery lifted her chin. "You always believed Jeff. So it's pointless for me to deny it, isn't it?"

"What do you expect when you told me nothing about it at the time?"

"I called you—"

"After you'd already packed up and left."

"Because at the time I thought—" She broke off.

"Because you thought what?"

Because she'd believed Jeff.

She'd been put off balance by his turning up at Guy's apartment, knowing it was her birthday and that she was having dinner with Guy—information he could only have gotten from one person. Guy. Then there'd been the way he'd made himself at home accepting her offer of a drink, his presumption that she'd let him make love to her because Guy had gifted him to her.

A monstrous lie.

But she'd been too taken aback to question it. She hadn't trusted Guy....

"I thought that you were into sharing me with your friends—I didn't want that. Jeff was very convincing. He made it sound like it was the kind of stunt you two pulled all the time," she said, trying to justify it. "In the end I had to fight him off."

"Fight him off?" Darkness—doubt?—entered his eyes. "Jeff's not aggressive."

"You think I'm making this up?"

He ran a hand through his hair. "God, I don't know what to believe. I keep thinking you must've misunderstood Jeff—or overreacted to a joke he made."

"He'd been drinking. He wasn't joking. I had to kick him to let me go."

"You should've called me."

"I told you, I rushed out without my cell phone. I just wanted to get out," Avery confessed. "And frankly I was so mad at you. Right then you occupied the number one spot on my all-men-are-bastards list. Once I reached the airport I cooled down a little and rang you from a pay phone."

She'd needed him.

That's when he'd told her he'd leave her bags with the doorman and said, *It was fun while it lasted. Don't call me again. Ever.*

And cut the connection.

That had convinced her that he was angry with her for not fulfilling Jeff's drunken fantasies, and that Guy Jarrod was a total, hedonistic bastard. That she was well out of the relationship. To top it off, she'd had to catch a cab back to his apartment to retrieve her bags from a curious doorman. It had been the final straw in her humiliation.

Guy raked his hands through his hair. "Avery. I've been in business with Jeff for three years. I've never known him to hurt a fly."

"So you don't believe me," she said tonelessly.

It stung that he hadn't accepted her word. But she'd expected this. She could hardly whine about it. After all, her pride had caused her to make that ridiculous intimation that she'd slept with Jeff.

And she hadn't trusted Guy, either. She'd been so busy

thinking of herself as the victim, that she hadn't even realized she'd done Guy a disservice too.

They were both a pair of fools.

"I didn't say that I don't believe you. But I have to give him an opportunity to give me his side of the story." There was a hesitant note in his voice.

Was it possible that she was gaining ground?

"You didn't let me give my side when I called from the airport," she pointed out.

"Because I barely knew—"

"Because you barely knew me," she finished for him. "I was only the woman who'd spent two weeks in your bed." The woman who'd fallen in love with him. "What's that compared to male friendship?"

"Hey, wait a minute, this has nothing to do with sexism."

"Doesn't it? You think Jeff is less likely to lie to you?" Irrationally she ignored the fact that he had known Jeff for a lot longer than he'd known her. That there might be merit in his argument. But she wasn't in the mood to be reasonable right now. Her throat was tight with unshed tears. Damn Guy Jarrod. He was breaking her heart all over again.

"The point you're not getting is that Jeff didn't just walk out without a word and leave. *You* did."

The silence simmered after his outburst.

Guy clenched his fists and let out a hissing breath. "Look, I didn't intend to say that. I think we both need to calm down. I'll put the hamper in the SUV. Why don't you change out of that damp swimsuit?"

Ten

Avery ducked under the large willow tree and swapped her still-damp bikini bottoms for a panties and jeans, and started to untangle her hair and finger-comb it out.

Why had Guy been so wound up by the idea that she'd walked away from him? She'd never thought that would've caused any resentment at all. He'd made it more than clear that she wasn't an important fixture in his life.

Had she misunderstood his casual, carefree manner? Had she meant more to Guy than he revealed?

Avery put her bikini in her tote and hefted it onto her shoulder, then shook her towel out. But the actions were performed without thought. She couldn't get Guy's face out her mind.

Surely what she was imagining was insane? Guy had never cared for her—not in any way that mattered.

The snapping of a twig caused her head to turn.

"Guy?"

Instead of Guy she found herself looking into the furry black face and inquisitive eyes of a bear.

A very young bear.

A cub.

Oh, help! Where was Momma? Her towel falling from her numb fingers, Avery started to back up.

The bear started to sniff at the hedge on the far side of the willow. Leaves rustled on Avery's left. She whipped around in time to see a second large cub come gamboling into the green cave under the willow.

Damn.

Momma definitely wouldn't be far away.

Her pulse pounding, Avery eyed the trunk of the willow tree. It wouldn't be too difficult to pull herself up onto the lowest branch. Then she remembered the bartender in town saying that a bear had invaded the tree outside the courthouse.

Momma bear would probably have her butt before she reached the first branch.

The newcomer leapt on the smaller cub and they started to roll around on the thick mat of grass. Then the smaller cub rolled onto his feet and shambled over to her towel.

Get away, she willed.

He didn't heed her silent urgings. After sniffing it, he pawed it. The other cub joined in and before long they were playing tug of-war with Avery's towel.

Where was Momma?

A loud snort answered that question. The bottom fell out of Avery's stomach as both cubs paused and pricked their ears, turning their heads toward where the sound had come from. Yes, that's right. Good babies. Go find Momma. Then they turned their attention back to the bright yellow towel.

Damn. Damn. Damn.

Avery knew she didn't have long before Momma came

looking for her recalcitrant cubs. But her legs didn't seem to want to work, a result of the adrenaline rush that the cubs' arrival had brought.

Dry-mouthed, she swallowed, but the coppery taste of fear stayed on her tongue.

She took another step back and came up against a wall of flesh.

"Easy," Guy whispered in her ear. "Keep still."

Her legs, already weak, turned to liquid with relief at the sound of his voice. Avery leaned back, grateful for his presence, the feel of his chest solid against her shoulders.

"Where's the mother?"

"At the river bank. I saw her when I came back."

Thank goodness he had.

"She'll come looking for her cubs."

Even as she spoke the cubs tired of the game of tugging and clawing at her towel. Dropping it, the larger cub trotted through the willow fronds and then after a few seconds the smaller cub followed.

"Whew." Avery darted forward to pick up her towel, then linked her trembling fingers through Guy's. "I have never been so glad to hear your voice."

"You kept your head. Although I will admit I got a shock when I saw the bear knowing you were nearby. When I heard the cubs cavorting I grew more worried. Luckily I found you before their mother did. Look," Guy parted the fronds of willow, "there's the sow."

Avery took in the black bear, her brown muzzle snuffling at her cubs.

"She can smell your scent on her cubs from the towel."

"Thanks—that reassures me."

Guy chuckled softly. "I'm not going to chase her away. Let's leave them to their world."

Avery was only too ready to follow him through the hedge

at the rear of the willow and scramble up the slope to where the SUV was parked. Once safely inside she said, "Strange as it may seem, I don't think I would've missed that experience for the world."

"What? You weren't terrified?"

"Oh, I was terrified all right. But it was worth it."

Guy shot her a narrow-eyed look. "You know what? I may still get you up in that balloon after all."

The first thing Guy did on his return to the resort was to close himself up in the wood-paneled study that had been his father's and put a call through to Jeff Morse.

Vivienne, his partner's very efficient PA, promised to have Jeff call him back shortly. An hour later, Jeff hadn't called. So Guy tried again. By the third call, Vivienne sounded uncharacteristically flustered as she advised that Jeff had just left to go hunting for a couple of days on a property that was out of cell phone range.

Guy set the phone down, propped his elbows on the walnut desk and stared for a long time at his steepled fingers.

Finally he moved to the computer in the corner of the study and booted it up. Fifteen minutes later he was satisfied with the e-mail he'd drafted. He hit Send.

Notifying Jeff of his intention to dissolve their Go Green partnership would provoke a response.

The picnic beside the river changed something between them.

Guy didn't raise the confession Avery had made about Jeff. But every night they met for dinner at Chagall's, obstensibly to discuss work, and afterward Guy would escort her to her room, and here they would make love. Not sex. Silent, desperate love.

After the first night Guy had refused to leave and they'd

ended up sleeping in each other's arms. Even though the next morning Avery had complained that he would be missed on the family floor.

"I have my own suite, it's self-contained," Guy said. "Melissa prefers the peace of Willow Lodge. Erica's moved out into Christian's house. Trevor's living in town. And Blake probably spends more time at airports commuting between Aspen and New York than he does at Jarrod Ridge. We're hardly living in each other's pockets. Too often I'm down in the kitchens checking the produce coming in from the markets early in the morning. Trust me, no one's going to miss me if I don't come to breakfast in the family kitchen."

When Guy put it like that, her reservations sounded absurd.

"You should move in with me."

"I don't want to be seen emerging from the private elevator early each morning," she said stubbornly clinging to her convictions. "People…staff…will talk."

"Then I'll fire them."

Her eyes went wide.

"Hey, that's a joke—bad one, but still a joke."

But it did remind her of the kind of power a man like Guy Jarrod had. He did have the power to make decisions about people's lives.

Even hers.

Later that day Avery felt restless and found herself needing more space than the resort, crowded with the continuous bustle of the Food and Wine Gala, allowed.

A drive into Aspen accomplished that. Without any conscious volition, Avery found herself back at the gallery where Margaret Jarrod's work hung. The gallery owner greeted her, and she smiled politely back before walking to the alcove in the back of the gallery to stare at the riverscape, as though that might give her the answers she sought.

Clearly Guy must've grieved when his mother had died. He'd missed her. Yet he never spoke about her.

Speak to me, Avery implored the painting. Help me understand.

But the picture remained a swirl of angry color and eventually Avery sighed and took herself off for a cup of coffee at a sidewalk cafe. Half an hour later she returned to her hatchback and made her way back to the resort.

On the stretch of tarmac just before the right turn onto the bridge that crossed the Roaring Fork River, a red sports car swerved to pass an oncoming white van.

Avery suppressed the fierce urge to scream. Faced by the sports car blocking her vision, Avery gritted her teeth and swung the steering wheel hard to one side.

The car bumped across the verge and lurched to a bone-jolting stop in a roadside ditch. Avery was flung forward as the airbags activated.

The radio hummed country music. Beyond the window she glimpsed bits of a tilted world. Dirt and shrubs and blue sky. Closing her eyes Avery said a silent prayer of thanks. When she opened them, it was to find herself staring through the windshield into a pair of feminine eyes.

"Are you okay?" The young woman asked, pushing her dark hair off her face.

"I think so."

Avery unclipped her seatbelt and tried to open the door. It was jammed solid. A wild sense of panic filled her. She had to get out!

"The car is on its side. You'll have to climb out. Are you sure you should be moving? Maybe it would be better to wait for the paramedics?"

"Yes, I'm fine." Avery couldn't bear the thought of being

trapped. The opposite door swung open. Avery clambered over the gearstick and hoisted herself out.

"I thought we were both finished when that idiot overtook me so recklessly." The other woman's expression turned to concern. "You're bleeding. There's a graze on your forehead."

Avery touched a hand to her head. "I'm fine—but I'm not sure if the other driver will be if I ever lay my hands on his throat."

"I've called 911, help is on its way."

Oh, thank God. "You must be an angel," Avery said with relief. "He was driving like a maniac, I didn't think I was going to be able to avoid a crash." Reaction was starting to set in.

"I thought we were all dead."

The brunette was ashen, too.

So she wasn't the only one who'd been terrified out of her wits for those moments, Avery realized. Moving off the verge, she flinched as she put her weight on her left leg. She felt unexpectedly shaky. "I'm going to sit down," she announced.

"Try putting your head between your knees."

Avery bent forward.

"Shock. My name is Nancy, by the way. Can I call someone for you? The tow trucks will probably be arriving soon."

"Guy."

"Which guy?"

Avery raised her head and caught Nancy's troubled look. The woman thought she was in shock. "Guy Jarrod—he lives at Jarrod Ridge."

"Okay." Nancy's face cleared, and she pulled a cell phone out the front pocket of her jeans.

Closing her eyes, Avery was dimly conscious of Nancy

telling someone what had happened. She concentrated on trying to stop the shaking that seemed to consume her.

At the sound of a vehicle slowing, she looked up.

"The paramedics are here," said Nancy, rising to her feet.

While the paramedics—a young beanpole of a man and a plump, motherly woman—tended to Avery, she tipped her head up to Nancy.

"How can I ever thank you enough for stopping to help me?"

The young woman shrugged. "It was nothing. It could as easily have been me who ended up in a ditch. And I didn't even get that idiot's license plate number."

"Me, neither."

They shared a smile.

The shaking had stopped. "Thank you for staying with me."

There was the sound of several vehicles pulling up. "Oh, and here's the tow truck, they'll probably take your car to town," said Nancy.

"I'll have to inform the rental company of the damage to the car." Avery winced at the thought. That was a call she was not looking forward to making. At least there would be insurance to cover the mess.

"Looks like your Guy is here too. So I'll be off."

Avery started, She was tempted to beg Nancy to stay.

"Is that sore?" The young paramedic asked, prodding gently around her knee.

"No."

"Avery!"

She jerked her head up at the sound of that all-too-familiar male voice.

"You are hurt!"

Guy moved faster than Avery had ever seen.

"Don't worry," she said, "it's only a graze—it barely stings."

"But that ankle will need X-rays," said the motherly paramedic. "We'll take you to the hospital."

"I'm fine."

"I'll take her." Guy was grasping her hand. It gave Avery an unexpected sense of comfort, of being cared for.

She let him help her to her feet but as she put her weight on her foot, her ankle crumpled.

"Ow."

"Definitely to the hospital." Guy's tone brooked no argument.

Yet Avery tried. "I don't need to go to the hospital. I'm sure it's nothing terrible—ice and elevation and it will be fine by tomorrow."

Guy shook his head.

"Guy, I'm fine. If you absolutely insist I can go to the medical center at the resort."

"You'll need X-rays."

"Don't be such a pessimist." Avery tried to make light of it.

But Guy only put his arm around her waist and said, "Lean on me. The sooner you get treatment, the better."

"He's right, my dear," added the motherly paramedic. "And if the only way to get you there is to let him take you, then so be it. But I need you to sign here for me." She produced a clipboard with a form.

With them all ganging up on her, Avery quit arguing and signed.

Once Guy had her in the SUV the drive to town went quickly. At the hospital a receptionist handed Avery a further sheaf of forms to complete. Full of questions about personal details. Medications. Consent.

Whether she was pregnant.

Pregnant. The word jumped out at her. If only...

She hesitated, before dismissing the sudden, startling fear. She wasn't pregnant. The test she'd taken—twice—had confirmed that. Before she could have second thoughts, she signed the form and gave it back to the receptionist with a smile.

"How long is the wait?" Guy loomed over the desk, his posture far from comforting.

"Not too long." The receptionist gave him a polite smile. "There's a coffee machine, feel free to help yourself."

Avery limped away to the seating area.

Guy came up behind her. "Can I get you a hot drink?"

"I'm fine."

Instead of settling beside her, Guy started to pace.

More out of a desire to give Guy something to do, than from thirst, Avery said, "I wouldn't mind a bottle of water, I saw a kiosk when we came in."

"Right."

Guy was gone before she could say more.

The receptionist caught Avery's eye and said, "Good idea to keep him busy."

Avery laughed in agreement. "I've only twisted my ankle, but he's behaving like it's broken."

The woman clucked. "Some men fuss when they're worried."

Avery didn't set her right. Guy wouldn't possibly be concerned about something so minor.

He still hadn't returned by the time Avery was ushered into an examining room. The doctor had kind brown eyes that looked years younger than her cropped, gray hair suggested.

"You've hurt your ankle."

Avery nodded and told her what had happened. "Just one

thing," she tacked on, "why do you need to know whether I'm pregnant?"

"So that we can take the necessary steps to protect the baby. It's always better to be safe than sorry. Is it possible that you may be pregnant?"

"I can't rule it out."

The doctor made a note on her pad. "We'll get that checked out to give some certainty in case we need X-rays. For now, let me take a look at that ankle."

Avery slipped her shoes off. "I took an over-the-counter pregnancy test—it was negative." The sinking regret that had swamped her returned for an instant. Reason told her that she wasn't pregnant. If she were, she'd be almost three months along by now. Surely she wouldn't have missed the signs?

It was impossible.

Yet since the first time Guy had raised the possibility of her pregnancy the thought had lingered, haunting her, refusing to dissipate, playing on her mind, recalling the dreams of motherhood…a family.

Wishful thinking?

No, it had been nothing more than dreams. Dreams that didn't—could never—include Guy.

Determinedly Avery shook herself free of the reverie.

"How does this feel?" The doctor's touch was cool on her ankle.

"No pain."

"What about now?"

Avery flinched. "That's tender."

There were more questions, and afterward the doctor said, "There is some swelling. It's probably only a twist, but I'd like to x-ray it just in case."

"It must've happened while I was trying to get out of the vehicle." Nancy had wanted her to wait for the paramedics, but she hadn't been able to bear the idea of being trapped inside the crippled car.

"The X-rays will confirm whether there are any fractures, but first let's get a specimen and check for pregnancy. I may have to examine you, too." The doctor lifted the handset of the phone on the wall. "Let me call the nurse to show you where the bathroom is."

Eleven

"You were right to be concerned," The doctor said ten minutes later as she leaned forward on her stool and studied Avery. "You are pregnant. When was your last period?"

Avery's ears started to ring and a numbness filled her. Frantically she calculated in her head. "I should've started my period this past weekend." But she hadn't. More desperately, she continued, "But the test—"

"When did you take the test?"

The test had failed. Despite the claims on the package of ninety-nine percent accuracy. How typical. Struggling with the daze of disbelief that had enveloped her, Avery tried to concentrate. "About two weeks ago."

"Too early to have shown." The doctor sounded very certain.

Avery stared at her in surprise. "What do you mean, too early?"

"By my estimation you're only about three weeks pregnant."

"Three weeks?"

That meant it had probably happened that night in the hot tub. Oh, God, how unlucky. And how lucky, too. She'd wanted a child…Guy's child…now it had happened, against all odds.

And against Guy's will.

Joy withered and dismay set in.

"I know it must be a lot to take in," the doctor said kindly. "There are always adjustments to be made." Glancing down at the form on her desk, she continued, "I see you work at Jarrod Ridge. I'll give you a card for a local prenatal group. Here's a diet sheet with suggestions of what might cause discomfort—don't forget to take plenty of folic acid." With a smile, the doctor added, "Congratulations. After you've had the X-rays done, come back and we'll talk about what to do to make that ankle as comfortable as possible. Ice and as much rest as possible for starters."

"Won't the X-rays harm the baby?"

The doctor shook her head. "You'll be protected by a lead apron. It will form a cone right down to your ankles. Baby will be perfectly safe."

Avery staggered back into the reception area, still reeling with shock.

Guy sprang forward,

"What did the doctor say?"

"Uh—" she gazed into his alarmed eyes. *I'm pregnant.* Yeah, that would allay his fears. Instead she forced a smile. "A twisted ankle. Nothing major."

Nothing major?

How on earth was she supposed to break the news? Guy had never wanted a long-term relationship. He considered her capable of sleeping with his friend, his business partner.

Of flirting with every eligible male who came her way. If he thought she was capable of that kind of treachery, surely he would never believe this baby was his? Particularly when she wasn't even sure whether he believed her about Jeff. Oh, God, Jeff was his friend, someone who was part of his everyday life. She'd prefer to see Jeff in hell. How could she bear to tell Guy that he was her baby's father when that would mean giving a creep like Jeff entry into her life? And her baby's life.

It was all enough to make her feel ill.

And that sensation had nothing to do with morning sickness—although that would probably not take long to follow.

Guy was staring at her expectantly. He must've asked her a question.

"I need to ice it and keep my weight off it, the doctor said," Avery bubbled, hoping that her response wasn't too far off what he asked.

His brow creased in a frown. "The room you have has a flight of stairs in the corridor. You can't stay there. Now you'll have to move in with me."

"No!"

Panic set in.

She couldn't bear to stay with him given all the tension between them.

"Avery, I swear I'll protect you. Your business credibility will not be compromised. But you need to be realistic. If you're going to have your foot up to rest it, you should have someone around."

"I'll be fine."

His jaw firmed. "We'll see."

A nurse came forward. "Ms. Lancaster? Follow me."

Guy caught her fingers. "Where to next?"

Avery shook her fingers free. "I'll be back as soon as the X-rays are done."

A backward glance revealed Guy pacing in the reception area, the bottle of water she'd requested still clutched in his hand.

"About time you got here."

Gavin, the next oldest Jarrod after him and Blake, came loping across the tennis court swinging his racket. Guy had called his brother to let him know that Avery had met with an accident, and he would be late for the game that had become a weekly fixture since their father's funeral.

"How is Avery?" Gavin brushed his light brown hair back from a face tanned to a shade of gold by the August sun.

"She banged her ankle." Guy shrugged, reluctant to let on how anxious he'd been. He hated hospitals. And all the while that they'd been there he'd kept worrying that something was going to go wrong. It had started with that dratted confrontation with the bear by the river. Hell, he'd almost been expecting today's call.

He had to get a grip.

Because Avery wasn't going to die.

She'd hurt herself—it was far from fatal. He wasn't about to share his baseless fear with Gavin, even though Gavin—not Blake—had been closest to him growing up. His twin Blake had always been able to say exactly what his father wanted to hear, whereas anything that Guy had said or done had been subject to criticism. His father had dismissed his drawings as useless. And when he'd told his father he wanted to be a photographer when he grew up, his father had bellowed so much that Guy had terminated his membership with the school camera club.

"She'll need to rest," Gavin said.

"I know." Guy unzipped his bag and pulled out his tennis

shoes. "But she's such a stubborn little thing, I doubt she'll listen."

Gavin gave him a swift look. "Sounds like you know her pretty well."

Oh, hell. That's right, Avery hadn't wanted his family—anyone—to know about them. He was so bad at keeping secrets. Especially from his family.

"Uh, we've talked a bit over the past weeks."

"A bit?" Gavin started to grin. "I heard about drinks in the sky lounge, dinners at Chagall's…you were even spotted out in town one night."

"All work—we were talking about the menus and beverages." It sounded so damn righteous. So he looked down and fastened his laces and added, "Truly."

The snort Gavin gave told him his brother hadn't bought it.

"I suggested that she stay in one of the family suites until her ankle gets better, but she refuses."

Gavin raised an eyebrow. "Your suite, I suppose?"

Avery would have his head if she overheard this conversation.

"The woman is injured." Guy tried to look affronted as he picked up his racket and zipped the cover off. "She will need help. Get your imagination out of the gutter, Gavin."

After giving him a penetrating stare, his brother said, "Perhaps she could stay with Erica and Christian."

Guy considered it. "Avery might feel like she's a third wheel—those two are nesting…planning their wedding."

"What about if she stayed with Melissa at Willow Lodge?" Gavin suggested.

"Willow Lodge is the cabin farthest from the Manor. It would be too hard for Avery to manage."

"Too hard for Avery to manage—or too far from your

suite?" Gavin taunted as they walked to opposite ends of the court.

Guy didn't answer. This was exactly the kind of talk Avery wanted to avoid. At Willow Lodge she'd have some space, some privacy. He concentrated on his serve. Fault.

After a double fault, he collected the balls and said, "You know, you might be onto something there. Willow Lodge would be perfect. Avery might be happy with that idea."

"You better take care," Gavin called a few minutes later when Guy served another double fault that gave Gavin the game. "You're distracted. Looks like woman trouble to me."

Ignoring the comment, Guy handed two tennis balls to his brother as they switched ends. "You still climbing the walls with nothing to do?"

Gavin said, "It's been extremely frustrating. A month ago I was in Namibia designing a wall for the biggest dam in that desert country. Now all projects are on hold. I'm twiddling my thumbs. Sitting around, waiting for Dad's estate to be wound up is driving me nuts." Opening his gear bag he pulled two bottles of water from the depths and handed one to Guy.

Pausing to open the pop-up top, Guy considered his brother's problem. "The Food and Wine Gala might not be the kind of thing that spins your wheels, but there must be some challenge you can sink your teeth into."

"I'll have to find something. Otherwise I might explore that old mine we played in as children. Maybe I can strike gold."

Guy laughed then tipped his head back and took a long swallow from the water bottle. Way back in 1879 Aspen had been the destination for a silver rush. Among the miners had been Eli Jarrod, their great-great-great-grandfather.

"Come on!"

With a start Guy realized that his brother was waiting to

serve. After tossing the bottle into his unzipped gear bag, he jogged back onto the court. "Ready."

The next few minutes passed in a flurry of action, during which Guy conceded most of the points to his brother. He sneaked a look at his watch. What would Avery be doing now? She'd gone to Tranquility Spa for a massage after their return. Surely that would be over by now?

A ball whizzed past him.

"Great ace," he yelled, hoping flattery would distract his brother from his moment of inattention.

"Ace? My eye." Gavin was laughing as he crossed to the other side and lined up for the final serve of the match.

This time the delivery was indeed an ace. No doubt about it. Guy shook Gavin's hand over the net and took the ribbing about where his thoughts had been for the duration of the game.

"You must be in love, brother."

Guy chuckled loudly. "Me? Not going to happen. I was thinking about what to do to keep you busy. Can't have you going insane with boredom."

He shifted under the unerring focus of Gavin's gaze.

"I always thought that when you fell for a woman you would fall hard," Gavin said finally. "Looks like it has happened at last."

"Don't kid yourself," Guy growled.

"Who's kidding whom?"

Guy had a sinking feeling that despite his wide-eyed mock innocence Gavin might be right, that he was indeed teetering on the edge of the precipice yawning ahead of him.

The vision was not comforting.

* * *

Guy paused for a moment at the door of the premier spa room that Melissa had told him Avery was using.

Avery was sitting on a ledge in a long pool. Water lapped at the top of her bikini-clad breasts in little waves. It rushed over an angled sheet of granite into the pool, sluicing over Avery below. Guy knew from experience that the water was hot—but not as hot as the next waterfall along.

Below the lime green triangles of her bikini top, her hands were touching her tummy with long, slow strokes that he found incredibly arousing. She wore a dreamy expression he'd never seen before.

"What are you thinking about?"

At the sound of his voice Avery started. Her gaze shot to his…then away.

"Guy."

She didn't sound delighted by his presence.

A feeling of déjà vu crept over him as he stepped into the room and closed the door.

Avery gave him an uncertain smile.

"How are you feeling?" he asked coming closer.

Her face cleared a little, and she laced her fingers together. "A lot better, thank you. Joanie has magic hands and Melissa made sure she pampered me to death."

His face softened at the mention of his sister. "Melissa has always been the nurturer in the family. I've just organized for you to stay with her for the night."

"But I can't just descend on her!"

"Of course you can—she's looking forward to the company."

"I'll consider it." Avery sank deeper into the water and her nose tilted up into the air.

He started to grin. Was it possible that his little spitfire was mad at him for doing something for her own good? "It's already sorted out."

She glowered at him.

She was cute when she was mad, and he had a feeling she was going to be madder still. Guy pulled his shirt over his head in one, swift movement, revealing a broad, muscled chest.

"What are you doing?" Avery shrieked.

"Easing out my tired muscles." In two paces he'd reached the door, and locked it. Next he toed off his sneakers. When he shucked off his tennis shorts, Avery closed her eyes.

He slid in behind her and pulled her up against his naked body.

"Guy!"

He kissed her nape. The skin was warm and steamy, and her hair was swept up on top of her head. Irresistible. "What?"

"You shouldn't be in here!"

They'd done this—and more—before. Already his body was hardening at the memory. But this time he had no intention of making love to her. Although Avery didn't know that. This time he just wanted to hold her.

"Give me one reason why not?"

"We work together—I don't want anyone to know we're involved."

"I'm not going to make love to you. I came to see if you're all right." He put on his most innocent expression, but it made no difference—she couldn't see it at this angle.

"I'm fine. And I sure thought you were making love to me. Because you're kissing the wrong part of me better."

His husky laugh caused the soft bits of hair at her neck to dance. "I'll kiss whatever part you want me to." He blew lightly onto her neck and felt her quiver. So responsive.

He tightened his arms convulsively around her.

"Thank goodness you're safe."

The images that had flashed through his mind when a young woman had called to say that Avery had been involved in a car accident…

Guy shivered. He never wanted to re-live those excruciating moments.

The thirty seconds it had taken to get confirmation that Avery was alive were amongst the longest of his life. The piercing pain had been a thousand times worse than the two hours he'd spent waiting for her at Baratin the night of her birthday. Because now he knew what it felt like to lose her…

He'd spent forty-nine days without her.

After the past three weeks he was starting to feel like he never wanted to let her go.

Avery tilted her head back. "I'm a lot tougher than I look."

"My mother thought she was, too." The words came from nowhere. He hadn't even thought about Mom for days. He usually tried not to talk about her at all. The topic always led to grim silences. But suddenly he couldn't prevent himself saying, "She promised me and Blake that she would beat the cancer."

Turning over, Avery looked up at him, her eyes luminous. "I'm sure she wanted to more than anything in the world. A woman with five young children would not want to leave them."

"I was foolish enough to believe her, in the way a six-year-old does. I thought she'd get better." How could he explain the devastation that he'd felt returning from a night at a friend's home to discover that his mother had been taken into the hospital, that she'd passed away? "She refused to have chemotherapy, you know. She chose to die, to leave us all. How can a six-year-old ever be expected to understand that?"

Avery slid up and pressed a kiss against his lips. "You poor little boy."

Hell. He didn't feel very much like a little boy right now. Not with her lying breast to hip along his body, her legs tangling with his. He gave a groan. "Avery, I got in here to hold you, to comfort you, not to make love. But you're making it very hard."

A wicked sparkle lit her eyes and she moved her body against his. "Am I?"

The little witch.

Guy groaned again. "Have mercy...and don't move."

"Why not?"

He swallowed. "You might jolt your ankle."

"My ankle is already feeling a lot better."

But she shifted and slid onto the seat beside him. Guy wished she'd stayed where she was. Yet if she had, the temptation would've been too great to resist. Instead he placed an arm around her shoulders, marveling at the tenderness that welled up inside him, the contentment that merely holding her brought. It wasn't something he'd experienced before.

Placing his index finger under her chin he raised it, and sealed her mouth with his kiss. Guy let himself sink into her... into the soft femininity that was Avery. Sweet. Feminine. Unique.

His.

When the kiss was over, he stared down into her blue eyes, stunned by how she'd inveigled her way into every crevice of his life in such a short space of time.

She blinked, and the spell was broken.

"There's something I have to tell you." She sounded subdued.

Guy wanted to shout "No." He didn't want to hear anything

that might break this accord that lay like a golden thread between them, joining them in a way that was somehow special.

Yet he found himself saying, "What is it?" while he hoped furiously that there were no further revelations about Jeff, or anyone else in her life, to follow.

The deep breath that she took warned him that he wasn't going to like it. But what she did murmur knocked the guts out of him.

"What did you say?"

She shifted in his arms, and Guy realized he was gripping her uncomfortably. He instantly slackened his hold.

"I'm pregnant," she repeated more loudly, edging away from him.

"How?" His head spinning, he asked, "Forget that. Have you known all this time?"

She blinked. "What do you mean 'all this time'?"

"Since being at Jarrod Ridge."

"Are you asking if this is the reason I came to Jarrod Ridge?"

He hadn't quite thought that far ahead. Now he considered it. Was this why she'd come? Guy shifted in the hot water. Had it been nothing to do with her Uncle Art at all?

Maybe it was what his subconscious mind was asking.

"Yes." His tone was terser than he intended as he tried to process the information that Avery was going to have his baby.

She slowly shook her head, and he could've sworn that the divide between them grew—even though she didn't move. "I only discovered today at the hospital."

"You've had symptoms?" And she hadn't bothered to reveal anything to him by word or action? He felt unaccountably put out.

"Nothing obvious. In fact, you started me worrying when

you asked whether there'd been any repercussions after our time in New York. I hadn't even thought about it. I bought a test from the drugstore—"

"So you had a suspicion that you were pregnant." Guy found himself glaring through the water to the pale skin of her stomach just visible through the swirling water. He couldn't see any sign that made her look remotely pregnant. "Thanks for letting me in on the secret."

"Hey, hear me out." She turned her head so that he looked square into her face. Her skin was dewy from the steam, and her eyes had darkened. She'd never looked more beautiful. "The test was negative—I took it twice. I wasn't pregnant then—"

"But you're pregnant now? How does that work?" Guy's brows shot up. "That *is* what you're trying to tell me?"

"Yes!" She was breathing quickly, her breasts rising and falling. "That's exactly what I'm saying. And before you even think of accusing me of trying to fob off someone else's baby on you—"

"That never occurred to me," Guy said heatedly, forgetting all about her breasts at the accusation. "Whatever gave you the idea I'd think that?"

"Your reaction to seeing me with Matt?"

Well, she had him there. He couldn't precisely argue without revealing his gut-grinding jealousy before he'd discovered Matt was her cousin.

"Your idiocy over Todd." She raised an eyebrow. "Warning me away from Louis? Need I go on?"

Guy started to feel very foolish. "Are you sure you're pregnant? It could be a mistake."

"Stop clutching at straws, Guy. I'm probably pregnant."

"Probably pregnant?"

But she didn't laugh as he'd intended at his emphasis on the absurd way she'd put it.

"I *am* pregnant, Guy. I know it's the last thing you want in your life. So I have no expectations of you. You are free. But you need to know I'm going to keep this baby."

He stared at her. What did she expect him to say to that?

Of course he didn't want a child—he didn't even want a wife, or a partner, or a significant other. He was quite happy the way his life was.

But he wasn't ready to lose Avery from his life either. For days he'd been dreading the idea of her leaving. He was no longer free—nor did he wish to be.

It struck him that the baby would give him a great reason to keep her in his life, without having to define to himself—or to her—exactly what their relationship was.

"Avery—" under the water he placed a hand on her thigh "—this gives even more reason why you should move in with me. You're pregnant with my child. That's hardly the kind of thing you can hide for very long. It's bound to come out."

Her thigh tensed. "You mean we should set up home together?"

Home? He wriggled like a trout hooked by a particularly attractive lure. "I was thinking we should live together and see how things work out."

She put her hands over her face. "Guy, a baby is about as lasting an arrangement as anything can be. It brings responsibilities like motherhood…and fatherhood. You don't have to assume that responsibility if you don't want to. I absolve you."

She was deliberately misunderstanding him.

Guy gave a sigh to vent his frustration and increased the pressure of his hand to make sure she didn't try to bolt. "Dammit—" he hesitated "—it's hard to take in. I never wanted a family."

"That's why I told you I'm not expecting anything of you."

Her hand closed over his. "Please understand I'm not trying to trap you."

"I know that." His certainty surprised him. His outburst had been boorish—the situation they were in was as much his fault as hers. He'd acted recklessly that night in the hot tub, and they'd both reaped the consequences. "And it's no longer about what either of us want. I'm sure this is every bit as much a trap for you as for me. The last thing you must want is a baby—particularly as your work is going so well."

After the Food and Wine Gala was over Guy had no doubt she'd have more work offers than she could handle.

"Not at all. I've always wanted a family…and kids." That dreamy look was back on her face.

Guy's heart stood still.

Sliding his hand out from under hers, he wondered if this had been a trap he hadn't even suspected? Giving her a narrow stare, he said, "Did you deliberately not use protection?"

"No! I stopped taking the Pill when I went back to California. I'd sworn off men." She gave him a wry smile. "And contrary to popular belief, I didn't come to Jarrod Ridge expecting to have an affair."

Ouch.

Was this a trap? If it was, hadn't he deserved to be caught? He hadn't taken precautions that night in the spa, even though he'd taken great care every time since. But once was all it took…

Avery stood up in the water and said, "I'll be going back to California in four days. There's no point in my moving in with you and telling the world that your mistress is pregnant with your baby."

Before he could temper his reaction, Guy burst out, "That's insulting to us both. You wouldn't be my mistress."

"Scared you couldn't afford me?"

Beads of water streamed over her curves…curves that

Guy knew intimately. But Avery was so much more than a sexy body.

He tore his gaze away. "Don't demean yourself! You're far too proper, with too much sense of your self-worth, to ever have accepted such an inequitable relationship—and I have too much respect for you to suggest it." Avery was far too independent to be any man's mistress. Although Guy was sure there were men who would've loved to have decorated her with diamonds and paid for her upkeep. She was smart, sexy and spirited. What more could any man want?

She looked stunned by his heated defense of her. What could he say? It had startled him, too. He justified it by adding, "My dad would've torn a strip off any of his boys for making a decent woman such an offer. He always said that honor was part of the Jarrod name."

Avery took two towels off a shelf, arranged one at the edge of the pool and sat down.

"A bit of a double standard, hmm? He must've kept a mistress, otherwise there would be no Erica."

"He didn't keep a mistress—not while my mother was alive." Guy glared at her for even suggesting that. Then he conceded, "But he did seduce another man's wife. Not much honor in that, I have to agree." Which was only one of the reasons he'd so resented Erica's existence. It went to prove that his father's high standards were nothing more than hypocrisy.

"Maybe he was lonely," suggested Avery.

"Lonely?" He shook his head. "That's stupid. He had a family—maybe we were farflung, but we were his children. He had Jarrod Ridge…the business empire he always wanted." Had it not been enough? Was Avery right? Had his father been lonely? Guilt pierced him. He shoved it aside, and focused on the woman who had turned his world upside down.

Leaning forward, Avery started to pat herself dry with the

second towel. "I think it would be far better for me to stay with Melissa as you've arranged, and for no one to be any the wiser about my baby."

Her baby? What about his rights? The surge of primal possessiveness took him aback. If Avery was planning to deny him access to his own child she was in for a surprise.

But it wasn't worth fighting now. They both needed time to absorb that they were going to be parents.

Finally he sighed and pushed his damp hair out of his eyes. "If you'd rather stay with Melissa, I'll take you to Willow Lodge."

Twelve

Willow Lodge oozed mellow serenity.

It was set away from the main resort complex, in a spot sheltered from the winds. Inside, the walls and floors were crafted from wood the color of honey and dramatic picture windows looked out over the willows for which the lodge was named. The fragrance of lavender and beeswax lingered in the air, and Avery found herself instantly unwinding.

And Melissa did everything to make her feel comfortable.

"Treat Willow Lodge like your home," Guy's sister said.

Avery took Melissa at her word. After sleeping under a down comforter and having a leisurely breakfast, Avery propped her leg up on a footrest in front of a window overlooking the willows and showing glimpses of the river beyond.

A constant trickle of visitors kept her entertained. Guy

was the first to arrive. Shortly after Melissa departed for Tranquility Spa, he came through the back door.

"How's the ankle?"

"Much better." Avery turned her head. Guy wore dark trousers and a black-on-white striped long-sleeved shirt with elegant European panache. The years he'd spent in France showed. She forced herself to stop gawking at the man like a lovelorn teenager.

He came closer and his breath was warm on the top of her leg as he leaned down. "No sign of swelling."

"Only a little bruising." With her fingertips Avery found the tender spot.

"It will go all the colors of the rainbow before it fades."

Avery groaned. "I hope not." He was so close that she could detect the subtle green notes of moss and musk in his aftershave. "I'm keeping it iced. It's helping—even though it's freezing."

"Good."

Avery wrinkled her nose at him. "You wouldn't be saying that if you were the one wearing an ice pack."

He hunkered down beside her, and put his hand on her ankle. "Probably not."

A delicious warmth cruised through her at his touch. Avery had thought her ankle too numbed by cold to respond to stimulus.

Not so.

When he started to move his fingers in little circular strokes her breath hooked in the back of her throat. His hand stroked up her calf, across the back of her knees, and tantalizing shivers followed. The taunting fingers stopped just below the hemline of her fitted dress, and she knew if she tried to protest her voice would be nothing more than a thin thread of sound. Then Guy would know precisely how much he was rattling her composure.

She glanced away, only to be transfixed by the sight of his long, square-tipped fingers caressing her flesh.

She inhaled a deep, steadying breath, and his heady male scent filled her senses.

How could one man have such an impact on her?

Only him.

Ever.

She feared it would only be Guy for her, all her life. And now she was pregnant with the baby he didn't want. It was over. He'd made it crystal clear he didn't want a wife… children…a family.

On Monday she was returning to El Dorado, to her family. Undoubtedly Guy would be amiable, offer support; Christian would be asked to negotiate the terms of any agreement, which she would insist on being kept confidential. Perhaps Guy would even offer to do his duty and see the child on the odd occasion. But Avery fostered no illusions that Guy would want to be actively involved with his child…or with her. She'd likely have more contact with Christian than with Guy.

At least she would have his baby….

She glanced up into his eyes. And stilled. There was an emotion she'd never seen exposed. A mix of tenderness and desire. Or something else?

Slowly he removed his hand from her leg. "I better get going. Otherwise I might not get to work today—and with the charity auction fundraiser tomorrow night, there's a lot to do."

Avery's heart skipped a beat.

For what seemed like a lifetime their eyes held. Then he leaned forward and kissed her. It wasn't like any of the kisses they'd shared before. It was gentle, tender, with the promise of passion in the way his lips moved on hers. And it left her yearning for more.

Then he pulled away and rose to his feet. "I'll be back later. Take care of yourself."

It was only as he walked away that Avery realized that despite his concern for her, he'd never once mentioned their baby….

After Guy had left, Erica dropped off a pile of magazines, and Avery discovered that they both shared a passion for collecting recipes and baking.

"Christian has a meeting in town tonight, so I'll come by with some ingredients to bake an apple pie," Erica promised.

Avery agreed in a rush. Guy had said he would return. The more people around to act as a buffer, the better. Guy clearly had no intention of talking about the baby, and nor did she. It would only cause tension and misery between them.

Erica had only just departed when Gavin and Trevor trooped in to see how Avery was getting along.

She was rather touched by the concern the Jarrods were showing her.

Late that afternoon Guy returned with food he'd had Louis rustle up in the kitchens at Chagall's. So by the time Melissa came home from the spa, the table was laid and candles lit, giving the honey tones of the lodge a cozy warmth.

"I seem to have taken over your home," Avery told Melissa apologetically.

"I don't mind." Melissa smiled at her. "It's nice to have company."

"But you've always said you wanted peace," Guy protested. "If you're lonely, you should come and stay in one of the family suites at Manor Lodge. In fact, there are two spare ones right now."

"I'm not lonely—and having Avery as company is different from living with you guys." Rolling her eyes, Melissa said to

Avery, "Believe me, sometimes a girl needs a break from her brothers. It was a pleasant surprise to discover I had a sister when Christian revealed Erica to us."

Avery slid her gaze to Guy to see how he was reacting to Melissa's revelation. But she detected none of the resentment she'd half expected.

"So that's a roundabout way of saying you're welcome to stay for as long as you like," Melissa smiled at Avery, "but my brothers are not."

Guy howled in protest.

Avery started to giggle. "Hey, I know exactly what Melissa means."

More laughter bubbled up in her throat as Guy glared at her.

"Traitor!"

"I was two when my parents died. I was lucky enough to be taken in by my aunt and uncle and I grew up with my cousins—four boys. Believe me, I always wanted a sister, too."

"Hey, now you're both ganging up on me."

"Wait until Erica arrives, you'll be outnumbered three to one," said Melissa with sisterly satisfaction.

Guy gave her an evil grin. "I'll have to call in reinforcements."

"No!" Avery and Melissa chorused. They glanced at each other and started to laugh.

When Erica walked in, she paused in the doorway. "Sounds like a festive dinner."

"Avery mentioned you were coming to bake a pie. There's more than enough food, so join us for dinner."

"That sounds like a great idea."

But Avery wondered if she was the only one to detect Erica's hesitation. Her hand touched her tummy. These people were her baby's family...she would've loved her baby to have grown up among them.

If only things could've been different. Not going to happen. Even though she'd needed Erica and Melissa present to stop the awkwardness between her and Guy, she was a little irritated that he'd made no attempt to corner her and discuss the baby.

It only underlined the fact that this was no romantic daydream; this was real life and sometimes it didn't work out quite as planned.

Guy had hoped for time alone with Avery.

The shock and terror that had followed her announcement that they were expecting a baby had started to wear off. Perhaps it was for the best that their talk didn't happen tonight. Avery deserved time to recover from the accident, and he could do with more time to get his head around the idea of the baby so that he could decide how he was going to handle the problem.

After they'd finished dinner, Guy found himself slouching on a barstool in the kitchen watching as the three women worked around the preparation island in perfect harmony. His sister, the half sister whom he'd treated with extreme wariness until very recently...and Avery.

Guy couldn't quite decide how best to describe his relationship with Avery.

He frowned as he watched her kneading the dough for the apple pie, her small hands moving with sensuous grace. Melissa had cut the apples into elegant slices and at Avery's insistence she settled down on the kitchen stool beside Guy and started to rub the small of her back.

"Did you hurt your back at work?" he asked.

"I'm not sure what I've done. It's aching a little."

For a split second the image of his mother rubbing her back in a similar fashion flashed through his mind.

"What is it?"

"Nothing." Then Guy shook his head to clear the image, and said more truthfully. "Actually, for a moment you reminded me of Mom doing that. I think she used to rub her back as well."

"How old were you when your mom died?" asked Erica from the other side of the kitchen island.

"Six."

Guy hadn't been there when she'd died. He'd been sleeping over at a friend's home. For years he'd been convinced if he'd been home she might not have died. It was his fault.

Blake had gotten to say goodbye. So had Gavin and Trevor and his father. Even Melissa, though she was only two at the time.

Guy had pretended he was fine, and retreated behind a happy-go-lucky facade that everyone except him accepted as the real Guy. He'd resolved never to give another human that much power over his life.

The only sound that broke the silence was the slap of the rolling pin on dough as Avery rolled it out.

Erica was sprinkling cinnamon over the apple slices. "I've heard plenty about your dad but not that much about your mom." Giving him and Melissa a swift glance, she added, "I don't mean to be nosy, but I've wondered, and you are my family now."

Melissa gave a sigh. "Dad changed after Mom died. He was very upset by her death, so we avoided talking about Mom at all."

"How sad!" Avery stopped rolling. "I never realized how lucky I was. My uncle told me all about what my mom had been like growing up. And both my aunt and uncle regularly pulled out the photo album and showed me photos of my parents' wedding, of my first birthday party. I always knew who they were."

"Guy used to stare at Mom's paintings."

Melissa clambered off the seat and started to cut the left over pastry into strips, while Avery pressed the dough into a baking tin. Erica carefully arranged the apple slices on top of the dough.

"He used to say they made him remember Mom, what colors she liked and how she smelled," Melissa continued after putting the pie in the pre-heated oven, "but Dad sold all the pictures—he didn't want anything to remind him of Mom. We've since managed to buy some back."

"Dad also got rid of the camera he and Mom had given me for my sixth birthday."

Melissa looked horrified. "I never knew that."

He didn't look at Erica…or Avery. "I used to say I wanted to take photos like Mom's paintings when I grew up. I suppose it was too painful for him to contemplate. Later I bought my own camera and joined the school's camera club."

"I remember that," said Melissa. "You wanted to be a photographer."

"But Dad wanted me to do a business degree. Like Blake." Guy shrugged. "Eventually we compromised. I did the business degree, but only after he agreed to let me go to culinary school."

"How could he do that?" Erica protested.

"Easily. He was Don Jarrod, he was used to imposing his will on everyone around him."

All three women had fallen silent, their eyes focused on him with varying degrees of…pity.

Guy forced an easy smile. "It was a long time ago. At least I got to do something that I loved. Something creative and satisfying, yet still lucrative."

"But you never forgot your mom," said Erica.

"No, I didn't, but it took a long time for me to stop resenting her for leaving us," he admitted in a rush of honesty. "Losing her wrecked Dad's life. I didn't like the kind of man Dad became after Mom died."

"How did he change?" Avery asked in a tentative voice. She'd propped her elbows on the island and her chin on her hands.

Guy shrugged. "None of us could do anything right."

"He had huge expectations of us all and wanted us to stay in the business doing what we were told," added Melissa, shaking out her blond hair. "Just like Guy said."

"And he let you go to France?" Avery's voice was filled with disbelief.

"He tried to stop me. He'd planned for me to stay closer. I won that battle." Even all these years later Guy could remember the satisfaction he'd gained in that moment.

"Guy wasn't the only one who left. Blake went to New York and I escaped to Los Angeles where I ran an ultra fashionable spa," Melissa added from where she'd perched herself back on the stool beside him. "And once Gavin finished university, he worked all over the globe, as far from home as possible. Only Trevor stayed in Aspen—yet even he wouldn't work for Dad at Jarrod Ridge."

"So Don Jarrod's empire was in danger of crumbling." Erica said, her hands busy as she wiped the surface of the island clean. "But he had the last say from beyond the grave, and forced you all to come back and work together if you wanted anything of the estate—"

"Don't forget his will also introduced you into the family," interjected Melissa. "You also stand to inherit a share of his empire."

Erica put the cloth in the sink and pulled a face. "Much to everyone's dismay."

"Not mine," said Melissa quickly. "I told you I always wanted a sister. You're part of the family now."

There was a silence.

Avery was looking at Guy expectantly. What did she expect him to say? That he wanted another sister? That he was glad to discover Erica's existence?

Hell, no. It only proved that his father had not been as inconsolable as Guy had foolishly believed all his life. So much for his resolve never to love a woman as faithfully as his father had loved his mother because he didn't want to risk the same heartbreak. He'd never been the kind of man who dug too deep into feelings, and he wasn't about to start now. It hurt too dammed much, revealed too much of what was missing in his life.

Except he couldn't for the life of him think of a flippant comment to make.

He turned away only to have Erica raise a questioning eyebrow at him from the other side of the kitchen, then glance meaningfully toward Avery. She was matchmaking! Erica had suspected his interest in Avery on the night of the oyster-and-champagne cocktail party, and it had become a certainty, he could read it on her face. Yet instead of irritation, Guy experienced a sudden unexpected bond with his half sister. And couldn't stop himself from winking at her.

Instantly Erica winked back.

"Okay, maybe it won't be so bad having another female in the family," said Guy with feigned reluctance.

"Good to know you feel that way." The sparkle in Erica's eyes outshone the radiance of the diamond solitaire on her ring finger.

Without intending to, Guy found himself seeking out Avery, and the approval in her sweet smile caused warmth to pool deep in his chest. For the first time since he'd come back to Jarrod Ridge he felt some degree of peace.

He had to remind himself that he wasn't the kind of man who indulged in emotion and soul-searching.

"The timer just went off," he said. "Which one of you three is going to cut me the first slice?"

Wearing her dressiest outfit the following night, a gold satin Versace dress that had been a gift from her aunt and uncle for her twenty-fifth birthday, Avery arrived early at the ballroom—more out of habit than anything else. She'd taken care with her makeup, and barely limped in the gold ballet flats she wore.

Camera crews were setting up for a segment that was to be filmed for a television show.

Guy was nowhere to be seen, and Avery rather suspected he was caught up in the kitchens overseeing the chefs, making sure that every detail was perfect. She was learning that the laid-back, carefree persona he cultivated concealed a far more complex, intense man. A perfectionist.

The wine selections had already been made—a collaboration between herself, Guy and Louis—and Avery was pleased with how well they complemented the dishes. Guy had been pleased, too.

She had done the job Uncle Art had wanted her to do. She would be leaving with her pride intact. Her heart was a different matter. There would be a large chunk left behind at Jarrod Ridge.

But she'd have Guy's baby to fill the hole.

Erica and a woman Avery had never seen before were fiddling with the flower arrangements.

"The flowers look beautiful," Avery told Guy's half sister. She smiled, and for the first time Avery saw a hint of Guy in her features. Her heart tugged. Would their baby have that look, too?

"Don't they?" Erica introduced Avery to the woman

standing beside her, a local florist, who was overjoyed to
have been given the job for the fundraiser.

"I only opened my shop three months ago, this is an
amazing break for my business."

"Avery is right, the arrangements do look beautiful. I'm
sure you'll get a lot of business." Undetected, Guy had come
up behind them. "Erica said from the start that you are very
artistic."

"Christian and I will be among those customers—for our
wedding. And heaven knows I'm not easily impressed." But
Erica looked delighted with Guy's praise. "I'm so glad we're
supporting local businesses."

"It was a great initiative."

Avery saw the glances Guy and Erica exchanged. There
was understanding…and fondness. She couldn't help feeling
pleased for Guy. The discovery of Erica's existence had been
a shock—but both of them had gained so much.

The ballroom started to fill.

By the silver flashes of light Avery gathered that the
beautiful group moving to one of the tables at the foot of the
stage must be movie stars.

Gavin and Trevor came over to join them, both tanned and
athletically built, with an appealing surf-and-sun openness
that made them look so similar. Avery looked from one to
the other, then to Blake and Guy. All four brothers were clad
in tuxedos and looked devastatingly handsome. But only one
held her heart….

"You know," she announced, "Gavin and Trevor should
be twins. They look far more alike."

Erica was the first to agree. "Funny, I had a similar thought
when I first arrived in Aspen."

"Let's go settle down at our table," Guy murmured to
Avery.

The siblings had divided themselves among different

tables, to spread the effect of having hosts throughout the ballroom. Avery hadn't inspected the final table lists, but it made sense for her to sit with Guy. After all, they were working together, and it would be downright weird if she objected.

And her only reason to object was one she didn't want made public: she loved a man who didn't love her, and she was expecting his baby.

He rested his hand under her elbow, and the contact sent a shiver of awareness through Avery. Oh, heavens, would this wretched wanting ever stop?

It grew worse when she discovered that she had been seated beside him. His thigh brushed hers as he sat down, and she was conscious of his dinner-jacketed arm beside her bare arm. She shifted a little away—the seat on her other side was the only one at the table not yet occupied. To her surprise she found a familiar face on the other side of the empty seat.

It broke the ice.

"Nancy!" She turned her head. "Guy, this is Nancy who rescued me…and called you." When the excitement settled, Nancy introduced the older couple beside her as her parents.

"We've been coming to this event for years," said Nancy's mother. "But this is only the second time Nancy's been with us."

"I've been working in Boston." Nancy rested her fingers on her mother's arm. "But I decided I missed home. So I came back to Aspen."

"I'm back after years, too—" At the arrival of the white-jacketed waiter, Guy broke off.

Avery chose a spinach-and-bacon salad as a starter, while Guy had wild mushrooms. The wines she'd selected worked well as an accompaniment and she couldn't stop herself from giving Guy a triumphant smile as he kissed his fingertips in appreciation.

He leaned toward her. "We make a good team."

"Glad you've got confidence in me."

"I have every confidence in you."

"You didn't to start with." She tossed her head and gave him a mischievous smile. "Are you ready to eat your words?"

Then she froze.

Beyond Guy a man was wending his way through the tables, a man she'd hoped never to see again. Avery whispered, "What's he doing here?"

A desperate look around showed that the only empty seat was the one right beside her.

Guy glanced up as the newcomer stopped beside their table, and cursed.

Thirteen

"What are you doing here, Jeff?" Guy demanded.

Jeff stuck his hands in his pockets and swaggered forward. "Already forgotten that you ordered me to come?"

Avery gasped.

Guy placed a steadying hand on Avery's arm and felt her tremble.

"I arranged our meeting for Monday afternoon—not tonight." A fierce emotion filled Guy. Jeff had come to cause trouble. Guy didn't doubt it.

Jeff had tried to pressure her to sleep with him, and Guy no longer had any choice but to break his partnership with Jeff, and walk away from the years of friendship they'd shared.

He believed Avery trusted that she'd told him the truth.

Avery came first.

Stunned, Guy looked at her. He took in the doll-like features, the blue eyes, the tendrils of blond hair that had escaped her upswept hairstyle. Why had he never realized how important she'd become to him?

Because he hadn't wanted any commitment.

Hadn't wanted the pain—the loss and loneliness—it might bring. Yet when Avery departed for California there would be a chasm in his heart that no one else would be able to fill.

The empty feeling had a name. Grief. He was already missing Avery. But this was different to his father's experience. His father hadn't had a choice in losing his Mom.

He did.

And he wasn't going to let Avery go.

Or the baby.

They were his…and he was going to keep them both safe. In any way he could. It was about far more than sex, about sating his senses with her. It was about waking with her beside him in the morning, sharing a joke with her. Simply knowing she was in the same room as him brought him joy. That could only be love.

He loved her.

He narrowed his gaze on his business partner.

Jeff glared back.

"You shouldn't have come tonight, Jeff," he said quietly. "I would've listened to your side of the story on Monday."

Avery clambered to her feet. "Excuse me, I need the bathroom."

Guy gave her a few seconds to get a head start. Then turning to Jeff, he said, "Maybe you're right. Let's talk now and finish it. Come."

Without a second look, Guy rose to his feet leaving his erstwhile friend to follow.

Avery was standing in the pre-function lobby off the ballroom. In the light of the chandeliers overhead, Guy could see that her face was pinched with strain. Placing his hand around Jeff's arm, Guy marched Jeff over to where she stood.

Her blue eyes went wide.

"Jeff, first, I think you owe Avery an apology," Guy said as they reached her.

Avery's lips parted in astonishment.

"I have nothing to apologize for," Jeff blustered. "She got what she was asking for."

Avery started to object, but Guy was too quick. He stepped forward until he stood nose to nose with his business partner. "Then why have you all but disappeared off the face of the earth since I tried to call you to confront you with what Avery told me? Why did it take an e-mail from me saying that our business partnership was over before you had Vivienne contact me to set up a meeting for Monday?"

Beside him, Avery gasped.

"She lied to you," said Jeff heatedly.

"I haven't even told you what she accused you of, so how can you know that she lied?" Guy asked gently.

Jeff pulled a handkerchief from his pocket and wiped the beads of sweat that had popped out over his forehead.

"You're not going to let a little bitch like her ruin what we've built up together?"

"Watch yourself!" Guy's tone was as dangerous as a lash. "And she didn't ruin anything. You did that all by yourself."

"You don't really mean to dissolve our partnership." The bluster had evaporated.

Avery's hand touched his sleeve. "Guy, you don't have to—"

"You don't need her." Jeff spoke right over Avery. "Surely you don't intend to be ruled by a piece of—"

"Don't say it." Even Jeff knew better than to argue with the lethal softness.

Guy rested his hand on Avery's waist and drew her close.

"We're both waiting for your apology, Jeff."

Jeff looked from Avery to Guy and his shoulders sagged. "I'm sorry."

Avery tipped her head up. "He told you he didn't—"

"No," Guy cut across Avery's words. "He didn't have to. I know you told me the truth when you said that he arrived at my apartment pretending that I'd asked him to pick you up, and fed you a pack of lies. You need to believe that I never sent Jeff to you as a birthday gift. I had something else planned."

A flicker of curiosity lit her eyes, and she opened her mouth to say something. But Jeff spoke first, "I'd been drinking. Sometimes I do really stupid things when I drink."

Guy remembered that years ago when he'd first met Jeff he'd sometimes gotten into sticky situations at parties. It had stopped soon after. He'd thought Jeff had simply grown up. He'd never suspected that Jeff had a problem.

"But why lie to me?"

"I made a move on Avery, and I knew that if she told you, you would get rid of your share in Go Green. I never intended for that to happen."

Guy gave a laugh of disbelief. His fingers itched to yank Jeff by the collar and shake him like a dog. Avery would not appreciate such violence. "That's it?" he asked. "That's all you can come up with?"

"I'm sorry." Jeff seemed to shrink still further. "Give me another chance. You can't end our partnership. I'll resume the counseling I gave up a few years ago."

"I'm glad to hear that, Jeff," said Avery. "You need help."

"Our business relationship is over," said Guy.

Jeff looked utterly miserable. "You don't need to dissolve the partnership—I'll agree to it. I'll sell out my share."

"That's certainly an option for us to discuss Monday afternoon. But I can't talk now, I have some things I need to say to Avery first."

"I don't think I should come back into the ballroom—I've lost my appetite. I'll find a hotel in town."

"Just stay out of the resort bars," Guy said.

"Here," Jeff passed him an envelope. "It's a contribution to the fundraiser."

Guy nodded. The friendship he'd shared for years with Jeff would never recover from his deception but the man faced a tough road to rehabilitation. Guy had stared down enough of his own demons since his father's death, to know he wouldn't want to be in Jeff's shoes. And, if he played his cards right, he'd get to keep Avery. He could afford to be generous. "Thank you. I'll see you Monday, we'll deal with Go Green then."

Jeff shook the hand he'd offered. "I'll understand if you don't invite me to the wedding."

"There isn't going to be a wedding—so you won't miss anything." Avery said from beside him, then walked away.

A sense of helplessness filled Guy. What the hell was he supposed to do now?

There wouldn't be a wedding—they both knew that. Avery had never expected it—hell, she'd even told him that.

Avery settled herself down in the seat that had been intended for Jeff, so that the chair she'd been sitting on before created a no-man's-land between her seat and Guy's. She needed that dividing space right now.

Pushing her untouched plate away, she turned to Nancy and started to chatter about the coming ski season.

Inside she was seething.

How dare Guy tell Jeff that he loved her? Pretending he'd never doubted her, and that he'd accepted her word? Then without missing a beat, shaking the man's hand? She'd half expected him to slap Jeff jovially on the back.

Men. Avery had stifled the urge to yell at Guy like a fishwife. To be honest, she'd wanted him to floor Jeff.

"Avery, we need to talk."

She'd been so engrossed in her murderous thoughts she hadn't heard him come up behind her. To buy herself time before responding, she leaned sideways and reached for her half-full wine glass and took a long sip of the apple juice it contained to fortify her for the "talk" he wanted.

He slid into the vacant seat beside her, the seat she'd deliberately left open. Putting his arm around on the chair back behind her, he leaned forward.

"I wish I could've spared you that unpleasantness."

Before she could respond Erica was beside them. "Sorry to interrupt…Guy you should be up on the stage. The bidding is about to begin. Have you forgotten you pledged to prepare a meal for two?"

He turned his head to his half sister. "Give me one minute."

"There isn't time," Erica protested. "Not now."

Guy raked his hand through his hair and gave an impatient sigh. "Okay." The blowtorch force of his gaze landed on Avery. "And don't even think of running out on me again. Do you understand?"

She nodded, still furious, but glad that she'd been spared a public confrontation.

Guy followed Erica onto the stage.

Avery still couldn't believe Guy had shaken that jerk's hand. She was glad he was gone.

The first item to be auctioned off was a case of French

red that went for a staggering sum of money. A weekend in one of the private, fully staffed, Jarrod Ridge lodges with a balloon ride and other trimmings went next.

Guy was up a few minutes later.

Back in New York Guy had promised to prepare her a feast in person. It had never come to pass. And now it never would. But a couple of complete strangers would enjoy his ministrations.

Gathering up her bag, Avery said goodbye to Nancy and her parents, and pushed her chair back. Skirting the edge of the ballroom she left the glamorous event.

She couldn't bear to watch.

The Sky Lounge was deserted.

For the baby's sake, Avery ordered a cup of hot chocolate rather than coffee or tea and retreated to a high-backed armchair in the corner by the floor-to-ceiling window. Kicking the ballet flats off, she tucked her feet beneath her, taking care not to put too much weight on her ankle, and stared out through the glass at the pinpricks of lights that twinkled in the darkness outside.

The day after tomorrow she would be gone.

She placed a hand on her stomach.

"Then it will be just you and me, baby," she whispered.

A picture of Guy as he'd looked on stage, debonair in a his perfectly fitted tuxedo filled her mind. That was how she would forever remember him. The bartender set her chocolate down on the round table in front of the armchair and Avery smiled her thanks as she picked it up.

Fleetingly she wondered how much Guy's donation had sold for. Cradling the mug in her hands, she pictured the lucky anonymous couple he would entertain and feed.

Avery grew still.

Was that it? Was it easier for Guy to cook for complete strangers than for a lover? Cooking for a lover implied caring. Guy didn't do caring—it smacked too much of commitment. She'd fallen for a man who was as far removed from her family dream as it was possible to get.

Then she remembered his over-the-top concern for her at the hospital.

That hadn't been the reaction of a carefree, commitment-fearing man.

Some men fuss when they're worried.

She stared thoughtfully at the frothy cream on the top of the hot drink. Even the receptionist in the doctor's rooms had noticed Guy's concern about her. And his every action since had shown his concern and caring.

Why?

Thank God you're safe.

That's what he'd said to her after he'd climbed in behind her in the spa and held her like he never intended to let her go. Avery took a sip of the drink, barely tasting it. Was it possible that Guy really did love her? He'd told Jeff he did but she'd been too angry to take it in.

Yet he'd never told her.

Perhaps he was one of those men who couldn't talk about love. Her head drooped. Then she rallied. It wouldn't be the same as the love she felt for him…but it was a start. She could work on it.

Like the shifting of the brightly hued splinters of a kaleidoscope the fragments of a new vision were forming.

Had Guy been irrationally afraid she might die?

His mother had died…

In the same hospital? Could it be that he'd envisaged his worst childhood nightmare recurring?

He'd never had a chance to say goodbye to his mother….

And she'd walked away from him in New York without saying goodbye.

What had he said just before he'd gone up on stage with Erica? *And don't even think of running out on me again. Do you understand?* And what had she done? She'd promptly walked out and retreated here to the Sky Lounge.

She'd left.

Again.

Horror filled her. Guy would believe she didn't care. If Guy truly loved her that would hurt, maybe cause him to withdraw behind the lighthearted mask that she was starting to detest.

Hastily she slipped her shoes back on and rose to her feet, only to stop in her tracks at the sight of Guy coming toward her.

The expression of apprehension on Avery's face caused Guy to rethink his plan of sweeping her off her feet and carrying her to his suite so they could have uninterrupted time for the talk he was determined to have with her.

Then he threw caution to the winds. He beckoned. "You're coming with me."

To his surprise, instead of arguing, Avery trotted over to him as quietly as a lamb.

"I shouldn't have left." The words bubbled from her. "I told you I was staying—then I didn't."

Guy shot her a puzzled look, but capitalized on her momentary meekness by grasping her hand in his. Her fingers tightened around his own.

"To hell with it."

She squeaked as he lifted her high into his arms, and strode out of the Sky Lounge ignoring the stunned expression of the bar staff.

It didn't take them long to reach the elevator to the private suites, and once inside the silence was electric. Guy gazed into her eyes. "We are going to talk."

"Yes."

"And you are going nowhere."

She nodded.

"You're not leaving, understand?"

"Yes, Guy."

"Good," he purred hoping that this unaccustomed subservience would last a little longer.

When the car came to a stop, he exited with Avery held high against his chest. Once through the hallway, he turned left and marched past the arched windows that looked out onto the starlit sky.

When he halted outside his suite, he said, "The access card is in my pocket." Then steeled himself as her fingers fumbled in his dinner jacket. Avery swiped it in the key slot, then he pushed the door open. Once inside the suite he closed the door, and let her slide down his body, before he leaned back against the heavy wooden door.

Avery narrowed the Barbie-blue eyes that had tied him up in knots. "Are you going to stand there all night long? Because it doesn't look terribly comfortable."

"I'm making sure you don't run out on me. Tonight you're staying with me all night long."

He heard her breath catch.

Then she said gently, "You don't need to worry. I have no intention of going anywhere."

The stiffness in his clenched jaw eased a little, and he stepped away from the door.

"I only have one demand," she said as she sank down on the sofa.

"What is that?"

"That you promise to trust me for as long as we are together."

"I trust you," Guy said with the solemnity of a vow. He knelt at her feet and picked up her left hand. "And I hate to admit it, but you were right when you taunted me about being jealous. I was jealous. But only because you are the only woman it hurt me to lose. I didn't know what had hit me."

"You didn't react when I said that Louis should take me on the picnic," she pointed out.

"Your mockery made me realize how much of an idiot I'd become. I didn't know what was happening to me. You're a terrifying little thing, you know."

She gave a gurgle of laughter. "Little things can't be terrifying."

"You are. You scared me to death," he confessed.

Avery leaned forward until the tip of her nose almost touched his. "You don't need to be jealous—there is only you, and I'm not going anywhere."

"Damn right you're not going anywhere," he growled. "At least, not without me."

"Then I'll stay."

"That will be forever. I want—"

"Guy—" she placed a finger against his lips "—you don't need to promise me forever. We'll take it one day at a time."

"But I want forever." He bent his head and placed a kiss on the ring finger. "Tomorrow we will go shopping for a ring."

"Guy!" Avery started to laugh. "You can't just tell me that. You need to ask me to marry you first. It's called a proposal."

He sat back on his heels and looked up at her, and shook his head. "I'm not taking any chance that you might say no."

Stretching out a hand, Avery stroked the engaging lock

that had fallen over his forehead back in to place. "I would never say no, trust me on that."

He drew a deep, shuddering breath. "I trust you with my life. Avery, I'm sorry for having been such a dumb idiot. I'll never doubt you again. Please marry me."

"Why?"

Here it was. She wanted blood. She deserved it. He shut his eyes. To his shock her lips touched his, and his eyes shot open. The butterfly kiss ended, and then she murmured, "I know I want to marry you because I love you."

Guy blinked at her. "Promise?"

"I promise."

"I love you, too," he said in a rush. Then he gave a shaky laugh. "That wasn't as hard as I thought it would be."

"It will get easier—and that's a promise too." She wrinkled her nose at him.

Linking his fingers behind her neck, Guy gazed deep into her eyes, enthralled by the understanding, the love, the devotion he glimpsed there. "I love you, Avery Lancaster-soon-to-be-Jarrod. I've fought it, I've distrusted my feelings, I've done and said some incredibly stupid things. But you have to believe I want you to be my wife. I want our baby… and whatever other babies might be in the future for us. I want us to be a family."

The smile she gave him was blinding.

"Sometimes dreams do come true," she whispered and leaned forward.

Guy met her half way. The kiss was hungry. Passionate. Perfect.

"I think it's time we went to bed," said Avery with a delicious smile.

Pale gold light from the bedside lamp broke the pre-dawn darkness in the bedroom. Avery pressed a button on her cell phone ending the call and set the slim phone down on the bed stand.

"Wake up," she urged the man sprawled on his stomach, his hand still resting on her thigh.

Guy groaned and cracked open an eye. "Good Lord, it's still night."

"Come, there's something we've got to do."

"At this hour? What?"

Avery gave him an impish grin as she clambered out of bed. "You'll see."

When they got down to the lobby fifteen minutes later, he stopped dead at the sight of the huddle of strangers in the lobby. "What is this?"

"We're going ballooning."

"No." Panic flared in his eyes.

"Hey, what's wrong? I thought this was what you wanted. You've been telling me I need to take more risks."

"I've changed my mind." His voice was muffled.

"Guy," Avery hooked her arms around his shoulders and drew his head down to look into his dark eyes. "What's wrong?"

"I don't want to lose you." His lips barely moved.

"You won't lose me."

"I have once—through my own stupidity when I didn't come after you and allowed you to go back to California. In the past few days I nearly lost you again—" he shuddered "—the car accident. I don't want you taking any risks."

"Well, you can hardly wrap me in cotton wool for the rest of my life," she said reasonably.

"I can damn well try."

"Too late." Avery wove her fingers through his and tugged. "It's all organized. We've got our own balloon and our own pilot."

"I must've been mad to suggest this," he muttered.

"Insane," she said cheerfully, "but you assured me it was safer than driving, remember? And you said it was a great way to see bears."

Guy groaned.

Within half an hour they were ready to ascend. The gas burner roared and the yellow envelope of the balloon was swollen and round. The first rays of the sun caressed Avery's uptilted face, giving it a radiance Guy had never seen.

She was exquisite.

And she was his.

"What about if I cook you a meal instead?" he asked with final desperation. "Whatever you want, you choose."

She met his eyes. Hers were sparkling with excitement. "What did you say? I'm looking forward to this. A little while ago I was dreading it, now I simply can't wait."

Damn, she hadn't even heard his final plea and he couldn't deprive her of the pleasure of the experience of a lifetime. Guy stopped fighting and took her hand in his.

"Stand beside me," she said, turning away to scan the valley below the resort, "I want you to feel exactly what I do."

Hell. His stomach churned. He didn't even want to think of her fear of heights. Instead he enfolded her in his arms from behind and crossed his hands over her belly. In his arms Avery—and his baby—would be safe.

The basket heaved and rose off the ground. Avery let out a whoop. The ascent went perfectly. Soon they were gliding over a grove of aspens.

Avery stuck her hand out and her fingers touched the topmost leaves.

"Come back here." Guy hauled her against his chest.

She turned into his arms so that she was facing him and

grinned at him. "I can't believe how fantastic this is. It's so smooth—despite the noise of the gas."

Resisting the urge to say "I told you so," he kissed the tip of her nose. "I'm glad you're having a good time." And he was.

"Well, I decided if you could overcome your fear of loving someone and admit you loved me, then it should be easy for me to overcome my fear of heights."

Her admission tightened his throat. "Avery—"

"Before you say I didn't have to do it, believe me I did. And it might've started off being for you. But now it's all for me. I feel utterly free—and it's not because I'm in the place I always considered to be the realm of angels." She gestured to the sky above them.

"It's been liberating for me, too," admitted Guy.

The sense of freedom was exhilarating. The burdens that had been pressing on him for years, the fear of commitment, the need to prove himself, had all lifted. Everything that mattered in his world was contained in the circle of his arms.

"I love you, Avery." This time the words came easily, as she'd promised. "And before I forget, I've got a date tonight."

She arched an eyebrow. "With me I hope?"

"With the winner of my auction donation."

"Oh." For a moment her eyes clouded over then cleared, and the blue eclipsed the cobalt sky above them. "I'll see you afterward."

"Don't you want to know who placed the winning bid?"

"Who?"

"I did."

Her eyes widened. "You did? But why pay for your-self?"

"We have unfinished business." At her puzzlement, he

added, "I have a birthday dinner to prepare for you. You missed out last time."

"That's what you were doing that night?"

He nodded. "I'd prepared you dinner at Baratin. But tonight will be better. Because as soon as we land we're going to go shopping for a ring. And later I'll place it here." He stroked her ring finger.

"We'll also need to tell your family about our engagement."

"They'll be delighted." Guy grinned as he imagined what Erica would have to say. "And tomorrow I'll fly to California with you to break the news to your family, too. Then we'll come back home."

Jarrod Ridge was home, would always be his home, Guy knew.

"There's a meadow beyond Willow Lodge overlooking Roaring Fork that I want you to see. If you like it we can build a home there."

"It sounds perfect." She gave him a gentle smile. "I'd like to keep the news about the baby to ourselves for now. It's so new, I want a bit of time for us to savor it alone. Is that selfish?"

"Not at all. The baby will be our secret," Guy said and he stroked her stomach, which still showed no sign of the life, the part of him and Avery that was growing inside. "The announcement will make a wonderful Christmas present for both our families."

"And in the meantime," her voice dropped to a breathy drawl that had Guy lowering his head to hear what she was saying, "we'll have plenty of nights to spend together."

Together. To Guy that sounded like heaven.

* * * * *

EXPECTING THE
RANCHER'S HEIR

BY
KATHIE DeNOSKY

Kathie DeNosky lives in her native southern Illinois with her big, lovable Bernese mountain dog, Nemo. Writing highly sensual stories with a generous amount of humor, Kathie's books have appeared on the Waldenbooks bestseller list and received the Write Touch Readers Award and the National Readers' Choice Award. Kathie enjoys going to rodeos, traveling to research settings for her books and listening to country music. Readers may contact Kathie at PO Box 2064, Herrin, Illinois 62948-5264, USA or e-mail her at kathie@kathiedenosky.com. They can also visit her website at www.kathiedenosky.com.

This book is dedicated to the wonderful authors
I worked with on this series, Maureen Child, Maxine
Sullivan, Tessa Radley, Emilie Rose and Heidi Betts.
It was a pleasure working with all of you.

And a special thank you to Charles Griemsman
and Krista Stroever for asking me to be
included in such a great project.

One

"Don't say pregnant. Please don't say pregnant," Melissa Jarrod whispered, afraid to open her tightly closed eyes. Maybe if she repeated it enough times she could will the white stick in her trembling hand to give her the results she wanted.

When she finally worked up the courage to take a peek at the pregnancy test she held, her eyes widened and it felt as if her stomach dropped all the way to her feet. The word *pregnant* in the little results window couldn't have been clearer.

"I can't be pregnant," she said disbelievingly as she glanced at herself in the bathroom mirror. "We've been careful."

But as her gaze dropped to her flat stomach, she

realized that the way her luck had been running lately, it was not only possible, it was highly probable. She and Shane McDermott had been in a physical relationship practically from the moment she returned to Aspen two months ago. She sighed heavily. Although they'd taken the proper precautions, there had been that one night only a few days after they'd started seeing each other when they'd gotten carried away and passion had overtaken them.

Hoping the results of the test might be wrong, she quickly picked up the box to check the directions. No, she had done everything correctly. She turned the box to the side to see if there was a disclaimer or some reassurance that the test could have given a false-positive reading. Her spirits sank further when she found what she was looking for. The percentage of error was so low, it was almost impossible that she wasn't pregnant.

Wandering into the bedroom, she sank onto the side of the bed. What was she going to do and how on earth was she going to tell Shane?

He had made it perfectly clear from the beginning that he wasn't interested in a serious relationship, and that had been just fine with her. When she'd first come back to Aspen for the reading of her father's will, she hadn't been certain just how long she would be staying. But she, her brothers and her newfound half sister had learned they were required to take over the running of the Jarrod Ridge Resort for at least one year or forfeit their inheritance of the thriving enterprise. Even so, it would have been utter foolishness to engage in anything long-term, knowing that she would eventually return to California at some point in the future.

But with the positive results of the pregnancy test, their casual affair had just taken a very serious turn and become a lifelong commitment. At least for her. But how would Shane react when he learned that in a little more than seven months he was going to be a father?

Lost in a tangle of disturbing thoughts and fighting a wave of sheer panic, Melissa jumped when her cell phone rang. Reaching to pick it up from the nightstand, she noticed the number for the Tranquility Spa on the caller ID.

"What's wrong this time, Rita?" she asked, taking a deep steadying breath.

Whether real or imagined, the assistant manager of Jarrod Ridge's elite spa had reported a crisis nearly every day since Melissa had stepped in to temporarily take over the manager's position. But for the first time in two months, she welcomed the insecure woman's concerns. Anything was a welcome distraction from her own current dilemma.

"I'm sorry to bother you, Ms. Jarrod, but the yoga instructor called in sick this morning and I haven't been able to reach our backup. We have a room full of guests and no one to lead the yoga class. What should I do?" Rita whined, her voice clearly filled with indecision, as well as a good amount of panic.

"First of all, breathe, Rita," Melissa said, rising from the bed to pull a leotard from her dresser drawer. "I want you to calm down, then escort the guests over to the juice bar for a complimentary drink."

"Then what?" the woman asked, sounding a little more in control of herself.

How on earth the woman had managed to land the assistant-manager position, Melissa would never know. Although Rita was very nice, she couldn't make a decision on her own if her life depended on it.

Melissa checked her watch. "I'll be there in ten minutes to teach the class."

The last thing she wanted to do was lead a yoga session this morning. She needed to figure out when and how she was going to tell Shane, as well as her family, about the pregnancy. But the choice had been taken out of her hands. The Tranquility Spa had a stellar reputation for giving Jarrod Ridge guests five-star treatment and she wasn't about to let that status slip on her watch.

Putting her long blond hair into a ponytail, she stuffed her things into her gym bag, then grabbed her car keys from the kitchen counter as she started out the door of the lodge. Since her return to Aspen, she had been staying in Willow Lodge, one of the exclusive log cabins owned by Jarrod Ridge Resort.

She could have stayed in her suite at the family estate, but that had never been an option for her. Jarrod Manor might have been where she grew up, but she had always thought of it as more of a prison than she had a home. She hadn't been back but a handful of times since moving out to go to college eight years ago and she didn't particularly care to go back now.

As she steered her SUV under the canopy of the resort's main entrance, she relegated thoughts of her dismal, lonely childhood to the back of her mind. Even though Willow Lodge was the cabin farthest away from the manor, she could have walked the short distance. But as soon as the yoga class was over, she fully intended to make the drive over to the next valley where Shane's ranch was located and tell him there had been an unexpected complication in their no-strings relationship. That is if she could find the place.

She had only been to Rainbow Bend Ranch once and that had been years ago. If she remembered correctly it was in a remote valley that was several miles off the main road.

When she parked the Mountaineer, her heart raced at the sight of the man standing beside the truck just in front of hers. Shane McDermott was handing his keys to one of the valets and she didn't think she had ever seen him look so darned sexy.

Tall and devilishly handsome, he was a cowboy from the top of his wide-brimmed black Resistol to the soles of his big-booted feet. Shane was the type of man she had always fantasized about, and if the expressions on the faces of the female guests standing by the resort's main entrance were any indication, he was the type of man they dreamed about, too.

No wonder he had a reputation for being a ladies' man. They were drawn to him like bees to pollen.

Her heart came to a complete halt when he walked over to open the driver's door of her SUV.

"Good morning, Ms. Jarrod," he said, removing his hat as any self-respecting cowboy would do when greeting a lady.

A slight breeze ruffled his thick black hair and it reminded her of how it had looked the other night after she had run her fingers through it when they'd made love. She did her best to ignore the tingle that coursed through her at the thought of what they had shared.

"Good morning, Mr. McDermott," she answered, getting out of the car to hand her keys to one of the uniformed valets.

"I thought Friday was your day off," he said, smiling congenially.

"It usually is." She breezed past him and hurried toward the resort doors. "One of the spa's yoga instructors called in sick this morning and I'm going to have to teach her class."

He fell into step beside her. "After you finish twisting the resort's guests into pretzels do you have the rest of the day off?"

"Yes."

She couldn't help but wonder where Shane was going with his line of questioning. In order to avoid gossip among the Jarrod Ridge employees and the disapproval of some of the older, less progressive-minded investors, they'd been extremely careful to conceal their affair. Not even her family knew about them, and they had managed to maintain the appearance of being nothing more than acquaintances by limiting being seen together. They hadn't even spent an entire night together for fear of someone seeing him leave her place. Thus far, they'd been successful by not being seen together at all.

But if Shane continued questioning her as they walked toward the spa, there was a very real possibility that someone would take notice, and by the end of the day, the rumors about them would be spread all over the resort, if not the entire town of Aspen. Or even worse, her nerves could very well get the better of her and she would blurt out in the middle of the crowded lobby that she going to have his baby.

Neither scenario was appealing. She knew for certain that she couldn't cope with the fallout that was sure to follow on top of everything else she had to deal with.

"I'll come by Willow Lodge later," he said, smiling. His icy blue eyes danced with mischief. "I have something I want to talk to you about, Lissa."

"Would you keep your voice down?" she hissed.

She quickly looked around to see if anyone overheard him. He was the only person who had ever called her Lissa and it never failed to send an exciting little thrill coursing through her.

"I have something I need to discuss with you, too, Shane. But I'd rather not go into it..." Her voice trailed off when a bellman seemed to take more than a passing interest in seeing them together. When the man moved on, she turned back to Shane. "I thought you were supposed to have a luncheon meeting today with some of the other Jarrod Ridge investors, Mr. McDermott."

"I do." He looked as if he didn't have a care in the world, and she couldn't help but wonder how quickly that would change when she shared her news.

"Then what are you doing here now?"

Melissa hadn't meant to sound so blunt, but if she didn't get to the yoga class pretty soon, poor Rita was sure to suffer a nervous breakdown and guests would start complaining. Besides, she needed to put some space between herself and Shane. The scent of leather and woodsy aftershave were playing havoc with her equilibrium and it was all she could do to keep from swaying toward him.

"I came early to see that the new herd of trail horses I sold the resort is living up to expectation." He arched one dark eyebrow. "Do you have a problem with that?"

Sighing, Melissa shook her head. "I'm sorry, I didn't mean to be so short with you. The yoga class was supposed to start fifteen minutes ago and I really do need to get to the spa."

"Then I won't keep you, Ms. Jarrod." His voice grew a bit louder as they reached the entrance to Tranquility Spa and she knew it was for the benefit of anyone who might be eavesdropping. He gave her a conspiratorial wink as he dipped his head ever so slightly and touched the wide brim of his cowboy hat. "It was nice running into you again. I hope you have a nice Labor Day weekend."

As she watched Shane turn and stroll down the hall toward the meeting rooms, Melissa sighed. The man looked almost as good from the back as he did from the front. His Western-cut, dark brown suit jacket emphasized the width of his strong shoulders and his blue jeans fit his long, muscular legs to perfection.

His well-toned physique rivaled that of a Greek god and she had intimate knowledge of the power and strength of each and every muscle when he had held her, kissed her, made love to her.

A tiny shiver streaked straight up her spine. She forced herself to ignore the sudden warmth that followed as it spread throughout her body. Opening the door to the spa, she took a deep breath and prepared to teach the yoga class.

Lusting after Shane McDermott was what had landed her in her current predicament. It would definitely be in her best interests to remember that.

"Melissa, did you hear me?" Avery Lancaster asked. Engaged to Melissa's brother Guy, the petite blonde had become a very close friend in the month since they met.

"Um, sorry," Melissa murmured as she took a sip of her water. With her mind still reeling from the results of the pregnancy test, she found it hard to concentrate on the conversation.

"I asked if you've tried the cucumber sandwiches Guy added?" her friend asked patiently as she pointed to the leather-bound folder Melissa held.

Perusing the new healthy-choices section her brother had added to the Sky Lounge lunch menu since taking over managing the resort's restaurants, Melissa shook her head. "No, I hadn't even noticed the new dishes."

Avery frowned. "Is something wrong?"

"Oh, just the usual stuff that goes along with managing a spa," Melissa lied, closing the menu and setting it on the table. She hated not being truthful with her friend, but she needed to talk to Shane about the pregnancy before anyone else.

"Still having problems with your assistant manager, little sister?" Guy asked, walking over to join them. He leaned down to kiss Avery, then seated himself beside her.

"Actually, Rita is doing a little better than she was," Melissa said, thankful to have something to focus on besides her own dilemma. "She did have a moment this morning when I thought her nerves were going to send her into a panic attack, but we got it straightened out."

"In other words, you took care of it," Guy said, knowingly.

"Well, yes," Melissa admitted. "But in all fairness to Rita, there wasn't anyone else to teach the yoga class this morning."

"Are you still taking the weekend off like you planned?" Avery asked.

"Blake thinks I should," Melissa said, shrugging. Guy's fraternal twin and the new CEO of Jarrod Ridge Resort, her oldest brother had pointed out at the last managers' meeting that she needed to back off to see if Rita could handle the assistant manager's position or if she needed to be replaced. "I'll only be a phone call away, so I don't suppose it would hurt to be off for a few days."

"You haven't taken any time for yourself since you started managing the spa," Guy pointed out. "We both know if Rita knows you're available, she'll call."

Melissa rubbed at the tension building at her temples. "I can't just leave her on her own. What if something happens like this morning?"

Guy looked thoughtful for a moment. "If Rita runs into something she can't handle, she can get hold of me or Blake. I'll be around most of the weekend, and you know that Blake will be, too."

"You and Blake both intimidate Rita." Melissa couldn't help but laugh. "Besides, what do you know about running a spa or teaching yoga?"

"Me? Intimidate someone?" Guy grinned. "Just

because I demand the best from my kitchen staff, it doesn't mean that I'm a tyrant." Reaching out, he patted her shoulder. "Don't worry. I'll take care of whatever comes up at the spa. You just relax and enjoy a little down time."

Never having been encouraged by their father to develop close family ties while they were growing up, Melissa and her four brothers had become a lot closer as adults. She couldn't help but wonder what it would have been like if they'd had a strong bond when they were children. Maybe growing up in Jarrod Manor wouldn't have been as lonely for her.

"Thanks, Guy," Melissa said, smiling. "If you need me…"

Her brother shook his head. "I won't." Checking his watch, he rose. "Break's over. Time to go back to the kitchen and see how things are going." He kissed Avery's cheek. "I'll see you this evening."

Watching Guy make his way across the crowded restaurant, Avery sighed happily. "Isn't he just the best-looking man ever?"

"You're in love," Melissa said, unable to keep from feeling a bit envious.

Although they'd had a rocky start, Avery and Guy had the kind of loving relationship she had always envisioned for herself. Unfortunately, what she and Shane had together would never go any further than what it was now—a strong physical attraction that would most likely cool considerably once he learned of her pregnancy.

As she and Avery finished lunch, they chatted about the upcoming dinner honoring the Food and Wine Gala investors. By the time they parted in the lobby an hour later, Melissa was more than ready to get back to Willow Lodge. Shane would be coming over soon, and although she had no idea how he would take the news about the baby, they needed to get used to the idea that in about seven months they were going to be parents.

Shane walked out of the meeting room toward the Jarrod Ridge lobby with a single-minded purpose—find Lissa and convince her to spend the three-day weekend with him at his ranch. The resort's annual Food and Wine Gala had been in full swing for the past couple of weeks, and everything had been extremely busy. The time they'd been able to spend together had been limited, and, now that the event was over, he fully intended to remedy that as soon as possible. He certainly wasn't looking for anything long-term to develop out of their affair, but he wasn't yet ready to give up on whatever they had going on between them, either. He had enjoyed spending time with her the past couple of months and looked forward to at least a couple more before they went their separate ways.

"Shane, my boy, it's good to see you again," a deep, booming voice said from somewhere behind him.

Stopping, Shane turned to smile at one of his

late father's oldest friends. "It's good to see you, too, Senator Kurk. How have you been?" he asked, shaking the man's hand.

"Can't complain," the senator said, smiling. Tall and commanding, the white-haired man had been a member of congress for as long as Shane could remember. "It's always good to get out of Washington for a few days and come back home to spend a little down time with my friends and family."

"I'm sure it is," Shane agreed. "I've heard they're keeping you busy these days with several important national issues."

Senator Kurk chuckled. "And if that isn't enough to keep me awake at night, I've been named the head of a new investigative committee." He looked thoughtful. "Aren't you an architect?"

Shane nodded. "I specialize in stables."

"Interesting," the man said. "I suppose your studies included other areas of architecture, as well?"

"Of course." When the man remained silent, Shane started inching away. "I'm sure you'll get to the bottom of whatever it is your committee is looking into, Senator," he said, hoping the man wasn't at liberty to share what the committee was investigating.

As much as he liked Patrick Kurk, the good senator could be as long-winded and boring as any other politician, and Shane had plans that didn't include listening to him drone on about what ailed the nation. The sooner he got over to the lodge, the sooner he would start what he was certain would be a very enjoyable weekend with one of the most exciting women he had ever had the pleasure of knowing.

"Excuse me, Senator," one of the man's aides said, hurrying up to join them. "The Rotary Club meeting is about to begin and your speech is first on the agenda, right after the opening remarks."

Relieved that his trip over to Willow Lodge wouldn't be delayed any further, Shane smiled. "I won't keep you, Senator. Maybe we can get together for some trout fishing on the Rainbow River the next time you're in town."

"I'll take you up on that the first chance I get," Senator Kurk said, turning to go. "It was good seeing you again, Shane."

Walking out of the resort, Shane forgot all about politicians and senatorial committees as he started out. He was on a mission to get Lissa to join him for the three-day weekend and he wasn't going to give up until he got what he wanted.

Given her concerns about feeding the gossip mongers at the resort, he was pretty sure it wouldn't be all that easy to talk her into staying with him at Rainbow Bend. But there wasn't a doubt in his mind that what they shared would be worth whatever he had to do to convince her.

Shane shook his head as he looked around to see if anyone was watching, then took the hidden shortcut back toward the luxury lodges. He had been jumping through hoops for the past couple of months just to please her, and it was beginning to get old.

Instead of going directly to the lodge where she was staying, it had become a ritual for him to head toward the stables, then cut back through a small patch of woods. She had insisted that no one would think anything of him going to check on the herd of horses he had sold the resort, and he supposed she was right. But he couldn't control other people's opinions of him and didn't give a damn what they thought anyway. Lissa, on the other hand, was a very private person and he respected her need for discretion even if he didn't completely understand it.

Slipping through the stand of pine trees behind Willow Lodge, he took the porch steps two at a time. Just as he raised his hand to knock, Lissa opened the door.

"What took you so long?" she asked, taking him by the hand to pull him inside.

As soon as they cleared the doorway, he took her into his arms and used his boot to shove the door shut behind them. "I don't know a man alive who doesn't want to hear a woman ask that question, angel."

She looked as if she had something more on her mind, but it would just have to wait. It had been almost three days since he had held her, kissed her, and he had every intention of immediately remedying that particular problem.

His mouth came down on hers, and she let out a

startled little squeak, but to his satisfaction, she didn't protest or try to push him away. Instead, she wrapped her arms around his waist and pressed herself against him.

Her response to him never failed to send a flash fire rushing from the top of his head straight to the region south of his belt buckle. Today was no different. In the blink of an eye, he was hotter than a two-dollar pistol on a Saturday night.

Shifting to pull her more fully into him, Shane deepened the kiss. As he stroked and teased, her sweet taste, the floral scent of her silky blond hair and the feel of her soft body pressed to his much harder one had him feeling as if his jeans had shrunk at least two sizes in the stride. He quickly decided that he would do well to end the kiss or there was a good chance he'd end up emasculating himself.

"I've been wanting to do that ever since I saw you at the resort this morning," he said, leaning back to smile down at her.

The dazed look in her vibrant blue eyes and the heat of passion coloring her creamy cheeks was one of the most beautiful sights he had ever been privileged to see. Soft and feminine, Lissa looked the way a woman was meant to look when a man kissed her.

She shook her head as if to clear it. "Shane, before this goes any further. We need to talk."

"Yes, we do," he agreed.

"There's something I need to tell you."

"Me first," he insisted.

He took her by the hand and led her into the great room. Settling himself into one of the oversize leather chairs in front of the stone fireplace, he pulled her down to sit on his lap.

"This is really important, Shane. There's been an unexpected development that—"

He placed his index finger to her soft lips. "It'll have to wait."

"This is something that can't wait."

He gave her a quick kiss to divert her. "I have something I want you to do with me this weekend."

The kiss distracted her just as he had intended. "W-what?"

"I want you to spend the next few days at my ranch with me." When it looked as if she was about to protest, he shook his head. "Hear me out, angel. Most of my ranch hands are off for the holiday weekend and the ones who aren't couldn't care less who I have staying with me. Cactus, my housekeeper, has already left to visit his sister in Denver for the next few days, and we'll have the entire house to ourselves. Unless you tell them, no one who cares will ever be the wiser that you stayed with me."

She looked thoughtful for several long moments before she finally nodded. "We need to discuss something at length and I think it would be a very good idea to have the privacy of your ranch to do it."

Surprised and more than a little pleased by how easily she had agreed, he hugged her close. "Talking wasn't what I had in mind when I asked you to go with me. But I guess we can hash over whatever you think is so important while we rest up from more pleasurable pursuits."

She gave him a warning look. "Will you be serious?"

"Angel, I thought you'd have figured out by now that when it comes to making love, I'm always serious," he murmured as he kissed the side of her slender neck. "But if you think it's necessary, I'll be more than happy to take a few minutes to refresh your memory."

"After I tell you what I discovered this morning, I think you'll agree that there should be less emphasis on teasing and making love this weekend and more concentration on making some very serious decisions about what we're going to do," she said, pulling from his arms to stand up. He watched her shoulders rise and fall as she took several deep breaths. "Shane, there's no easy way to put this and I doubt you'll be happy to hear about it."

His smile slowly faded. Her body language and the seriousness of her tone warned him that whatever was on her mind was most likely something unpleasant. But he had never been one to avoid an obvious problem. He preferred to hit the difficulty head-on, deal with it and move forward.

"Why don't you just tell me outright and get it over with, Lissa?"

"A-all right."

The slight tremor in her voice and the lone tear slowly slipping down her cheek when she turned to face him caused his heart to stutter and had him moving to get to his feet in the blink of an eye. But her next words stopped him stone cold.

"Shane, I'm…pregnant."

Two

Feeling as if he had taken a sucker punch to the gut, Shane stared at her as he sank back down into the plush chair. Rarely at a loss for words, he suddenly couldn't have strung two words together if his life depended on it.

Pregnant. Lissa was pregnant. That meant he was going to be a…he swallowed hard against the knot forming in his stomach…a daddy.

Un-freaking-believable.

He shook his head in an effort to make some sense of his tangled thoughts. He wasn't sure what he had expected her to tell him, but the fact that she was having a baby—his baby—certainly hadn't been it.

Hell, he had never expected any woman to announce that he had made her pregnant.

"The baby belongs to you," Lissa said, sounding a little defensive.

He shook his head. "There wasn't a doubt in my mind about that, angel. When did you see the doctor?"

"I haven't." She bit her lower lip to keep it from trembling and he knew she was thoroughly stressed. "I just took the home test this morning."

"Maybe it was wrong."

"I don't think so. I've missed one period and getting close to missing the second." Her shoulders slumped. "Besides, the test boasts the highest accuracy rate of all the in-home brands."

Suddenly needing a good dose of fresh air and a little time to come to grips with her news, Shane rose to his feet. Walking over to her, he used the pad of his thumb to wipe the tear from her cheek.

"Why don't you pack a bag for the weekend while I go get my truck?"

"But what if someone sees us leaving town together?" she asked, looking uncertain.

"We've got bigger things to worry about than what some busybody with nothing better to do than spread gossip is going to say about seeing the two of us together," he interrupted, anticipating her argument. Taking her into his arms, he pressed a quick kiss to her forehead. "Once we get to Rainbow Bend, we can discuss things, sort it all out and decide what we're

going to do. For now, get your things together and be
ready to go when I get back." Without waiting for her
to change her mind or find an excuse to stay at the
resort, he quickly released her and walked outside.

Pulling the door closed behind him, Shane stood
on the deck for several mind-numbing moments
and gazed at the panoramic view of the Rocky
Mountains against the bright blue September sky.
Splashes of gold from the aspen trees making their
annual autumn transformation painted the slopes and
quavered delicately in the slight breeze. He saw none
of it.

He was too focused on the fact that he had done
the one thing he had sworn he would never do. Hell,
he had never even considered fathering a child as part
of his life plan.

But he had just learned that particular horse had
left the barn and there was no sense in closing the
gate now. As he saw it, all there was left to do was
man up, accept his responsibilities and do the right
thing. It was what his morals demanded and his father
would have expected of him.

Filling his lungs with the crisp mountain air,
Shane straightened his shoulders and descended the
steps. Walking toward the main part of the resort,
he knew exactly what he had to do.

He had made Melissa Jarrod pregnant. Now, it was
time for him to make her his wife.

The drive to Shane's ranch was mostly spent
in quiet reflection as they both contemplated the

ramifications of the unexpected turn in their no-strings affair. By the time they reached Rainbow Valley, Melissa felt as if her nerves were stretched to the breaking point. Grappling for something—anything—to keep from thinking about their dilemma, she glanced around.

She had only been to the Rainbow Bend Ranch once before and that had been several years ago when her father had coerced her into accompanying him on a horse-buying trip for the resort. It had been a lame attempt on his part to bridge the ever-widening gap between them. She hadn't wanted to be there and spent the time wishing she was anywhere else, instead of taking in the gorgeous scenery.

But as Shane drove the truck over the ridge and down the winding road leading into the picturesque valley, she couldn't get over the breathtaking view. "This is beautiful, Shane. You're so lucky that you got to grow up here."

"I like it," he said, stopping the truck beside a rustic two-story log ranch house. "But not everyone appreciates the isolation."

Melissa frowned. "You make it sound as if it's stuck out in the middle of nowhere. I wouldn't consider ten miles outside of Aspen all that far from civilization."

"That's because you haven't been here in the winter," he answered, shrugging one shoulder. "When we get a heavy snow, the road up on the ridge can be closed off for weeks at a time, making trips into town few and far between."

"How did you get back and forth to go to school when you were a child?" she asked, remembering that he had graduated with honors.

"When I was younger and winter hit, I stayed in Aspen with my dad's sister and her family until they moved to New Mexico." He got out of the truck and walked around to open the passenger door for her. "By the time they left Colorado, I was almost out of school and old enough to stay on my own."

"That's when you stayed at Jarrod Ridge, wasn't it?" she guessed. Required by her father to work at the resort after school and on weekends, she vaguely remembered seeing Shane working with the horses the few times she had escorted guests to the stables.

Nodding, he reached into the bed of the truck for her overnight case, then placed his hand on the small of her back as he guided her toward the house. "My dad and yours had an agreement that I could stay at Jarrod Ridge the winter of my senior year, in exchange for me wrangling on the weekends and acting as a guide on some of the trail rides."

"Considering how much you've always loved horses, you probably didn't have much of a problem with that," she said, smiling as they climbed the steps to the wraparound porch.

He shook his head, then reached around her to open the front door. "Since the resort buys all of its stock exclusively from Rainbow Bend, it was like taking care of my own horses."

When they entered the house, Melissa got her first glimpse of Shane's home and it came as no surprise that everything from the pieces of antique harness and tack decorating the walls to the foyer's chandelier made of elk antlers was rugged and thoroughly masculine. Just like the owner. There wasn't so much as a hint that a woman had ever lived there and she couldn't help but wonder what had happened to his mother.

Melissa tried to think if she had heard anything about the woman. Nothing came to mind. Had his mother passed away when Shane was a child like her mother had?

"Cactus left this morning for Denver, so we'll be on our own for meals," Shane said, interrupting her thoughts. He hung his wide-brimmed hat on a peg beside the door, set her small bag on the floor and reached to help her out of her jacket. "Just let me know when you get hungry and I'll throw a couple of steaks on the grill."

She frowned. "For the past couple of weeks, it seems that I'm hungry all of the time."

"Is that because of the pregnancy?" She watched his gaze zero in on her midsection as if he was looking for a significant change to have taken place in the past few days. Apparently finding none, he raised his gaze to meet hers. "I remember one of my hired men joking about his wife eating like a field hand when she was pregnant with their little boy."

"I wouldn't say I'm that bad yet, but I do think the pregnancy could be the cause for the increase in my appetite." She nibbled on her lower lip as she tried to remember what some of her friends had mentioned about the early stages of their pregnancies. Nothing came to mind about constantly being hungry. "Since I've never been pregnant before, I'm not really sure," she said, shrugging.

He stared at her for several long seconds before nodding. "We'll have to check with your doctor about that when you go for your first visit." Looking thoughtful, he added, "In fact, it would probably be a good idea to start making a list of the things we need to ask him."

"Whoa, there, Cowboy. What do you mean by 'we'?" She shook her head. "I don't remember inviting you to go along with me."

"Doesn't matter. I'm going," he stated, as if it were a foregone conclusion.

"Why?"

"We'll discuss my reasoning later, as well as make a few important decisions," he said, giving her the same charming grin that never failed to make her pulse race. He picked up her bag and ushered her toward the stairs. "Right now, I'll show you to the bedroom and let you freshen up while I put the steaks on to cook."

When he guided her up the steps and down the

hall, she was a bit surprised that he opened a door and showed her into one of the guest rooms. They'd never spent an entire night together and she had assumed when he asked her to spend the weekend with him, he had intended for her to sleep in his room. But after hearing the news of her pregnancy, she had no doubt that his previous insatiable desire for her had cooled considerably.

He set her bag on the bed, then turning to go, took her into his arms. "When you get ready, come down to the kitchen. I should have supper ready in about twenty minutes." Then, before she could react, he softly kissed her cheek and left the room.

As she unzipped her case and started to put her clothes away, a sadness she couldn't quite understand filled her. Why did Shane's diminishing interest in her bother her so much?

It wasn't as if they were in love. They had both agreed before beginning their affair that the time they spent together would be relaxed and casual with no emotional involvement getting in the way of their respective careers.

Now that she had been given the responsibilities of running the resort's world-class spa, she had her hands full. She would love to have a husband and family of her own one day, but now just wasn't a good time to do it. Besides, Shane wasn't the right man to make that dream come true. His reputation for moving from one woman to another was only slightly better than her brother Trevor's.

Along with raising championship quarter horses, Shane was a highly successful architect specializing in the design of exclusive stables. His client list included some of the richest, most famous people in the equine world and he simply didn't have time for more than a casual relationship, anyway.

Melissa bit her lower lip to keep it from trembling. It was times like this that she missed having a mother the most. She would love to be able to turn to her mother and ask for her advice. Unfortunately, Margaret Jarrod had died of cancer when Melissa was two and she had grown up without the love and nurturing guidance of a mother.

Shaking off her uncharacteristic gloominess, she finished unpacking, then took a deep breath and stepped out into the hallway as she headed for the stairs. She had known her time with Shane would end at some point. She just hadn't realized it would be so soon. Nor could she have anticipated that she would be pregnant with his baby when it happened.

"When do you intend to call the doctor's office for your first appointment?" Shane asked, reaching for his glass of iced tea. Lissa had been extremely quiet for most of the meal and it was past time they addressed the issue that had been on both of their minds since she made her announcement that afternoon.

When she looked up from the bite of steak she had been pushing around the plate with her fork, she shook her head. "I really haven't thought that far ahead. I only took the test this morning. Then, before I had the chance to recover from the shock of the results, I was called to take over the yoga class at the spa and later met Avery for lunch."

"Shortly after you finished that, I showed up at your door and here we are," he guessed.

She nodded. "I still haven't had time to fully comprehend the fact that I'm actually going to have a baby."

"It is pretty unreal, isn't it?" He was having a hard time wrapping his mind around that fact himself.

Her vivid blue gaze reflected some barely contained panic and he was fairly certain he had that deer-in-the-headlights look about him, as well.

"I knew it was possible," she said, finally laying her fork down. "But seriously, only one time unprotected and I get pregnant? The odds against that happening have to be pretty high."

"Looks like that's all it took for us." He reached across the table to cover her hand with his. "But I want you to know, you aren't going to have to go through this alone. We're in this together. I'll be there to support you every step of the way, Lissa."

"I appreciate that." She stared at him for several long moments before she finally sat back from the table. "But if you mean monetarily, I think we both know that isn't necessary. I'm financially independent and have more than enough to handle whatever expenses there are before and after the birth."

Given their initial agreement to keep things casual, he could understand her misinterpretation of his promise, as well as her reluctance to believe he would commit himself to anything more than monetary assistance. But the idea that she considered him so shallow and irresponsible that he would just walk away from her and the child they created still didn't sit well.

"I'm not talking about child support," he stated, doing his best to keep his tone even.

"What *are* you talking about, Shane?" she asked, looking confused.

Rising to place their plates on the kitchen counter, he turned to face her. "I'm telling you that I'll be with you for doctor appointments, the baby's birth and raising him."

"In other words, you're telling me you're going to want joint custody." She nodded. "I can understand that and I don't see a problem. I'm sure we can work something out."

"Custody is going to be a nonissue," he said, shaking his head. He walked over to squat down beside her chair, then reaching up to brush a strand of long blond hair from her cheek, he smiled. "I'm pretty sure that sharing the responsibility of a child is automatic when his parents are married."

Her eyes widened and her mouth opened and closed several times as she obviously tried to find her voice. "Married?" she finally gasped.

"Yes."

Her expression stated louder than words ever could that she didn't believe him. "*Married* as in the tiered cake, white dress and 'I do'?"

"Yup."

"No."

"Why not?"

She closed her eyes, then opening them, shook her head as she pinned him with her crystalline gaze. "Have you lost your mind, Shane? You can't possibly be serious."

"Angel, marriage is one subject I never joke about," he said, meaning it.

"We can't get married, Shane," she insisted. "Beyond the basics, we really don't know that much about each other."

"Sure we do." He stood up and, lifting her into his arms, sat down in the chair to settle her on his lap. "I know you like when I do this." Kissing the side of her neck, he was rewarded with her soft sigh. "And you really like this," he added, slipping his hand beneath the tail of her aqua T-shirt. He used his fingertip to trace the satiny skin covering her ribs. As he slowly lowered his head, he moved his hand. "But you love this."

His mouth covered hers at the same time his hand cupped her breast and to his immense satisfaction, Lissa didn't so much as put up a token protest. Encouraged by her response, Shane deepened the kiss and once again marveled at her sweetness and the feeling of completion he always experienced when he held her.

He had kissed a lot of women in his time, but not one of them made him feel the way Melissa Jarrod did. Her slender body fit perfectly against his and her passion never failed to excite him in ways he could have never imagined.

His lower body tightened predictably and he decided he had better break the kiss before things got out of hand. At the moment, Lissa needed his comfort far more than she did his lust.

Drawing in some much-needed air, he smiled. "I told you I knew a lot about you."

She shook her head as if to clear it. "I wasn't talking about pleasing each other sexually and you know it."

"Correct me if I'm wrong, but isn't that a huge part of marriage?" he asked, unable to keep from grinning.

"Maybe for a man, but a woman needs more from a relationship than just good sex," she insisted. "*I* need more."

He raised one eyebrow. "Would you care to enlighten me?"

Leaning back, she stared at him for a moment as if she thought he might be a little on the simple side. "Do you realize we've never spent more than a few hours together at any one time? I may know you intimately in bed, but I don't know anything about you otherwise. I don't know what you like to read, what kind of movies you prefer or even what your favorite color is."

He frowned. "I don't see how any of that would make or break a marriage."

She pulled from his arms and stood up. "Don't you see? Those are the kinds of things you know about the person you are committing to spend the rest of your life with." Sighing heavily, she turned to face him. "I don't even know what side of the bed you sleep on or if you snore."

"So you're telling me that knowing whether I snore or not is more important than a gratifying love life?" he asked, laughing.

If looks could kill, the one she sent his way would have him laid out in two shakes of a squirrel's tail. "Will you be serious, Shane? I'm trying to explain what constitutes a committed relationship."

Oh, he knew exactly what she was driving at. Lissa thought she needed to know what made him tick. But she was wanting more from him than he was comfortable giving. He had never been in the habit of sharing more than the surface details about himself with anyone and he wasn't inclined to do so now.

Unfortunately, if he wanted her to go along with his plan, he was going to have to give her something she considered relevant. "Nonfiction, action-adventure, red and left."

She looked confused.

"I mainly read nonfiction and my favorite movies are action-adventure. I like the color red and I prefer the middle of the bed. But if I had to choose a side, it would be the left." He grinned. "As for the snoring, you can let me know about that tomorrow morning."

"Those things are nice to know," she said, looking a little more satisfied with his answers. "But that's just the tip of the iceberg."

Before she could press him further and delve into areas he would rather not go into, he decided to turn the tables and ask a few questions of his own. "What about you? What is there about Lissa Jarrod that you think I need to know?"

He gave himself a mental pat on the back at her pleased expression. "Let's see. I like pizza, I hate Brussels sprouts—"

"Who doesn't?" he said, making a face.

She laughed. "And I adore romantic movies."

"What about horses?" he asked, wondering if they had that in common. "Do you like to ride?"

"I haven't ridden in several years, but I used to enjoy going on some of the trail rides offered at Jarrod Ridge." Smiling, she added, "I even had a favorite horse named Smoky Joe that I always rode."

Shane stood up and took her into his arms. "I don't remember you going on any of the rides I guided."

Loosely wrapping her arms around his waist, she gazed up at him. "That was because I was too young. When you were eighteen and leading those trail rides, I was only eleven."

"Now hold on just a minute," he said, frowning.

"Didn't you tell me one time that you worked at the resort when I did?"

"Yes." He felt her body tense. "Of course, I wasn't on the payroll. But I started doing simple things like delivering messages from one office to another. That was when I was eight."

"Ah, the pre-e-mail and text-messaging days."

She nodded. "By the time I turned ten I had graduated to showing guests how to find their way around the resort grounds. Then, at sixteen, I started working the front desk."

Shane wasn't opposed to a kid doing a few chores. Hell, his dad had him mucking out stalls and feeding horses from the time he was old enough to carry a feed bucket. But it sounded as if Donald Jarrod had his kids doing more than just simple chores.

"Whose idea was it for you to go to work at such an early age?" he asked, remembering that he had seen all of the Jarrod children working various jobs around the resort.

She shrugged one slender shoulder. "My father wanted all of us to know the business inside and out. I suppose he thought by starting us out young, we would learn what made Jarrod Ridge the premier resort in Aspen."

He could tell by the tensing of her muscles and the tight tone of her voice that they were skirting a touchy subject. "Do you think it would be all right for you to go riding tomorrow?" he asked, deciding to lighten the conversation. It was obvious she didn't care to talk about her father or the resort and he would have a much better chance of her agreeing to marry him if she were in a better mood. "I'd really like to show you the rest of the ranch. But if you think it would hurt you or the baby, we can wait," he hastened to add.

Her expression brightened. "I would really like that. I'm pretty sure it will be all right. I have a friend in California who rode her horses until she was six months pregnant and everything was fine."

"Great." He pressed a kiss to her forehead. "If you think what you saw of the ranch from the top of the ridge is beautiful, you'll really like seeing Rainbow Falls."

Her eyes twinkled with excitement, making him glad that he had thought of taking her to see it. "You have a waterfall on your property?"

"Yup."

"I love waterfalls. They're always so peaceful and relaxing. We even have the sound of a waterfall piped into the massage rooms at the spa."

"We'll have to get up early," he warned. "It will take us several hours to get there because of the terrain, but believe me, it's well worth it." For reasons he didn't understand and wasn't inclined to dwell on, he wanted to make the outing special for her. Thinking quickly, he added, "I thought we could pack a few sandwiches and have lunch by the falls."

"That sounds absolutely wonderful, Shane." She

covered her mouth with her hand to hide a yawn. "I can't wait."

"I think you'll have to." He chuckled. "Aside from the fact that it's already dark outside, you'd probably fall asleep in the saddle before we rode out of the ranch yard."

"You're probably right." She yawned again. "For the past few days, it seems that I can't get enough sleep."

"Is that because of the pregnancy, too?" He knew a whole lot more about pregnant mares than he did about pregnant women, but he figured it could be the reason behind her fatigue.

"I assume that's the reason," she said, resting her head against his chest.

Shane tightened his arms around her and lowering his head, covered her mouth with his for a quick kiss. Then, reluctantly stepping back, he turned toward the kitchen counter. "Why don't you go into the living room and put your feet up while I load the dishwasher and clean up?"

"Are you sure I can't help?" she asked, sounding tired.

"Positive. It won't take but a few minutes." He rinsed their plates and started stacking them in the dishwasher. "There is one thing you could do for me, though."

"What's that?"

"Turn on the sports channel and see if you can

catch who won the game this afternoon between the Rockies and the Cardinals."

"You're a baseball fan?"

Looking at her over his shoulder, he grinned. "I like baseball as much as the next guy. But this game is kind of special. I have a bet going with Cactus and I'd like to see who wins. He thinks the Cardinals will sweep the Rockies in this three-game series and I say they won't."

Laughing, she shook her head as she started toward the living room. "Men and their sports."

As he started the dishwasher, he couldn't help but think about how fast his plans had changed. When he had first come up with the idea of bringing Lissa to the ranch for the weekend, he had thought they would be spending the majority of their time within the confines of his bedroom. But that had changed in the blink of an eye with her announcement that she was going to have his baby.

Now, even though it made him as jumpy as a day-old colt, his main priority was convincing her to let him do the right thing by her and the baby. He wiped off the counter, then turning out the kitchen light, headed for the living room.

He had three days of uninterrupted time with her to figure out how to get her to say yes. Given her argument about their not knowing enough about each other, it probably wasn't going to be easy.

Smiling to himself as he walked down the hall, he decided he was more than ready for the challenge.

His personal code of honor demanded that he make her his wife and help her raise their child. And there wasn't a doubt in his mind that before he took her back to Aspen, she would agree to be just that.

Three

When Shane turned off the television, Melissa asked, "How much money did you win from your housekeeper?"

"None. If he had won, I was going to have to cook for the next month." Shane laughed. "But since he lost, the old boy is going to have to keep the driveway cleared of snow until spring."

"How old is Cactus?" she asked, hoping he was younger than Shane made him sound.

"I'm not sure," he said as he rose from the couch to take her hand in his. "He's a little sensitive about his age, but I'm pretty sure he's at least seventy and probably a few years older than that."

"He's that old and you're going to make him get

out in the cold to clear the snow?" she asked, allowing him to help her to her feet. She didn't like the idea of Shane taking advantage of the older gentleman. "Tell me you're going to take pity on him and let him out of this stupid bet."

"Not on your life." Grinning, he shook his head. "I don't feel the least bit sorry for him. He'll be on a tractor with a heated cab, a built-in CD player that he can crank up as loud as he wants with his favorite bluegrass music, and if I know Cactus, he'll have a Thermos of Irish coffee to keep him company."

"You make it sound like he was going to win either way."

Shane nodded as they climbed the stairs. "We go through this every fall. He'll come up with a bet he knows he can't win in order to do something he enjoys."

She didn't understand that kind of logic. "Then why doesn't he just volunteer for the job?"

"Because that's not how the old guy works," he explained. "When his arthritis started making it hard for him to do some of the ranch work, I knew he didn't want to leave the ranch. It's been his home for as long as I can remember. So I started complaining about needing someone to cook and take care of the house." Shane grinned. "I didn't really need anyone to do that, and he knew it. But he couldn't come right out and ask me for the job."

"So that's when the bets started?" she guessed.

Shane nodded. "He bet me that I couldn't beat his

time at saddling a horse. If he won, I had to buy him a new pair of boots and if I won, he would take the housekeeping job."

She liked that Shane would go to those lengths to preserve the older man's dignity. It told her a lot more about his character than he realized.

"You did it to save his pride."

"Exactly." Chuckling, Shane opened the door to the room he had shown her earlier. "So, with this latest bet, he not only gets to drive the tractor and pretend he's doing ranch work again, he has something to gripe about while he's doing it. And if there's anything he likes better than complaining, I don't know of it. He got his nickname because he's prickly as a cactus."

Melissa smiled as she entered the room. "He sounds like quite a colorful character."

"He is." Leaning one shoulder against the doorframe, Shane folded his arms across his wide chest. "He can be an ornery old cuss, but he's got a heart of solid gold. I'll make sure you get to meet him sometime."

"I'd like that." When he stood there as if he waited for something, she rose up on tiptoes to kiss his cheek. "Good night."

Before she could back away, he put his arms around her. "It will be once we go to my room."

"I don't understand." With his strong arms around her and the feel of his hard body pressed to hers, she suddenly felt winded. "If you wanted me to spend the night in your room…why did you put my case…in here?"

"I thought you might like to have the privacy this afternoon when you freshened up," he said, nuzzling the side of her neck. "I never intended for you to sleep here."

When his lips skimmed the hollow below her ear, a tingle raced up her spine. "Oh, I thought—"

"—I'd want you to leave my bed once we'd made love," he finished for her. "Not a chance, angel."

That wasn't what she had been thinking, but it was better than telling him that she thought he had lost interest in her now that she was pregnant. Some men couldn't get away from a woman fast enough when they learned of an unplanned pregnancy. Not knowing him any better than she did, what else was she to think?

But apparently she had been wrong about his desire waning. She sighed. It was just one more example of their lack of knowledge about each other, not to mention a serious breakdown in communication.

Before she could point that out, he asked, "Where's your bag? I'll take it to my room."

Taking a step back, she walked over to open one of the dresser drawers and removed her nightshirt. "After I unpacked, I put it in the closet."

He frowned as he pointed to the garment she held. "I've never known you to wear nightclothes."

"That's because you always left my place before I put them on," she shot back. "And since you seemed surprised to learn that I do wear a nightshirt, I assume you don't wear anything to bed."

"Nope," he said, grinning. "I don't like the encumbrance."

She shook her head. "This is what I was talking about earlier, Shane. If we had spent more time getting to know each other, we would know these things."

"You never wanted me to spend the night because you were afraid someone at the resort might find out and start gossiping about it," he pointed out.

She couldn't argue with him about that. It had been at her insistence that he leave Willow Lodge each night after they'd made love.

"But that's water under the bridge now," he said, shrugging.

Too tired to debate the issue any further, she nodded. "I suppose you're right."

He put his arm around her shoulders and steered her out into the hall. "I'll help you move your things to my room in the morning before we leave. Right now, we need to get to bed. We'll have to be up early if we're going to have lunch at the falls tomorrow."

When he led her into his bedroom and turned on the bedside lamp, she took a moment to look around. A lot could be learned from someone's personal space.

She wasn't at all surprised to see the large room was decorated in the same rustic, masculine style as the downstairs. A king-size log bed with a Native American–print comforter and pillows dominated the room. The bright colors of the matching drapes contrasted perfectly with the dark log walls and heavy, peeled-log dresser and chest of drawers.

If she had ever had any doubts about Shane being the quintessential cowboy, they were gone now. One look at his choice of decor was all it took to know that he was a lot like the land he loved—rugged and a little wild. The type of man that was dangerous to a woman's peace of mind. The very type women just couldn't seem to resist.

"How long has your family owned the ranch?" she asked.

"A little over a hundred and twenty-five years." He unbuttoned his shirt. "Hasn't your family owned Jarrod Ridge about as long?"

Fascinated by the play of his chest muscles when Shane shrugged out of the shirt, it took a moment for her to realize what he had asked. "Y-yes, my father's great great-grandfather started it and every generation since has expanded the business."

"What do you think your generation will add to the resort?" he asked, unbuckling his belt and reaching for the button at the waistband of his jeans.

"I don't know," she said absently. She was far too engrossed in watching him reveal his magnificent body to worry about what would happen at Jarrod Ridge.

When he pushed the denim down his thighs, her heart skipped a beat. She had watched him strip off his clothes many times since they began their affair.

She had even helped him take them off a few times, but the sight of his well-developed physique never failed to take her breath away.

"Aren't you going to change?" he asked as he reached for the waistband of his boxer briefs.

He either didn't know the effect he had on her or he was intentionally trying to drive her crazy. She suspected it was the latter.

Suddenly feeling as if she would burst into tears and not entirely certain why, Melissa quickly took off her clothes and pulled the nightshirt on. Walking around to the right side of the bed, she got in and closed her eyes. She was on Shane's ranch, in his bed and pregnant with his baby. It was all too much to comprehend.

Overwhelmed by the events of the day and completely exhausted, she couldn't stop a tear from slipping from beneath her lashes. She swiped it away with the back of her hand and turned onto her side in hopes that he hadn't noticed.

"Lissa, are you crying?"

"N-no."

She felt the other side of the bed dip as Shane stretched out beside her. A moment later, he wrapped her in his arms and turned her to face him.

"What's wrong, angel? Why are you crying?"

His concerned tone and the feel of him holding her so tenderly against him was all it took for the floodgates to open. Sobbing her heart out and unable to stop herself, she clung to him as the torrent of emotion ran its course.

"I—I don't know…why…that happened," she said when she was finally able to get her vocal cords to work. She had never been more embarrassed in her entire life.

"I think I do," he said as his hand continued to stroke her hair in a soothing manner. "You've had a hell of a day and you're so tired you can barely keep your eyes open."

His understanding words and the gentle tone of his deep voice helped ease some of her humiliation. "You're probably right. I think this has quite possibly been the most stressful day I have ever endured."

He reached over to switch off the lamp. Then, cradling her to him, he kissed her so tenderly another wave of tears threatened.

"Try to get some sleep, angel." His arms tightened around her. "It's all going to work out. I give you my word on that."

Too exhausted to think about everything that had happened since her return to Aspen two months ago for the reading of her father's will, Melissa snuggled against Shane and closed her eyes. Maybe with the morning light things would be clearer. Maybe then she would be able to cope with the fact that her life had spun completely out of control and there didn't seem to be a single thing she could do to stop it.

When Shane led the gelding out of the barn and over to the fence, he smiled. "Does this horse look familiar?"

Lissa's blue eyes twinkled with excitement. "He looks just like Smoky Joe."

"That's because he's old Smoky's little brother," he said, handing her the reins. After hearing that the blue roan had been her favorite at Jarrod Ridge, Shane purposely chose the horse for her to ride to Rainbow Falls.

"Thank you," she said as she softly stroked the horse's velvet muzzle. "What's his name?"

"He's registered with the American Quarter Horse Association as Smoke Storm, but we just call him Stormy." Walking back into the barn to get a saddle and blanket from the tack room, Shane returned to placed the saddle over the top fence rail. Then, smoothing the saddle blanket over the gelding's back, he added, "I don't want you to worry that he might be more than you can handle. In spite of his name, there's nothing stormy about him." He picked up the saddle and positioned it on the blanket. "I've seen kittens with more piss and vinegar than this guy."

Lissa smiled as she hugged the animal's neck. "Smoky Joe was that way, too. You could do just about anything with him."

Shane nodded. "That's why we bred the same mare and stallion several different times. The colts they foaled were all good-natured and perfect for people who aren't used to riding a lot."

"In other words, perfect for the inexperienced guests at Jarrod Ridge," she guessed.

He pulled the cinch tight. "That was the idea."

While Lissa and Stormy got to know each other, Shane quickly saddled his sorrel stallion. "Need a leg up?" he asked, turning to see if she needed help mounting the roan.

"I think I can get this," she said, slipping her booted foot into the stirrup.

He stepped behind her in case she had problems and immediately decided that he would have done well to take her at her word. When her perfect little blue-jeans-clad bottom bobbed in front of his face as she climbed onto the saddle, the air rushed out of his lungs like helium from an overinflated balloon.

Holding her soft body to his throughout the night, then waking up with her in his arms this morning without once making love to her, had been a true test of his control. But Lissa hadn't needed his lust. She had needed his comfort and he had been determined to give it to her or die trying.

Exhausted, emotionally spent and extremely vulnerable, she had tried to give the impression that she was fine. He knew differently and once he had taken her into his arms, she had finally let down her guard and accepted the support he had promised her. But not without considerable cost to his well-being.

With her breasts pressed to his chest and her delicate hand resting on his flank, he had spent the entire night aroused. And if that hadn't been enough to send him hovering on the brink of insanity, he had awakened this morning with one of her long, slender legs intimately lodged against his overly sensitive groin.

That had sent him straight into the bathroom for a cold shower. By the time he finally stepped from beneath the icy spray, his teeth had chattered uncontrollably and he would have bet everything he had that he could spit ice cubes on command.

Unfortunately, his gallantry was beginning to wear thin. He wasn't sure how much longer he would be able to play the consummate gentleman without going stark, raving mad.

"Earth to Shane. Come in please," Lissa said, bringing him back to the present.

"What?"

She laughed. "I asked if you are going to just stand there daydreaming or if we're going for a ride?"

"Uh, sorry," he muttered. He couldn't tell her that he had been thinking about how much he wanted to hold her, how much his body ached to be inside her. "There are a couple of different ways to get to the falls and I was trying to decide which would be the fastest," he said, thinking quickly. There was only one trail leading to the waterfall, but she didn't know that and he wasn't about to admit that he'd been fantasizing about stripping them both and making love to her until they both collapsed from exhaustion.

"How far is it to Rainbow Falls?" she asked as he mounted the stallion and they rode through the corral gate.

"It's only about three miles as the eagle flies, but having to skirt some of the steeper terrain and due to all of the bends in the river, it takes a few hours," he explained.

She gave him a wistful look. "I wish I had known about this trip before we left the lodge. I'd have brought my camera. I'm sure the scenery is going to be gorgeous."

He decided not to remind her that once he made her his wife, she would be able to take as many pictures of his ranch as she wanted, any time she wanted. But he wasn't a fool. If he did remind her of that fact, she would most likely come up with more ways they didn't know each other and be on the defensive.

That was the last thing he wanted. His plan hinged on the element of surprise. When he played his ace in the hole, he had no doubt he would have her agreeing to marry him faster than he could slap his own ass with both hands.

"Shane, this is absolutely breathtaking," Melissa said as they rode single file over the ridge and around a switchback into the upland valley.

"It isn't much good for pasturing the horses, but I like to camp out here occasionally," he said, leading the way down the slope.

"I love camping out," she said, remembering the wonderful time she'd had when her father allowed her to go on a couple of overnight trail rides with some of the resort's guests.

It had taken considerable thought on her part and several arguments with her father to convince him that she would be there to address any special needs of the Jarrod Ridge guests. He had finally relented, but only after she had pointed out that she would technically still be working for the resort and not just frittering away her time. God forbid that she did something with her time that she actually enjoyed, she thought, unable to keep from feeling resentful.

"What's wrong?" Shane called over his shoulder.

Jarred back to the present, she focused on the man riding the big red stallion ahead of her. "Nothing. Why do you ask?"

Stopping his horse, he turned in the saddle. "I've seen happier faces on condemned felons."

"The sun was in my eyes," she said, hoping he would drop the matter.

"If you say so." His expression told her that he wasn't buying her excuse, but to her relief, he let it go.

She didn't want to discuss the unreasonable demands Donald Jarrod had placed on his children. It was something she had spent her entire adult life trying to forget and she certainly didn't want to ruin an otherwise glorious day thinking about her childhood. Besides, she didn't know Shane well enough to share the dirt on a family that, up until her father's death and the subsequent discovery that she had an illegitimate half sister, had an impeccable reputation.

They rode in companionable silence for some time before he pointed to the river. "As soon as we go around this bend, you'll see Rainbow Falls just off to the right."

Riding side by side once they cleared the tree line, Melissa's attention once again turned to Shane. He was an expert horseman and handled the stallion with ease. But aside from admiring the way he sat the horse, she simply loved watching him.

With his black Resistol pulled down low on his brow to shade his eyes and a day-old growth of beard, he looked a little wild, possibly dangerous and totally delicious.

A tremor coursed through her and she had to remind herself that lusting after the man was not conducive to getting her life back under control. Not only had she become pregnant because of it, the physical attraction she had for him was in danger of transforming into something deeper, something more meaningful.

Even though what she felt for him was probably nothing more than a temporary infatuation, in the end it could still do a lot of emotional damage and leave behind some deep long-lasting scars.

As devastatingly handsome and charming as Shane was, he just wasn't the type of man for her. He had the reputation of moving from one woman to another, leaving a string of broken hearts in his wake. Given the circumstances they found themselves in now, that was one complication she could definitely do without.

He had made it clear right up front that he wasn't looking for a lasting commitment. Neither was she. She had her own business in California and she might be returning to her life there once the year required to obtain her inheritance was over. She'd reasoned that it was better not to look for anything deeper than a casual relationship until she had decided what she was going to do. After witnessing what some of her friends went through as they tried to maintain long-distance commitments, she had quickly decided it wasn't for her. Things never seemed to work out, and the hurt and disillusionment that went along with a breakup was something she definitely wanted to avoid.

Besides, she hadn't really taken Shane's proposal seriously. That's why she had dismissed outright his outrageous suggestion that they get married. It had to have been a knee-jerk reaction to the startling news, and once he had more time to think about it, she was certain he would see reason. He would probably even be relieved that she'd had the foresight to turn him down.

The sound of rushing water brought her out of her disturbing introspection and, looking up, Melissa realized they had ridden around the bend in the river and arrived at Rainbow Falls. It was everything Shane had told her and more.

Cascading from the ridge high above, the water fell a good seventy-five feet onto the massive boulders below, then slowing, it formed the lazy river that meandered across the valley floor. What caught and held her attention more than anything was the faint rainbow caused by the sun reflecting off the mist created by the falling water.

"It's absolutely beautiful," she said, understanding why it had been named Rainbow River.

"I was pretty sure you would like it." She could hear the satisfaction and pride in Shane's voice and knew he was pleased that she hadn't been disappointed.

They stopped the horses along the riverbank just out of the icy mist and dismounted. As soon as her feet hit the ground, her legs felt as if the tendons had been replaced with stretched-out rubber bands and her muscles had turned to Jell-O.

When she took a wobbly step, Shane was immediately at her side to support her. "Are you all right?"

Nodding, she took another tentative step. "I should go riding more often. Maybe then I would be in better condition."

Shane took her into his arms. "I think you're in great shape, angel." He laughed. "You'd have to be to twist yourself up like a Christmas bow in those yoga classes."

"Yoga is more about stretching and relaxing the muscles." Smiling, she enjoyed the feel of him holding her to him. "Horseback riding takes a certain amount of tensing the thigh muscles to help you stay balanced in the saddle."

"Your thigh muscles don't seem to be all that weak when you hold on to me," he said, nuzzling the side of her neck. His deep baritone sent shivers of excitement streaking up her spine and her legs threatened to fail her for an entirely different reason this time.

Before Melissa had the chance to respond to his suggestive words, his mouth came down on hers and she forgot all about her weak knees or the internal lecture she had given herself about lusting after the man. All she wanted, could even think about, was the feel of his lips moving over hers with such gentle care.

When he used his tongue to coax her to allow him entry to her tender inner recesses, she wrapped her arms around his waist and held on for dear life. As he teased and coaxed her to answer his exploration with one of her own, a lazy heat spread throughout her body and her lower stomach tightened with the ache of unfulfilled desire.

But the spell that seemed to hold her in its grip was broken when he moved his hands to lift the tail of her pink T-shirt and the icy mist coated her bare abdomen. The breeze had shifted, carrying the spray farther than when they first got off the horses and they were both getting wet.

Shane quickly moved them out of the way, but the mood was effectively shattered and not a moment too soon. What on earth had she been thinking?

She had forgotten all about why going blithely along as if nothing had happened wasn't going to solve her dilemma. They hadn't fully discussed or made any decisions about her being pregnant, and that was something they were going to have to address in the very near future. The pregnancy couldn't be hidden indefinitely. Once she started showing, people were going to start talking and asking questions. She wanted to be ready with some answers when they did.

Unfortunately, it was always this way when Shane held her, kissed her. Sound judgment and common sense seemed to take a backseat to the passion and desire he created within her.

"I think we'd better…break out those sandwiches we made…before we left your house," she said, trying to catch her breath. "I'm starting to…get hungry."

His mouth curved upward in a wicked grin. "To tell you the truth, Lissa, I am starved to death right now. But my hunger hasn't got a damned thing to do with food."

Doing her best to ignore the excitement that his candid comment evoked, she walked over to the roan and began unpacking one of the saddlebags. "You, Mr. McDermott, are incorrigible."

He laughed as he helped her spread a blanket for their picnic. "More like insatiable, angel."

"That may be, but do the best you can to contain yourself," she said, smiling as she carried their lunch to the blanket.

Kneeling at the edge of the fleece, she avoided his intense blue gaze as she placed the sandwiches on plates, then opened two small bottles of apple juice. If she looked at him, there was a very good chance she would abandon her resolve and that was something she couldn't afford to let happen.

"We have things to talk about and decisions to make," she said, taking a sip from her juice.

His expression turning serious, Shane lowered himself to sit on the blanket beside her. "Let's put a hold on that for right now. We'll have plenty of time to make our plans tomorrow." Smiling, he reached for a sandwich. "You need to take today to relax and regroup, anyway. Yesterday was a pretty rough day for you."

It was the first reference he had made to her melt-down the night before, and she was grateful that he didn't seem overly interested in pursuing it now. "Maybe you're right."

"I know I am," he said, sounding so darned sure of himself, she wasn't sure whether she should kiss him or take something and bop him with it.

Either way, she decided to take his advice. There would be plenty of time tomorrow to figure what to do about a carefree affair that had unexpectedly become a very serious issue.

Four

The first shadows of evening had just begun to stretch across the valley when Shane and Lissa rode back into the ranch yard. All in all, it had been a pretty good day, he decided as they dismounted. He had been more than a little pleased by her reaction to his ranch and looked forward to showing her more when they had time.

"I've been thinking that supper in front of the television would be nice tonight," he said, leading their horses into the stable. "We can watch a movie on one of the satellite channels or pop a DVD in the player." Unsaddling the stallion, he carried the tack and blanket into the tack room, then returned to the center aisle of the stable to do the same with the roan. "Although, I think I had better warn you. I don't have much in the way of romantic movies in my collection."

"Why doesn't that surprise me?" she asked, laughing as she reached for a brush to groom the gelding. "I have to admit though, a night of vegging out does sound nice. And whatever you choose to watch is fine with me. I'll probably fall asleep before the opening credits even get started."

Finished with brushing the stallion, Shane led the animal down to his stall, then returned for Stormy. "Why don't you go on to the house and take a hot shower? It will only take me another few minutes to feed and water the horses."

Without waiting to see if she took him up on his suggestion, Shane walked Stormy to his stall, then set about giving the animals oats and filling their water troughs. He was surprised when he turned around to find that Lissa had sat down on a bale of straw beside the tack room door to wait for him.

"I thought you were going to take a shower and change," he said, walking up beside her.

Shrugging, she smiled. "I thought we could go back to the house together."

He liked the sound of that and without hesitation, he picked her up and sat down to settle her on his lap. Her arms automatically circled his neck and she laid her head on his shoulder.

Damn, but he loved holding her like this. "Legs still a bit wobbly from riding so much?"

"A little. But not as bad as the first time I dismounted." She snuggled closer. "Thank you for today," she said softly. "I really enjoyed seeing your ranch and Rainbow Falls. It's all very beautiful."

Her warm breath whispering over his neck and the feel of her cradled against him sent his hormones racing. His arousal was not only immediate, it left him feeling light-headed from its intensity.

"I'm glad you had a good time," he said, shifting to a more comfortable position.

"I've been thinking, Shane."

He didn't like the sound of her tentative tone. "About what?"

"This weekend should probably be our last time seeing each other."

Her voice was so quiet he wasn't sure he had heard her correctly. But a bucket of ice water couldn't have been more effective at putting an end to his overly active libido.

Sitting her up on his lap, he met her gaze head-on. "You want to explain yourself? What do you mean this is our last time together?"

She sighed. "Jarrod Ridge is a family-oriented resort. Some of the older investors would likely take a dim view of our having an affair."

"What do you think is going to happen when they find out you're pregnant out of wedlock?" he shot back. The way he saw it, they'd take the news a whole lot better and be less likely to condemn if she had the baby's daddy standing beside her.

She nibbled on her lower lip a moment before shaking her head. "I've thought about that, too. I'm hoping they won't find out."

A chill raced up his spine. She wasn't talking about…

"I'll have to check with our attorney, Christian Hanford, to see if there's a way to keep from losing my inheritance if I move back to California. But having the baby out there would keep the talk down around the resort," she said, oblivious to the fact that she had damned near given him a coronary before she finished explaining. "You and my family will be the only ones who know that I've had a child. I know they'll keep that kind of news quiet in order to keep from jeopardizing our business."

Why did everyone's opinion matter so much to her? For that matter, why did the whole family protect the Jarrod Ridge reputation as if it were as valuable as the gold in Fort Knox?

"Why the hell are you protecting the resort above all else, Lissa?" he asked before he could stop himself. But once the words were out, he couldn't really say he regretted the question.

She looked stunned. "What do you mean?"

"Why are you scared to death about what everyone is going to say or think?"

Shane knew he was treading on dangerous ground, but he had a feeling that it had been drilled into her as a child that appearances were everything and the reputation of the resort came before anything else.

Even if it meant sacrificing her own happiness or well-being.

Her body stiffened and he knew he had hit the nail on the head. "My father's death caused enough upheaval. Jarrod Ridge doesn't need unrest among the people with a vested interest in its success," she insisted. "We need their funding to bring more events to the resort."

He could tell she was avoiding having to answer his questions. He decided to let that slide for now. But eventually she was going to have to stop putting that damned resort and its precious reputation ahead of her own wants and needs. And if it took him having to bring that to her attention, he was up for the challenge.

"I'm one of the investors in the resort and I couldn't care less what the majority of those old goats think."

He pulled her close and wondered what kind of childhood she'd had. If being put to work at the age of eight and her unrealistic concerns about gossip were any indication, it had to have been miserable.

"But we aren't going to talk about any of that now," he said, determined to change the subject. "This afternoon, we made an agreement to get this all straightened out tomorrow. I'm going to hold you to that."

Deciding not to give her the opportunity to argue the point further, he captured her mouth with his. Resistant at first, he felt her begin to relax against him as he traced her perfect coral lips with his tongue, then coaxed her to open for him. His blood heated and his body reacted as it always did when she was in his arms. When he stroked her tongue with his, he could tell from her soft moan that she was as turned on as he was.

Unfortunately, sitting on a bale of straw in a stable had to be one of the least sensual places on earth. Cursing himself as nine kinds of a fool for starting something he couldn't finish until they went to the house, he groaned and reluctantly broke the kiss.

"I think it's about time we took that hot shower," he said, setting her on her feet.

"We?" she asked as he rose to take her hand in his and hurry her toward the stable doors.

He didn't even try to stop his wicked grin. "I've decided it's about time for the ranch to 'go green.' We'll save water by showering together."

When they reached the house, Shane stopped only long enough to remove their boots, then led Melissa toward the stairs. No matter how foolish it might be, she willingly followed him straight into the master bathroom.

She was determined not to think about this weekend being the end of their affair or the loneliness she would suffer once it was over. It might not be smart, but she wanted to store up the memory of his tender touch and the strength of his lovemaking. She would need them on those lonely nights that lay ahead of her once they stopped seeing each other.

"You do realize you're way overdressed for a shower, don't you?" he asked, his blue eyes twinkling with mischief as he closed the door.

She smiled. "I could say the same thing about you, Cowboy."

"Really?" He reached for the snaps on his chambray shirt as he took a step toward her. "I'm pretty sure I can remedy that."

"Don't." She reached up to remove his hat, then hanging it on the doorknob, took his hands in hers and lowered them to his sides. "Let me see if I can take care of it for you."

Releasing the first closure, she kissed his tanned collarbone. "That wasn't too difficult," she said, lightly skimming her nails along his skin as her fingers traveled on to the next snap. She flicked it open, then pressed a kiss to the newly exposed skin. "Neither was that."

His abdominal muscles contracted when she continued on to the next one. She smiled as she slowly released each closure to nibble and kiss his perfect torso. "I think I'm starting to get the hang of this."

"Oh, I would say you've become quite proficient at it." His voice was husky and when she glanced up, the heated look in his blue gaze stole her breath.

As they continued to stare at each other, she finished unsnapping his shirt and tugged the tail of it from the waistband of his jeans. Parting the lapels,

Melissa moved to push the garment over his shoulders and down his arms.

Her heart skipped a beat as she gazed at his sculpted chest and abdomen. Unable to resist, she touched the hard ridges of his stomach with her fingertip, then traced the thin line of hair from his navel to where it disappeared into the waistband of his jeans. She was rewarded with his sharp intake of breath.

"You've got a good start there, angel," he encouraged. "Don't stop now."

"I don't intend to." Unbuckling his leather belt, she shook her head. "I was always taught not to quit until a job was finished." She released the button at the top of his jeans and toyed with the metal tab below. "And to make sure the job was done to the best of my ability."

Slowly, intentionally, she pulled the zipper downward. By the time she eased it over his persistent arousal to the bottom of his fly, Melissa wasn't certain which one of them was having more trouble drawing their next breath.

"Oh my, Mr. McDermott," she teased as she lightly touched the bulging cotton of his boxer briefs. "You seem to have a bit of a problem."

His big body jerked as if an electrical charge had coursed through it. "You caused my current dilemma. Now what are you going to do about it?" he asked through gritted teeth.

The feral light in his eyes caused a delicious

warmth to spread throughout her being. "What would you suggest I do?"

"Finish what you started."

Smiling, she put her hands on his sides, then slipping her fingers inside both waistbands slid his jeans and underwear over his hips and down his legs. He quickly stepped out of them, then kicked them to the side.

She took a moment to appreciate his perfection. Her heart skipped several beats as she let her gaze slide from his handsome face down his torso and beyond. Muscles developed by years of hard ranch work padded his shoulders and chest and his stomach was taut with ridges of toned sinew. Every cell in her body tingled as she took in the beauty of Shane's male body and his strong, proud arousal.

"I love your body," she found herself murmuring.

"It was made just for yours, angel." Lifting the hem of her T-shirt, his grin was filled with such promise it sent goose bumps shimmering over her skin. "Since you've been so nice and helped me out, I think it's only fair that I return the favor."

"I think so, too," she said.

As methodically as she had removed his clothing, Shane removed hers and tossed them into the growing pile on the bathroom floor. When he removed the last scrap of silk and lace, he stood back.

"You're absolutely gorgeous, Lissa." He pulled her into his arms, and the feel of hard masculine flesh touching her much softer feminine skin caused a need within her so deep it reached all the way to her soul.

"I think we'd better take that shower while we still have the strength," he said, his voice hoarse.

She waited until he adjusted the water, then stepped under the luxurious, multiheaded spray. When he joined her, Shane turned her away from him, then reached for a bottle of shampoo. As his large hands began to gently massage her scalp and work the shampoo down the long strands, Melissa didn't think she had ever felt anything more sensual than having him wash her hair.

Neither spoke as he rinsed away the last traces of shampoo, then reached for the soap. Working the herbal-scented bar into a rich lather, he held her gaze as he slowly smoothed his hands over every inch of her body and by the time he was finished she felt more cherished than she ever had in her entire life.

"My turn," she said, taking the soap from him.

Treating him to the same sensuous exploration, she took the time to commit to memory every muscle and cord of his perfect physique. When she finally touched him intimately, she watched him tightly close his eyes. His head fell back and a groan rumbled up from deep in his chest a moment before he took the soap from her, rinsed them both thoroughly, then gathered her to him.

He lowered his head and the moment his mouth came down to cover hers, she put her arms around his wide shoulders and her eyes drifted shut. She could feel herself being lifted and automatically brought her legs up to wrap them around his lean hips. They fit against each other perfectly, and when he entered her with one smooth stroke, Melissa reveled in the feeling of being one with him.

As water sprayed over them from all sides, their wet bodies moved together in perfect unison, and all too soon, she felt herself start to climb toward the peak of completion. Her muscles tensed as the need grew and intensified. Then, as if something inside of her broke free, pleasure filled every fiber of her being and stars danced behind her tightly closed eyes.

Almost immediately Shane's body surged within her a final time and he crushed her to him. She held him just as tightly as he rode out the storm and found his own shuddering release.

When she finally gained the strength to move, Melissa leaned back to look at his handsome face as he still held her to him. For the past couple of months, she had told herself their affair was strictly physical and she could walk away from it at any time with no regrets. She now realized that she had been deluding herself. From the moment he introduced himself at a meeting between her family and the Jarrod Ridge investors, she had not only been attracted to him physically, she had been drawn to his charming personality and easy sense of humor.

"You're amazing," he said, giving her a tender kiss as he lowered her to her feet. He turned off the shower, then helping her out of the enclosure, patted them both dry with a large, plush towel. "Why don't I pop a pizza in the oven and find something for us to watch on one of the movie channels, while you dry your hair and get dressed?" he asked as he wrapped the towel around her, then tucked it under her arms.

"That sounds wonderful," she said, realizing she was actually quite hungry.

He gave her a smile warm enough to melt the polar ice caps. "I'll meet you downstairs on the couch in about twenty minutes."

Feeling more relaxed than she had since taking the pregnancy test, Melissa picked up the hair dryer and turned it on. She wasn't going to think about their predicament, what they were going to do about it or that in less than two days she would no longer be enjoying a few stolen hours with Shane. Tonight she was going to concentrate on the moment and face tomorrow when it came.

"What's your life like out in California?" Shane asked as the movie he had selected for them ended.

The film's storyline had been about a woman returning to her hometown and the life she had left behind to do that. That got him to thinking. He knew what it had been like for Lissa since returning to Aspen for the reading of her father's will. She had to stay for at least one year and manage the Tranquility Spa in order to inherit her share of Jarrod Ridge. But her life in Los Angeles remained a complete mystery to him.

"Life in southern California is, in a word, hectic." She shrugged one slender shoulder. "I've been there since I started college and you would think I'd be used to the pace after all this time."

Her answer surprised him. "But you're not?"

"Not really." She shook her head and shifted on the couch to face him. "Everyone is always in such a hurry to get somewhere or to do something. Then, when they do accomplish whatever they set out to do, they are in a huge hurry to do something else."

"Life in the fast lane can be draining," he said, wondering why she had chosen to go to college so far from home. "But I think it's that way in most urban areas."

She nodded as she removed the fluffy tie holding her hair in a ponytail. "It's a little better in Malibu where I live now, but life still moves a lot faster than Aspen."

"That is a nice area." He had been to Malibu a few times and although it was way too crowded for his taste, Shane had found the view of the ocean to be beautiful. "Do you live near the beach?"

"I have a condo not too far from the Malibu Pier." She smiled. "I like living on the beach and my spa and yoga center, Serendipity, is only a couple of miles away. That's another plus for me."

"Who's running things while you're away?" he asked, reaching out to tuck a wayward strand of hair behind her ear. "I'm sure you left someone you could trust in charge."

He ran his index finger over her hair. He loved the feel of the silky golden threads against his skin. He drew in some much-needed air and forced himself to concentrate on what she was saying. Lissa felt it was important that they talk and learn about each other. Besides, if he was going to get her to go along with his plans of getting married, he was going to have to pay a little closer attention.

"I have two wonderful assistant managers." She smiled fondly. "Michael is very efficient at managerial duties and in the treatment room his hands are pure magic."

"Oh, really?" For reasons he didn't quite understand and wasn't ready to analyze, the only hands Shane wanted her to consider magical were his.

Her enthusiastic nod caused a slow burn to start in the pit of his stomach. "Michael warms the oil with his hands, then when he puts them on your body and starts kneading the muscles…" She closed her eyes and smiled as if imagining the man's hands on her. "…it's pure heaven."

The irritation in Shane's gut exploded into all-out anger and he couldn't figure out why. Maybe it had something to do with the fact that Lissa seemed to enjoy having the man's hands on her a little too much. It might even be the probability that she had been alone with the guy in a dimly lit room with nothing but a thin sheet draped over her nude body. Or more likely, it was a combination of all of it. Whatever the reason, he didn't like it one damned bit.

But Shane couldn't understand the proprietary feeling he had toward her. It wasn't as if he hadn't been with his share of women before Lissa returned to Aspen. It would be ridiculous of him to expect her to have gone without companionship before they started seeing each other. Yet he couldn't quite shake the territorial feeling that ran through him.

"Aren't some of the women who work for you just as good at giving massages?" he asked, wondering why she hadn't asked one of her female employees.

She nodded. "In their own way, yes, they are very good. But being a man, Michael naturally has more strength in his hands and gives a more thorough deep-tissue massage."

"How long has he worked for you?"

"Let's see, he and his life partner, Hector, moved from Florida into the condo below mine about three years ago, and I hired them both shortly after that," she said, looking pleased with herself. "I was really lucky to get them before another spa snapped them up. Besides Michael being the best masseuse I've ever seen, Hector is a master yoga instructor and conducts most of the yoga and meditation classes at Serendipity. He's my assistant manager for the yoga center."

Shane's anger cooled immediately when he realized neither of the men were interested in Lissa. The fact that he felt such relief was almost as disturbing to him as his possessiveness had been. He had never been the jealous type and couldn't imagine what the hell had gotten into him.

Deciding it was time for a change of topic, he asked, "Do you miss not living near the beach?"

"Absolutely," she said, nodding. "Listening to the waves is nice, especially at night when I'm ready to go to sleep. I like to sit on the beach sometimes and watch them roll in to shore. It reminds me of how small and insignificant my problems are compared to the big picture."

"Don't you miss watching the seasons change, angel?"

"They do change," she admitted. "But it's subtle and not nearly as big of a change as here. It's beautiful here in the fall." She grinned. "And I do love Aspen in the winter. There's nothing like flying down the mountain on a pair of skis after a new snow."

"You like the fresh powder?"

"Absolutely." She tilted her head. "What about you? Do you like to ski?"

He gave her a mischievous grin. "I have been known to tear it up on a few of the slopes around here. I've also done a little cross-country skiing."

Yawning, she leaned her head back against the couch. "I've missed being able to participate in the winter activities we have in the mountains."

"They have some nice skiing in California," he reminded her.

"Yes, but I would have to drive several hours to

get there." She smiled. "I like having a ski slope practically in my backyard."

"Then why did you go to college in California in the first place?" he asked before he could stop himself.

Shane had a feeling it had something to do with her getting away from home and the control of Donald Jarrod. But she'd shied away from discussing her relationship with her father, and from her expression, she wasn't interested in discussing it now.

She hesitated as if choosing a suitable answer. "I was young and wanted to spread my wings a bit." Hiding another yawn behind her hand, she gave him a sheepish grin. "I think I need to go up to bed before I fall asleep right here."

He knew she was making an excuse to escape before he had the opportunity to ask any more questions. "You're probably right." Turning off the television, he rose to his feet, then helped her to hers. "What do you say we go upstairs and see just how good I am at giving a massage?"

"But I don't have a problem with tightness in my shoulders or neck," she said as he led her toward the stairs.

"Angel, I wasn't talking about massaging your back." He couldn't stop his wicked grin. "The areas I had in mind are on the front side of your body and a whole lot more interesting."

Shane lay staring at the ceiling long after the woman in his arms drifted off to sleep. The evening had been perfect and given him a glimpse of what life could be like once he and Lissa were married.

Married. The word alone should have had him running for the hills, and he still couldn't quite believe that he was actually going to take the plunge.

Two days ago, the idea of marriage and having a child never crossed his mind. It was simply something he had never allowed himself to contemplate. He had witnessed the hell his father went through when his mother left and that was more than enough to convince Shane he wanted no part of the institution.

He could remember the nights he had lain in bed as a small boy listening to his mother and father argue about how unhappy she was living out in the middle of nowhere. Eventually her pleading for his father to sell the ranch and move them all to a metropolitan area had turned to threats of her leaving.

Then, one day when he was nine, Shane came home from school to find his mother gone and his father passed out with an empty whiskey bottle at his feet. Cactus had stepped in to watch over him and when his father finally sobered up after a two-month bender, Shane asked several times where his mother was. "Gone" was all he could get out of his father each time he asked. Shane finally gave up and stopped asking.

But Hank McDermott was never the same after that. Other than being there to raise his son and instill a strong set of values in him, it was as if his dad had quit caring about everything else and reminded

Shane of a horse that had its spirit broken. Once full of life, his father rarely left the ranch and removed everything in the house that hinted a woman had ever inhabited the place.

Shane had never wanted to give that kind of power over him to any woman. Never wanted a child of his to lie awake at night wondering where his mother was and why he never heard from her again. But with Lissa's announcement that she was pregnant, he suddenly found himself determined to do the very thing he had vowed never to do—get married.

Glancing at her head resting on his shoulder, he took a deep breath and tried to relax. As long as he kept everything in perspective and his feelings for her under control, everything should be fine.

He would be a good provider, a faithful husband to her and a loving father to their child. That's all any woman could ask of a man and all Shane was ready or willing to give.

Five

"It's about time you hauled your sorry butt out of bed."

At the sound of the elderly gentleman's comment, Melissa stopped abruptly just inside the kitchen doorway. Standing at the stove, wearing nothing but a pair of long underwear and boots that had seen better days, the man had his back to her and apparently only heard her approach. She assumed he was Shane's housekeeper, Cactus, and he obviously thought that Shane had come downstairs for breakfast.

How could she let him know that she wasn't who he thought she was without startling him?

When he suddenly turned around, they both jumped. "God's nightgown! Where in the name of Sam Hill did you come from?"

"You must be Cactus," she said, unsure of what else to say. "Shane's told me a lot about you."

"Well, he never told me a damn…danged thing about you," he stammered. "If he had, I sure wouldn't be standin' here in nothin' but my long johns." His wrinkled cheeks turned fiery red above his grizzled beard. "Excuse me, ma'am. I'll go get myself decent."

The man disappeared into a room off the kitchen as quickly as his arthritic legs would allow. A moment later, Shane walked up behind her to wrap his arms around her waist.

"How did you manage to get breakfast started so fast?" he asked, kissing her nape.

Her skin tingled from the contact. "I didn't. It appears that your housekeeper, Cactus, has arrived home a little earlier than expected."

He sighed as he rested his chin on her shoulder. "I'm sorry, Lissa. I should have known this would happen. Whenever he goes to see his sister they always get into an argument and he ends up coming home early about half the time."

"It doesn't matter." She turned within the circle of his arms to smile up at him. "Cactus probably doesn't know anyone affiliated with the resort. Besides, I seriously doubt that he would tell them I was here, even if he did."

Shane kissed the tip of her nose. "Why is that, angel?"

"Because he knows I could tell them I caught him

cooking breakfast in his long underwear," she said, laughing. "If his blush was any indication, I think I embarrassed him all the way to the roots of his snow-white hair."

Rolling his eyes, Shane shook his head. "He definitely marches to the beat of his own drum. But don't worry. He'll get over it."

"Boy, I got a bone to pick with you," Cactus groused as he limped back into the room. "Why didn't you tell me you were gonna have a lady friend comin' for a visit this weekend?"

"I didn't figure it would matter, since you weren't supposed to be here," Shane answered, unaffected by the older man's irritation. Releasing her, he walked over to the coffeemaker. "Have a seat at the table, Lissa, while I pour us a cup of coffee. Lissa, this is Cactus Parsons, my housekeeper and the orneriest old cuss you'd ever care to meet."

"It's nice to meet you, Cactus," she said, smiling.

He nodded. "Ma'am."

Remembering something one of her friends had mentioned about not drinking caffeinated beverages while pregnant, Lissa shook her head. "Thank you, but I think I'll pass on the coffee."

When Shane walked over to sit beside her at the table, Cactus asked, "How do you like your eggs, gal?"

"Say scrambled," Shane whispered. "That's the only way he knows how to cook them."

"I heard that, and it ain't true," the old gentleman retorted. "I know how to put cheese in 'em or if your lady friend would like onions and green peppers, I can make 'em that way, too."

Shane laughed. "But they're still scrambled."

"It don't matter," Cactus insisted, his toothless grin wide. "They're still different than just plain old eggs."

Having grown up in the house where teasing and good-natured banter hadn't existed, Lissa enjoyed listening to the exchange between the two men. It told her a lot about the kind of man Shane was.

Besides going out of his way to preserve an old man's dignity by making bets they both knew were a complete farce, Shane went along with and even encouraged the man's complaints because he knew it made Cactus happy.

That was something her father certainly would have never done for one of his employees. For that matter, he hadn't bothered to do anything even remotely similar to that for his own children.

There wasn't a single time in her life that she could remember her father teasing or playing with her or her brothers. He had reminded them on a daily basis from the time they were old enough to listen that if they weren't excelling academically or working to somehow improve Jarrod Ridge, they were letting themselves down and disappointing him.

"Here you go, gal," Cactus said, interrupting her

thoughts as he placed a plate of bacon and eggs in front of her.

As soon as the plate touched the table, the food that had smelled so delicious only a few moments before caused a terrible queasiness in the pit of her stomach. Glancing at Shane, she watched his easy expression turn to one of concern and she knew she must look as ill as she felt.

Unable to make an excuse for leaving the table, Melissa jumped from the chair and ran as fast as she could for the stairs. She barely managed to make it into the master bathroom and slam the door before falling to her knees.

She had never in all of her twenty-six years been as sick as she was at that moment. If the fact that she was pregnant hadn't sunk in before, it certainly had became very real now.

Feeling as if the blood in his veins had turned to ice water, Shane took the stairs two at a time as he chased Lissa. What the hell was wrong with her?

She had seemed fine when they got up and came downstairs for breakfast. Then, without warning, she'd turned ghostly pale and bolted from the room like a racehorse coming out of the starting gate.

As soon as he entered his bedroom he heard her and found the bathroom door locked. "Lissa, let me in," he demanded.

"Go…away…Shane." Her voice sounded weak and shaky.

"Not until I know you're going to be all right." If he had to, he would break the damned door down. But he wasn't going anywhere until he found out what was wrong with her.

"I think…I have…morning sickness," she said, sounding downright miserable. "Please leave…me… alone so I…can die…in peace."

Feeling completely useless, Shane drew in a deep breath and walked over to sit on the end of the bed while he waited for her nausea to run its course. He felt guilty. If not for one of his swimmers, she wouldn't be in there feeling as if death would be a blessing.

He rested his forearms on his knees and stared down at his loosely clasped hands. He wished there was something he could do for her, but he was at a total loss. Horses didn't suffer through morning sickness and, since he never intended to have a wife and kids, he had never bothered to learn more than the basics about human pregnancies. Now he was going to have to play catch-up and learn all he could on the subject.

Several minutes later as he sat there mentally compiling a list of things that he wanted to research, he heard the bathroom lock click open and Lissa slowly opened the door. His heart slammed against his ribs at her appearance.

She looked as though she had just been through hell. Her usual peaches-and-cream complexion was still a pasty white, perspiration dotted her forehead and her long blond hair hung limp around her shoulders.

"I asked for privacy," she said, sounding completely spent.

"I gave you as much as I thought you needed." He might fall short with his lack of knowledge, but there was no way he would have left her on her own and gone back downstairs. "Does morning sickness last the entire length of the pregnancy or is it a short-term thing?"

Walking over to sit down on the bed beside him, she shook her head. "Every pregnancy is different. Some women have it for the entire nine months and others aren't bothered by it at all. My friend in California only had a problem with morning sickness for a month or so before it disappeared."

Nine months of being sick every morning? Just the thought made his skin crawl. In his estimation even a day or two was way too much.

"Is there something the doctor can give you to keep it from happening?" he asked, hoping there was.

He put his arm around her shoulders and tucked her to his side. Surely in this day and age there had to be something to help a woman get through it.

"I think there is medication to help with the nausea, but since I haven't been to the doctor yet, it's irrelevant at the moment." She yawned. "Maybe it would be a good idea for you to take me back to the resort this afternoon."

Shane didn't have to think twice about his answer. "No way." Rising to his feet, he pulled her up with him, then walked her around to the side of the bed. "There's no one there to take care of you and as sick as you are, I don't want you being by yourself."

"If I need something or someone, I can call Erica," she said, referring to the half sister the Jarrod children had learned of during the reading of their father's will.

"We both know you wouldn't do that," he stated, pulling back the comforter. "Your sister would want an explanation, and you aren't ready to give her one." He motioned for her to lie down. "I told you that I was going to see you through all of this and that is exactly what I intend to do, angel. Now, stretch out and take a nap. Maybe you'll feel better when you wake up."

"You're not going to be a bully about this, are you?" she asked. He thought she might dig her heels in and try to resist him telling her what to do, but to his satisfaction she climbed into bed. "Because if you are, I'm not—"

"Only if I have to be, to make sure I keep you and the baby safe and well," he said, careful to keep his voice gentle. Pulling the cover up over her, he sat down on the side of the bed. "Now get some rest, Lissa." It was only after he kissed her smooth cheek that he realized she had already fallen asleep.

Shane wasn't certain when he had developed the fierce protectiveness that coursed through him now, but there was no denying its presence or its overwhelming strength. Staring down at the blond-haired woman in his bed, he silently made her a promise. No matter what it took, he would do everything in his power to keep her and their child safe and healthy.

"Where's Cactus?" Melissa asked when she came downstairs to find Shane sitting at the computer in his office.

"He and a couple of the men who stayed around for the weekend are playing poker down at the bunkhouse," Shane answered, looking up from the screen.

"What excuse did you give him about my…sudden exit from the room?" She could only imagine what the outspoken old man had to say about that.

"He didn't ask," Shane said, shaking his head. "He muttered something about it being my fault he burned the bacon as he scraped your plate into the garbage disposal." He shrugged. "I didn't bother to correct him." His expression changed to one of concern. "Are you feeling all right?"

His consideration touched her deeply. She had awakened to find a plate of crackers and a cup of weak tea on the bedside table, along with a note from him, telling her not to get up until she had consumed both. Apparently Shane had found the home remedy on the Internet, and whether it had been the nap or the crackers and tea, she did feel a lot better.

Nodding, she sat down in one of the two leather armchairs in front of his desk. "Right now I'm doing fine. I don't know for certain, but I assume since it's called 'morning sickness' that I won't be bothered again until tomorrow when I wake up."

"Good." He stood up and walked around the desk to sit in the chair beside her. "I've been checking the Web for information on pregnancy and doctors. If the tea and crackers work to help alleviate the worst of the nausea, it's best to stick with that, rather than a prescription medication. I'll set my alarm to get up earlier and have them waiting on you when you wake up tomorrow."

She smiled. "It sounds like you've done quite a bit of research."

"You wouldn't believe how much information there is on pregnancy." Clearly amazed, he shook his head. "The first thing we need to do is make an appointment with an obstetrician and get you on prenatal vitamins. Then, we'll have to review your diet to see where nutritional adjustments are needed."

Melissa stared at him a moment as she tried to assimilate Shane the ladies' man, with Shane the expectant father. "I intend to call for an appointment as soon as you take me back to Aspen," she assured him. "And I'm certain I'll be given instructions on what foods I should avoid and what I should add to my diet, when I see the doctor."

Nodding his obvious approval, he went on. "We'll also need to—"

She held up her hand to stop him. "Back up, Cowboy. Where is all this 'we' stuff coming from?"

"I told you, angel. I'm going to be with you every step of the way." He reached over to take her hand in his. "You're not going through this alone."

"I truly appreciate your willingness to help," she said slowly. "But if I'm in California and you're here in Colorado—"

"That's unacceptable," he interrupted, shaking his head. "I'm not going to let you risk losing your inheritance, Lissa."

"And I can't take the risk of having even one of the investors pull out of the upcoming projects planned for Jarrod Ridge."

Unable to sit still, Melissa rose to her feet to pace the floor in front of his drafting table. They had reached the moment she had been dreading. Decisions were going to be made that would affect the rest of their lives, as well as that of their child's. She just hoped with all of her heart they made the right choices.

"There are a lot of people dependent on the resort's success." She needed to make him understand. "Jarrod Ridge is the single largest employer in Aspen. If future projects like the Food and Wine Gala are canceled because the investment capital isn't there, people will start losing their jobs."

"None of that is going to happen," he said calmly.

Turning to face him, she couldn't believe his assertion. "You know Elmer Madison and Clara Buchanan. They are huge investors in Jarrod Ridge and two of the most puritanical members of the group, not to mention the most influential. We both know they'd disapprove of me becoming an unwed mother and convince several of the other investors to take their money elsewhere. I can't be responsible for—"

"The first thing I want you to do is calm down," he cut in. "Stress isn't good for you or the baby." His commanding tone indicated that the issue wasn't up for debate. "And the second is, you're worrying for nothing. Once they learn we're getting married, there's nothing they can say without looking like the pompous, judgmental asses they are."

"Shane—"

"Hear me out, Lissa." He rose to his feet, then walked over to loosely wrap his arms around her waist. "There's no way I'm going to allow you to go back to California to have our baby alone."

"You're starting to sound like a bully again," she warned. No one had told her what she was or wasn't going to do since she had left home after high-school graduation, and she wasn't inclined to let Shane pick up where her father had left off.

"I'm not being a bully. I'm trying to get you to see reason." His tone was less dictatorial and he had apparently gotten the message that she wasn't going to be ordered around. "This is my child, too, Lissa. We may not have planned on you becoming pregnant, but that doesn't mean I don't want to be just as much a part of his life as you do."

She had always wanted children some day and prayed that their father would be more interested and involved than her own father had been with his. That would be next to impossible with her living in one state and Shane in another.

Nibbling on her lower lip, she shook her head. "I'm sure we could work something out that gives us both equal time."

"Don't you see? Marrying me solves everything, angel." He drew her close to press a kiss to her temple. "You get to keep your inheritance, the resort keeps its investors and our baby gets a full-time momma and daddy to raise him."

Either her resistance was down or what he said was beginning to make sense to her. She did want to maintain her share of Jarrod Ridge and she could likely only do that by remaining in Aspen to manage Tranquility Spa. If she married Shane, some of the investors might grumble about her becoming pregnant before the marriage, but it should be enough to keep them from pulling their funding.

Leaning back, she gazed up at his handsome face. She had always hoped to have a husband and family, but in her dreams she had imagined marrying for love, not to save the resort's reputation and funding.

He must have sensed her resolve was weakening. "I give you my word that you won't regret becoming my wife, Lissa," he promised. "We can make this work. We already have a lot more going for us than other couples have."

His statement took her by surprise. "We do?"

He nodded. "We get along well, we enjoy and appreciate some of the same things, we have a fantastic love life and a baby on the way. The way I see it, that's a damned fine start."

"But there's still a lot we don't know about each other," she said, unwilling to give in so easily.

"We'll learn as we go," he said with a knowing grin.

The skunk knew she was going to agree with his plan. Was it too much to ask that he not gloat about it?

"How would we tell everyone the news?" she asked, wondering what her family would say.

Shane looked thoughtful for a moment. "I can make reservations to throw a dinner party in the Sky Lounge. I'm a Jarrod Ridge investor and given the way your family feels about losing its backers, I'm sure your brothers, sister and their significant others will feel compelled to attend."

If there was one thing she was certain of, it was the compliance of her family with one of the resort's investors. Shane and his father before him had contributed quite a lot of money to special events at

Jarrod Ridge. There was no way her brothers would risk losing that.

"I can't think of a single reason that anyone in my family would turn down your invitation."

"Good." His grin widened. "Now, can you think of anything else we should do before we tell your family?"

She shook her head. "Not at the moment."

"Then there's only one thing left to do." He dropped to one knee and taking her hand in his, smiled up at her. "Melissa Jarrod, would you do me the honor of becoming my wife?"

Staring down at Shane, she couldn't help but wonder what she was getting herself into. "I can't believe I'm about to say this," she murmured. Closing her eyes, she took a deep breath. Then, straightening her shoulders, she opened her eyes and nodded. "Yes, Shane, I'll marry you."

Six

The following week as he sat thumbing through a magazine in the obstetrician's waiting room, Shane took note of the pregnant women around him. Their stomachs were various sizes, and he couldn't help but wonder what Lissa would look like in the months to come.

Tossing the magazine on a table beside his chair, he glanced over at her, sitting beside him. He tried to envision her slender figure growing large with his child. From his research, he had learned that some women didn't start showing their condition until late in the pregnancy, while others blossomed early. He wondered which way Lissa would carry their baby.

His speculation was cut short when a nurse called

their names. "Melissa and Shane, if you'll follow me, we'll get your blood work taken care of and weigh you before the doctor does your examination."

Once the woman had drawn Lissa's blood and collected what she needed for a variety of other tests, they were ushered into a small room at the end of the hall. Taking both of their health histories, the nurse finally gave Lissa instructions on preparing for the examination and left the room.

"I think they know more about me now than I do," Lissa said as he helped her lay back on the uncomfortable-looking table.

"If you stick with the same doctor, they'll have all the information on record and it won't take as long the next time," he said, seating himself in a chair beside her.

Raising up on one elbow, she looked at him as if he had sprouted horns and a tail and carried a pitchfork. "Next time?"

"Well, I assumed you'd want more than one child," he said, wondering what the hell had gotten into him. They were just at the beginning of one pregnancy and he was talking about another?

If someone had told him a week ago that he would be sitting in a doctor's office, waiting to find out when his baby was due, he would have laughed them into the next state. Now, he found himself looking forward to learning the approximate time he would become a daddy and discussing the possibility of even more children.

Unreal.

"Let's get me through this pregnancy first," she advised, lying back down against a pillow. "Then we'll discuss our options."

He was saved from opening his mouth and making things worse with her when an attractive middle-aged woman, wearing a set of scrubs and a lab coat, walked into the room. "I'm Dr. Fowler," she said, smiling.

For the next half hour, the doctor examined Lissa, told them what to expect during the first trimester and answered their questions. Then, giving them an approximate date in April for the birth, she handed them a list of do's and don'ts and told them to make an appointment to see her in a month.

"I think I'm on information overload," Shane said as he escorted Lissa across the clinic parking lot to his truck. He helped her up into the cab, then walked around to the driver's side and slid in behind the steering wheel. "What do you say we go to the ranch and chill out until the dinner party tomorrow night?"

"That sounds good," she said, buckling the shoulder belt. "I don't particularly want to run into any of my family until after we tell them our news."

"Why not?" he asked, starting the truck. Never having had a brother or sister, sibling dynamics were something of a mystery to him.

"My brothers probably haven't noticed my frequent absences from the spa this week, but I know my sister, Erica, and my brother's fiancée, Avery, have." She shook her head. "They're sure to ask why I canceled our lunch date today, and I don't want to lie to them."

"I don't blame you." He liked that she was honest and preferred not to say anything, rather than tell a lie.

"Have you told Cactus anything about all of this?" she asked, hiding a yawn behind her delicate hand. "I'm sure he's curious."

Shaking his head, Shane turned the truck onto the road heading west out of Aspen. "No, but he has to know something is up."

"Has he said anything?"

"Not a word."

"Then how do you know he's aware there's something going on?" She looked bewildered and so darned cute, it was all he could do to keep from stopping the truck in the middle of the road and kissing her senseless.

"I've never brought a woman to the ranch before," he answered.

"Never?"

Shane shook his head. "Nope."

"So that's why Cactus was so surprised to see me that morning," she said, sounding sleepy.

"Yup. He hadn't seen a woman in that house since my aunt and her family left Aspen to move to Santa Fe."

He wasn't sure why, but he had never before felt

compelled to bring a woman home with him. Nor had he ever been tempted to take a woman to see Rainbow Falls. At least he hadn't until he met Lissa.

Glancing over at her, he realized she had fallen asleep. What was it about her that was different from other women he had been involved with?

As he steered the truck onto the private road leading over the ridge to the ranch, Shane decided that he was probably better off not knowing. There were some questions that were better left unanswered and he had a feeling this was one of them.

"Melissa, you look amazing," Avery Lancaster said, when she and Melissa's brother Guy walked up to her outside of the doors to the Sky Lounge. "Is there a new facial treatment in the spa I haven't heard about?"

Hugging her brother's fiancée, Melissa smiled as she shook her head. "I've just been getting more rest and eating a bit healthier."

It wasn't a lie. Of late, all she wanted to do was sleep and she had added an extra serving of fruits and vegetables to her diet each day.

"Well, whatever you're doing is working," Avery said, laughing. "You're positively glowing."

"You do look different," Guy agreed, frowning.

The fact that her brother thought he noticed a change in her was a bit of a shock. Since meeting the beautiful wine expert at his side, he was barely aware of anything else around him.

Melissa's brother Trevor chose that moment to stroll over to them. "Do any of you know what this party is all about? I've never known McDermott to be overly social. Usually the guest lists for his get-togethers consist of himself and the lady of the moment."

"Are you sure you aren't talking about yourself?" Guy asked, grinning.

Unrepentant, Trevor laughed. "I never said I thought McDermott was in the wrong on that."

"To answer your question, I have no idea what this dinner is about," Guy said, opening the door to the lounge. When the three went inside, he held the door for Melissa. "Are you coming?"

"I'll be there in a minute," she said, spotting her half sister, Erica, and her fiancé, Christian Hanford, as they got off the elevator.

Listening to her family speculate about Shane's invitation was the last thing she needed. Her nerves were already as tight as a bowstring. Once they made their announcement about getting married and having a baby, the course would be set. She just prayed with everything that was in her it was the right one.

"Avery and I missed you at lunch yesterday," Erica said, hugging Melissa close. "Are you all right?"

Feeling guilty for avoiding her newfound sister for the past week, she nodded. "I'm fine. I've just been preoccupied lately with...a new project."

Melissa truly liked her half sister and regretted that her father hadn't let them all know about her.

But whatever Donald Jarrod's reasoning had been, the family hadn't learned of her existence until the reading of their father's will two months earlier.

"Let's go in and see what McDermott has up his sleeve," Guy's twin, Blake, suggested as he joined them. As usual Blake had his trusted secretary, Samantha Thompson, at his side, and Melissa wondered for at least the hundredth time since meeting her how long it would take for Blake to realize what a beautiful woman Samantha was.

As the five of them entered the Sky Lounge, Melissa immediately spotted Shane at the doorway of one of the private gathering rooms, greeting her family as they arrived. He always looked good to her, but tonight he looked positively devastating in his black suit and tie. Very few men could look at ease in business suits as well as jeans and a work shirt. Shane managed to do it effortlessly.

"Where's Gavin?" he asked when they reached him.

"He should be here shortly," Blake answered, shrugging. "As we were getting on the elevator, I saw him in the lobby, talking to an old friend of his."

Motioning toward a large round table in the center of the room, Shane smiled congenially. "Have a seat and we'll get started as soon as he gets here." Trailing behind the two couples, Melissa stopped when Shane touched her arm. "I want you to sit in one of the two chairs tipped up against the table," he whispered close to her ear.

Seeing the chairs with their backs leaning against the table's edge, she nodded. Walking over, she set the chair upright and seated herself. She knew from the look on Erica's face that her sister expected Melissa to sit in the empty chair beside her. She hated that she might have hurt Erica's feelings, but she was sure her sister would understand once she and Shane explained the purpose of the party.

"Sorry I'm late," Gavin apologized as he and Shane approached the table together. "I ran into one of the guys we graduated high school with and stopped to say hello."

Once her brother was seated with the rest of her family, Shane straightened the chair beside her, but instead of seating himself, he remained standing. "I know you're all wondering why I invited you here tonight," he said, making eye contact and smiling at each individual at the table.

"Well, now that you mention it, we did—" When his oldest brother elbowed him, Trevor stopped short to glare at Blake.

Shane smiled. "I don't blame you. I would have been curious, too, Trevor."

Melissa tightly clenched her hands, resting in her lap. He was about to reveal the secret they'd kept for the past two months, and although it would be a relief to have their affair out in the open, she just hoped they were doing the right thing.

Lost in thought, she was surprised when Shane reached down to take her hand in his and pull her up to stand beside him. "Since your sister's return to Aspen a few months ago, we've been seeing each other and our relationship—"

"I knew it!" Trevor said triumphantly. Obviously proud of himself for noticing what the others had missed, he added, "When I saw the two of you together back in July, I knew something was going on."

"Don't break your arm patting yourself on the back there, Trevor," Gavin said drily. "I suspected Melissa was hiding something, too. I just didn't know what it was."

When the laughter at the table died down, Shane put his arm around Melissa's shoulders and gazing into her eyes, announced, "Lissa and I wanted all of you to be the first to know, we're getting married and will be welcoming our first child next spring."

Before anyone could react, Shane lowered his head and gave her a kiss that caused her head to spin and her toes to curl inside her sensible black pumps. When he finally raised his head, there was a hushed silence. Then, everyone started talking at once.

"Congratulations you two," Guy said, grinning from ear to ear. "It looks like my pastry chef is going to be busy for quite some time making nothing but wedding cakes."

"That's great," Trevor said happily. "Now that McDermott is off the market, I won't have as much competition with the ladies."

"I'm so happy for you," Erica said, rushing around the table to hug Melissa.

Avery was right behind Erica to wrap her arms around Melissa. "I never suspected a thing. I don't know how you managed to keep quiet about a relationship as serious as this." Giving her a watery smile, Avery added, "I think it's wonderful."

As her brothers and Christian took turns shaking Shane's hand, Melissa noticed that although Blake's secretary, Samantha, added her congratulations, the woman seemed uncharacteristically quiet and subdued. What could possibly have the vibrant brunette so down in the dumps?

Before she had a chance to speak to the woman and ask if everything was all right, Gavin wrapped Melissa in a brotherly bear hug. "I wish you every happiness, little sister."

Tapping on his water glass with the edge of his knife, Blake drew everyone's attention. "I'd like to make a toast."

To her surprise, one of her brothers had ordered a bottle of champagne and the waiter had just poured them all a glass of the sparkling pink wine. All except for her and Avery. Their glasses held sparkling white grape juice.

"I'm pregnant," Melissa said, pointing to Avery's glass. "What's your excuse?"

Her friend made a face. "Remember, champagne makes me sneeze."

Melissa didn't have time to dwell on the matter when Blake raised his glass.

"To Melissa and Shane," he said, smiling. "May you have a long and happy life together.

Everyone raised their glass in agreement, then taking a sip of wine, settled down to dinner and conversation. As it always did, talk turned to plans for expanding the resort's services and special promotions. Melissa tuned most of it out as she watched her family.

Apparently so did Erica and Avery. They'd been huddled together since finishing their desserts and she wondered what the two of them were up to.

All in all, the evening had gone quite well, she decided, feeling more at ease than she had in several days. It was a huge relief to have her and Shane's relationship out in the open.

As the evening drew to a close and everyone gathered their things to leave, Erica and Avery pulled Melissa aside. "Let's get together for lunch on Wednesday," Avery said, her eyes twinkling.

"We want to start making plans for a baby shower," Erica added, just as excited.

Melissa was touched by their enthusiasm and happiness for her. "I'd like that, but don't you think it's a bit early to start planning something like that? I'm only a couple of months along."

"You can never start planning the perfect party too early," Avery said, laughing.

"Besides, from everything I've been told, it will

start getting extremely busy in a couple of months when the ski season starts," Erica agreed. "If we get most of the details worked out now, we won't be so rushed later on."

Agreeing on a time for their lunch, Melissa watched her sister and future sister-in-law leave the restaurant. She loved finally having female family members. After growing up as the only girl in a house full of boys, it was definitely a welcome change.

"I think everything went pretty well tonight," Shane said, walking up to put his arm around her. "At least, none of your brothers threatened to grab their shotguns and run me out of town."

She laughed. "I doubt that any of them own a shotgun." As they walked from the Sky Lounge, she added, "I'm just glad everything is out in the open and we don't have to sneak around anymore."

"Yeah, I'm not going to miss those midnight treks from the stables through the woods to Willow Lodge one damned bit. It's a wonder someone hadn't noticed and thought I was a Peeping Tom." Waiting for the elevator, his laughter turned into a grin that held such promise it stole her breath. "From now on, I'll just roll over and turn out the light."

"Really?" she asked, laughing at his lascivious grin.

"Most definitely." He leaned close to whisper, "And just in case you have any doubts about that, I intend to give you a demonstration as soon as we get back to the lodge."

* * *

Using Lissa's key, Shane let them into Willow Lodge, then closing and locking the door behind them, took her into his arms. He nibbled kisses from her neck up to her delicate earlobe.

"I've been wanting to have you all to myself all evening." Used to being alone with her, he'd had the devil of a time keeping his hands to himself.

"The dinner party did seem to drag on, didn't it?" She put her arms around his waist and snuggled close. "Thank you, Shane."

He leaned back to gaze down at her. "For what?"

"For taking charge tonight when we told my family about us." She kissed his chin. "I wasn't quite sure how to go about it."

"I never said I hadn't rehearsed a few dozen different speeches before I settled on one." He grinned. "When you're in a room full of men who just might take your head off and shout down your neck because you got their little sister pregnant, it inspires you to think things through."

"You did just fine," she said, unknotting his necktie. He loved the feel of her fingers brushing his throat as she removed the silk tie.

Placing his hands on her shoulders, he turned her around. "As good as you look in this dress, I think you'll look much better out of it."

Slowly sliding the zipper down from her neck to her lower back, he sucked in a sharp breath. "Good thing I didn't know earlier that you weren't wearing a bra," he said, kissing the back of her neck. "I'd have never made it through the evening."

When he started to slide the black dress from her shoulders, she caught the front to her and shaking her head, stepped away from him. "Why don't you build a fire in the fireplace while I change?"

As she walked from the room, Shane blew out a frustrated breath and slipping off his suit coat, unbuttoned and rolled up the sleeves of his dress shirt. Building a fire hadn't been high on the list of things he'd had planned for the evening. In fact, it hadn't been anywhere on it. But it was something Lissa wanted, and he was finding more and more that he was willing to do whatever it took to make her happy and see her pretty smile.

A nice fire had just started crackling in the stone fireplace when the lights in the great room went out. A moment later, Lissa walked up and knelt down beside him in front of the hearth.

"I thought these might be nice to snuggle up with," she said, setting a stack of pillows and a couple of fluffy blankets on the floor beside him.

Glancing over at her, he did a double take. She was wearing the sexiest black satin robe he had ever seen. One side of the slinky little number had slipped down over her bare shoulder and he knew as surely as he knew his own name, she didn't have a stitch of clothes on beneath it.

"Do you want me to make some hot cocoa?" she asked before he could find his voice.

Shane swallowed hard and shook his head. The shimmering light cast by the fire seemed to bathe her in gold, and he knew for certain he had never seen her look more beautiful.

"The only thing I want is right here beside me," he said, pulling her to him. He brushed his mouth over hers. "Do you have any idea how sexy and desirable you are?"

"I haven't really thought about it," she said, toying with the top button of his shirt. "I've been too busy thinking about how much I think you deserve a good, relaxing massage."

His mouth went as dry as a desert in a drought. What man in his right mind would turn down having a beautiful woman run her hands over every inch of his body?

Without a word he stood up, and while she arranged the blankets and pillows on the hardwood floor in front of the fireplace, he made short work of taking off his clothes. It was only after he lay facedown on the soft blankets that she slipped the robe off. Dropping it beside him, she picked up a bottle of oil that he hadn't noticed before. He felt her pour several drops of the warm liquid onto the middle of his back.

At the first touch of Lissa's palms on his bare skin, Shane felt as if he had died and gone to heaven. Her gentle, soothing touch was driving him crazy and his reaction was not only completely predictable, it was immediate.

By the time she worked her way down the back of his thighs and calves, then told him to turn over, he felt as if the temperature in the room had gone up several degrees. Never in his entire life had he experienced anything as exciting and arousing as having Lissa's hands gliding over his body.

Their eyes met and, holding his gaze with hers, she drizzled a small amount of the oil onto the middle of his abdomen. As she caressed his shoulders and pectoral muscles, Shane ached with the need to hold her, to touch and excite her as she was doing to him.

"Enough," he said, catching her hands in his to pull her down beside him.

Covering her mouth with his, he traced her soft lips with his tongue. He didn't think he had ever tasted anything sweeter. When he coaxed her to open for him and the tip of her tongue touched his, he felt as if a charge of electric current coursed from the top of his head all the way to his feet.

He broke the kiss and turned her to her back. Deciding to treat her to a little of the same sweet torture she had put him through, he picked up the bottle of oil. Smoothing the slick liquid over her satiny skin, he paid special attention to her breasts and tightly puckered nipples. By the time he moved down to her flat stomach, he wasn't certain which one of them was suffering more.

The blood rushing through his veins caused his ears to ring as he stared down at her. Her expressive blue eyes reflected the same hunger that filled him and her porcelain cheeks wore the blush of intense passion. Shane knew for certain he would remember her this way for the rest of his life.

The evidence of her desire fueled his own and the need to once again make her his was overwhelming. Using his knee to part her thighs, he settled himself over her.

"P-please," she murmured.

"What do you want, angel?"

"You." She reached to put her arms around him. "I want you, Shane."

His breath lodged in his lungs as he pressed himself forward and her supple body accepted him. Closing his eyes for a moment in a desperate attempt to hang on to his rapidly slipping control, he held himself completely still. He wanted to make this last, to love her slowly and thoroughly. But when she wrapped her long legs around his hips to hold him to her, Shane knew he had lost the battle.

With his pulse pounding in his ears like a sultry jungle drum, he slowly began to rock against her. The way she met him stroke for stroke, their bodies perfectly in tune, sent a flash fire to every fiber of his being and clouded his mind to anything but the mind-blowing pleasure surrounding them.

All too quickly, he felt her body tighten around his. Her feminine muscles clung to him, driving Shane over the edge, and he felt as if he had found the other half of himself when together they found the release they both sought.

Melissa couldn't help but smile when she snuggled against the man sleeping next to her. After they made love in front of the fireplace, he had carried her into the bedroom to make love to her again. Then, true to his word, he had rolled over and turning off the bedside lamp, pulled her close and gone to sleep.

As she studied his handsome face, she thought about how wonderful he had been at dinner. He had seemed genuinely happy when he told her family about their upcoming marriage and the baby they'd have in the spring.

Placing her hand on her still-flat stomach, she couldn't help but marvel at the fact that she was going to be a mother. For as long as she could remember, she had hoped to one day have a precious little miracle of her own to hold and love. She reached out to touch Shane's strong jaw with her fingertip. He had made that happen and she couldn't help but love him for it.

Her heart skipped a beat. She had known from the beginning of their affair that she was in danger of getting in over her head. He had been clear that their involvement was temporary and she had wanted that, too. But the attraction she had felt for him was too strong, had been too immediate not to pose a serious threat to her peace of mind.

She had told herself she could control her infatuation and avoid falling in love with him as long as she kept things in perspective. She knew now that she had been lying to herself all along.

If the truth was known, she had fallen in love with him the moment they laid eyes on each other two months ago. He was the most charming, considerate man she had ever met and the longer she was around him the deeper her feelings had grown.

Her chest tightened and a tear slid down her cheek. She quickly swiped it away with the back of her hand. In the coming months, she was going to have almost everything she had always hoped for. She was going to marry the man she loved, have a home in one of the most beautiful places on earth and start the family she had always longed for.

So why couldn't she be happy and content with that?

Melissa knew exactly what was keeping her picture-perfect fantasy from becoming reality. She wanted it all. She wanted the home, the family and the one thing she wasn't sure Shane would ever be able to give her…his love.

Seven

"It looks like I'll just have to take a couple of the appointments myself," Melissa said as she and Rita went over the afternoon reservations.

"I'm so sorry, Ms. Jarrod," Rita apologized for at least the tenth time. "I don't know how I could have made that kind of mistake."

"It's all right, Rita. These kinds of things happen from time to time," Melissa assured her. "Just look a little closer next time to make sure there's an opening at the time requested by the guest."

Rita was beginning to gain more confidence and improve her managerial skills, and Melissa was hopeful that would continue. She knew the woman was a single mother and needed the job to support herself and her son. She certainly didn't want to cause Rita any more stress by having to replace her.

"Ready to go?"

Looking up, Melissa smiled at Avery as she entered the Tranquility Spa's reception area. "Would you mind if we have lunch in the Sky Lounge today?" she asked. "I only have an hour or so before I have to be back."

"Problems?" Avery asked.

Giving Rita an encouraging smile, Melissa shook her head. "Not really. I'm afraid there was a mix-up and we're overbooked this afternoon. It seems all of the Jarrod Ridge guests want a spa treatment before this weekend's dinner honoring the investors. I'm going to have to do a couple of the massages and at least one of the facials myself."

"Wow! You are busy," Avery said, her eyes widening. "But that actually works out better for me, too." She grinned. "In fact, I was going to ask you if the Sky Lounge would be okay. I wanted to stop by and talk to Guy for a few minutes after we eat."

"What about Erica?" Melissa asked, grabbing her purse. "Is she going to be able to meet us?"

Avery nodded. "I called her this morning and asked her to get a table by one of the windows and that we'd meet her in—" she looked at her watch "—oops. Five minutes ago."

"Then I suppose we'd better get going," Melissa said, laughing. She loved that in the past couple of months she had gained a sister and a future sister-in-law that were also quickly becoming her best friends.

A few minutes later, as they got off the elevator and entered the Sky Lounge, they immediately spotted Erica and hurried over to the table she had been saving.

"I'm sorry we're running late," Melissa apologized as she slid into one of the empty chairs.

"You can blame me for that," Avery said, seating herself. "Guy was running late leaving to go to the restaurant this morning because I…that is we…I mean—"

Grinning as they watched Avery squirm, Melissa and Erica both propped one elbow on the table, cupped their chins in their hands and asked in unison, "Yes?"

"Uh, never mind." Avery's cheeks were pink as she shook her head and quickly picked up a menu. "I think I'm going to have the tuna melt."

"Nice save," Melissa said, laughing as she picked up her menu.

After they placed their order, the conversation turned to plans for the baby shower. "I won't know for a few more months whether to decorate in pink or blue," Melissa said, shrugging.

Erica smiled. "What are you hoping for? A boy or a girl?"

"I haven't really given it much thought," Melissa admitted. "But it doesn't matter to me as long as the baby is healthy."

"That's all that's important," Avery said, nodding.

Choosing a date in February for the shower, they discussed nursery themes and shops where Melissa should register. By the time they finished lunch and left the restaurant, she had only a few minutes to get back to the spa.

"I suppose I'll see you both on Saturday evening at the dinner?" she asked as they got off the elevator in the lobby.

"Christian and I wouldn't miss it," Erica said.

"We'll be there." Avery grinned. "I'll probably have a hard time keeping Guy out of the kitchen, though. You know how he is about wanting every dish to be perfect."

"Since Guy took over managing the resort's restaurants and brought in Louis Leclere as chef, the efficiency of the kitchen staff has improved greatly," Melissa said.

"The new items they've added to the menu seem to be a big hit, too," Erica added.

Melissa checked her watch. She had only a few minutes to make it to the first massage appointment. "I'm really sorry, but I have to run. See you on Saturday."

As she hugged them both and headed down the hall toward the spa entrance, something Erica asked her at lunch kept running through her mind. It didn't matter to her whether their baby was a boy or a girl.

But did it matter to Shane whether they had a son or a daughter?

Like most men, he would probably prefer to have a boy. But she didn't think he would be disappointed either way. Unfortunately, it was hard for some men to hide their feelings. She had always suspected that her father had been disappointed she was female.

Of course, she couldn't say he had treated her brothers much better. He had driven all of his children to be overachievers and in the process alienated them from the very thing he had wanted them to embrace—Jarrod Ridge.

Shaking her head, she relegated thoughts of her late father to the back of her mind as she walked through the reception area of Tranquility Spa and prepared to go back to work. The sooner she finished for the day, the sooner she and Shane could leave for the ranch.

For some reason he had insisted they have dinner at Rainbow Bend, which was fine with her. She loved the peace and quiet of the remote ranch and after a day filled with booking mix-ups, Melissa couldn't wait to get there.

"Dinner was delicious, Cactus," Lissa said as she helped clear the table. "How did you know I love country-fried steak smothered in milk gravy?"

The elderly man beamed. "I didn't, but I sure am glad you liked it, gal."

Shane sat back and watched the exchange with

interest. Cactus didn't care for most people and the fact that he was falling all over himself to please Lissa said a lot. If Shane didn't know better, he would swear the old boy was completely smitten.

Of course, he couldn't blame Cactus. With each passing day, Shane found himself thinking about her more often, wondering what she was doing and counting the hours until they could be together again. It was something he wasn't sure he was comfortable with, but there didn't seem to be anything he could do to stop it, either.

Deciding that it would be better for his peace of mind to simply not think about it, he left the table. "Lissa, I have something that I'd like for you to take a look at."

"Can it wait?" she asked, handing Cactus a plate to rinse. "After that wonderful meal, the least I can do is help Cactus with the cleanup."

"Don't you worry about it, gal," Cactus said, shaking his head. "Since Shane got me this here dishwasher, I don't mind doin' kitchen chores near like I used to."

"Are you sure?" When Cactus nodded, she surprised the old man by kissing his wrinkled cheek. "Thank you for dinner. It was wonderful."

Shane had known Cactus all of his life and he'd never known the man to be at a loss for words. He always had something to say, whether it was to give his unwavering opinion or complain—which was usually the case. But the old geezer couldn't seem to find his voice. He just stood there wearing the sappiest expression Shane had ever seen.

"You wanted to show me something?" Lissa asked, drawing Shane's attention. She had walked over to him and he had been so astounded by Cactus's atypical behavior, he hadn't noticed.

Smiling at her, Shane nodded. "But there is something I think we need to do first."

"What's that?"

"We are going to make Cactus's day," he whispered close to her ear. Shane put his arm around her shoulders and tucked her to his side. "Cactus, what would you say if I told you that pretty soon you'll be able to cook for Lissa a lot more?"

"That'd suit me just fine," Cactus said, nodding his approval. "She's a danged sight more appreciative 'bout my cookin' than you are."

Shane laughed. "So you want me to start kissing you now after every meal?"

"Try it and you'll be missin' your front teeth," Cactus warned, turning back to the dishes in the sink.

"Then I guess after we get married, I'll just have to leave the kissing up to Lissa," he said, anticipating the old gent's reaction. Shane didn't have long to wait.

He hadn't seen Cactus move as fast in years as when he spun around to face them. "Well, I'll be damned." If he'd had teeth, his ear-to-ear grin would have lit a city block. "Married, you say?"

Shane glanced down at Lissa and winked. "Do you think I should tell him the rest?"

"You might as well," she said, smiling.

"There's going to be a baby joining us in the spring." A sudden, unfamiliar feeling settled in his chest and Shane realized that he was actually beginning to get excited by the prospect of becoming a daddy.

"I guess now that there's gonna be a woman and youngin' underfoot, you're gonna expect me to stop my cussin', scratchin' and spittin'," Cactus said, his grin belying his complaint.

"It probably wouldn't be a bad idea." Laughing, Shane turned Lissa toward the hall, then called over his shoulder, "You'll have to give up cooking breakfast in your long johns, too."

As they walked down the hall to his study, he chuckled. He could still hear Cactus grumbling about kids, women and bone-headed ranchers who expected him to give up everything worth doing.

"What did you want to show me?" Lissa asked, when they entered the study and he closed the door.

She looked so sweet and desirable, he didn't think twice about taking her into his arms and kissing her until they both gasped for breath. When he finally raised his head, Shane drew in some much-needed air.

"I've been wanting to do that all day."

Her smile sent his temperature skyrocketing. "I've missed you, too."

"How was your day at the spa?" he asked, a bit surprised that something so mundane suddenly felt important to him.

She shook her head. "Don't ask. You really don't want to know."

Leaning back, he frowned. "That bad, huh?"

"Just tiring." She explained about the booking mix-up, then smiling, asked, "How about you? Anything interesting happen?"

"I got a call from Sheik Al Kahara." He shrugged. "He wants to hire me to design all new stables for the Thoroughbred farm he just bought in Kentucky."

"That sounds like a challenge," she said, sounding genuinely interested. "Do you have to do a lot of traveling with jobs like that?"

"I have to travel occasionally, but not more than once or twice a year." He shook his head. "Most of my clients e-mail the size of stable they want and what they want included in the design. I send them a quote and then once we sign the contracts, I go to work on the design. But the sheik's is going to be a piece of cake. He basically wants the same setup I designed for the stables at his palace in Almarif."

Her eyes widened. "Do you have a lot of foreign clients?"

"I have quite a few."

"Are they all royalty?"

Her curiosity about his career pleased him more

than he would have thought. "Not all of them are royalty, but I have designed stables for several members of this or that monarchy." Taking her hand, he led her over to the other side of the room. "But I don't want to talk about sheiks or stable designs right now." He motioned for her to sit in one of the chairs in front of the fireplace. "I want your opinion on something."

"I can't guarantee how much help I'll be, but I'll try," she said, smiling as she settled into the high-backed leather armchair.

"Oh, I think your opinion on this counts for a lot more than you think." He turned to remove the small, black velvet box he had placed on the fireplace mantel before leaving to pick her up after she got off work. Flipping the box open, he turned to hold it out to her as he watched for her reaction to the pear-shaped diamond solitaire in a white-gold setting that he had bought for her the day before. "Do you think you would be interested in wearing this to the investors' dinner on Saturday evening?"

If the look on her face was any indication, he had hit a home run. "My God, Shane, it's beautiful."

Removing the sparkling jewelry from the box, he took her left hand in his to slip the ring on her third finger. To her delight and his relief, it fit perfectly.

"How did you know my ring size?" she asked, jumping from the chair to throw her arms around his neck.

"I guesstimated," he said, catching her to him. "So you like it?"

"I love it." She leaned back to stare down at her hand. "It's exactly what I would have chosen." Then, looking up, the smile she gave him lit the darkest corners of his soul. "Thank you."

"Are you ready for my other surprise?" he asked, kissing the tip of her nose. He decided there wasn't anything he wouldn't do just to see her smile at him like she was at that very moment.

Her eyes widened. "There's something else?"

He took her by the hand and led her out of the study to the front door. "I want you to close your eyes and keep them closed until I tell you to open them."

"What are you up to now?" she asked, laughing.

"If I told you it wouldn't be a surprise." Shane grinned. "Would you rather I blindfold you?"

She shook her head. "No, I promise I'll keep my eyes closed."

Once she did as he asked, he helped her down the porch steps and across the yard. "Don't peek," he warned, releasing her hand to untie a set of reins from the corral fence.

"Shane, what on earth—"

Placing the leather straps in her hand, he said, "Okay, you can open your eyes."

When she did, she looked puzzled. "I don't understand."

"Stormy is yours now, angel." The look on her face was everything he had hoped for.

"He's mine?" Her eyes sparkled as she stared at the blue roan, standing saddled in front of her.

"Yup." Shane grinned. "I've already sent in the paperwork to transfer his registration to you."

She glanced at the sun sinking low in the Western sky. "Do you think we have enough time to take a short ride?"

Grinning, Shane nodded. "I thought you might want to do that. That's why I had one of my men saddle Stormy and have him ready." As Lissa mounted her horse, Shane walked into the stable. He returned with his stallion and swung up onto the saddle. "We should have time to ride to the trailhead that leads to Rainbow Falls and make it back before dark."

"Thank you for everything." Riding the roan up beside his sorrel, Lissa leaned over to kiss his cheek. "This is the nicest, most thoughtful thing anyone has ever done for me." Her delighted expression suddenly turned to a teasing grin. "You are going to get so lucky tonight."

"Then let's get the hell out of here," he said, nudging his stallion into a lope.

"What's your hurry, Cowboy?" she asked, laughing as she urged Stormy to follow.

"I want to get back." When she caught up to him, he grinned. "I could really use some…luck."

* * *

As they rode across the valley back to the stable, Melissa couldn't keep from smiling. "I love it here."

"Really?" It sounded as if Shane had a hard time believing she meant what she said.

"Who wouldn't love this?" Twisting around in the saddle, she took in the majestic beauty of the surrounding snowcapped mountains. "This has to be the quietest, most peaceful place on earth."

"Some people would rather live where there are people around and things to do besides sit and listen to the grass grow," he said, staring straight ahead.

She shook her head. "I'm not one of them."

"That reminds me. There's something else we need to discuss before we get married," he said slowly. "Where do you want to live?"

Confused, she stopped her horse. "This is your home. I assumed you'd want us to live here."

Reining in the stallion, Shane turned to meet her questioning gaze. "I do want to live here. It's home. But I also know and accept that once the snows start, I may only get out of the valley a handful of times until the spring thaw. I accept the fact that there isn't a convenience store just around the corner. It's a good ten-mile drive if you forget to buy something while you're in town."

It was almost as if he was trying to talk her out of living on the ranch. Once they were married, didn't he want her to live with him?

"I remember you telling me the first day you brought me here that the road leading into the valley sometimes gets closed off for several weeks."

His intense gaze caught and held hers. "Do you think you can stand being snowbound for that long?"

She stared at him for several moments before she spoke. "I can't answer that right now because I've never been in that situation, Shane." She flicked the reins to urge Stormy into a slow walk. "What I can tell you is this. I understand all the drawbacks of living here and I'm still more than willing to give it a try."

Each lost in thought, neither had much to say as they rode into the ranch yard. Dismounting the horses, by the time they had the animals groomed and turned into their stalls, Lissa had started yawning.

"I have to send an e-mail to a potential client. Why don't you go on upstairs and take a hot shower?" Shane asked, when they entered the house. He caught her to him for a quick kiss. "I promise I won't be long."

"I think I'll do that," she said, hiding another yawn. She smiled apologetically. "I'm beat."

"I know, angel." Kissing her again, he released her and took a step back. "I'll be up in a few minutes."

Shane watched her climb the stairs before he went into his study and opened his e-mail. Quickly composing a message with a quote for his architectural services, he pressed the send button, then turning off the computer, sat back in his desk chair.

The evening couldn't have gone more perfectly. Lissa had loved the engagement ring he'd bought her and couldn't have been happier when he gave her the roan gelding. The ride to the trailhead had gone well, too—right up until she mentioned how much she enjoyed the peace and quiet of his ranch.

What had gotten into him anyway? Why couldn't he have taken her at her word that she wanted to live on the ranch? Why had he felt compelled to point out all the drawbacks of living on the Rainbow Bend?

Something he had overheard his father tell Cactus right after Shane's mother left kept running through his mind. At first, Carolyn McDermott had loved living on the ranch and hadn't minded the isolation. But as the years went by, being snowbound for weeks on end and having no neighbors close by had taken its toll and she had come to hate the picturesque valley.

After living on the ranch for a while, would Lissa end up feeling the same way? Would her resentment grow to the point that she left and never looked back?

Unlike his mother, Lissa was from Aspen and well aware of what the weather was like in the Rocky Mountains. But she had lived in California for the past eight years and although she said she missed the winter activities, she also liked living on the beach. After being snowbound a few times, what if she decided she preferred the more temperate climate of Malibu? And what if instead of leaving her child behind as his mother had done, Lissa took their son with her?

Staring at the dark computer screen, Shane drew in a deep breath. He didn't think Lissa would do that to him. Even before he'd convinced her to let him do the honorable thing and make her his wife, she had told him that arrangements could be made for him to be part of their child's life.

Rising from the chair, he turned off the desk lamp and left the study to head upstairs. Lissa had told him she wanted to try living on the ranch and that was really all he could ask of her. Only time would tell if her enthusiasm would turn to loathing. As long as he kept that possibility in mind and didn't allow his fondness for her to develop into a deeper emotion, he should be fine.

Unfortunately, he was finding that harder to keep in check with each passing day. Lissa was quickly becoming an addiction, and one that he wasn't sure he would ever be able to live without.

Eight

"How was your meeting with the other Jarrod Ridge investors this afternoon?" Melissa asked when Shane stopped by the spa the following afternoon.

"Long and boring as hell." He chuckled. "At least it was right up until I made my little announcement about our engagement." Laughing out loud, he shook his head. "You should have seen Elmer Madison's and Clara Buchanan's faces."

"Let's go into my office and you can tell me all about it," she suggested, not wanting to talk in front of the spa staff and resort guests.

They had agreed that he would tell the other members of the investment group they were getting married, but decided to wait until after the wedding to let them know about the pregnancy.

Once they entered her office and closed the door, she turned to face him. "Tell me what happened."

"When Elmer asked if there was any more business we needed to discuss, I stood up and announced that I'd asked you to marry me and that you had said yes."

He took off his cowboy hat and sailed it over to land on the couch. Then, pulling her against him, he kissed her until she saw stars.

"I—I want...details," she said, trying to catch her breath when he finally lifted his head. "What could they possibly find wrong with our getting married? You didn't mention the baby, did you?"

"No, that would have probably sent both of them into outer space." Shane shook his head. "I think they are both scared to death that, by marrying you, I'll get in on an investment they won't."

"That's ridiculous." She frowned. "All investments for special events are done through the group. They can pull out of the group at any time or choose not to support a project, but we offer all investment promotions to the group as a whole, not to individuals."

"I know, angel." He shrugged. "It might be they are afraid that once I'm married to you, I'll start contributing more and end up getting a bigger return on my money. Either that or they're both a few cards shy of a full deck." He grinned. "My guess is it's a little of both."

"Did they say anything?" She couldn't imagine what it would be if they had.

"Nope. They didn't say a word."

"Then how do you know they had a problem with our getting married?" Maybe Shane had misinterpreted their reaction.

His blue eyes twinkled with humor. "When I said that you and I were getting married, old Elmer turned so red in the face, I thought he might bust that blood vessel that stands out on his forehead whenever he gets upset."

"What about Clara?" Melissa asked, trying not to laugh at the visual picture Shane was painting. "What was her reaction?"

"She was taking a drink of water and got so choked, I thought I was going to have to perform CPR on her." He made a face. "I'd rather climb a barbed-wire fence buck naked than put my mouth on hers."

"And all this time, I thought you had a secret crush on Clara," she teased.

His exaggerated shudder and horrified expression had her laughing so hard, she found it hard to breathe. "Not in this lifetime. Just the thought of getting 'cozy' with that old bat is enough to make a man swear off women for good."

She couldn't stop laughing. Clara was at least twice Shane's age and always looked as if she had just sucked on a lemon.

His expression suddenly turned serious. "Lissa,

I want you to know that although the pregnancy brought about our decision to get married, you don't have to worry. I give you my word that I'll always be a good provider and a faithful husband."

Taken aback by his unexpected proclamation, she stared at him. "I'll be a good, faithful wife to you. But what brought this on?"

"I know that my reputation of moving from one woman to the next is only slightly better than Trevor's," he explained. "I just wanted you to know that I honor my commitments. You never have to worry about me going out and finding someone else."

After spending so much time with him in the past couple of weeks and seeing him interact with Cactus, she knew for certain Shane wasn't that kind of man. "It never crossed my mind that you wouldn't be anything but faithful to our marriage."

The sudden knock on the door came as no surprise. The spa had been extremely busy all day with guests getting ready for the dinner tomorrow night.

Reluctantly leaving Shane's arms, Lissa walked over to open the door. "Is there a problem, Rita?"

"I hate to bother you, but Joanie just got sick and had to go home," her assistant manager explained. "She has two half-hour facials booked and I'm afraid all of the other girls' schedules are full. Will you be available to take her place or should I cancel the appointments?"

"I'll be right there, Rita." When the woman went

back to the reception desk, Melissa closed the door and turned to Shane. "I'm really sorry, but I have to get back to work. We've really been slammed today. It looks as if I'm not going to get out of here for at least another couple of hours."

He picked up his hat from the couch and walked over to where she stood by the door. "I need to go anyway." He gave her a tender kiss, then reached for the doorknob. "I have to pick up my tux at the cleaners and then I have a couple of things Cactus wanted me to get before we go back to the ranch for dinner." Shane grinned. "He's planning on making you his world-class beef stew and sour-dough biscuits."

Just the thought made her mouth water. "That sounds scrumptious."

Nodding, Shane opened the door. "I'll be back to pick you up this evening around five."

Walking out into the reception area, Melissa sighed as she watched Shane leave. She loved him and if she hadn't known that before, she would have after his reassurance that he would be a good husband.

Cowboys had a reputation for their word being their bond. If it was important enough for him to tell her he would be committed to their marriage, then he fully intended for it to work out between them.

It hadn't been the declaration of love she would have preferred, but it was enough to give her hope. Maybe one day he would say the three words she longed to hear.

* * *

"When would you like to get married? Shane asked as he and Lissa sat in front of the Willow Lodge fireplace. After having dinner with Cactus, he had driven them back to the cabin for a nice quiet evening alone in front of a crackling fire.

"So much has happened over the past couple of weeks, I haven't had time to give it a lot of thought," she said, snuggling against him. "But I'd like to wait until after Erica and Christian's wedding. I don't want to take anything away from their special day."

He nodded. "I can understand that. When is it?"

"Christmas Eve." She looked thoughtful for a moment. "What would you think of a New Year's Eve wedding?"

"Sounds good to me," he said, kissing the top of her head. "Do you want a big wedding?"

"Not really." She sat forward and reached for her mug of hot cocoa. "I think I'd like something small with just family and close friends."

"Whatever you want, angel." He grinned as he leaned over to kiss away a smudge of melted marshmallow from the corner of her mouth. "I guess the next question would be where do you want the ceremony?"

He watched her look around the great room of the lodge. "I think right here would be nice."

"You don't want to get married at Jarrod Manor?" He'd thought she would want to have it at the family mansion.

KATHIE DENOSKY 141

"No." Her emphatic answer surprised him.

They stared at each other for several silent moments before he asked, "Why not, Lissa?"

She hesitated, then just when he thought she was going to avoid answering his question, she shook her head. "I don't have a lot of pleasant memories there."

"But that's where you grew up." He reached for her cup of cocoa to set it on the coffee table, then took her hands in his. "What was there about it that made you unhappy, angel?"

"There wasn't any one thing," she said, sighing. "It just never felt like much of a home to me."

"Why is that?"

He watched her shrug one slender shoulder before she met his questioning gaze. "I think you've probably figured out by now that I wasn't overly close with my father."

Shane nodded. From what she'd said about her dad wanting his children to start learning about the resort at such an early age and her obsession with how other people's opinions of her could reflect badly on Jarrod Ridge, he'd come to the conclusion that Donald Jarrod had placed his business above all else and taught his children to do the same.

"I've been told that when my mother was alive my father wasn't as focused on Jarrod Ridge as he became after her passing," she said quietly. "But for as long as I can remember, he never had time for us. He was always too busy either working or traveling to promote the resort." Her expression turned resentful. "And he expected us to make Jarrod Ridge our number-one priority, as well."

He had dealt with Donald Jarrod on several occasions through the investors group, as well as when the man bought horses for the resort stables, and he didn't think he'd ever met a bigger workaholic. But surely Jarrod had realized his family was more important than business.

"Maybe he was unaware—"

"Oh, I think he knew." She rose from the couch to walk over to the floor-to-ceiling windows of the great room. "Unfortunately, it's too late now to do anything about repairing our relationship."

Shane got up from the couch to walk up behind her. Wrapping his arms around her, he pulled her back against him. "I'm sure your dad was just trying to be a good provider for you and your brothers, angel."

She sighed. "That might be, but tell that to a child wanting nothing more from her father than his love and attention."

Although Shane's dad had lost interest in almost everything in life after his wife left, he'd still been there to raise his son. And, in his own way, Shane was certain his father had loved him. But apparently Lissa hadn't had that assurance.

"You at least had your brothers," he said, tightening his arms around her.

Nodding, she rested the back of her head against his shoulder. "I did, but they were all older. Besides, they were boys and didn't want to play with dolls or have tea parties."

Shane chuckled. "No, I can't imagine any of your brothers wanting to do that."

She turned within the circle of his arms to face him. "Just the thought is pretty amusing, isn't it?" she asked, the ghost of a smile curving her coral lips.

He nodded. "Blake would have probably shown up in a suit and tie and Trevor would have invariably brought a date."

Her smile broke through. "Of course."

Happy to see that her mood had lightened considerably, Shane pressed his lips to hers. "So it's decided, then. We'll get married here on New Year's Eve with family and close friends."

Resting her head against his chest, she nodded. "I think I'm going to invite Hector and Michael. They're two of my closest friends in Malibu, and besides, I'd like to talk to them about running the spa for me with the option to buy after a specified length of time."

"Are you sure you want to get rid of your business?" It pleased him that she intended to make her move to Colorado permanent, but he hated to see her give up a business she'd built from the ground up and was obviously quite proud of.

"It's not so much that I want to get rid of it," she admitted, yawning. "But I grew up with a father who was more absent than not and I don't want that for our child from either of his parents. Besides, I'll have

Tranquility Spa, and if we stay as busy as we are now, I'm going to talk to Blake about expanding."

"Uh-oh. It looks like the sandman is about to pay you a visit," he said, chuckling when she yawned again. "We had better get you to bed."

"I hope I can stay awake during the investors' dinner tomorrow evening," she said when he rose and guided her toward the hall.

"Yeah, it would be a shame to fall asleep during one of the speeches." Shane laughed.

"Maybe I better plan on taking a nap tomorrow afternoon," she said as they entered the bedroom.

"I'll plan to take one with you," he said, giving her a wicked grin.

"You're insatiable, Mr. McDermott," she said, shaking her head.

He took a step toward her. "And I intend to show you just how ravenous I am as soon as we get into bed."

As he and Lissa walked into the Jarrod Ridge Grand Ballroom for the festivities, Shane knew beyond a shadow of doubt that he was with the sexiest, most beautiful woman in attendance. Lissa had put her long blond hair up in some kind of soft, feminine twist, exposing her slender neck. He would like nothing more than to kiss every inch of it.

But the long, shimmery black evening dress she wore was what had his libido shifting into high gear. Slinky and form-fitting, it emphasized every one of her delightful curves and each time she moved it reminded him of a sleek jungle cat's elegance and grace.

Remembering where they were, he tried to rein in his unruly hormones. If he didn't get things under control soon, everyone in the whole damned place would know exactly what he had on his mind.

He spotted Clara Buchanan on the other side of the room and concentrated on how she would react to the evidence of his wayward thoughts. That was enough to take the wind out of any man's sails.

"There's Blake and his secretary, Samantha," Lissa said, bringing him back to reality. "They'll be seated at the head table with Erica and the rest of my brothers."

"What about us?" he asked. "Is that where we're sitting?"

"No. As an investor, you'll have your own table and I told Guy to have the kitchen staff put my place card next to yours."

"You're both looking very nice tonight," Trevor said, walking up to them. Lissa's brother had a pretty, young brunette clinging to his arm.

"Good to see you again," Shane said, shaking Trevor's hand.

After a few minutes of exchanging small talk, Trevor and his date moved on. "I wish he would settle down a bit," Lissa said quietly. "I've seen Elmer and Clara watching him, and they don't look all that pleased."

Putting his arm around her bare shoulders, Shane kissed her temple. "I agree that your brother is known to play it pretty fast and loose with the ladies, but it's really none of Elmer's or Clara's business what he does or how he chooses to conduct his life."

Before Lissa could respond, several of the regular resort guests came over to greet them and pay their compliments to Lissa's family on another spectacular event.

"The food in past years has been very good, but the cuisine this year is outstanding," George Sanders, a food critic from Los Angeles, said enthusiastically. "As soon as I find him, I intend to let Guy know the resort's pursuit of culinary excellence will be the focus of my next column. The crème brûlée is to die for."

"I'm sure Guy will be very pleased to hear that," Lissa said, smiling.

Once the portly gentleman stopped gushing about the food and moved on, Shane placed his hand on Lissa's back. "Why don't we find our table and see who our dinner partners are?"

He could use a reprieve and he was sure Lissa felt the same way. Besides, hearing himself repeat the same greeting at least twenty times, his face felt as if it had frozen in a permanent grin.

When they found their table close to the main table at the front of the room, Shane held Lissa's chair, then settled himself onto the one beside her. "It looks like we're hosting the politicians," he said, glancing at the place cards on the elegantly set table.

She nodded. "I just hope they put their political differences on hold for the evening."

"I'll see what I can do about that," Shane offered. "I happen to know that Senator Kurk and Representative Delacorte are both into fly-fishing. If it looks like the conversation is going to turn into a debate, I'll invite them both to go fishing next spring on the Rainbow."

"Thank you," she said, looking grateful. "I would really like for the evening to remain free of controversy."

"Shane, my boy, I hoped I would see you here this evening," Senator Kurk said, approaching their table. "I think you know my wife, Beatrice?"

Shane stood up while the older woman sat down. "It's nice seeing you again, Mrs. Kurk," he said nodding. He shook the senator's hand, then sat back down. "I'm glad you could join us."

"The way I hear it, congratulations are in order. A little bird told me you're planning on taking a trip down the aisle," the man said, smiling at Lissa. "Is this lovely girl your bride-to-be?"

"Senator Kurk, Mrs. Kurk, I would like for you to meet my fiancée, Melissa Jarrod," Shane introduced them.

"Melissa?" Beatrice Kurk exclaimed, disbelievingly. "I didn't recognize you, dear. You're all grown up. I think the last time we saw you, you were getting ready to leave for college."

As Lissa and the senator's wife exchanged pleasantries and caught up, Representative Delacorte and his wife arrived. Dinner was served shortly afterward and to Shane's immense relief, the two politicians seemed to have put their opposing political views aside for the evening.

While the women asked Lissa about new services at the spa and plans for their upcoming wedding, Shane found himself enjoying the men's stories of fishing for trout in the various rivers and streams in the Rocky Mountains. He was even surprised to learn the men were pretty good friends when they weren't at loggerheads over political issues.

As they waited for dessert to be served, the two men and their wives politely excused themselves. Shane knew they were going to work the room and try to secure votes for the upcoming elections before the event's closing speeches began.

Relieved to once again be alone with her, Shane turned to Lissa. But her attention was trained on her brother Trevor seated at the head table with her other siblings and their respective dinner companions.

"I can't believe what he's doing," she said, shaking her head. Seated beside a shapely redhead, the brunette that had been clinging to Trevor earlier was nowhere in sight. "I can only imagine what Elmer and Clara are thinking right now."

Watching his future brother-in-law whisper something to the redhead, then while her head was turned, wink at a blonde seated a few tables to the left of the head table, Shane had to admit the man was asking for a boatload of trouble. He saw nothing wrong with a single man playing the field. Hell, he'd had his own share of women before he met Lissa. But Shane had at least had the good sense to limit himself to being with one woman a night.

If Trevor wasn't careful, he was going to set himself up to be right in the middle of a class-A catfight. And once the women figured out he'd been playing all of them, they would stop blaming each other and turn on him with claws bared.

"Shane, could I speak with you in private for a moment?" Senator Kurk asked, standing at Shane's shoulder. Engrossed in the show at the head table, he hadn't seen the man approach.

"Of course," Shane answered, somewhat puzzled by the senator's serious demeanor. Rising from the table, he kissed Lissa's cheek. "I'll only be a few minutes."

He hated leaving her alone, but relieved to see Avery Lancaster heading toward their table, Shane turned his full attention to the man walking beside him. He had never seen Patrick Kurk look as serious or as determined as he did at that moment.

When Avery sat down in the chair next to her, Melissa couldn't help noticing the scene playing out just beyond her friend's shoulder. Her brothers Guy and Gavin had walked up behind Trevor at the head table. One of them spoke to him, then all three men left the room.

"What's going on?" she asked, turning to her friend.

"Guy and Gavin are going to strongly suggest that Trevor use a little more discretion with the female guests here tonight," Avery answered quietly.

"I'm glad," Melissa said, meaning it. "He's not doing the resort's reputation any favors."

"You mean 'come to Jarrod Ridge and get your heart broken by one of its handsome owners' isn't going to be the resort's new slogan?" Avery asked sardonically.

Melissa loved Avery's quick wit. "I somehow doubt that would help business," she said, laughing.

"Where's Shane?" Avery asked, looking around.

"Senator Kurk wanted to speak to him in private about something." Unconcerned, Melissa took a sip of her water. "He's probably hitting Shane up for a campaign donation or wants him to volunteer to hold some kind of fundraiser."

Avery nodded. "It's not enough that politicians want our vote, they also want our money."

"Are Guy and Gavin having their talk with Trevor?" Erica asked as she joined them.

Melissa smiled at her sister. "I'd say it's hitting the fan, even as we speak."

Erica winced. "I'd hate to be in poor Trevor's shoes right now."

"Me, too," Melissa and Avery both spoke at the same time.

"I'm glad I have you two together," Melissa said, deciding it was time for a change of subject. Even though Trevor deserved getting the warning about his notorious behavior, she took no pleasure in it having to be done. "One of the guests at the spa left a magazine in the reception area and it had pictures of a nursery decorated with an 'under the sea' theme," she explained. "I really liked it and I think that's what I want to use for the nursery. It incorporated all of the pastel colors and had the cutest baby sea creatures."

"I looked at that just the other day," Avery said, nodding. "It's adorable."

Melissa briefly wondered why Avery had been looking at nursery themes, but dismissed the thought. Her friend had probably been looking for ideas to use for the baby shower.

"I love the little pink sea horse and blue octopus," Melissa added, knowing she had settled on the theme she wanted for the nursery.

"It would be perfect for a boy or girl, too," Erica agreed enthusiastically. "And we can use all of the colors when we decorate for the shower."

Melissa hugged both women. "You two are the best. Thank you for planning this baby shower for me."

"Uh-oh. It looks like I'm going to have to go soothe the savage beast," Avery said suddenly, pointing toward Guy as he walked back into the ballroom.

"He doesn't look as if the encounter with Trevor was pleasant."

"I doubt that it was," Melissa said, hating that her family had to deal with yet another conflict.

"I'm afraid I need to get back to Christian," Erica apologized, rising to her feet. "I see he's been cornered by someone, no doubt looking for free legal advice."

As she watched her two best friends walk back to their fiancés, Melissa wondered where Shane was. She checked her watch. He had told her he would only be a few minutes and that had been a half hour ago.

Deciding he would probably be back soon, she left the table to freshen up before the closing speech began. As she started down the hall toward the ladies' powder room, she couldn't help but recognize Shane's voice coming from just around the corner.

"I'm flattered that you asked me to help with the investigation, Senator," Shane said. Melissa started to join him and the senator, but his next words stopped her in her tracks. "I have a couple of stables to design, but after I send the blueprints to the contractors, I'll have all the time in the world to devote to the investigation."

"There could be times when you'll have to do some frequent traveling," Senator Kurk warned.

There wasn't even so much as a moment's hesitation before Shane answered the man. "That won't be a problem. There's nothing keeping me from spending all the time needed on the job sites and giving them my undivided attention."

Lissa couldn't stand to hear any more. She and their child were nothing? Hadn't he listened to what she'd told him just the night before?

Feeling as if her heart had shattered into a million pieces, she turned and walked straight to the resort's lobby. Shane was no different than her father had been. He intended to put work ahead of his family, and that was something she just couldn't accept.

At the front desk, she asked for a piece of the resort's letterhead and an envelope. When she finished scribbling the note, she sealed it in the envelope and handed it to one of the clerks working the reservations desk.

"I want this delivered to Erica Prentice at the head table in the Grand Ballroom," she said, surprised that her voice sounded so steady. "Take it now before the closing speech starts."

"Yes, Ms. Jarrod," the young woman behind the counter said. "I'll take it to her right away."

As the woman hurried down the corridor leading to the ballroom, Melissa thought about walking to the lodge, but decided against it. She had left her light wrap at the table and the temperature outside had already dropped considerably. Besides, she didn't relish the idea of walking that distance in three-inch heels.

She turned to the concierge. "I want someone to drive me to Willow Lodge."

The man nodded. "It may take a few minutes to—"

"Now!" If she didn't get back to the lodge soon, there was a very real danger of her falling apart right there in the middle of the lobby.

Never having heard her bark orders at anyone, the man moved faster than she had ever seen him and in no time Melissa found herself seated in the back of one of the resort's courtesy limousines. She forced herself to remain stoic on the short ride up the road to Willow Lodge. She knew that she had already caused enough gossip and speculation among the employees with her outburst at the concierge. She didn't want to add more by dissolving into a sobbing heap in the back of the limo.

When the driver stopped in front of the lodge, she got out and hurriedly let herself inside. Only after she had closed and locked the door did she give in to the emotions that she had held in check since overhearing Shane and Senator Kurk.

First one tear and then another slipped down her cheeks and Melissa rushed into the bedroom to collapse on the bed. As she stared at the diamond ring on her left hand the loneliness of a lifetime came crashing down on top of her. She had never been able to live up to her father's expectations and it appeared that she wasn't enough for Shane now.

Nine

When Shane and the senator returned to the ball-room the closing speech had just begun and all eyes were focused on Blake Jarrod, Lissa's brother, the new CEO of Jarrod Ridge. As he thanked the guests and investors, Shane looked around for Lissa.

Where the hell had she gone? Had she become ill and had to leave? If so, why hadn't she found him to take her back to Willow Lodge?

As he scanned the crowd to see if she might be sitting at another table, he glanced at the head table. Lissa's sister, Erica, was staring at him and he could tell from her expression that she knew something about where Lissa might be.

Frustrated by the fact that he couldn't get to

Erica to ask where Lissa had gone until after Blake concluded his speech, Shane barely heard his name being called when the investors were asked to stand and be recognized. By the time Blake gave his closing remarks, Shane was already on his feet and threading his way through the crowd to the head table.

"Where did Lissa go?" he demanded when he reached Erica.

"Just before Blake's speech she sent me a message that she was having someone take her back to Willow Lodge," Erica said, looking worried. "Do you think she's not feeling well?"

"I don't know, but I'm sure as hell going to find out," he said, already turning toward the door. "Thanks."

"Please let me know if she's all right," Erica called after him.

Nodding that he would, Shane impatiently made his way through the crush of people leaving the ballroom. Was there something wrong with her or the baby?

As all of the things that could go wrong during the first trimester ran through his mind, he quickly decided that he'd done a little too much research about pregnancy. Apparently, ignorance really was bliss. It had to be better than the hell his imagination was putting him through now.

It seemed as if it took an eternity to make his way across the crowded lobby and out the resort's main doors. Unwilling to wait for the valet to bring his truck around, Shane broke into a run as he headed for the lane leading up to the private lodges.

Why had Lissa sent her sister the message saying she was leaving instead of him? What had happened between the time he and the senator stepped out into the corridor and the time they reentered the ballroom?

As he sprinted up the steps and across the deck of Willow Lodge, he fished for the key Lissa had given him from his pocket. His fingers felt clumsy as he rushed to unlock the door and let himself in.

"Lissa?" he called when he finally opened the door.

The silence was deafening. He glanced around the room. Her handbag was lying on the couch as if she'd tossed it aside so he knew she was there.

"Lissa, where are you?" he called, his heart thumping against his ribs as his fear increased. When he found her in the bedroom, she was lying on the bed, sobbing uncontrollably. "Lissa, angel, what's wrong?"

Before he could sit on the side of the bed and take her into his arms, she raised her face from the pillow she clutched. "D-don't, Shane." Shaking her head, she scooted to the opposite side of the mattress. "P-please just...go home."

What had gotten into her? When he left the table at the dinner, she had been fine.

"What's wrong?" he demanded.

"I want you…to leave," she sobbed. "Just go… back to your ranch…and leave me alone."

"Angel, you're not making sense," he said, trying to maintain a patient tone. "Calm down and tell me what happened to make you so upset."

Pushing herself to a sitting position, she swiped at her eyes with the back of her hand, then shook her head. "I overheard you and Senator Kurk."

"And?" He couldn't think of a single thing they had discussed that would send her into such an emotional meltdown.

"There's nothing to keep you from traveling extensively?" She shook her head. "What about me? What about our baby? Are we always going to come in a distant second to whatever project you're working on? Aren't we important enough to you that you want to be with us?"

"Calm down, Lissa."

"Don't tell me what to do, Shane. All my life I've come in last place behind a man's work and I won't do it again." Her eyes flashed with a mixture of hurt and anger. "Answer my question. Do you or do you not want to be here with me to make a marriage between us work?"

He had told the senator he was free to travel and devote his time to investigating design flaws in several federal and military buildings. But he couldn't tell her the reason he'd agreed, because he didn't like admitting—even to himself—that he needed distance to regain his perspective.

When he remained silent, Lissa's crushed expression caused his gut to twist into a painful knot. "I think your silence is answer enough, Shane." Removing the engagement ring he had given her, she reached across the bed to place it in his hand. "I'm just glad we discovered that it wouldn't work out between us before we actually got married."

"Lissa—"

"Don't, Shane," she said, sounding completely defeated. "There's really nothing left to say."

Staring at her for several long moments as he tried to put his tangled thoughts into some semblance of order, he shook his head. "This isn't over, Lissa."

Silent tears slid down her smooth cheeks. "Yes, it is, Shane."

He could tell from the look on her face she wouldn't listen to anything he had to say, even if he had been able to explain himself. "What about the investors and your family? What are you going to tell them?"

"That's really no longer any of your concern," she said flatly. "I'll handle whatever announcement I need to make regarding our breakup."

Suddenly angry, he asked, "What about the baby? I want to know—"

"From now on, anything you have to say to me can be done through Christian Hanford. Closer to the baby's birth, I'll have him contact your attorney to work out a custody agreement." She took a deep breath and pointed toward the door. "I'd really like to be alone now, Shane. Please lock the door as you leave."

He stared at her for a moment longer before turning to walk out of the bedroom. Placing the door key she'd given him on the kitchen counter, he let himself out of the house and descended the porch steps.

As he slowly walked down the lane toward the resort's main building, the engagement ring he still held felt as if it burned a hole in his palm. When he'd given it to her, he could tell it meant the world to her and he'd suspected then that she'd fallen in love with him.

He knew now that his instincts had been right on the mark. Lissa did love him and he could tell that it had broken her heart when she'd taken off the ring and handed it back to him only minutes ago.

His anger escalated, but it wasn't directed at anyone but himself. What the hell was wrong with him? How had he let things get so out of control?

He'd known for the past couple of weeks that he was walking a fine line, and keeping his feelings for Lissa in check was going to take monumental effort on his part. That's why he'd eagerly agreed to accept Senator Kurk's offer. He'd suddenly needed the distance between them to pull back before he found himself in far deeper than he'd ever intended to go.

But was it already too late? Had he done the unthinkable and fallen in love with her?

Shaking his head, Shane wasn't sure. And until he

got it all figured out, it would be best to leave things as they were between them. He'd already hurt her terribly. He'd rather give up his own life than do it again.

Standing on the deck at Willow Lodge, Melissa stared at the mountains beyond. How could her life have changed so dramatically, yet everything around her stayed the same? She had never experienced such emotional pain, never felt so alone as she did at that moment, yet the birds still sang and the sun still shone on the golden aspens whispering in the crisp mountain breeze.

Why had she deluded herself into thinking that Shane would be as committed to making their marriage work as she intended to be? How was it possible that she had missed seeing he was as driven by ambition and work as her father had been?

Shane had told her he would be faithful, and she had no doubt he'd meant what he said. But fidelity was one thing. Spending the time together that a couple needed to make a marriage work was something else entirely.

She had been willing to give up the life she'd built for herself in Malibu to remain in Colorado so that they could be a family. Was it too much to ask that he make a few concessions, as well?

The night he'd given her the engagement ring, he'd told her that his career required only occasional travel. But at the first opportunity that had come along for him to spend more time away from her and their child, he hadn't been able to agree fast enough.

All her life she'd come in a distant second to her father's ambition to make Jarrod Ridge the number-one resort in the Rockies. She refused to settle for second place with her husband.

"Melissa, is everything okay?" Turning at the sound of her sister's voice, Melissa watched Erica climb the steps and walk across the deck toward her. "You left the dinner so suddenly yesterday evening, I was afraid you might not be feeling well. Are you all right?"

"No, and I'm not sure I ever will be again," she said honestly. "But I'll survive. I always do."

"What's wrong?" Erica asked, clearly alarmed. "Are you feeling ill? It isn't anything with the baby, is it?"

Melissa shook her head. "As far as I know the baby is fine."

Erica looked around. "Where's Shane?"

"I don't know. Probably at his ranch." Since learning she had a half sister and welcoming Erica to the family, the two of them had grown fairly close and Melissa did need to talk to someone. "I broke off our engagement last night."

"Oh, no!" Erica immediately wrapped her arms around Melissa. "I'm so sorry. You both seemed so happy."

Melissa shrugged one shoulder. "It's probably

better that it happened now instead of after we got married."

"That's true," Erica agreed. "But it's still so sad." When the breeze picked up, she suggested, "Why don't we go inside and I'll make us both a cup of herbal tea?"

A few minutes later Melissa sat at the table, staring at the steam rising from the mug Erica had placed in front of her.

"Are you sure the two of you can't work things out?" Erica asked quietly.

"I don't see how." Over the course of the longest, loneliest night of her life, she had asked herself a thousand times if she'd made the right decision. Each time the answer had been that she had. "We both saw our relationship differently and I'm not sure that could ever change."

They were silent for several minutes before Erica asked, "Is there anything I can do?"

Melissa nodded. "You can be there for me when I let the rest of the family know the marriage is off."

"You know that Avery and I will both be there to support you no matter what," her sister said without hesitation. "For that matter, I can't imagine any of our brothers being anything but supportive."

"I hope so." Erica hadn't grown up in the same house with their father and therefore had no way of knowing how much emphasis had been placed on appearances and the family's reputation. "I've decided that I'll be going back to California soon.

I can have the baby out there without causing any disruption with the investors."

"Melissa, you can't do that. You'll lose your share of the resort." Erica shook her head. "No one wants to see that happen."

"If I don't, we could lose a considerable amount of funding for highly successful events like the Food and Wine Gala." She rubbed the tension building at her temples. "We've probably already lost one of our biggest investors."

Erica frowned. "Who's that?"

Melissa gave her sister a sad smile. "Shane."

"Do you really think he'll stop funding special promotions because the two of you are no longer involved?" Erica looked doubtful. "I'm sure he's made a lot of money from helping fund Jarrod Ridge projects. I wouldn't think he'd want to give that up."

"I don't know. It could be a bit uncomfortable for both of us." She took a sip of her tea. "But aside from Shane pulling out of upcoming projects, some of the others aren't going to look kindly on me being pregnant and single."

Erica touched Melissa's hand. "I think you're giving those people too much power over you. It's none of their concern what you do in your personal life."

"Shane said virtually the same thing," she admitted.

Maybe she was giving too much credence to what others thought of her family. But it was hard to cast aside a lifetime of instruction on the importance of others' opinions of her. For as long as she could remember her father had lectured his children on how their actions directly affected the resort and how important it was to protect Jarrod Ridge's reputation above all else.

"The main thing is you don't have to make a decision about any of this right away," Erica said, rising to place her cup in the sink. "You have plenty of time to weigh your options, then you can decide what *you* want to do."

After Erica left, Melissa sat at the table contemplating their conversation. In this day and age, many women chose to be single mothers and no one thought anything about it. So why was she afraid of what two busybodies had to say about her? And why was she willing to lose her inheritance because of it?

She wasn't. The only opinions that really mattered were those of her family. They loved each other and since their father's death the bonds between them were strengthening. Maybe her brothers would stand behind her and her decisions if she stayed in Aspen.

Sitting up straight, she came to a decision. She didn't care anymore what people like Elmer Madison and Clara Buchanan had to say about her becoming a single mother. They weren't living her life. She was.

If they pulled out of the investment group because of her pregnancy, it would be their loss. There were probably several other townspeople who would readily take their place and reap the rewards of investing in Jarrod Ridge. And if not, the family could pick up the slack themselves.

Feeling slightly better, she sighed. If only she could resolve her feelings for Shane that easily. But making a rational choice to change your attitude about something was far easier than trying to change how you felt about a person.

There was no way around it and no way to stop it. She loved Shane with every fiber of her being and always would.

"Cactus, this is the worst meat loaf I've ever tasted," Shane complained, pushing his plate away.

The truth was, the meal could have been prepared by a gourmet chef and the results would have been the same. Everything he'd tried to eat for the past few days had tasted like an old piece of harness.

"It's been three days since you and that little gal parted ways and I swear you're in a worse mood now than you was when you first told me she wouldn't be around no more," Cactus grumbled as he cleared the dinner table.

Shane sighed and tuned Cactus out as the old man continued his rant. He knew he was being unreasonable about everything with everybody. But he couldn't seem to stop himself. He couldn't eat, couldn't sleep and nothing he did seemed to relieve the hollow ache that had settled in his chest when he walked away from Willow Lodge the other night.

"I'm sorry if I've been a little irritable," he said, knowing there was no excuse for taking out his bad mood on Cactus.

"A little irritable?" The old man looked disgusted. "Boy, I've seen pissed-off grizzly bears with better attitudes than yours."

Rubbing the tension at the base of his neck, Shane nodded. "I know. And I'm really sorry about that."

"Well, knowin' and doin' somethin' about it are two different things." Dishes clattered as Cactus dumped them into the sink. When he turned to face Shane, he pointed a wooden spoon at him. "Seems to me that if you're that miserable, you'd get your sorry hide back to town and see what you could do to patch things up with that gal."

"It's not that easy."

"Why ain't it?"

Shane wasn't surprised that Cactus thought it could be that easy. The old man saw things as black and white, right and wrong. If something went wrong, a person fixed it and moved forward. But some things just weren't that easy to repair.

"For one thing, I doubt that Lissa would open the door if I did go by her place."

"Then you catch her out somewhere and talk to her," Cactus shot back. "And if you have to get down on your hands and knees to tell her how sorry you are, then do it."

"How do you know I'm in the wrong?" Shane asked, feeling a bit affronted. He hadn't told the old man anything more than the wedding was off and Lissa wouldn't be visiting Rainbow Bend anymore.

"Far as women are concerned, it don't make no never mind who started it or what it's about," Cactus said sagely. "To their way of thinkin' it's always a man's fault."

"I'll take that under advisement," Shane said, starting down the hall. He didn't need to hear more of Cactus's advice on relationships. He already knew who was to blame for his and Lissa's breakup.

Once inside his study, Shane closed the door and walked over to his drafting table to sit down. He'd tried for the past couple of days to work on the plans for the sheik's stable, but hadn't accomplished a damned thing. For a man accused of being ambitious and driven, he certainly wasn't living up to expectations.

Staring off into space, he couldn't stop thinking about Lissa and the shattered look on her pretty face when he hadn't been able to answer her questions. He had a good idea he knew exactly why he had agreed to the senator's request to help with the investigation and it wasn't something he was proud of. Accepting the job had been his way of running, of trying to escape what he knew now to be inevitable.

He took a deep breath. A man never liked admitting, even to himself, that he was a coward. But the truth of the matter was, he was just plain scared.

Lissa made him feel too much. She made him want to reach out for the things that he had told himself he would never have.

Propping his elbows on the drafting table, Shane buried his head in his hands. Somehow when he wasn't looking, Lissa had gotten past his defenses and he'd done the unthinkable. He'd fallen in love with her.

His heart pounding in his chest like a jackhammer, he rose from the drafting table to walk over and stare out the window at Rainbow Valley. He hadn't wanted history to repeat itself, hadn't wanted to go through the same hell his father had by loving a woman.

But with the exception of trying to drink her memory away, Shane found himself in the same position. He loved Lissa and was finding it damned near impossible to live without her.

As he watched an eagle make a soaring sweep of the valley, he thought about something Lissa had said when she broke off their engagement. She felt she'd taken a backseat to a man's work all of her life. Now he was doing the same thing her father had done. From what he could remember, Donald Jarrod spent every waking minute overseeing every aspect of the thriving enterprise. And instead of the preferential treatment some men would have shown their own kids, Jarrod had seemed to expect his children to work harder and do more than anyone else.

It was no wonder when Lissa heard his conversation with Senator Kurk that she had assumed he was as driven and ambitious as her father. She had no way of knowing that he'd been running from himself and not striving to build his career.

He shook his head. Although he wanted to excel in his field, Shane had no intention of ever letting it take over his life. But he hadn't told her that the other night. Now, he wasn't sure she'd give him the chance.

But he had to try and he knew exactly where to start to make things right between them. Turning to walk over to his desk, Shane picked up the phone.

"Senator Kurk? This is Shane McDermott."

Ten

"Blake, is this a good time?" Melissa asked from the door of her brother's private office.

"What's up?" he asked, looking up from the papers on his desk that he and his assistant had been going over.

"There's something I need to tell you," she said, walking into the room.

"I'll leave the two of you alone," Samantha said as if sensing that Melissa's business with Blake was of a personal nature.

Of all of her brothers, Blake had turned out to be the most like their father. He was the consummate business man and had been the best choice to step in as CEO of Jarrod Ridge. He was also a bit intimidating.

Settling herself into the chair in front of his desk, she took a deep breath. "I wanted to let you know that I've ended my engagement to Shane."

His concerned expression when he got up and walked around the desk encouraged her. "I'm sorry to hear that, Melissa," he said, sitting down in the chair beside her. "Are you all right?"

The genuine concern she heard in his voice had her fighting back tears. "It's been a rough few days," she admitted. "But I'm doing okay."

"Is there anything I can do?" he asked.

"Not really." She shrugged one shoulder. "Although I'm sure once the word gets out around the resort there will be a lot of talk and speculation. I just thought you needed to know before that happens."

Blake nodded. "I appreciate that, but I'm more concerned about your welfare than I am the rumor mill."

"I hope you mean that, because I've made a decision I'm not entirely certain you'll be happy with." She met his puzzled gaze. "I'm staying here in Aspen."

His complete confusion was written all over his face. "Where else would you go?"

"At first I thought it might be best if I went back to California to have the baby." She stared down at her hands clasped tightly in her lap. Making the decision to place herself ahead of the resort was new to her and she only hoped her brother understood. "I know some of the investors aren't going to look favorably on my being a single mother, but—"

"I couldn't care less if those people contribute another penny to Jarrod Ridge," he interrupted.

Shocked at her brother's statement, she stared at him. "Really?"

He nodded. "They knew Dad would sell his own soul for this resort and its reputation. For years they've used that to hold us all hostage with the threat of withdrawing from the investors group. That ends now."

His decisive tone left no doubt in her mind that Blake meant what he said. "It won't make a difference if they do stop investing in special events, will it?" She didn't think it would, but she wanted to be sure.

Blake laughed. "Not hardly. Our great great-great-grandfather started the investors group when he needed capital to build Jarrod Ridge. We've grown way beyond needing anyone else's money to do whatever we want with the place."

"Then why hasn't the group been dissolved?" she asked, unable to understand why her father hadn't done so years ago.

"The same reason you were willing to give up your share of Jarrod Ridge and go back to California," Blake said. "Dad was afraid of what disgruntled investors like Clara and Elmer might say against the resort."

For the first time since walking into her brother's

office, Melissa felt some of her tension ease. "I take it you don't care what they say?"

"The locals aren't the ones keeping Jarrod Ridge going, nor do they make or break our reputation," he said, grinning as he shook his head. "The tourists do that. We keep the townspeople afloat with the clientele we bring in. I seriously doubt they're so vindictive they would bite the hand that feeds them."

"I hadn't thought of it like that." Rising, Melissa hugged her brother. "Thank you, Blake. Our talk has helped me more than you can imagine."

"That's what family is for, Melissa," he said, returning to sit at his desk. "And I'm sorry things didn't work out with you and McDermott."

"Me, too," she said sadly as she left his office.

As she walked back to the spa, Melissa wondered why her father hadn't seen what Blake pointed out about the resort's importance to the town. Or maybe he had and used the fear of ruining the resort's reputation to manipulate and control his children. Either way, the next generation of Jarrods weren't going to have to live under the threat of other people's opinions.

But the resolution to that problem brought little relief. In fact, it only gave her more time to think about Shane and the incredible loneliness and heartache she'd felt since breaking off their engagement.

Lost in thought, she was halfway across the reception area when she realized her assistant manager had called her name. "Is something wrong, Rita?" she asked, turning to face the woman.

"Ms. Jarrod, I'm afraid I've made another mistake with this afternoon's schedule," Rita said, looking as if she might burst into tears. "I don't know how it happened, but we have a guest in the Green Room, waiting for a massage and there isn't a masseuse available. Could you take the appointment?"

Sighing, Melissa nodded as she headed for the Green Room at the back of the spa. "Not a problem, Rita. Just double-check before you book next time."

In truth, she was glad to have something to take her mind off of how much she missed Shane. Anything was better than sitting in her office, thinking about all the things that could never be.

As soon as she opened the door to the dimly lit therapy room, the piped-in sound of a waterfall seemed to wash over her and caused her to catch her breath. She'd probably never be able to hear the sound again without thinking of Shane and the afternoon they'd spent together at Rainbow Falls.

Glancing at the massage table, she did a double take. There wasn't anyone there. The sound of the door being closed and the lock being secured had her spinning around to face whoever was in the room with her.

"Hello, Lissa." The male voice was so low, so warm and intimate, it felt as if he caressed her, and it caused her heart to skitter to a complete halt.

"Shane, what on earth do you think you're doing here?"

The sight of him was both heaven and hell rolled into one. She'd missed him so much, but the thought that they'd never be together caused such emotional pain, it was all she could do to keep from crying out from its intensity.

"I told you the other night that our discussion wasn't over," he said, advancing on her.

She quickly skirted the massage table to put it between them. "And I told you there wasn't anything left to say."

Wearing nothing but a towel wrapped around his waist, he folded his arms across his wide chest and shook his head. "Maybe you don't have anything more to add, but I have plenty."

Melissa closed her eyes and tried not to think about how wonderful it felt to be wrapped in those arms, to lay her head on that bare chest and have him hold her throughout the night. Opening her eyes, she shook her head. "Please, don't do this, Shane."

"Don't do what, Lissa?" he asked calmly. "Explain why I agreed to help Senator Kurk with the investigation? Or don't tell you about the war I've been waging with myself about why I hesitated to answer your questions?"

Why was he doing this to her? Couldn't he see it was tearing her apart just being in the same room with him and knowing they could never have a future together?

"None of it matters, Shane," she said, trying desperately to keep her voice from cracking. "You can't change, and I won't settle."

"Yes, it does matter, angel," he said, his deep baritone wrapping around her like a warm cloak.

Knowing that he wasn't going to leave her alone until she heard what he had to say, she pointed to his towel. "Do you really think this is the kind of conversation we should be having with you wearing nothing but that?"

"I don't have a problem with it." He moved his hand to release the terry cloth where it was tucked at his waist, causing her to go weak in the knees. "But I can take it off if you want me to."

"N-no," she said hastily, holding her hand up to stop him. "The towel will be fine. Just tell me what you came here to say, then leave."

He motioned toward the lounge chair in the corner. "This might take a while. Why don't you sit down?"

With her legs feeling as if they might not support her much longer, she conceded and walked over to lower herself onto the lounger. When he started to walk over to her, she shook her head. "You can say what you need to from over there."

If he got any closer there was a good chance he would reach out and touch her. That was something she couldn't allow to happen. If he did, she knew for certain she'd lose every ounce of her resolve.

She watched him take a deep breath. The movement of his rippling abdominal muscles sent a shaft of longing straight through her. Quickly averting her eyes, she concentrated on his suddenly serious expression.

"First of all, I want you to know that I'm not like your father, Lissa. I'm not driven to work every waking minute." He shook his head. "Don't get me wrong, I enjoy my career and I'm good at what I do, but that's just a part of my life. It's not all that I am."

"That isn't the message you were sending the other night," she interjected. "The way it sounded when you agreed to help with the congressional investigation, you couldn't wait to get started."

He nodded. "I know that's the way it seemed, but I wasn't taking the job because I couldn't resist the chance to work. I took the job because I felt the need to run."

It felt as if her heart shattered all over again and Melissa wondered how he thought his explanation was better than her assumption. "Y-you didn't have to…go to those lengths to get away from me," she said, hating that she could no longer keep her voice steady. "All you had to do was tell me you'd changed your mind."

"No, Lissa, I wasn't wanting to run from you," he said softly. "I wanted to run from myself."

Confused, she frowned. "I don't understand."

"Let me tell you a story that might help clear things up," he said. She didn't understand how that was going to make his explanation any clearer, but she could see from his expression that he thought it was very relevant. "When my mom and dad got married and he brought her to Rainbow Bend, she told him she loved living there. And who knows? Maybe she did for a while."

"Who wouldn't love living there?" she found herself asking.

"After a few winters of being stuck in the house with no way to get out of the valley for several weeks at a time, my mom found it intolerable." He gave her a sad smile. "You know, I can't remember a night when she was still with us that I didn't lie awake listening to her beg my dad to sell the ranch or, later on, threaten to leave if he didn't."

"Oh, Shane, I'm sorry," Melissa said. "That's why you kept warning me about being snowbound, isn't it?"

He nodded. "I wanted you to know up front what you were getting yourself into."

"Your mother wasn't from around here, was she?" she asked suddenly.

"No, she was from somewhere in Florida," he said, looking puzzled. "But why does that matter?"

"Because she wasn't used to the type of weather we have here." Melissa wasn't excusing the woman's behavior, but she was certain the differences in climates had to have come as quite a shock. "I grew up here. I'm used to deep snows and the difficulties that poses to traveling. She wasn't."

Shane seemed to mull that over a moment before he nodded. "You might be right about that. But it doesn't excuse her from leaving her husband and son and never looking back."

"You never saw her again?"

"No. I was notified a few years ago that she had been killed in a car accident."

Melissa could understand a child not seeing their mother due to death. Her own mother had died of cancer when she was two and she'd known Margaret Jarrod only through the pictures her father had kept. But how could a mother willingly walk away from her child and never contact him again?

"How old were you the last time you saw her?" she asked.

"Nine." He met her gaze head-on, and she could tell that he was still haunted by the abandonment. "But I actually lost two parents that day."

"But I thought your dad didn't pass away until your last year of college," she said, confused.

"His spirit was gone long before that," Shane said, sighing heavily. "After he finally crawled out of the whiskey bottle and burned everything that hinted at a woman ever living in the house, he did two things for the rest of his life. He worked and slept. Beyond that, he didn't have a lot of interest in life."

With sudden clarity Melissa knew exactly why her father had turned into a workaholic. He'd been trying to fill the void left by his wife.

"Did your father leave a picture of her for you?"

Her father hadn't been able to get rid of anything that had belonged to her mother.

"No, I barely remember what she even looked like." Shane shrugged. "But I made a vow that I'd never put myself in the position for the same thing to happen to me. I wasn't going to give that kind of power over me to any woman."

Afraid that his next revelation would be that he could never give her what she needed most—his love—she bit her lower lip to keep it from trembling a moment before she asked, "W-what does that have to do with you helping the senator?"

Shane walked over to kneel in front of her. "I was trying to run from the fact that I'd done the very thing I'd swore never to do, angel."

Melissa closed her eyes and tried not to read anything into what he had just said. She couldn't bear it if it turned out she was wrong.

"What were you trying to run from, Shane?" she finally found the courage to ask.

"I was trying to run from loving you, Lissa," he said, taking her hands in his. "There isn't much of anything in this life that I can honestly say I'm afraid of. But the thought of loving you the way I do and having you leave me one day, scares the living hell out of me."

Tears filled her eyes. "You love me?"

Nodding, he took her into his arms and crushed her to his broad chest. "I love and need you more than I need my next breath."

Before she could tell him that she loved him, too, he covered her mouth with his. Heat streaked throughout her entire body when he traced her lips with his tongue and she readily opened to grant him the access he sought. As he tasted and teased, her heart filled with the knowledge that Shane loved her. She'd never felt more complete than she did at that moment.

When he finally broke the kiss, Melissa leaned back to cup his face with both hands. "Shane McDermott, I love you with all my heart and soul."

"And I love you, angel." He gave her a quick kiss, then lifted her left hand to slip her engagement ring back onto her finger. "Promise me you won't give this back to me ever again."

Throwing her arms around his neck, she shook her head. "Never." It suddenly occurred to her that he had been wearing nothing but a towel from the moment she walked into the room. "Where did you keep the ring while you were telling me about your parents?"

He laughed. "You didn't notice that I kept my left hand closed?"

"I...well...not really." She smiled. "I was too busy looking at your...um, heart."

"Like that, do you?" he asked, grinning. He took her hand to place it on his chest. "It belongs to you now, Lissa. My heart, my soul, all of me belongs to you for the rest of our lives."

"And I'm yours, Shane," she promised. "I have been from the moment we met."

Lifting her, he sat down and settled her on his lap. "We have a few more things we need to discuss."

"What would that be?" she asked, laying her head on his shoulder.

"I believe you when you say that you love the ranch," he said slowly. "But I think we'll build a house here in Aspen to live in during the snow season."

Sitting up, she frowned. "But I won't mind being snowed in as long as it's with you."

He laughed. "I know, but I'm thinking down the line." He placed his hand on her still-flat stomach. "When our baby is old enough, I don't want to have him or her living with relatives to attend school like I had to do."

"I hadn't thought of that," she said, liking the idea that he wanted them to all be together.

"I also think it would be a good idea for us to spend this winter at Willow Lodge." He kissed her nose. "That way we won't miss any doctor appointments because of weather."

"You're just full of good ideas, aren't you," she said, unable to stop smiling. "That way while you're traveling for the congressional investigation, I'll at least have Erica and Avery over from time to time."

"You can have your family over as much as you like, but I'll be there, too," he said, pressing his cheek to her temple.

"You will?"

Grinning, he nodded. "I called Senator Kurk this afternoon and told him that after careful thought, I wouldn't be available for the job after all."

"Did he understand?" she asked, wondering if he'd made an enemy out of an old family friend.

"He told me he was disappointed, but he understood that being a newlywed I wouldn't want to be away from you." Shane kissed her temple, her cheek and the tip of her nose. "And that brings me to the last thing we need to talk over."

"A wedding date?" she guessed.

He nodded. "Are we still good for New Year's Eve, angel?"

"Absolutely."

He nibbled kisses along the side of her neck. "Why don't I get dressed and you take off the rest of the afternoon. I'd like to take you back to Willow Lodge and catch up on the three days we've been apart."

"That sounds like your best idea yet, Cowboy," she said, loving him more with each passing second.

He was her heart, her soul, her very life. She couldn't wait to be back in his arms again, celebrating the happiness of finding each other, the life they had created and the love she knew for certain they would share for the rest of their lives.

* * * * *

MILLS & BOON®

Want to get more from Mills & Boon?

Here's what's available to you if you join the
exclusive **Mills & Boon eBook Club** today:

- ✦ *Convenience – choose your books each month*
- ✦ *Exclusive – receive your books a month before anywhere else*
- ✦ *Flexibility – change your subscription at any time*
- ✦ *Variety – gain access to eBook-only series*
- ✦ *Value – subscriptions from just £1.99 a month*

So visit **www.millsandboon.co.uk/esubs** today
to be a part of this exclusive eBook Club!

MILLS & BOON®

Need more New Year reading?

We've got just the thing for you!
We're giving you 10% off your next eBook or
paperback book purchase on the Mills & Boon
website. So hurry, visit the website today and type
SAVE10 in at the checkout for your exclusive

10% DISCOUNT

www.millsandboon.co.uk/save10

Ts and Cs: Offer expires 31st March 2015.
This discount cannot be used on bundles or sale items.

MILLS & BOON®
By Request

RELIVE THE ROMANCE WITH THE BEST OF THE BEST

A sneak peek at next month's titles...

In stores from 20th February 2015:

- **Royal and Ruthless** – Robyn Donald, Annie West and Christina Hollis

- **At the Tycoon's Service** – Maya Banks

In stores from 6th March 2015:

- **He's the One** – Cara Colter, Barbara Hannay and Jackie Braun

- **The Australian's Bride** – Alison Roberts, Meredith Webber and Marion Lennox

MILLS & BOON®

Why shop at millsandboon.co.uk?

Each year, thousands of romance readers find their perfect read at millsandboon.co.uk. That's because we're passionate about bringing you the very best romantic fiction. Here are some of the advantages of shopping at www.millsandboon.co.uk:

* **Get new books first**—you'll be able to buy your favourite books one month before they hit the shops

* **Get exclusive discounts**—you'll also be able to buy our specially created monthly collections, with up to 50% off the RRP

* **Find your favourite authors**—latest news, interviews and new releases for all your favourite authors and series on our website, plus ideas for what to try next

* **Join in**—once you've bought your favourite books, don't forget to register with us to rate, review and join in the discussions

Visit **www.millsandboon.co.uk**
for all this and more today!